The Regency

LORDS & LADIES
COLLECTION

*Two Glittering Regency
Love Affairs*

Lady Clairval's Marriage
by Paula Marshall
&
The Passionate Friends
by Meg Alexander

The Regency

LORDS & LADIES

COLLECTION

The Regency

LORDS & LADIES
COLLECTION

*Paula Marshall &
Meg Alexander*

MILLS & BOON®

First published in Great Britain 2005 by
Harlequin Mills & Boon Limited,
Eton House, 18-24 Paradise Road, Richmond, Surrey TW9 1SR

THE REGENCY LORDS & LADIES COLLECTION
© Harlequin Books S.A. 2005

The publisher acknowledges the copyright holders of the individual works as follows:

Lady Clairval's Marriage © Paula Marshall 1997
The Passionate Friends © Meg Alexander 1998

ISBN 0 263 84572 9

138-0905

Printed and bound in Spain
by Litografía Rosés S.A., Barcelona

Lady Clairval's Marriage
by
Paula Marshall

Paula Marshall, married with three children, has had a varied life. She began her career in a large library and ended it as a senior academic in charge of history in a Polytechnic. She has travelled widely, has been a swimming coach, and has appeared on *University Challenge* and *Mastermind*. She has always wanted to write, and likes her novels to be full of adventure and humour.

Prologue

There was no reasoning with him. The steward panted up the tower stairs after his master.

'M'lord, I beg of you. Do not be overhasty. M'lady. . .'

He got no further. The face the Marquess of Clairval turned on him was a baleful one, suffused with so much anger that it was no longer purple, but almost black. He flourished the whip in his right hand at his overbold servant.

'Be silent!' he roared. 'Or I'll use this about *your* sides instead of on hers. She will obey me today, or the worst will befall her.'

The Marquess possessed a turn of phrase which would not have disgraced a Drury Lane melodrama, but this was no play but real life; the blows he intended for his abused wife were real ones, not the acrobatic tricks of an actor – as the steward well knew. But he had never used a horsewhip on her before. . .

The man fell silent. He followed his master up the stairs with a sinking heart, condemned to witness whatever cruelty Clairval decided to inflict on his helpless wife. The steward had watched her turn from a pretty young bride into a gaunt shivering wraith, unrecognisable to anyone who had known her before she became Clairval's lady.

Best to be silent. The monster in front of him would doubtless double the punishment he intended for her simply because a servant had been foolish enough to plead on her behalf.

They were past the turn of the steep stone staircase: an oak door strengthened with great iron hinges stood before them.

'Unlock it!' snarled the Marquess, standing back.

The steward put the key in the massive lock, and threw the door open. Clairval strode by him, cracking his whip. The room he entered was small, with a curtained recess in one corner which held a rude bed. It contained a deal table, two chairs, a candlestick, a shelf on which a few books stood, a washstand and an iron pail. A chest for clothes stood in another corner. The only daylight came from a slit in the massive walls.

There was no sign of the woman held prisoner in this grim cell.

'In bed, one supposes, the idle bitch,' sneered the Marquess. 'Come out, madam. I would speak with you. Delay can only make matters worse.'

There was no answer. The steward coughed nervously, and his master turned on him. 'Be quiet, damn you. I would have her answer me, not listen to your rantings and snivellings.'

He raised his voice. 'Come out, madam, or I will drag you out to give you the punishment you deserve for disobedience,' and he cracked the whip again.

Still no answer.

With a muttered oath Clairval strode over to the recess, pulled back the curtain to find. . .nothing.

Both recess and bed were empty.

The bed had been carefully made. A ragged cotton

nightgown was folded neatly on the pillow. But of its maltreated owner there was no sign.

'No!' This came out as an animal howl as Clairval staggered back into the room to stare round it, to gaze at the low ceiling as though his wife might somehow be hanging there. He even strode over to the bookcase to pull it from the wall lest she had found a way to conceal herself in the small space behind it.

Common sense told him that there was nowhere that she could hide; that his wife had, by some means he had yet to discover, escaped from the prison he had made for her these past two years.

Someone would pay for this, by God! and that someone was cowering behind him, as apparently shocked and surprised as his master. But no matter, in lieu of anyone else, his back would serve as well as hers to bear the brunt of Clairval's anger on discovering that his bird had flown.

Not only did he use his whip to beat his steward senseless, but at the end, he threw him, unconscious, down the stone stairs, where he lay unmoving, before he descended them himself, roaring vengeance on those who had helped her to escape. For sure, she could not have found her way out of her prison alone.

Nor had she; but how she had done so, and with whose help, Clairval was never to discover, only to suspect – and if any of his vast staff of servants knew who it was who had risked everything by rescuing his unfortunate wife, they never betrayed him by word or deed.

All Clairval's bellowings and threats were in vain. They could not make his servants tell him what they professed not to know. No one had seen his missing wife for at least two days, and although he organised a search immediately, no trace of her could be found.

'For,' said his secretary, a cowed man of middle age who could not hope to find new employment if Clairval dismissed him, 'the turnpike road from York runs south not far from here. She may have taken the coach for London – and if she has it would be difficult to trace her. But that, of course, is merely my supposition.'

'To hell with your suppositions, man! You know no more than I do. A madwoman is loose, and that madwoman is my wife. Have bills printed, offering a reward for her return. See to it. At once.'

'Yes, m'lord. At once, m'lord.'

His secretary knew better than to do other than to try to placate him. That the bills would be lies, and that the mad person was the Marquess of Clairval, not his unfortunate wife, was a truth that no one, in that part of Yorkshire which Clairval owned and controlled, dare utter. His excuse for imprisoning her had been that she was mad, and the law in 1827 said that a man might do as he pleased with his wife without let or hindrance. She had no separate existence but was his to do with as he wished. He might imprison her, or turn her out of the house, penniless. All this the law allowed

And now his wife had disappeared from Clairval Castle, and the law gave him the right to drag her back to the prison from whence she had fled – particularly since he had branded her as a madwoman.

But although the Marquess of Clairval might be the Lord of all around him, the months dragged by, and still the Marchioness remained lost. . .and daily he grew more grimly determined to find her.

And if he ever found her. . .what then?

Chapter One

'**I** must say, Luke,' remarked Cressy, Lady Lyndale, carefully laying a flawless blue wash of sky on the water colour painting before her, 'that I never thought that you would still be unmarried at nearly thirty.'

'Nor did I,' replied Luke Harcourt cheerfully. He, too, was busy painting the same beautiful scene. It was a fine day in a spring which had arrived early that year. They were both sitting on the terrace overlooking the park at Haven's End, the Lyndales' home in Wiltshire. Behind them was the great house from which the estate took its name. Before them the ground fell away towards open country, lush and wooded.

There seemed little useful to reply to that, so – remarkably – Cressy said nothing, although she was used to expressing herself freely and forcibly. She merely frowned, and gazed into the middle distance where her husband, James, Earl of Lyndale, sat propped against a tree, reading.

Beyond him, at the point where the parkland ended and the open country began, two of his small sons were flying a kite with the help of their tutor. His daughter, demure and well-behaved, sat beside her governess sewing a fine seam, not far from Cressy and Luke.

Five minutes later Cressy tried another ploy.

'You have met no one who really interests you, perhaps?'

Luke, intrigued by her persistence, for she had never spoken to him on such a subject before, looked across at her and said slowly, 'I believe that to be a correct description of the matter.'

He thought that to speak so baldly and shortly might be thought of as a snub, so he added, carelessly, 'I like my freedom, you know, and would not lightly surrender it to the claims of domesticity.'

Now this, Cressy knew, was a surprisingly pompous statement from Luke, who despite his immense learning, always avoided any appearance of pedantry. Cressy also knew that he was not speaking the exact truth, but she did not like to say so.

Instead she continued painting, and willed herself to wait for any further comment on the subject to come from him – if he wished to make any, that was. She knew that she had been treading on forbidden ground, but Luke's continuing refusal to commit himself to anyone was beginning to worry her – not the least because she feared that she might in part be responsible for it.

She also felt responsible for *him* – and his refusal to marry.

Luke's surname might be Harcourt, and it was generally and politely assumed that he was a distant relative of the Lyndale family, but he was actually her husband's illegitimate son, who happened to be exactly the same age as Cressy was. The politeness consisted in everyone in society accepting the distant-relative explanation of his existence.

Luke had never given any sign that he was hurt by his dubious status or that he resented the fact that he would never inherit his father's title or the beautiful house which had always been his home. Nor had he ever reproached his father for his illegitimacy. He knew that James had been forcibly prevented from marrying his mother, and that when his mother had died in childbirth James had adopted and educated him.

More, once his father had succeeded to the earldom he had settled enough money on Luke to give him an annual competence, large enough to keep him in comfort. He had also been given one of the Lyndale family's many surnames. His wit and charm had made him popular, and he was accepted everywhere in good society.

So far however, he had not chosen to marry, something which worried his father because he felt that his son's consciousness of his illegitimacy was responsible for his remaining single.

He had recently told Cressy so. His wife had looked thoughtfully at him – and did not tell her husband what she knew was the real reason. She had first met Luke when they were both eighteen, when she was already in love with his father despite the difference in their ages.

Luke had fallen passionately in love with Cressy from the very first moment that he had met her – but he had also seen that her love was given, once and for all, to his father. He had behaved impeccably towards them both, but Cressy, wise beyond her years, had rapidly divined the secrets of Luke's heart. Now she was beginning to suspect that his never-to-be-fulfilled passion for his father's wife had rendered all other women pale beside her.

This she deeply regretted.

Luke ought to marry. He was everything a good

husband and father should be – but she could not tell him so. Nor could she tell James Luke's secret.

What she *could* do was to try to turn Luke's thoughts towards marriage. Now this, she knew, was meddling, and something which she normally avoided, but she could not resist saying, 'There must be some young woman somewhere, Luke, who could possibly . . .' She paused for a moment, not knowing how to finish the sentence. Luke finished it for her.

'Prevent me from turning into a crusty old bachelor.'

'Exactly.' Cressy was relieved that Luke had done her work for her. 'That is the point.'

Luke turned his head in her direction and gave her his infectious grin. ' James thinks that I am that already. Or rather, a crusty young one. You know what his nickname for me is?'

Cressy's smile was rueful. 'Oh yes, the "Man of Letters"!'

'No "Man of Letters" ought ever to have a wife. Bachelorhood, a tortoiseshell cat, a faithful and elderly housekeeper, and a band of bachelor friends are all he deserves.'

'You deserve more than that,' was Cressy's quiet response, and the pair of them fell silent again, concentrating on their painting until the arrival of Cressy's elder son, Robert.

'Mama, Luke! What are you doing? Oh, please let me look,' he exclaimed as he reached them. He was dragging his kite behind him, and Will, his younger brother, was panting in his rear. Their tutor was engaged in conversation with James who, having finished reading, was walking towards the little group on the terrace.

He arrived in time to hear Robert say excitedly, 'Oh,

Mama, you should see what Luke has done. It is most remarkably like.'

'More like than mine?' questioned Cressy, lazily waving her brush.

'Oh, but he has not painted the same picture as you, Mama. Do show her, Luke.'

Luke thus urged, turned his painting round for the whole party to view it. There, caught for all time, was Cressy, her head bent over her work, an expression of still and utter concentration on her face. It was an expression that all three men had seen many times before: it was the other side of her usual lively vivacity.

But the portrait was something more than that. It was a revelation of the painter's feelings for his subject. Each delicate stroke was a witness to Luke's love for Cressy. His talent for drawing was not the equal of hers, but as with his writing he was able to translate on to paper the deepest feelings of his heart.

Looking at it, James knew at last why his son had never married. Cressy merely said, rather feebly as she afterwards thought, 'I had supposed that you were painting the scene before us.'

'And so I was,' replied Luke, deliberately misunderstanding her. 'Here, it is yours,' and he handed it to her.

James said quietly, 'I paid Lawrence a small fortune for an oil which never showed the truth of my dear wife half so well.'

Something in his voice moved Luke, who said, 'A fluke, sir. I could not do such a thing again.'

Afterwards he was to think that the small painting was in some way a farewell to an impossible dream. He was never to know that he had betrayed himself to his father – although Cressy did.

That evening, as they sat alone in her room, James

asked Cressy a question. 'How long have you known, my dear?'

'That Luke is in love with me? Since I first met him, James. But he has never said a wrong word to me. Luke is a man of honour – like yourself.'

'I know. That he is a man of honour, I mean. And that is why he does not marry?'

Cressy rose and strode restlessly about the room. 'That, too. Oh, James, I pray that he will find someone to love, and who will love him. I do so want him to be happy – as we are.'

James put out a hand. 'Sit by me, my dear, and do not fret. The matter is not for us to settle.'

'No, I know that. He is a grown man.'

'And a good one. The only thing which worries me is whether he has enough steel in his character.'

'Oh, as to that,' replied Cressy, and her answer was in her dominant mode, 'we none of us know that until we are tested, I suppose. I dont think that Luke has been tested yet.'

This was what Luke always called a Cressyism. Something so obvious, and yet so profound that it came out almost like a hammer blow. James remembered what she had said some years ago when he had unexpectedly told her that he wished to resume his Parliamentary career, 'I always knew that one day you would wish to be more than a simple squire on your acres. I think that I would make a good hostess for you, don't you?'

He had been fearful that she would argue with him, or object – and all the time she had been waiting for him to make such a decision. And now she had summed up Luke.

He rose, 'To bed,' he said, 'and before that we will

pray for our son. That all will be well with him when
he returns to London tomorrow.'

'Or offer a libation to the gods for him,' responded
Cressy, who, like her late father, was something of a
heathen. 'Between us we ought to secure him a happy
future!'

Luke arrived at his London lodgings in a downpour.
The warm and verdant spring of Haven's End seemed
far away; even his landlady's cheerful greeting hardly
lifted his depressed spirits.

'Come in, Mr Harcourt, come in, out of the rain!
Your journey has not been too troublesome, I hope.
You must allow me to put the kettle on. A cup of tea
always works wonders for the weary traveller.'

Luke put down his bags and smiled gratefully at her.
Mrs Britten was more than his landlady – she was his
friend. A middle-aged widow whose parson husband
had died early, leaving her only a small annuity, she let
the first floor of her comfortable home to a respectable
gentleman in order to supplement her income. For the
last five years that gentleman had been Mr Luke
Harcourt.

Mrs Britten sometimes thought that it had almost
been worth coming down in the world to have him in
the house. He never caused her any trouble – unlike
some of her earlier lodgers. The parties and dinners he
gave were always discreet. He showed no signs of
wishing to marry, and it was to be hoped that he never
would. She thought that she would never be so lucky
again as to have someone in her home who was so
charming and so considerate.

Luke followed her into her pretty drawing-room. She
had obviously been expecting him, for a tea tray was
laid out on a small gate-legged table before the fire. He

did not, at first, notice that there were three cups, saucers and plates waiting, not two, nor that on his entrance a young woman rose from the big armchair by the fire.

So quiet, indeed, was she, that afterwards he was to think that his first meeting with her was almost symbolic in nature, in that she was a woman who improved with knowing – unlike some who, after a first splendid impression, grew less and less attractive.

On seeing her, Luke bowed in her direction, and Mrs Britten, before picking up the silver tea-pot, introduced them to one another.

Mrs Cowper, a widow and now her parlour boarder, Luke was rapidly informed, sat down again quickly, allowing him to do so.

She was young, for a widow, with a delicate oval face, dark hair neatly dressed, and the appearance of one who had been recently ill. Her pallor was extreme and she was painfully thin. Her blue eyes were fine, but strangely shadowed. Her clothing was plain and shabby. Her gown was grey, with a wide white linen collar like that of a Quakeress. She had a small piece of fine sewing in her hand.

Luke was later to discover that Mrs Cowper earned a living as a sempstress, making the most exquisite garments. Baby linen, small girls' frocks and little boys' frilled shirts were among her specialities.

'Mrs Cowper is a distant relative of mine,' Mrs Britten explained, handing Luke his tea. 'After her sad loss she fell ill, and I am only too happy to give her a home for as long as she wishes.'

'Mrs Britten has been very good to me,' remarked Mrs Cowper quietly. 'I am deeply grateful to her. She also tells me that you have lodged here for some years,

Mr Harcourt, and that you are a famous writer.' Her voice was low and pretty.

'A writer, but hardly famous,' he replied, 'one day, perhaps, but not yet.'

'He is too modest, my dear Anne,' interjected Mrs Britten robustly. 'He is responsible for a remarkable tome on politics which I understand caused quite a stir when it was published, and now he writes for all the best magazines. He had a piece in Blackwood's recently.'

She could not have gazed more proudly at Luke if he had been her own son. She and Mr Britten had been childless: a great grief to them both.

Luke waved a hand as a mild disclaimer. The fine eyes, he saw, never looked directly at him – which piqued him a little. It was not that he was vain, but it would have been dishonest for him to pretend that he was unaware of his good looks. With his dark, lightly waving hair, amber eyes, a sensitive shapely mouth, and a physique which was notable for its strength, he was accustomed to draw all feminine eyes – but not, apparently, Mrs Cowper's.

Her gravity, too, was extreme, as became plain when the conversation continued. 'This book you wrote, Mr Harcourt? May I ask what its subject was?'

'A philosopher who has been greatly neglected,' he told her. 'An Italian, Niccolò Machiavelli, whom I consider understood the practical art of government better than anyone else whose works I have ever read.'

'Old Nick,' she said suddenly. 'The devil was nick-named after him, I believe – or he was nicknamed after the devil!'

This surprised Luke so much that he said without thinking, 'Now that *is* truly remarkable, Mrs Cowper. Not many with whom I have spoken have known that.'

For the first time she looked straight at him: not at her work, or the opposite wall, or the fire.

'My father gave me a good education, but he also believed that I should acquire what he called the womanly arts – which was prescient of him, because a lady who wants bread may earn it by sewing, not by an understanding of political philosophy!'

'Very true,' remarked Luke, 'if unfortunate – for the lady, I mean. Our society does not much consider what a gentlewoman is to do to keep herself alive if she has no husband or father to look after her.'

Mrs Britten, surprised a little by the animation of her friend – but not completely so, because she privately thought that Mr Luke Harcourt could charm birds off trees if he so wished – made her contribution to the discussion.

'You may well say that, Mr Harcourt. I do not know what I should have done if Mr Britten had not left me this house and a small competence. They have enabled me to live in comfort, rather than merely existing. Gentlewomen are not supposed to speak of these things, I know. I also know that you, Mr Harcourt, will not think us wrong to do so.'

'Gentlewomen are not supposed to think of many things,' said Mrs Cowper equably, examining her beautiful stitching. 'But we have to eat – just like gentlemen. And there are so many things that we may not do to earn our daily bread.'

She paused and stitched on for a moment without looking up. Then still in that gentle voice, she said, 'I am surprised, Mr Harcourt, that you did not choose to become an MP. Mrs Britten tells me that your patron, Lord Lyndale, controls several seats, any one of which you might have chosen to grace.'

'Despite the fact that Mr Pitt was Prime Minister at

four and twenty,' riposted Luke with a smile, 'I feel that I am still too young to grace the House – later, perhaps.'

'You have no wish to put your Machiavellian notions into practice, Mr Harcourt?'

He thought there was just a touch of criticism in her tone, and, indeed, after saying this she avoided Luke's eyes completely.

He gave a light laugh and replied, a slight melancholy in his voice, 'I think that perhaps you do not judge me to be sufficiently serious.'

Her fine brows rose. 'On such a short acquaintance, Mr Harcourt, I have no right to judge you at all.'

Luke had no answer to that. Mrs Britten, apparently unaware of any odd undercurrents running between her two protégés, offered happily, 'I am sure, Mr Harcourt, that if ever you do become an MP you will make a splendid one.'

Whether or not Mrs Cowper agreed with her was not revealed. She stitched on for a few moments before rising to her feet, saying, 'You will both excuse me, I know, but I must complete this little garment for tomorrow, and although I have enjoyed Mr Harcourt's conversation I must absent myself from it in order to concentrate on my work.'

Luke stood up immediately and watched her walk to the door.

He thought that she limped slightly but not enough to mar the air of contained grace which sat so much at odds with her humble occupation and her dowdy dress. He had the uncomfortable impression that if he had not been present she would have been content to remain and chat with Mrs Britten.

How he knew this was a mystery to him – as much a mystery as Mrs Cowper was. She turned at the door, gave a little bow, saying as she rose from it, 'It has been very pleasant to meet you, Mr Harcourt. I wish that I could say that I had read your book.'

'Oh, if you would like to do so, Mrs Cowper, then I have a copy in my room which you may borrow. We could have a little chat about it later.'

For a moment he hoped that she was going to smile, but she thought better of it. 'If so, Mr Harcourt – ' was her parting shot ' – you must be kind to me when you do. Mrs Britten has already told me that you were expected to be a great scholar at Oxford, once you gained your degree there, but disappointed everyone when you decided to live in the world and be a writer instead. I have no guns as large as that to counter you with.'

She had surprised him again. There was a delicate edge to everything she said. If only she would look at him! But she was gone, the door closing behind her, and he was left with tea, cakes, and Mrs Britten.

'Come on, Harcourt, old fellow! You must be tired. I've not known you so quiet since Examination Day at Oxford! Surely a couple of months in the country haven't ruined your appetite for fun.'

Luke looked up at his friend and fellow scribbler, Patrick O'Hare. Pat had a pretty opera dancer on his knee and was tenderly feeding her brandy from the glass in his hand. They were in a dubious hell off the Haymarket, and Pat's destination for the evening was obvious. For some unknown reason, or perhaps the memory of a pair of blue eyes, Luke had no taste for amorous adventure that night.

He had spent the first part of it listening to Mrs Britten telling him that Mrs Cowper's life had been a sad one. 'I believe that her marriage was an arranged

one and not too happy. She was left virtually penniless
as a result of her late husband's lack of consideration
for her in making his will. After his death she became
ill, and is only just recovering. She deserves our utmost
sympathy.'

Mrs Britten spoke with such passion and feeling that
Luke felt that she considered that he had been a little
rough in his treatment of Mrs Cowper, and if so, he
reproached himself. It had not been his intention to
disturb her.

He would take more care in future – although he
doubted whether in his busy life he would run across
her very often. After all, she was Mrs Britten's friend,
not his.

Feeling a little lonely after leaving the loving cocoon
of Haven's End, he had gone on to The Coal Hole
where Renton Nicholson kept open house. There he
had met Pat, who had a fine tenor voice, and had
entertained the company with songs both sentimental
and bawdy. Half-cut before he met Luke, Pat had
insisted that the pair of them seek livelier entertainment than even Nicholson provided.

Luke had demurred a little and then agreed. It was
not his habit to go trawling for loose women, or barques
of frailty. Until his recent visit to Wiltshire, he had had
a long-term relationship with a pretty milliner who
called herself Josette.

He had wined and dined her at Cremorne Gardens
the night before he had left London for the country,
but when the meal was over, she had put a hand over
his, and had said earnestly, 'Luke, there is something I
have to tell you.'

What a simple-minded ass he had been!

'Can't it wait until we go home?' he had asked, home

being the two rooms he had rented for her in a house off the Haymarket.

She had shaken her head, and had said, 'Oh, no, Luke. We must say goodbye here. It would be kinder to both of us.'

'Goodbye?'

He remembered how puzzled he had been. Nothing had been said between them to suggest that she was about to end their happy arrangement.

'Yes, goodbye.'

He remembered her unaccustomed firmness. 'I shall shortly be going back home, Luke, to Kent, to marry my childhood sweetheart, now that I have saved enough to help us to start married life together.'

Luke was a kind young man, but his life had always been easy. The only hard thing in it had occurred when he had fallen deeply in love with Cressy, so deeply that he had resigned himself to remaining unmarried.

Nevertheless, the loving relationship which he had enjoyed with Josette LeClerc – her real name was Jean Clarke – had come to mean a great deal to him. He had found it impossible not to say what would hurt her, although afterwards he had cursed himself for his cruelty.

'And does this young man know how you have earned the money which you have saved?' he had asked her coldly.

Josette had flushed and had pulled her hand away from his. She had hung her head a little and had said in a low voice, 'No, and I hope that he never does. He thinks that I saved it out of my pay for working in Madam's shop.'

She had paused before continuing. 'I had not thought that you would be unkind, Luke, because you have always been so good to me. But you and I both know that you would never have married me. I want a real home of my own, and babies, and Nat will give me both of them.'

He had not been able to contradict her, for it had been nothing less than the truth. But something important was going out of his life, and when he returned to London it would not be to Josette's welcoming arms.

Was it that which was haunting him? He had taken Josette's hand in his again, had stroked it, and had said, as lovingly as he could, 'Forgive me, my dear, but I was shocked at the thought of losing you.'

And that had been the truth. He had not been lying to please her.

'Yes,' she had told him steadily, 'for you had all the pleasures of marriage, did you not? And none of the pains.'

Luke had not thought her to be so shrewd. Then he remembered how quickly she had learned the manners and carriage of a lady. She had persuaded him to teach her how to read and write, and had asked him for advice on dress. Would she unlearn it all for Nat – or use just enough of it to help him in her new life?

They had parted kindly enough at the end, though the parting had been bittersweet and had pained them both. He had pulled out his purse and had tipped a pile of golden sovereigns into her hand. 'For you,' he had said, kissing her on the cheek. 'For your new life.'

'Oh, no, Luke, no need for that. You must know that it was never just the money with you.'

He would not let her say him nay. 'I am not trying to pay you off, Josette. What I give you is in gratitude for the happiness we have shared. Try to think of me occasionally – but not if it spoils your new life.'

'And that is how I wish to remember you, Luke. You were always kind to me. Not like many.'

So it had ended. . .

'Still silent, Harcourt? It's not like you.' It was Pat again, reproaching him cheerfully for his moodiness. Luke acknowledged that it *was* unlike him, and called for another drink. Remembering how he had lost Josette had quenched whatever appetite for 'fun' which he had arrived with.

'You're right, Pat,' he said. 'I *am* tired. Forgive me. I'll call a cab and try to get a good night's sleep.'

It was not so very late, after all, but opening the door into Mrs Britten's, he was as quiet as he could be, tip-toeing up the stairs so as not to disturb the sleeping house.

Not quiet enough perhaps, for the door of the small library-cum-study on the first floor was opened as he passed it – and there was Mrs Britten's new lodger.

She was still in her day dress, although it was just past midnight, and her dark hair was in a cloud about her shoulders. She had a candle in her hand.

'Oh, it's you, Mr Harcourt. I thought it might be a burglar. Indeed, I do not know what I thought.'

'I am sorry to disturb you,' he said. 'Although I see that you were not asleep.'

'Not in the library, no.' She was looking away from him again. 'I fear that I often find sleep difficult. I will try not to disturb you if the need to arise and find something to entertain me in the night's watches should occur again.'

He could not prevent himself from a pleasantry – if only to find out how she reacted to it. 'I see that I must lend you my book as quickly as possible. It is sure to send you to sleep!'

This sally brought the shadow of a smile to her pale face.

'Nothing about Old Nick could possibly send me to sleep, Mr Harcourt. Indeed, I would consider that it is sure to keep me awake.'

They had been conversing in whispers in order to avoid waking those already asleep. Luke was suddenly conscious that to be found on the first landing with Mrs Cowper after midnight could scarcely help her reputation.

'I will bid you goodnight, Mrs Cowper. It would not do for us to be found alone together in the dark.'

She looked him straight in the eye for the first time. 'Oh, Mr Harcourt, think nothing of *that*. So much worse things might befall a lady than talking to a perfect gentleman such as yourself after hours.'

Luke was not sure by her words or her manner whether she was funning or not – or reproaching him. There was something fey about her dry manner, and the tilt of her head when she had finished speaking. It was as though she was making an arcane joke imposs-ible for him to understand.

His only response was to bow, bid her goodnight again, and leave her. From something Mrs Britten had said earlier; he gathered that Mrs Cowper had two rooms on the second landing. Whether or no she was repairing to them immediately was no business of his.

On the other hand, she had succeeded in driving his lost Josette from his mind. Instead, he was puzzling over what was so strange about Mrs Cowper because, for all the slight acerbity of her speech to him, he had gained the impression that he frightened her.

Which was not the usual effect Mr Luke Harcourt had on ladies, married, single or widowed!

Chapter Two

Luke saw little of Mrs Cowper for the next two weeks. Like the man and woman moving in and out of a weather house, she was never in the drawing-room when he was there, and presumably always inhabited it when he was out. They never even passed on the stairs. It was difficult not to believe that she was avoiding him. To his surprise, Luke found himself looking out for her. Perhaps it was because her manner to him was so enigmatic that he had come to think of her as a puzzle to be solved.

Luke loved puzzles, both in life and in literature, and he was good at solving them, which was what his new employer found useful in his writing. He had recently been trying to sell the series of articles which he had written whilst he had been staying at Haven's End. They were analyses of the various programmes for electoral reform that had been proposed over the last few years, and he had finally succeeded in placing them with Pomfret Bayes, who edited *The Pall Mall Gazette*.

Bayes had suggested that he might write short stories, political satires or sketches of high life for him. 'You bein' so acquainted with society, Mr Harcourt, would make you just the feller to have a go. I could get young Cruikshank to do the drawins for you, so I could. There's money, there, Mr Harcourt. Not, I understand, that you're short of tin, but a young gent like yourself could always do with more, I'll be bound.'

Luke was thinking over this offer all the way back to Islington. He was beginning to dislike being so dependent on his father, and the idea of making himself less so had its appeal. Mrs Britten put her head round her drawing-room door when he came in.

'Oh, there you are, Mr Harcourt. I was hoping that you might arrive early. I've just laid out tea and a little something to eat for Mrs Cowper and myself, but, alas, I've been called out. Why don't you take it with her? She'll be down in a moment.'

Is it possible that the old dear is matchmaking? was Luke's amused thought. And what if she were? It would be an act of charity to take pity on a lonely widow woman, would it not? After all, they could always engage in small talk about his book which he had left with Mrs Britten some days earlier for her to pass on to her protégée, who was so intent on avoiding him.

He was examining the small china ornaments on the mantelpiece with apparently passionate interest when Mrs Cowper arrived. She took one look at him, and stood back – again as though his mere presence disconcerted her. To reassure her, he bowed and indicated the seat in front of the tea table.

'Mrs Britten has been called away, and has asked me to keep you company. If that is not what you wish, then I will leave – but I must say that I would find it exceedingly pleasant to take tea with you.'

He noticed how graceful she was when, a little hesitantly, she sat down: she possessed the manners and speech of a perfect lady. She had brought her work basket with her, so he assumed that she would have spent the rest of the day keeping Mrs Britten company.

For the first time Luke appreciated how lonely life must be for the two women. He had his work, his friends in the world of journalism, his club, his visits to the gym and fencing academy where he kept himself in trim, and the entrée into high society where he was frequently asked to dine, or to attend receptions. His life was so busy that finding time to work was his problem, play consumed so much of it! Not so with Mrs Cowper. Her work was her life.

Because he was silent, she was silent too. She seemed to find speaking difficult, and only did so when she thanked the maid, Mary, who came in with the hot water for the tea, and a plate of muffins, already split and oozing butter.

'Pray offer the muffins to Mr Harcourt first, Mary,' she ordered. 'I am sure that Cook would like him to eat them whilst they are still hot.'

Luke took a muffin, thanking both women, and then bit into it. Alas, it was so well filled that it almost exploded, showering him with butter. Mary could not resist a giggle at the spectacle of him trying to do two things at once: mop himself clean with his spotless table napkin, and try to prevent his muffin from landing on the carpet.

Quite deliberately Luke made a little pantomime of his misfortune before looking up to see that, for once, Mrs Cowper was showing some genuine animation. She was trying hard not to laugh.

His napkin in the air, his muffin in pieces at his feet, he smiled and murmured reproachfully, a twinkle in his eye, 'My dear Mrs Cowper, if you wish amusement you should visit the theatre to watch a genuine *farceur* who is paid to entertain you. My efforts are poor by comparison.'

Her dark eyes shone as she replied to this feeble attempt at wit. 'But yours are so much more spontaneous, Mr Harcourt, do admit. And spontaneity, like brevity, is surely the soul of wit.'

'Now how do you know that I had not planned that little contretemps simply to see you smile, Mrs Cowper? It becomes you, you should do it more often.'

No one was more surprised than Luke when this shot out of him.

'One must have something to smile at, Mr Harcourt. Besides, you could not have known that you were about to be provided with the means of causing me amusement. On the stage, now, you would have practised that little turn for several days before you dared to delight an audience with it.'

Luke's own amusement was unfeigned. Neither was his admiration of what her pleasure at this exchange was doing to her face. She looked years younger than the pale and gaunt drudge whom he had met a fortnight ago. For the first time he wondered exactly how old she was. He had assumed her to be at least thirty: now she appeared to be much less than that. Very much less.

His company, the tea which she was sipping, the muffin which she was eating, the entertainment he had by chance provided, had all combined to make him look more closely at her, and what he saw pleased him. She also seemed more at ease with him than she had been in their previous encounters, so much so that she initiated further conversation by asking him whether he was having any luck with his writing.

'Mrs Britten told me that you were being interviewed by the editor of *The Pall Mall Gazette*, this afternoon with a view to his publishing your work in his magazine. I trust that the interview proved successful.'

'Very,' replied Luke, drinking his second cup of tea but wisely refusing further muffins. 'He has accepted the articles which I wrote when I was staying in Wiltshire recently. I had thought he might find them rather wanting in general interest, perhaps even a little dull.'

Mrs Cowper wiped her hands delicately on her napkin before resuming her sewing. Her eyes on her work, she said, 'Having read your book, Mr Harcourt, I cannot believe that . It seemed very witty to me, but I wonder that you can approve of those whose attitude to life and politics is so immoral.'

'Both of them, in general, being so immoral, seeing that they are concerned with power, which of itself possesses no morality, one cannot be surprised that a philosopher, writing of them, is also immoral,' replied Luke.

He was being deliberately provocative, he knew, but he wished to see her face animated again, and hoped that she would rise to the bait he was offering her.

She stitched very carefully for a few moments before answering him. When she did so, looking straight at him for once, Luke was surprised to see that her eyes were full of tears, her voice trembled, and was so low that he could scarcely hear what she was saying.

'Oh, of course, if power is involved, one must be surprised at nothing which those who hold it do to retain it, or if not, to gain it. Tell me, Mr Harcourt, do you think that it is ever possible for men to use power wisely?'

Luke wondered what he had said to move her so.

'One must hope so. For example, if our laws and constitution were both reformed to give ordinary men more say in ruling the country by allowing them to vote, instead of confining that to the few, then I would hope to see power used more responsibly.'

'And women, Mr Harcourt? You said nothing of women. Are women always to be left powerless – and exploited? Does your radicalism – for I see that you are a radical – extend to that?'

She said this with great fire. Her dark eyes shone, her cheeks glowed. For the first time she was attacking him, not simply reacting passively to what he had said.

'Well, as to that, Mrs Cowper, seeing how difficult it is being to extend the power to vote to men, then it must be almost impossible for women to be granted more freedom – yet. And, after all, women are fortunate in having men to look after them and shield them from the harsh realities of life.'

He knew, as soon as he had finished speaking, that his answer to her had been superficial and patronising. He was punished for it immediately. Her fine eyebrows rose. Her stitching lay abandoned on her lap. Her mouth twitched ironically.

'Ah, yes,' she murmured. 'The harsh realities of life. You reassure me, Mr Harcourt.'

She paused, and Luke knew that she was mocking him. 'As I am being shielded, and Mrs Britten – and the women who walk the Haymarket at night to earn a pitiful living? And the women whose husbands beat them regularly, and to whom the law offers no redress? Whose husbands may turn them out of their home, penniless, and keep their children from them? I think that you know better than that, Mr Harcourt.'

Her scorn was so fine and fierce that it transformed her. To his astonishment Luke felt helpless before it. There were a thousand arguments which he could have used to try to refute her, to point out that if the Rights

of Man were not yet granted then the Rights of Women
were hardly likely to gain a fair hearing.

What he actually said was, 'You shame me a little,
Mrs Cowper, for I am well aware of the disadvantages
which married women suffer – and widows, too,' he
added with a placatory smile.

Luke was used to skating on the surface of life when
he spoke to women, and mousy Mrs Anne Cowper was
the last person whom he would have expected to have
mounted such a fierce and logical attack on him. Her
usually quiet and apologetic manner had deserted her.
But only for the moment, apparently.

For she had taken up the sewing which she had laid
down, and was stitching rapidly away, while murmuring, 'Pray forgive me, Mr Harcourt. I should not have
spoken so rudely to you. It is not your fault that the
law is so unequal, and as a radical you are trying to do
something to reform it. Pray let us speak of more
pleasant things. I see that there is a *Book of Beauty* at
your elbow. We could perhaps admire the plates in it
together.'

She was mocking him again! He was sure of it. By
assuming the rather vacant tones of a pampered
woman, and by referring to the *Book of Beauty*, a
publication which was perhaps the greatest example of
the superficialities of an idle gentlewoman's life, she
was reproaching him by suggesting that such super-
ficiality was all that he expected from a woman.

He countered her with her own tactics. 'By all
means,' he replied politely, picking the book up, 'if that
is what you really wish.'

Her smile at him was a watery one. 'It is one way of
calling truce, Mr Harcourt, and raising a new topic of
conversation.'

'So it is,' he said softly. 'So it is.'

He opened the book at a poem of such vapidity, that he almost laughed aloud, and to test her decided to read it aloud. What new situation that might have created was not to be known, for Mary came in with more hot water, and Mrs Britten was on her heels, demanding tea and fresh muffins.

Their contest was over for the day, since Mrs Cowper immediately resumed her role of 'patience on a monument' as Shakespeare once had it, and fell silent again, leaving their landlady to quiz Luke on his afternoon, and to offer him fresh tea, before he returned to his room.

Not to work, but to ponder on the enigma which Mrs Anne Cowper presented to him.

And what do I make of Mr Luke Harcourt? mused Mrs Anne Cowper when Luke had sauntered out after telling them that he was due to attend a great ball at Leominster House – the season having already begun – and would arrive home tolerably late, but would try not to disturb them both when he did.

He was charming and *galant* in the French sense, full of good manners and perfect tact. He was handsome, but not offensively so. His dark good looks, proudly held head and excellent physique showed to full advantage in his careful, but not too careful, fashionable dress.

He had a good and original mind, no doubt of that, either.

Every page of his book bore witness to his intellectual powers. On the other hand, he was plainly a *dilettante*, idling his way through life. The book had been written three years ago when he was still only twenty-four, and he had produced nothing since but light sketches, articles on reform and other political matters of the day which must have been child's play for the young man who had written as he had done of ·Machiavelli.

The reason for his mode of life was plain. His guardian, Lord Lyndale, of whom he always spoke with gratitude, had settled on him a competence just large enough for him to be pleasantly idle on, to enable him to play at life rather than work at it. She was unaware that he was Lyndale's son, and equally unaware that she was echoing his father's worries about Luke's steel – or lack of it.

Perhaps, she thought, he has not been tested – and perhaps he never will be, which would be a pity. Even as she had been thinking of him, she had stopped sewing and had allowed her work to lie neglected on her lap. A log fell on the fire, and the noise returned her to the present, for thinking of Luke's possible lack of steel had made her remember all too vividly one who might be seen as possessing too much of it.

Mrs Britten, watching her, knew when her protégée's thoughts became painful and took a dark turn. She said lightly, 'Come, my dear Anne, do not repine. For the present you are safe here. Do not think of the past, I beg of you.'

'I was not thinking of the past,' Anne replied, 'or rather, for only a moment. I was wondering why Mr Harcourt does not make the best use of his undoubted talents.'

One might think my dear girl to be sixty-two, not twenty-two, to have such grave thoughts, was Mrs Britten's inward and immediate response. But suffering matures one, no doubt of that.

Aloud, she said, as unemotionally as she could, 'My own opinion is that Mr Harcourt is a gifted young man who has not yet found his way in life. It is to be hoped that he will. He has a good heart, as well as a good mind.'

Now which of those two attributes, she privately wondered, has caused my poor Anne to show, for the first time since she sought shelter here, an interest in the outside world?

And what might be the outcome of that?

Luke made his way through the crowds at Leominster House, greeting and being greeted. He was looking for James and Cressy, whom he was sure would be there. James was found soon enough, among a crowd of Parliamentary colleagues talking politics – but Cressy, where was she?

At last he saw her. She was over by one of the tall Corinthian pillars, which held up a vast glass dome, chatting to Lady Jersey. His stepmother was looking as delightful as ever in an apricot toilette. She waved at him with her fan, inviting him to join them.

Nothing loth, Luke obeyed her. But as he did so, the oddest thing happened. For nine years, ever since he had first met her, Luke had only to see Cressy to know how much he loved, admired and desired her, and to feel the deepest despair that she could never be his. But...but...tonight the admiration was there, and the love, although that, too, had changed, but desire and despair alike had fled.

Before him was a beautiful and clever woman whom a man loved as he ought to love his father's wife, as he might love a grown-up sister, if he had one. What in the world had come over him? Had he changed? Or had Cressy? It was as though he had been holding a kaleidoscope, which showed him a beautiful and desirable object, and somehow the kaleidoscope had tilted

so that he still saw the same equally beautiful object –
and yet it was quite changed.

The chains which had bound him to Cressy had fallen
off. It was not that she was less to him than she had
been – far from it – but that he valued her after a
different fashion.

She was smiling at him as she re-introduced him to
Lady Jersey, who greeted him in her usual familiar
manner. 'You come pat, Master Luke,' she said. 'We
have both been deserted by our husbands, and need
someone to escort us to the cold collation. Lady
Leominster's cold collations are famous. It would not
do to miss them. Besides, we need a man to talk
scandal to.'

Sally Jersey was fond of indulging in this sort of
nonsense; her satiric nickname was Silence, meaning
that she was a chatterer. In his new role of society
satirist, Luke was pleased to listen to her. He offered
her his arm, and the three of them made for the
refreshment room.

'You see,' she began, 'we have so much to occupy us
tonight. They say Clairval is invited, doubtless hoping
to discover whether his wife is here, disguised as a page
imitating poor Caro Lamb chasing Byron, or perhaps
hidden behind the arras – like a character in a play.'

She saw by Luke's expression that he was not quite
following her. 'Ah, I collect that you are not long back
in town and so are unaware of the latest *on dits*. Which
of us shall enlighten you? Dear Lady Lyndale, perhaps.
Although, as you know, she likes to listen to gossip,
not spread it.'

Cressy said quickly, 'It is an unhappy story. We
should not joke about such a sad misfortune.'

'Ah, but exactly whose sad misfortune? The husband's or the wife's? You must know, Mr Harcourt,

that the Marquess of Clairval's wife has run mad, has been confined to her room to spare both her and the neighbourhood – and has disappeared. . .completely.'

Lady Jersey paused dramatically, aware that she had an interested audience.

'Run mad and disappeared,' repeated Luke slowly. 'Yes, truly a sad story. She ran away, I suppose, with someone – but who?'

'Who knows?' was the lady's somewhat arch answer. 'All that we do know is that Clairval has advertised this very day for knowledge of her whereabouts and is offering a large reward. He has set the Runners after her – she has been gone these six months, they say.

'They also say. . .' and she leaned forward confidentially '. . .that she ran so mad that for the last three months of her confinement she was imprisoned in one of the tower rooms at Clairval Castle. Or so the story goes in Yorkshire.'

'If,' Cressy remarked drily and practically, 'the lady has run so very mad, then surely she would be a conspicuous figure in any society in which she chose to settle, and therefore Clairval should have little trouble in finding her! Furthermore, I do not like him,' she continued, putting down her lobster patty in order to speak more plainly.

They were now sitting in an alcove watching the passing show. 'He has neither manners nor small talk.' She picked up her patty again, and said before eating it, 'He has no large talk, either!'

'Who does like him?' asked Sally Jersey spitefully. 'Everyone was sorry for the poor little wretch who married him.'

'Poor?' said Luke being about to seize a buttered roll, seized on this apparent fact instead.

'I speak figuratively, of course. She was actually

extremely wealthy. Clairval was the poor one in the marriage. She was the daughter of old "Grecian" Temple. He had been an underpaid Greek scholar at Oxford – hence the nickname – until a distant cousin died and left him a large fortune. He had only this one daughter, who is now Lady Clairval. Her mother died when she was born. She was left quite alone when her father died and her guardians were happy to marry her off to Clairval. She had an odd name, I remember. . . Anticleia.'

'Not odd at all,' announced Cressy firmly. 'It is the name of Odysseus's mother, the wife of Proteus. Everyone knows *that*.'

Luke's lips twitched as this learned Cressyism was thrown so casually into Sally Jersey's light gossip, but he made no comment, only asked her, 'Clairval is in his forties. How old was Miss Anticleia Temple?'

'Barely eighteen, a poor innocent child to be married to such a brute. They say that her relatives were determined to have a title in the family. Those who witnessed the ceremony said that she looked like a schoolgirl – more suited to be his daughter than his wife.'

'Well, then, there's no wonder that she ran mad,' remarked Cressy irrepressibly. 'I'm sure that I should have done so if I had been married off to Clairval. Yes, I suppose that it was the title which attracted them.'

'And the money him,' put in Sally Jersey, determined to have the last word. 'And look, here he comes, arm in arm with my husband, who I know does not care for him in the least. Only his rank allows him to be tolerated by us at all.'

Luke could not remember having seen Clairval before – other than in the distance. The man looked like the brute gossip had suggested he was. He was massive, not only tall but broad and running to fat. He had conceivably been an athlete in youth but was so no longer.

His face resembled, Luke thought irreverently, a side of tough beef, being streaked reddy-purple and dirty cream. Although his clothes were impeccable, they somehow served not to enhance him, but to demonstrate instead how much his body had gone to seed.

He was reputed to have been handsome in his youth, but little evidence of it remained. His hair was a shopworn tawny streaked with grey. His manner when he spoke was bullying and intimidatory. One could only pity the poor mad wife. Luke remained quiet whilst Clairval was introduced to Cressy and himself. His own bow was as deep as it ought to be to a nobleman of such consequence and betrayed none of his true thoughts.

Lady Jersey commiserated with him on the loss of his wife. 'And I understand that you have no news of her, none at all. Most worrying for you.' She almost added, Not to know whether she is dead or alive, but thought that under the circumstances it might not be tactful.

Clairval bowed, shook his massive head and put on as melancholy a face as he could before replying in a broken voice, 'Particularly as my poor lady is so lacking in wits that any passing stranger must be considered as able to take advantage of her. I tremble for her – wherever she is.'

He paused, passed a handkerchief over his face, and said sadly through it, 'I blame myself, you must understand. If I had been willing to admit straight away that her mind was unhinged, then I could have called in a mad doctor earlier, and much misery might have been saved us both. As it is. . .' and he shrugged '. . . I can only pray that she is still in the land of the living.'

'Poor man,' sighed Lady Jersey after Clairval had walked off, still arm in arm with Lord Jersey who did not look as though he appreciated the honour. 'One really feels for him. He seems quite broken by her loss. Perhaps we have misjudged him.'

No one answered her. Even Cressy made no comment at all – unusual for her, Luke thought. Perhaps, like himself, she believed that Clairval protested too much over his wife's loss, since his remarks on it were a counterpoint to every conversation in which he took part at Leominster House that night.

How sincere Clairval's very public grief was Luke begged leave to doubt.

His doubts were reinforced a couple of days later when James told him that, after leaving the Leominsters, the gossip was that Clairval had made straight for Laura Knight's high-class brothel and had spent the night there with not one, but several of her girls.

A garbled version of this story was also passed on to him by Bayes, who was now urging him to write about Clairval's marriage for his radical weekly newspaper, *The Clarion.* In it, Bayes attacked everyone in high life whom he considered was representative of the corruption of those who ruled England.

'The gossip is,' he whispered confidentially, his finger beside his nose, like a criminal from the parish of St Giles conspiring with one of his fellows, 'that the lady was not mad at all, but that Clairval was saying so to gain the balance of her fortune which was settled on the child they never had. That he was imprisoning her in order to drive her mad, not because she was mad.'

'Oh, come,' protested Luke. 'I can hardly believe

that, even of Clairval. I have met him, and he's scarcely likeable...but...'

'There were odd stories about him years ago,' continued Bayes. 'I'll pay you highly if you discover anything new. Imagine how much it would help the cause of reform to expose such a grandee as Clairval.' He was already thinking about writing a poem satirising the wicked Marquess and his unfortunate child bride.

But it was not Luke's notion of what he wanted his life's work to be. He was being asked to dabble in a sewer. It was one thing to write high-minded articles about the noble cause of extending the vote to the common people of England, or comment wittily on the minor *on dits* of society. It was quite another to write salacious pieces about Clairval's private life and dubious sexual habits. He knew that Bayes would find someone else to do it if he refused, but that was not his business.

'You'll end up in prison for criminal libel, like Leigh Hunt did when he attacked the Prince Regent,' he warned.

'But think how many copies of the paper I would sell first,' wheedled Bayes. 'And there's nothing like being a martyr to a cause to advance it!'

As a consequence of this long conference with Bayes, Luke arrived back in Islington late enough for Mrs Britten to offer him supper.

'I have more than enough soup and rolls,' she told him cheerfully, 'to feed the three of us, and besides, my dear Mrs Cowper needs cheering up a little. We should both, I am sure, like to hear of what passed at Leominster House the other night. They say that there was a great crowd there, and that the King himself attended.'

Not for the first time Luke wondered from whence

Mrs Britten gained her knowledge of current high life. But soup, and Mrs Cowper's company, sounded pleasant, so he agreed to her request – and the dish of soup turned out to be only a small part of the repast.

'So, Mr Harcourt,' said Mrs Britten, shooting him a conspiratorial glance as Mary removed the soup plates preparatory to bringing in a tureen of stewed pike, 'were you fortunate enough to meet the King the other night?'

'No, indeed,' he replied, joining in the game of cheering Mrs Cowper up. 'I only saw him from a distance, but I did have the honour of meeting the subject of the current most titillating rumour in society.'

'Indeed.' said Mrs Cowper drily, wiping her lips with her napkin. 'And was the subject of your conversation fit for a humble dinner table in Islington?'

Yes, she *was* roasting him, no doubt of that! Luke returned the compliment. 'Oh, our conversation was mild enough for a schoolroom, I assure you, but the rumours about him were something else again.'

Mrs Cowper's fine brows rose. 'A him? And what him was this, pray? Rumours usually have a female subject!'

'Oh, a female subject was also involved,' replied Luke gaily. 'In this case it was the gentleman's or rather nobleman's, wife. It was the Marquess of Clairval to whom I was introduced, and who has most carelessly mislaid his. It appears that not only is the poor lady mad, but also that she has run away, has disappeared quite. Clairval claimed to be most distressed at her loss, was almost in tears as he spoke of it. . .'

He stopped speaking. What had he said? Mrs Britten was looking daggers at him. Mrs Cowper, on the contrary, had dropped her head and was examining the tablecloth with an earnestness usually reserved for the perusal of a fascinating book. Only the entry of Mary with the pike, potatoes and a dish of anonymous greens lightened the atmosphere.

'Oh, splendid!' cried Mrs Britten gaily. 'I'm sure that they did not serve you anything half so fine the other night. Come, Mr Harcourt, allow me to help you to a succulent piece of pike. It is quite a favourite of mine when well cooked.'

She continued to talk nineteen to the dozen in a feverish and urgent voice, most unlike her usual cheerful one. It seemed, Luke thought drily, that as a topic of conversation the reception at Leominster House had changed in one short minute from being most desirable to something which was not to be persevered with at all.

His belief that this was so was enhanced by Mrs Britten launching into a long and rambling story about a neighbour who was trying to organise a protest against the annual Fair, which was due to take place in Islington the following week.

How he set about it, and his lack of success – since most of the citizenry of Islington welcomed it – took up the next twenty minutes, but, as a ploy to cheer Mrs Cowper up, it hardly seemed to be working, since she remained quiet and apparently uninterested in anything except her dinner.

Finally Mrs Britten ran down. Silence reigned. Luke wondered whether to break it, but was saved from having to make a decision by Mrs Cowper raising her head, fixing him with her fine eyes, and asking him, 'And what, Mr Harcourt, was your impression of the Marquess? I should be interested to learn it, since I thought that I detected a touch of criticism in your original remark.'

So much for Mrs Britten trying to dismiss the subject of Clairval and his wife!

'You are correct in your supposition,' said Luke. 'I must confess that I was not taken by the noble Marquess, and I thought that his tears over his lost wife were crocodile ones. Particularly when I was informed that he had almost certainly married her for her money and that she was young enough to be his daughter.'

He did not mention the rumour that Clairval had driven his wife mad, or had imprisoned her in order to do so. He saw the gleam in Mrs Cowper's eye and wondered what was coming next. What further question might he expect from her?

Nothing more about Clairval, but before she resumed eating her supper she asked him quietly, 'And what is your opinion of people who peddle gossip, Mr Harcourt?'

Now here was a hard question for him to answer, seeing that Bayes was prepared to pay him good money to do so in *The Clarion*! Luke decided to be honest with her.

'You have me in a cleft stick there, Mrs Cowper, since the editor to whom I sell my articles on politics has promised me even greater fees if I am prepared to write about society scandals instead. He believes that to expose those in high life will eventually bring about a better life for us all.'

'And have you agreed, Mr Harcourt? To make a living out of the miseries of others – such as Clairval's poor wife, whether she be mad or no? Are you ready to do evil so that good may come of it?'

'That is a very harsh statement, Mrs Cowper,' was his uneasy reply.

There was nothing mute or passive about her now. The almost holy calm which she had always maintained before him was quite gone. A becoming flush coloured her usually pale cheeks, her eyes shot fire, her shapely mouth was curled in scorn, not in cool acceptance.

Seen thus she was more than pretty: she was beautiful. Apparently the mistreatment of another woman had brought her to life. And what she had just said to him was no more than the question he had been asking himself.

He was coming to understand that in some ways he was as passive as she was: content to go with the tide, to live his quiet pleasant life, not asking much from it, nor getting much either. He was dodging commitment because to commit himself might disturb the even tenor of his way. Which was what Josette had hinted to him when she had finally turned her back on him in order to marry the man who was prepared to commit himself to her.

He knew what was causing his passivity, but what was causing Mrs Cowper's? The loss of her husband, her consequent collapse into poverty and the necessity to work long hours to gain some kind of a living, so that she must remain quiet in order to endure what must be endured because it could not be cured?

Except – and why was that? – Luke thought that there was more to Mrs Cowper than appeared on the surface: that there was some deeper explanation for her way of life and her presence at Mrs Britten's.

All this flashed through his mind as Mrs Cowper made no answer to him, having decided to concentrate on eating her supper, rather than discuss moral problems over it. The fire and vivacity which had transformed her had died down and she was a humble sempstress again.

Clairval banished from the table, Mrs Britten heaved a great sigh of relief and steered the conversation into quiet backwaters where no monstrous fish, a distant cousin of the pike which they had just eaten, lurked ready to devour anyone who ventured into his territory. Merely to speak of one such as Clairval was enough to grant him power over lives which scarcely touched his. Far better to talk of the coming Fair and wonder what new delights might be on show there.

Perhaps she could persuade Mr Harcourt to escort Anne Cowper and herself to it. Ladies at a fair were always in need of a man's protection.

There seemed no escape from Clairval for Luke. Pat O'Hare told him bluntly during a jolly evening at The Coal Hole that he had accepted a commission from Bayes to write about Clairval's lost wife and his marriage.

'Bayes said that he offered it to you first but that you went all moral on him. Not turning Methodee, are you, Luke?'

'Didn't fancy prying into bedrooms and boudoirs,' retorted Luke curtly.

'A man has to live, and Clairval's reputation was hardly savoury before this,' said Pat lightheartedly. 'I've winkled out of a friend in the know that he's got a former Bow Street Runner trying to trace her. He thinks that she might have fled to London, apparently.

'What few relatives the poor bitch has have told him that if she turns up wanting help from them they'll hand her over to him. Seems that they think that she's not shown much gratitude to him for having made her his Marchioness. A bit rich, that, when another friend of mine tells me it's common knowledge in Yorkshire that he treated her worse than a slave. Locked her up in a cell in a tower.'

Luke thought of Clairval and winced. Shrewd Pat saw him do so.

'Yes, I know. It's a dirty business. But think of it this way. If we can expose him as a cur who has maltreated his wife then we might be able to stop his little gallop. . .'

'No chance of that.' Luke was curt again. 'She's his wife and the law says that he can do as he pleases with her. You know that as well as I do. It's a bad business, but that's the way of it.'

So the question of whether or not he ought to write about Clairval had been settled for him. He went to see Bayes to tell him that he would prefer to continue writing articles on politics or philosophy, and that others could deal with society scandals if they wished.

'Your funeral, not mine.' Bayes was philosophical. 'I suppose you've enough tin to pick and choose, though!'

For some reason this dismissive comment, implying that he was a mere amateur, hurt Luke. He tried to work out why all the way home to Islington in a hansom cab which dropped him off in the High Street. He finally gave up, after deciding that Bayes was wrong. Even poverty, he hoped, would not have seen him scandalmongering to earn a living.

Satisfied by this decision, he settled his top hat at a jauntier angle, and strode for home. If he were lucky, Mrs Britten might invite him to tea and he would have a further opportunity to discuss difficult moral subjects with Mrs Cowper whilst she sewed diligently away.

He had reached a cross path when the noise of an altercation drew his attention. A small crowd had gathered around a low stone wall before a piece of waste ground. In the middle of it a burly man in the leathers of a saddler was shouting at a woman seated on the wall. The watchers were either hallooing him on, or bellowing support for the woman by urging him to 'leave the gal alone!'

Intrigued as ever by the busy parade of low life which filled Islington's streets, Luke stopped to discover what all the fuss was about.

The woman was crouched over something in her lap, her face invisible, but Luke knew immediately who she was. He moved towards her at the same moment that the shouting brute in front of her reached out a hand to seize her roughly by the left wrist, twist it brutally, and pull her to her feet.

Luke thus saw her face for the first time, and yes, as he had somehow strangely known, it was Anne Cowper, and the something which she was holding was a small and shaggy mongrel dog.

'Let go, you bitch. That cur is mine to do as I please with,' the ruffian – for so he appeared to be – howled at her, still clutching her roughly by the wrist. It was plain that he dare not treat her more harshly, or snatch the dog from her because the crowd around him, still growing, was by no means all on his side.

He turned to shout at them. 'Tell her to give it back.'

Anne Cowper spoke at last, her voice low and breathless but quite calm. 'Indeed not. You were thrashing it to death until I picked it up to try to save it.'

The man appealed to the crowd again. 'Aye, and what's that to you? A man may do what he pleases with his own – dog, horse or wife – when they're disobedient. That's what the law says and I'll set the law on yer.'

Luke, fascinated, saw that Anne's pallor was that of fear, but she answered him bravely enough. 'Because a man *may* do what he pleases with his own does not mean that he *should*, if what he does is wicked.'

This brave statement brought answering growls of encouragement as well as jeers from those who supported the notion that right was might where horses, dogs and women were concerned.

Luke thought that he ought to intervene, if only because it was becoming plain that sooner or later the man would use violence to drag the animal from Anne's arms. But the crowd was now so large that it had drawn the attention of a man of law, some sort of beadle, who pushed his way forward demanding to know 'What's a-goin' on, 'ere?'

Even as the dog's owner began to speak, to explain what had happened, to re-state his right to have his dog back and to do as he pleased with it – to kill it if he so wished – Luke pushed his way to where Anne and her tormentor stood.

He said in as dominant and commanding a voice as he could, 'Allow me to try to settle this unhappy business. I know the lady and will vouch for her good character. More than that, I am prepared to pay enough money to buy the dog from you, sir, and end this whole wretched business.'

The crowd had receded from him as he walked forward, pulling off his hat. He was so very much the gentleman and aristocrat in his splendid coat, buckskin breeches and shining boots that his good looks, as well as his commanding presence, had the women present oohing and aahing and poking one another.

The man said rudely, 'Who the devil are you, that you want to buy a worthless cur from me? You've got more money than sense, like all you young gents, I'll be bound.'

'No more of that,' ordered Luke curtly. He had reached Anne Cowper by now and had put a hand on her trembling arm. The dog gave a frightened bark as he did so.

'Mind that,' cried his owner. 'He's as ill-favoured a

brute as a dog can be. Give me a guinea, though, and he's yours.' The beadle, and most of the crowd, nodded agreement at this preposterous proposal, seeing that the dog was worth nothing.

Luke did not attempt to argue with him over the price demanded. He fished a guinea out of his pocket and held it up. 'It's more than you deserve,' he announced severely. 'And more than the cur is worth. But take this, and the dog is the lady's. But you'll get nothing until you release her wrist.'

'A fool and his money are soon parted,' sneered the man, but he threw Anne from him and took the offered coin. She gave a small cry of pain on being released and fell against Luke, her face grey.

'Damn him,' grated Luke, moved both by her suffering and by the determination with which she was still clutching the dog. 'He's hurt you. If I had known that, I'd not have offered him a penny.'

'Too late,' triumphed the man, and made off at the run, grasping his new-found wealth tightly. Luke, pleased to be rid of his presence, contented himself with saying gently, 'Pray allow me to take the animal from you, Mrs Cowper, and then we must try to find you a surgeon so that he may examine your wrist.'

He helped her to sit on the wall again, as the crowd, fun over, began to scatter, but she refused to hand him the dog even when a portly man came forward, saying, 'If the lady is hurt, then allow me to assist her. I am Adam Dobson, a surgeon.'

Mrs Cowper shrank away from both of them, her eyes shadowed. 'No, please. No. I am not hurt, only a little shocked.'

Both Luke and Mr Dobson, however, could see that her wrist was swollen and bruised. Finally Luke managed to persuade her to allow the surgeon to examine it, and she reluctantly held out her arm. At his first touch, though, gentle as it was, she gave a great shiver, and hid her face.

Whilst Mr Dobson carefully flexed and manipulated her wrist, Luke pulled off his cravat so that by the time the surgeon had finished examining her and had pronounced her wrist to be sprained, he was able to hold out an improvised sling for the surgeon to put on.

'Your wrist has been broken in the past, madam, has it not?' asked Mr Dobson as he finished securing the sling. Anne did not answer him directly, but simply nodded her head. She was still clutching the dog to her with her good hand.

'It was not properly set,' he told her severely, 'which is why it has become damaged again so easily. Some country fool made a botch of it, I suppose. Fortunately, being your left wrist, no great harm has been done. But you must not use it again until I give you permission.'

Still she made him no answer, nor did she look directly at Luke. The surgeon had not done with her, for as she stood up he said, 'Pray allow your friend to hold the dog for you, since you will find walking difficult with both a sling and the animal to manoeuvre.'

Lips quivering, but the colour slowly returning to her wan face, Anne handed Luke the dog, which barked its protest at losing its new friend, but quieted when Luke stroked its shaggy head. He privately agreed with its original owner that it was the most ill-favoured animal which he had ever encountered, but never mind that: it seemed to be pleasing Mrs Anne Cowper simply by existing.

After taking down Anne's address so that he might call to examine her wrist in a few days' time, Mr Dobson bade them good bye, quietly pocketing the guinea which Luke slipped to him. After which Luke, slightly hampered by the dog, helped Mrs Cowper to walk back to their lodgings.

'I haven't thanked you,' Anne said shyly. 'You really were a good Samaritan, Mr Harcourt. I cannot say how sorry I am that I have teased you so cruelly about your good faith ever since I first met you. I am properly shamed.'

'Oh think nothing of that,' exclaimed Luke, who had suddenly begun to think of Mrs Cowper as Anne from the moment when he had seen her crouched on the wall, braving a bully twice her size and weight. 'But you were risking yourself, you know, to defy such a brute.'

'I know,' she admitted 'But I cannot bear to see anything beaten. And such a little creature. He would have killed it, I am sure.'

Luke could not but agree. 'All the same,' he told her, a trifle severely, 'I want you to promise me that you will never do such a reckless thing again. I might not be there to help you the next time.'

'No, indeed. The problem was that I could not afford to buy the poor little creature from him, you understand. You will allow me to pay you back a little at a time, will you not?'

'Certainly not!' replied Luke warmly. 'Think of it as a reward for your courage. Particularly when you bore the surgeon's manipulations so bravely. I could see that he was hurting you.'

Anne's smile was wan, but a smile. 'A trifle, a mere trifle,' she told him. 'And now I have only one worry. What in the world will Mrs Britten say when I arrive home with my poor little charge?'

'Oh, no need to trouble yourself on that score.' Luke's reply was as confident as he could make it. 'I know that there is an empty kennel in the back yard.

Her dog died of old age about six months ago and I cannot think that she will turn this poor scrap away.'

Nor did she. Exclaiming alternately over Anne's poorly wrist, the dog, and Mr Harcourt's fortunate arrival on the scene, Mrs Britten also made sure that all four of them, including the dog, had an even better supper than usual, and Anne was sent to bed with a glass of hot toddy to ease the pain of her damaged wrist.

What troubled Luke a little, although he said nothing to anyone about it, was not only the knowledge that Anne Cowper's wrist had been broken before, but the fact that as a result of tiredness and strain, her slight limp was a little more prominent than usual as she bade him goodnight. He was sure from everything he saw of her that her married life had not been happy. The other thing which he was sure of was her uncomplaining courage.

What she needed was someone to look after her, he concluded, since it was plain to him that no one had ever looked after her before.

The dog, christened Odysseus – Dizzy for common use – spent a happy night in his new home.

Chapter Three

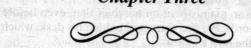

Pat O'Hare was sitting quietly in his rooms in Stanhope Street, near to Regent's Park, when he heard a banging on the house door. Next the door itself was flung open, and a man's voice began to shout imperiously at his landlady. In the commotion he heard his own name shouted.

He walked to the head of the stairs – his rooms were on the first floor – and called down, 'What is it, Mrs Rouncewell? What's the trouble?'

'No trouble,' said the imperious masculine voice, 'and now I know that you are at home, O'Hare, I shall come upstairs to see you at once. Fernando, Jem, follow me.'

Fernando and Jem were two burly men who followed their master upstairs. Pat knew at once who his visitor was. He had seen him about town, in Laura Knight's exclusive brothel, and driving a curricle in Hyde Park. It was the Marquess of Clairval, all fifteen stone of him – he was even larger than his two footmen who resembled pugilists more than house-trained servants.

One of them was a boxer whom Pat had seen in Jackson's gym. On Clairval's orders they stood, one on each side of the door into Pat's study, like a pair of Praetorian guards, armed with muscles not swords.

Clairval threw his hat and whip on to Pat's desk, remarking conversationally, 'That stupid bitch downstairs said that she wouldn't let me up until she had first announced me. Who the devil does she think you are? Fat King George himself incognito, instead of a jumped-up cur of a journalist who spends his time slandering his betters?'

He was so plainly bent on mischief that, even before his last words, Pat had retreated behind his desk, which stood in the bow window.

'Aye you may well run away from me,' sneered Clairval, hurling some galley sheets from the printer towards Pat, half of them landing on the floor, the other half on his desk. 'I've just been interviewing the toad who owns *The Clarion*. He confirmed, oh so politely, what an informant of mine had already passed on to me: that his scandal sheet was ready to publish filth about my marriage. Filth which you had written. Shall I give you the taste of the whip which I gave him?'

Pat said from behind the shelter of his desk, 'I'll set the law on you if you do, Marquess or no Marquess.' He wasn't feeling half so brave as he sounded.

Clairval said in a bored voice, 'I thought that you might threaten me with that. So did Bayes, but I persuaded him that, if he did, I knew some scandal about him which might land him in Newgate. I can't say that he took his medicine like a man.'

He gave a great exaggerated yawn. 'Now, I couldn't find anything to blackmail you with – not that you're as pure as the driven snow, mind – so instead I've brought Jem and Fernando along with me. I hear you consider yourself a student of the Fancy so you may face the pair of them at once and take your medicine like a man.

'Any complaint from you and they will swear that

what was done to you was done by accident in sparring practice. That little lesson should cure you, once and for all, of peddling inaccurate scandal about me and mine.'

'Here?' queried Pat desperately, his voice rising. 'They're going to thrash me here? Mrs Rouncewell might tell a different tale from theirs.'

'It's my experience,' said Clairval, bored again, 'that the Mrs Rouncewells of this world will say anything if the money offered them is right.'

He looked at Pat, began to crook a finger at his bully boys, and then dropped it. 'On the other hand, you can save yourself a beating, which might leave you with a broken wrist, which would prevent you from writing anything at all – let alone about me – if you will only do as I wish. Not only that, if you agree to my proposal, I shall see that you will receive a reasonable reward.'

Pat looked at the two bruisers, who were plainly eager to set about him immediately, and decided on surrender. He knew that it was useless to plead with the monster before him.

'What is it that you want of me?' he asked. He could only hope that what was required of him didn't compromise his already-stained honour overmuch.

'A small enough favour.' Clairval's tone was almost indifferent. 'As you well know, my poor mad wife escaped from her home where I was making sure that she received every attention her sufferings and her rank deserved. I have reason to believe that she fled to London, the more easily to hide herself away. I dare not think what ill fortune might befall the poor little thing in this corrupt city.' He heaved a great sigh.

'Now I know you go out and about in society. You hear all the gossip and the rumours – ' and he pointed at the scattered galley sheets ' – so, I wish you to try to discover where she may have hidden herself. Someone must know, for I am convinced that she is not alone. I have an ex-Runner on the job, but he only has access to criminal haunts and the like, not those in society like you. And you are shrewd, as your writing proves.

'Bring me anything you find as soon as you find it – and don't try to trick me. Jem and Fernando are disappointed, I know, that they may not use you for sparring practice. Don't give them the opportunity to do so.

'You will also oblige me by writing a pamphlet setting out the true history of my poor mad wife – that should silence the lies of the gossips and the Radical writers when I publish it.' His grin at Pat was feral.

All Pat knew was that he had been reprieved, but only at the expense of tracking down the *poor mad wife*, whom rumour said had been brutalised by the man before him, and by doing his dirty work for him into the bargain. Yet what alternative had he? Like many young gentlemen with little money, Pat desperately needed what he earned from his journalism to stay afloat and not end up in a spunging house. He had been counting on this money from Bayes, and now he had lost it.

Besides, it was always possible that Clairval was telling the truth about his wife: that she was mad and needed the protection which he could give her. . .

He nodded agreement, and as a reward Clairval tossed him a purse of guineas: it was far more than Bayes would have paid him.

Pat took it and felt like Judas.

'I must say,' remarked Luke, 'that Dizzy improves with knowing – and with all the good food he has been scoffing.'

He was in Mrs Britten's small back yard, watching Anne put out a large bowl of scraps for the happy cur, who barked his pleasure whenever he happened to see either of them.

'I don't think that he had ever been fed properly before,' replied Anne, 'or looked after, either.'

'No, indeed. Care and attention works wonders for us all.'

Luke forbore to add that the remarks which they had made about Dizzy could have been made about Anne. In the few weeks since he had first met her, everything about her – her looks, her skin and her general appearance – had improved wonderfully. The gaunt and haggard scarecrow was slowly changing into an attractive young woman.

Every week he revised her age downwards. From first judging her to be in her early thirties and then in her late twenties, Luke now thought it possible that she was in her early twenties. And this despite the fact that her conversation and her general demeanour were those of a woman much older than that.

For her part Mrs Cowper – who was not to know that Mr Luke Harcourt now always thought of her as Anne, however punctilious he was in addressing her as Mrs Cowper in conversation – thought that Mr Harcourt also improved the more one knew him.

He was so kind! She had not thought that a man could be kind, let alone as kind as Luke Harcourt was. Such had not been her experience of life. The fear which she had thought that she would always feel for all men deserted her when she was with him. She could almost bear for him to touch her. When he had helped her home after they had rescued Dizzy she had found, to her astonishment, that the strong arm on which she leaned was welcome to her.

Last night, when they had been talking after supper, which Luke now invariably ate with her and Mrs Britten instead of having it brought to his suite of rooms, he had told her that he had refused to write about Clairval's marriage.

'Not, you must understand,' he had said, 'that that means that no one will do so. He has already commissioned a friend of mine to undertake what I refused to do.'

'I am sorry to hear that,' she had said.

'Let me be honest,' Luke had told her earnestly. 'Had I needed the money, as my friend does, I doubt whether I should have allowed my scruples to overcome my need to earn a living. But I do have private means, and Pat does not, so you must not think too harshly of him. A man needs to eat. Bayes twitted me by saying that my small fortune enabled me to be nice in my conduct.'

He had paused – Why was he telling her this? – but something drove him on. 'I am not a very noble fellow after all, you see.'

Anne had done something which had surprised him. She had put out a hand to cover his where it had rested on the tablecloth. 'Necessity drives us all on to do things of which we are not proud, and none of us may judge another lest we ourselves are ready to be judged. At least you resisted temptation, for I think that you were tempted to accept Mr Bayes's commission, were you not? As at times we are all tempted.'

Luke had given a little laugh. 'All of us, Mrs Cowper? No, I cannot believe that you are to be included in the all of which you speak.'

Her smile for him had been a sad one. 'We none of us know the secrets of another's heart, Mr Harcourt. In that respect we are less fortunate than poor Dizzy, who has no secrets at all, and does not know whether any others of his kind have secrets, and is therefore, in that respect, always happy!'

How is it, Luke had thought afterwards, that Mrs Cowper and I so often end up speaking of such serious and moral matters? Not that I mind doing so, of course. Now Josette and I, until our last meeting, never really spoke of any serious matters at all. Cressy and I did, though. As do Cressy and James.

Mrs Britten had ended their conversation, deliberately Luke had thought, by talking nonsense about the odd-job boy who claimed to be frightened by small harmless Dizzy, and shot past his kennel as though a fire-breathing dragon dwelt there.

Anne had finished feeding Dizzy. Luke offered her his arm back into the house, and said, to show that he could make light conversation, 'You will accompany Mrs Britten and myself to the Fair next week, will you not? She seemed to think that you might refuse.'

She did not tell him that she had an aversion to going into large gatherings or being in a public place where she might be seen – and recognised – even though only recently she would have done. On the contrary, for some reason the thought of being escorted to a fair by Mr Luke Harcourt was a strangely exciting one.

'Oh, no,' and the bright blue eyes which looked up at him were sparkling. 'I shall be delighted to accompany you. I have never been to a fair. My father disapproved of them, and my late husband considered them beneath his notice. I have never been to Astley's Circus, either, and I suppose it is the notion that they were both forbidden to me which makes them seem so attractive.'

'Never been to a fair or to Astley's!' echoed Luke in a teasing and disbelieving voice. 'What a gap in your education, madam. I see that we must fill it. But I must warn you, you are not to put on your best bonnet, nor wear your most elaborate toilette, for if you do you are likely to become a target for pickpockets.'

She gave him a smile as teasing as his own. 'Then I pity the poor thieves, Mr Harcourt, for they will find nothing in my pocket to pick! They will have to rely on yours.'

'Oh, I am not so well breeched these days,' he retorted truthfully; the reason being that he was trying to live on his own earnings and not on the money which his father had settled on him. 'Fear not, though, I shall have enough to enable the three of us to join in all the fun of the fair.'

He bowed to Mrs Britten, who was watching them both from her chair by the window, an odd smile on her face.

Later, as he was leaving to join Pat O'Hare for a night on the town, Mrs Britten approached him as he was shrugging his greatcoat on.

'A word with you, Mr Harcourt, if you please.'

She was so grave that Luke wondered for a moment if she had suffered some bereavement and needed assistance. Not so, for taking his silence for consent, she continued. 'I know very well that you are as good-hearted a young gentleman as ever I let rooms to, and that is why I am daring to speak to you on this matter.

'I hope that you will take no offence at what you might see as meddling, but I must beg of you not to take any advantage of Mrs Cowper. I have seen the pleasure which you take in each other's company – which is very fine – but I would not wish your acquaint-ance with her to go any further than it has done. Mrs Cowper has had a hard life, with a great deal of suffering in it, and I would not like her to suffer any further pain.'

Luke said, as coolly as he could, although he was stung by the notion that his landlady thought that he was trifling with her friend, 'Would it reassure you, Mrs Britten, if I tell you that my intentions towards Mrs Cowper are strictly honourable?'

'Indeed, Mr Harcourt, I never thought that they were otherwise. It is simply that I trust you not to. . .' and she searched for the right phrase to use that would not offend him '. . .raise her expectations, as it were.'

'Oh, you may trust me not to do that,' he replied drily, so drily that Mrs Britten, her face troubled, caught at his arm.

'Oh, Mr Harcourt, do not take what I have just said so amiss that you cease to speak to Mrs Cowper at all. Since you returned from Wiltshire, she is a changed woman, and it is mostly your doing. Put down what I have said to you as the fears of an older woman for her protégée who deserves more than the unhappy life which has been hers so far.'

So, he had been right in his suppositions. Mrs Cowper's married life had not been a happy one. He said impulsively, for he knew his landlady well enough to be aware that she was no mere busybody, 'No offence taken, madam, I assure you. I have noted what you say and you may trust that my behaviour to her, as to all women, will be as proper as a gentleman's should.'

This seemed to reassure her, for she bowed her head, saying simply, 'Thank you, Mr Harcourt. I knew that you possessed a good heart.'

Luke smiled at her little compliment, and added a rider to his reassurance. 'You will allow me, I trust, to escort you both to the fair. I know that Mrs Cowper is looking forward to her visit very much.'

'Of course, Mr Harcourt. And I am greatly looking forward to going with you as well.'

He bowed and she curtsied. The strange little interview was over, leaving Luke with the distinct impression that, yes, there was some mystery about Anne Cowper which was making Mrs Britten so determined a protectress of her. He absolved himself of any wrong thoughts about her, since he had never viewed her as prey.

But it was also apparent that something must have changed in the manner in which he and Mrs Cowper spoke to one another and which had caused Mrs Britten to be troubled enough to speak to him.

Well, at least they had parted friends, although what she had said caused Luke to lie awake that night after an unsatisfactory evening's pleasure, and ask himself exactly what his intentions were concerning Anne Cowper.

To which he found no satisfactory answer.

Islington Fair was not so big as Bartholomew Fair – nor Greenwich Fair, for that matter – but it was big enough. Half of the citizenry welcomed it, the other – respectable – half most emphatically did not, since fairs not only attracted a small army of pickpockets and cutpurses, but also a band of gypsies. These were even more suspect than the thieves, but with less reason.

The smaller, uncovered booths were arranged down the High Street in front of the shops; another source of annoyance to the local townspeople, since they provided a fierce source of competition for them.

The larger covered booths, and the main attractions such as the menageries, and the small theatres under canvas called penny gaffs, were sited in the market place and on a piece of waste ground near by. The fair was officially opened by the Town Crier, a ceremony which Anne witnessed by accident when she delivered her latest batch of work to the shop in the High Street which had commissioned it.

She had never seen anything like it in her short, unhappy life, as she dawdled, wide-eyed, back to Mrs Britten's down the row of booths which were selling everything from gingerbread, sweets, oysters, wicker baskets and pegs to books and pamphlets.

The strangely dressed people who were tending the booths, the noise, and the sight of a troop of gypsies arriving on horseback, all held her entranced. It was as though the little joys of childhood that she had never been allowed to experience were being gifted to her now that she was a grown woman. More than one man gave her bright and sparkling eyes a second glance as she wandered along, and said to himself, 'Why, there's a pretty gal!'

'My dear, I thought that you were lost,' exclaimed Mrs Britten breathlessly when Anne finally arrived home with a pair of gingerbread men wrapped in a screw of paper which she handed to her friend.

'Oh, I see that you have been enjoying yourself at the Fair. Mind, the best of it will not be ready until later today when Mr Harcourt will be our escort. But was it wise of you to be alone for so long in such a public place among so many?'

Anne's smile was apologetic. 'I must confess that I never thought of that, but I can't believe that anyone would come to look for me in Islington.'

'Hmm,' snorted her friend. 'From what you have told me, I think that *he* might follow you to Hell, let alone Islington, in order to find you.' She was always careful never to name Anne's pursuer, even in the safety of her own home.

'But you will let me accompany you and Mr Harcourt this afternoon, won't you?' wheedled Anne.

'I'm not sure that I am wise to encourage you, and I admit I did agree that we should all three go, but dear Anne, do take care. Even with Mr Harcourt, take care.'

Anne dared not admit to herself what Mrs Britten might be hinting, and said, 'I cannot believe that Mr Harcourt has any sinister motives where I am concerned.'

'He is a young and handsome man, and that is enough,' declared Mrs Britten robustly. 'I know that he is a good-hearted one, but even good-hearted young men have their limitations and temptations.'

She would never have agreed to Mr Harcourt taking the pair of them to the fair if she had realised how far matters had gone between him and Anne – never mind that they were largely unspoken. She considered that the most dangerous thing of all was that neither Luke nor Anne fully understood what was happening to them. A foolish thought, perhaps, given Luke's undoubted experience of life and love, but meeting Mrs Anne Cowper had taken the pair of them into unknown territory.

Mrs Britten was concerned that they did not become lost there.

She was even more concerned when she saw the easy pleasure with which they greeted one another when the time came for them to visit the fair.

Luke had followed his own advice to Anne and had dressed down rather than up in a pair of grey woollen breeches which had seen better days, leather gaiters, heavy half-boots and an old brown coat. They were clothes which he wore when he visited Haven's End and engaged in country pursuits; they had never seen any better days at all, only worse ones.

'Why, Mr Harcourt,' Anne told him merrily. 'I don't think that I would have recognised you were it not that you are in Mrs Britten's hall waiting for us to come down.'

She put her head on one side, and rallied him by saying, her mouth curling with amusement as she finished, 'I do believe that I admire your hat most of all!' It was the kind of hat a haymaker might wear – or perhaps a coachman – brownish in colour, with a wide round brim and a low crown. But he had swept it off to greet them with all the flourish of a dandy of the *ton*.

'Now, Anne,' reprimanded Mrs Britten with a smile which robbed her tone of offence, 'you must admit that whatever he wears, Mr Harcourt always looks the gentleman.'

'Oh, dear, then I have quite failed in my objective,' mourned Luke. 'I did not wish to appear gentlemanly at all. Up from the country, rather. An honest yeoman, hardly worth robbing.'

He held out his arms for them to walk one on each side of him. 'Come, ladies, yeoman that I am, I shall be the envy of all at the Fair this afternoon.'

Luke thought that Anne had never looked better. Her gown was a pale mauve one, as befitted a widow, and was certainly not cut in the latest mode, or, indeed, in any known mode at all. The only thing which relieved its plainness was the cream-coloured collar which she had crocheted herself. Her bonnet was a tiny straw with a black velvet band and a couple of mauve silk pansies – also made by Anne – decorating it.

But it was not her clothing which was giving her a new glow; it was the slight blush in her cheeks which enhanced the ivory pallor of her face. Her face had lost its hollows, and her tender mouth was curving up, not down, as it had done when he first met her.

Humour informed it, and that humour had spread to her eyes, which sparkled and shone at him beneath her finely arched eyebrows. However was it that he had once thought her plain?

Islington Fair was roaring when they reached it. The noise was so great that before the day was over most of the small shopkeepers would be petitioning for it to be restrained. Children, eating gingerbread men or sucking sweets, ran about shouting. Men and women stood before the gaudily decorated booths, proclaiming their many attractions at the top of their voices.

All the small entertainments were in full swing. A gypsy fiddler was playing for an impromptu dance being performed by soldiers and their young women alongside a man who had three inverted thimbles before him on a small table.

Fascinated, Anne asked Luke what the man was doing. He smiled and told her, 'He lifts the thimbles to show you that there is a pea under one of them. He then covers them, moves them round and asks you to bet under which thimble the pea is to be found. If you guess correctly, you will win the bet, and he will pay you.'

'I know –' and Anne's voice was guarded ' – that I am an innocent, but I would have thought that the man with the thimbles would make only a poor living, since it would be easy for anyone who watched him carefully to know exactly where the thimble with the pea is.'

'You think so?' Luke smiled at her. 'Come, let me pay for you to try to find the thimble with the pea.' He laughed gently at her hesitation. 'It will not be a costly lesson, I assure you, but a useful one.'

He threw a florin on to the table, saying to the man, 'The lady wishes to play the game.'

'And so she shall, young sir.' The man, thickset and

wearing a battered top hat, crooned his patter at them. 'Look, pretty lady,' and he lifted the thimbles to show that the pea was under the middle one.

'Mark well what I do.' He began to move the thimbles rapidly around whilst Anne stared hard at the one under which she knew the pea was hidden, until he stopped suddenly, lifting his hands and leering at her.

'Now, pretty lady, where is the pea?'

'There!' And Anne confidently pointed at the right-hand thimble.

'Lift it, then, my pretty dear – and see whether you have won your bet.'

Anne lifted the thimble, to find beneath it – nothing!

'No, that can't be,' she wailed at Luke. 'I watched his hands so carefully that I was sure that it must be there.'

Luke and Mrs Britten were both laughing at her surprise. Grinning, the man said, 'Let me show the pretty lady where the pea is. Watch, dearie,' and he lifted the other two thimbles to reveal that the pea was under the middle one.

'I could have sworn that it was in the thimble on the right,' lamented Anne as they walked away. 'And I lost your florin for you, Mr Harcourt. I'm so sorry.'

'Oh, think nothing of that,' Luke said tenderly, pressing her hand which had somehow found its way into his. 'For it was I who was tricking you, as well as the thimble-rigger – which is what the man who runs that game is called. You see I knew that you couldn't win, because whichever thimble you had lifted you would have found nothing. The man palms the pea – that is, removes it and hides it in his hand – when he turns the thimble over at the beginning.'

'Oh, but, Mr Harcourt,' cried Anne, 'how can that be? There *was* a pea under the middle thimble, and look, someone has just won!'

She pointed at the thimble-rigging man who was handing money over to an ill-favoured rogue in a blue and white spotted neckerchief, who had been among those around the stall while Anne had been playing there.

'He simply palmed the pea again,' Luke informed her, 'and put it under the thimble even as he seemed to uncover it. The man who appeared to win was the thimble-rigger's assistant, there to make you think that *you* can win.

'There is a similar trick involving three playing cards, one of which is the Queen of Hearts, called Find the Lady. The fair people call those who bet on such games, marks – which means innocents. You see, there is an old saying, "The quickness of the hand deceives the eye ."'

Anne was secretly amused. A game called Find the Lady, indeed! Despite herself, she began to laugh. 'I was a mark, was I not? Were you educating me, Mr Harcourt, so that I should not bet my non-existent fortune, and lose it all?'

'I was teasing you, because I wanted to see your face when the man lifted the thimble and the pea wasn't there. It was, indeed, a picture I shall always treasure.'

Forgetting everything – Mrs Britten, the deportment which had ruled her life and which had seemed to bring her nothing but misery – Anne did something which she had never thought she could or would. Her face alight with mischief, she slapped lightly at Mr Luke Harcourt's hand. 'Oh, you wicked creature, to tease me so. You are as big a rogue as he is.'

Also forgetting himself and everything which he had promised to Mrs Britten so recently, Luke caught the slapping hand, bowed over it and kissed it before he could stop himself. 'So pleased to have amused you,' he murmured. 'Now, what shall I follow that with?'

'Nothing,' said Mrs Britten smartly. She had been watching her lodgers and was displeased with them both. They seemed to have lost the sense they had been born with. Particularly Anne, who also appeared to have forgotten how precarious her position was. 'You must allow the showmen to entertain us now.'

And so they did. Luke, who knew all about fairs and had visited many before, found his enjoyment in watching Anne's. Eyes wide, lips parted, her face rosy with pleasure, she found entertainment in everything she saw.

She hid her face in Luke's chest when the sword swallower began his act. 'Oh, no. I can't endure the sight of that,' but surprisingly was enchanted when Luke paid for them to enter the booth where Madame Giradelli, The Fireproof Lady, performed her magic tricks, holding her hands in the flames of a brazier and apparently swallowing fire without any ill effect.

She wore the oddest costume which Anne had ever seen: an elaborately frilled gown which ended just below the knee to reveal a pair of heavily frilled pantaloons. Her feet were bare, and she had a ring with a giant winking stone on one of her toes.

After that, Luke bought them all oysters from one of the large booths, which boasted gaily striped coloured awnings, and where a pretty girl danced up and down before it, trying to persuade the passers by to sample the goods. She winked at Luke, calling him 'a fine upstanding young feller,' when he handed his money over.

Anne had never eaten oysters in the public street before, nor had she ever visited a menagerie, so her pleasure was guaranteed, as well as his, when they entered the big tent where Mr Wombwell had assembled in tiny cages some of the most ferocious animals on earth. Or so his posters, and the barker outside, informed them.

Next Luke took them into Mr Richardson's penny gaff which gave Mrs Anne Cowper more pleasure than the one visit to the theatre which she had been allowed as a young girl before she had been married.

She joined in hissing the villain, cheering the handsome hero, and in clapping the happy ending when the hero and his pretty girl were reunited after he had killed the villain in a duel. Never mind that both hero and heroine were rather long in the tooth, their remarkable and garish costumes more than made up for that.

'Oh,' sighed Anne blissfully when they were in the open again. 'I did enjoy that.'

Luke, about to offer her his arm, was struck, as though by summer lightning, with a most blinding revelation. She was standing by him so that he was seeing her in profile, and the expression of pure delight on her delicate face had an extraordinary effect on him. As thunder follows lightning, so Luke was overwhelmed by the realisation that this, this, was nothing other than love.

He also knew that he had never truly experienced it before. What he had felt for Cressy had been something quite different. Most of all he wished to protect the innocent creature beside him. He had never felt the need to protect Cressy, for she had never been vulnerable, had always been self-sufficient. But Anne – oh, that was a different matter.

And yet, at the same time, he wanted her. He wanted to be as near to her, as close to her, as a man might be to a woman. He wanted her in his arms, not only to tell her that he wished to love and care for her, but so that they could join together in experiencing all that men and women were made for: the age-old ceremony where they would become not two, but one.

All this in a moment of time. He was saved, either fortunately or otherwise, from saying or doing anything by a familiar voice hailing him.

It was Pat O'Hare.

Chapter Four

'Good day to you, Harcourt, and to you, mesdames,' cried Pat, all Irish charm as he swept off his hat. 'I believe you know my friends, Jackson and Thomas. What the devil are you doing in that get-up? Rehearsing for a part as a yokel in Drury Lane's next pantomime?'

His keen eyes swept over Luke and the two modestly dressed women with him. The younger one looked rather like a slow-burning charmer, one of those who improved as you got to know her. Trust Luke Harcourt to know where to find them!

'Come, O'Hare,' retorted Luke. 'You know how many pickpockets and cutpurses haunt these fairs. I'm less likely to be a target than you are, togged out fit for a reception at Devonshire House.'

'Pooh, nonsense,' was Pat's reply. 'Aren't you going to introduce us to the ladies?' His smile at Anne was a winning one.

He didn't win Anne. Inwardly she shrank away from him. She had been so happy alone with Luke and Mrs Britten. She still feared all men except Luke, so she stood mumchance, head bent, until Pat decided that he had been mistaken about her. She was simply a dowdy-goody with an attendant friend to whom Harcourt was being stupidly kind by taking them to the Fair.

All in all, the next quarter of an hour was not a happy one for Anne until Jackson proposed that they visit the penny gaff. It enabled Luke to say that they had already visited it and that he had promised Mrs Cowper that she should see The Learned Pig, who had so recently impressed a crowd of assorted scholars and savants, so they begged to be excused.

Excused they were, and Luke could not resist a quiet smile when, as he left them, Pat went to pull his watch out of his pocket – and found that it, and his handkerchief, had disappeared quite.

The grin which he gave Luke's party was a rueful one. 'You are not to crow over me, Harcourt,' he offered sadly. 'I doubt whether I could bring myself to wear that get-up, even to save my watch.'

This sally set Luke's party, as well as his own, laughing.

Anne, her arm tucked in Mrs Britten's, whispered to her kind friend, 'Mr O'Hare seemed a pleasant enough gentleman, but I am not sorry to see him and his party leave us. It is so much cosier when there are only the three of us.'

Mrs Britten silently agreed with her. She was only happy when Anne Cowper was not in too much company. Even to be at the fair at all was perhaps a mistake. On the other hand, this friend of Mr Harcourt's could scarcely be seen as endangering her. . .

Anne enjoyed seeing the animals most of all, from the monkeys on sticks to The Learned Pig who turned out to be just as learned as promised, proudly displaying his knowledge of French and German. She also admired the farm animals, from sheep to cattle, whose owners all boastfully proclaimed that they were the largest of their kind in the world.

It was when they were inspecting a ewe so large that it appeared almost deformed that a man whom Anne had already seen watching them, and who had a most fearsome appearance, walked up to Luke. He said in the strangest accent she had ever heard, 'All you *gorgios* look alike to me, but I knew at once that you were the only one who ever ate a *hotchiwitchi jogray* with us and claimed that you enjoyed it. Welcome, brother Luke,' and he held out his large hand.

Seen near to, he was no less fearsome, but beneath the long hair on his head and face he possessed a kind of hawklike handsomeness. He was wearing a jacket like Luke's, only the buttons on it were half crowns – and as if that were not enough, those on his flashy waistcoat were spaded half guineas.

His breeches were similar to a gamekeeper's, except that they, and his jacket, were made of velveteen, and his leggings, unlike Luke's, were not leather, but of a buff cloth, furred at the bottom.

But it was his hat which was the strangest thing of all. It had a high peak like a Spaniard's. The whip he carried was ornamented with a huge silver knob. His holland shirt was finely made and was a brilliant white. All told, he made Luke look shabbier than ever.

A couple of other men, as strange and fine in dress and appearance as he was, stood a little way behind him, like the courtiers in the playlet which they had recently seen in the penny gaff.

'Jasper!' cried Luke. 'You're a long way from home.'

'Oh, brother Luke,' smiled Jasper. 'All places are home to us. You should know that. And this is your pretty wife?'

Anne blushed and looked away. Luke said briefly,

'This is my friend, Mrs Anne Cowper, and our landlady, Mrs Britten. They are doubtless wondering what a *hotchiwitchi jogray* is.' He turned to them, explaining, 'You have Jasper Petulengro, the king of the gypsies, no less, to tell you what it is.'

'A hedgehog stew,' translated Jasper. 'And you know, brother Luke, that we Romanies have no king. True it is, though, that I am their Pharaoh. I am sad, Luke, that you have not yet found your mate – but you will bring your pretty *rackley* and her friend to drink tea with us, will you not? We are camped yonder on the nearest thing to a heath that we could find. Come.'

'You may not call yourself a king, Jasper,' Luke riposted, 'but you behave like one – and that is all that matters in this world!'

Mrs Britten, fearful of the gypsies, as so many townspeople were, whispered to Anne, 'If we were not with Mr Harcourt, I should be afraid to go to their camp, but I don't think that he will allow any harm to come to us.'

Even as she spoke, a group of gypsies on horseback galloped up, led by one of the most handsome men Anne had ever seen. He said something in a strange language to Jasper and to Luke, whom he greeted with a flourish of the hand and a bent head. There was nothing humble about his manner, and he nodded condescendingly when Luke replied, haltingly, in the same strange language.

When Jasper saw that Anne was listening, fascinated, to them both, he said, 'They are speaking Romany, pretty lady, the language of the gypsies. Brother Luke is one of the few *gorgios* – that is, people who are not Romanies – who has taken the trouble to learn it. We honour him for doing so.'

Led by the horsemen, they reached the encampment,

which was made up of small tents, with wagons drawn up behind them. Before the tents were tripods from which iron cooking pots hung.

A small woman, who greeted them, turned out to be Jasper Petulengro's wife. She was finely and strangely dressed. Her dark hair hung in long braids, and she had huge gold hoops in each ear. Anne wondered if the pearls around her long, proud neck were real. If so, they were worth a small fortune, as were the gilt ornaments on her dress.

She kissed Luke on his cheek, before taking his hand and bidding them all to sit so that they might drink tea and break bread with them. The handsome horseman had dismounted, and was staring boldly at Anne, so boldly that, a little afraid, she turned her head away.

Luke saw that the man's attention worried her. Quietly he said, 'Do not be afraid. His name is Tawno Chikno which means The Small One, although he is so tall – just as we call Lady Jersey, who chatters so much, Silence. He has an ugly middle-aged wife who adores him, and he her. Jasper has told me that many *gorgio* women have begged him to marry them, but he has always refused! So, you see, there is nothing to be afraid of.'

Jasper overheard Luke, and also tried to reassure Anne. 'Brother Luke tells you true. But then he always does. He should have been one of us.'

He handed Anne tea in a fine china cup and saucer. 'Eat and drink with us, my pretty.'

Anne thanked him shyly. Luke thought that he had never seen her look so well. There was a slight flush on her face as she drank her tea and ate the coarse bread which Mrs Petulengro gave her. The woman had been watching her carefully, and spoke at length to Luke and Jasper in Romany.

Luke listened to her, then told Anne, 'Mrs Petulengro thinks that you have an interesting face, and that she would like to read the leaves in your cup after you have drunk your tea. She is a *chovihani* or a fortune teller. They call fortune telling *dukkerin* in their own language.'

He did not tell her that Mrs Petulengro had also said, 'Yon *rackley* will be your doom, brother Luke,' meaning that Anne was his fate, or his future. When he had shaken his head at her, she had lifted her shoulders and said, 'You may not alter the future, brother Luke, howsoever you might try to. But it is no great matter since you have no wish to do so. I see your heart and her name is written there.'

She leaned forward when Luke had spoken, holding out her hand to take Anne's cup. Hesitantly, Anne gave it to her. She did not believe that the woman could tell her fortune, and she hoped that she could not tell her past. She watched Mrs Petulengro stare at the pattern of the leaves at the bottom of her cup as intently as she had previously stared at Anne and Luke.

'Your hand,' she said at last, putting the cup down. 'Give me your hand, my pretty dear, that I may read it, for the tea leaves are not as plain as they ought to be.'

She spoke as though she were intoning some strange ritual, and her eyes were as fixed as though she were looking, not at Anne, but at some distant horizon. Anne found herself falling into something resembling a trance as Mrs Petulengro took her hand and fixed her strange yellow eyes on her.

At last she spoke in a lilting, singsong fashion, not at all like that of her normal voice. 'I see you imprisoned on high in a strange place far from here. You have come to us after a long and dangerous journey. You look small and frail but you have a courage as strong

as that of a Romany's. Two treasures are yours, and
the second is not gold. A faithful loving heart is better
than riches, and that, too, you possess.

'All before you, and all that is past is dark and
mysterious, but at the end is light, and you shall have
your heart's desire, but not before much suffering.
Suffering, they say, purifies, and suffering has already
purified you and will purify you more. I will give you
the power, not only to endure, but to see the truths of
life and love.'

She dropped Anne's hand and looked into her eyes
for a long minute, as though she were searching her
very soul. She spoke again, her voice so faint that only
Anne could hear her.

'Most strange it is, dearest *chal*. Through the darkness around you I can see that your destiny and ours
are entwined, though how and why, I do not know.
You are in great danger, but fear not, all shall be well.'

She paused, spoke only to repeat what she had said
earlier,

'At the end is light. . .and that is all I can see. . .that,
and the gift that I bestow on you.'

Silence followed, until, 'Did I speak?' she asked
Anne. 'Did I prophesy?'

'You spoke darkly of the past – and of the future,'
replied Anne. 'But I think that I understood you.'

Oh, yes, the woman before her had somehow seen
something of her past life. Anne had said nothing to
her beforehand which might have hinted of imprisonment, suffering and flight – but she had seen them. She
had also spoken of a future where Anne would achieve
her heart's desire – but only after more suffering. Her
heart's desire! What would that be?

Anne looked up, and saw Luke's eyes on her. In that
moment she knew, not only that she loved him, but

that he loved her. She looked at the handsome young gypsy, and knew that what Luke had told her was true. He loved his plain and middle-aged wife dearly. It was as though many things which had been hidden from her, so that she had walked the world as though she were asleep, were made plain.

And Mrs Britten, what of her? For the first time Anne could see quite clearly the goodness of her: a goodness which few possessed. She twisted her hands together. Could she live with this new power?

Mrs Petulengro was still watching her even though she had sunk exhausted to the ground. She said, again for Anne's ears only, 'Oh, *chal*, *chal*, do not repine. Accept, and although everything has changed it will be as though nothing has. But the power will not leave you.'

Anne looked at Luke again, and the revelation was still there, but did not blind her. Accept, yes, she would accept.

'*Chal*?' she asked him. 'And *rackley*? What do they mean?'

'*Chal* means child,' Luke said. '*Rackley* is woman.'

He could see immediately that Anne had changed again as she had been changing since he first met her. But this change had been rapid, not slow, and he could not put a finger on what it was. Always he had been aware of her brave spirit behind the submissive face that she showed the world, but now that spirit was suddenly visible.

In some way she had been blessed. He had not heard what Mrs Petulengro had said to her. No one had for, although Anne had heard her voice as loud and compelling, the others had heard only a low muttering. He knew, though, that the change was connected with the *chovihani* and her divination

Jasper Petulengro, who had been intently watching all that had passed, said gently, 'Eat, my children, eat. The breaking of bread together seals friendship. My wife has made your lady one of us, as you are one of us, brother Luke, so is she our sister. There is always a home here for you.'

Mrs Petulengro suddenly spoke in her prophetic voice again.

'Aye, and it may yet be needed. Give me your remaining bread, *chal*. I feel faint and you have had some of my strength.'

Anne handed the bread over, and Mrs Petulengro tore at it as though she had not eaten for days. She rose and walked towards the tents, saying 'I must sleep.'

Her husband, his face troubled, watched her go. He said to Luke, 'It is not often that the strength leaves her after the spirit has spoken, yet it has done so today. But remember this, she always speaks true.'

In a lighter tone, he added, 'Come, pretty lady, brother Luke and the lady's protectress, come and see Chikno school the horses. It is a sight to please mortal men and women more than a little.'

So they did, and a fair sight it was, and after that one of the gypsies came with his fiddle and escorted them back to the Fair, bowing low before he left them, blessing them in Romany.

Anne's long and happy day was over, and exalted, she walked back to Mrs Britten's, her hand in Luke's, knowing that not only did she love, but that she was loved.

Before they had parted Jasper had bid her farewell, adding, 'Remember, pretty lady, that though the *chovihani* spoke so surely of the past and the future, all that we mortals ever have is the present. Enjoy that, for the past is gone, and may not be relived, and the truth of the future is unknown, even though we may have had a glimpse of it, since sometimes that glimpse may be deceitful. Meet your doom as it comes to you. Seize the day.'

That night, for the first time since she had arrived at Mrs Britten's, Anne's sleep was peaceful, her dreams were happy ones, and Luke walked through them all.

'Pray, Mr Harcourt, did you enjoy the hedgehog stew of which Mr Petulengro spoke?'

It was the following afternoon. Luke had come down to the drawing-room where Anne was working. Her face had lit up when he entered, for her visit to the gypsies had liberated her, and she no longer feared to let him know how much she enjoyed his company.

'Not very much,' he answered her, 'but it would not do to say so. I was only a boy when I first met the gypsies, and Tawno and his men cured me of my fear of horses. My gratitude to them is so great that I would do nothing to hurt them. Letting me eat with them and share their life a little is an honour not given to many *gorgios* and I am very sensible of that.'

'Afraid of horses,' echoed Mrs Britten incredulously. 'You do surprise me, Mr Harcourt, you ride so beautifully.'

By her expression Luke saw that Anne, too, was surprised by his confession.

'Oh, yes,' he went on. 'I had a bad fall when I was very young, and although my guardian thought that I had recovered from it, my recovery was only a physical one. I had to exercise my will every time I went riding. I dare not confess my cowardice until one day, when I was at the gypsy encampment on the heath near my home at Haven's End, Tawno Chikno dared me to ride

one of their half-broken horses. I think that he sensed
my fear and wanted me to confront it.'

He paused, and continued as though the memory
still pained him. 'I will not bore you with the details of
how he cured me. Suffice it that he did, and that the
lesson was long and hard. Afterwards I found riding a
joy, and not a penance, and he taught me some of the
simpler equestrian tricks he knew.

'They do not share the whole of their knowledge
with us, only a little. They are fearful that, if too much
is shared, the spirit of the Romanies will die, and they
will become like *gorgios* – than which there is no worse
fate.'

Anne bent her head over her work. She did not want
to discuss the Romany's powers. She had thought that
the ability to read men and women would pass from
her as soon as she left the gypsy camp, but it was still
with her. She found that she even knew what Dizzy
was feeling – she could not call the blur which surrounded him thinking! But his happiness when he saw
her was more tangible than ever.

What touched Anne was discovering how careful of
her Mrs Britten was, and that she was determined to
protect her from Luke in case he began to think wrong
thoughts about her. She had also found that she had
another talent. If she wished, she could blank out her
awareness of other's feelings.

I wonder what she is thinking, mused Luke, watching
the slight play of emotion on Anne's face. He sighed.
He really ought to be paying attention to his own
problems, not troubling about Anne's. Ever since he
had turned down Bayes's commission to write scandal
about Clairval, he had been finding it difficult to write
at all.

Anne heard the sigh. It told her that Luke was

worried, but not what was worrying him. She looked at him under her lashes. His brow was furrowed, and there were signs of strain on his handsome face. Even her new powers of intuition were not powerful enough for her to divine exactly what was wrong with him: that having decided he would no longer live on his father's bounty, he was finding it impossible to make a living at all.

And then she knew! She said, as off-handedly as she could, 'Pray, what new articles are you writing for Mr Bayes? Or have you accepted a commission for another editor? Do not answer me if you think that I am prying into your affairs.'

Luke decided to tell her the truth. He might feel better if he shared his feelings of despair with someone. 'You are not prying, Mrs Cowper. Indeed, it is kind of you to ask. No, I have not begun any new articles for Mr Bayes, or for anyone-else. Nor am I like to. The nub of the matter is that I seem to have lost all my powers of invention and I am beginning to wonder whether I ought to have settled in the safe haven of Oxford's cloisters after all.'

'You are not writing of society's scandals, then?'

Luke stirred restlessly in his chair. 'That is part of my problem. It is not the kind of work which I wish to engage in, but refusing it seems to have dried up my muse. I wish. . . I don't know what I wish. . .'

Anne put down her sewing, and said earnestly, 'I think I understand you, Mr Harcourt. It occurs to me that, since writing scandal about high life is not your true *métier*, you might be happier engaged in writing the truth about low life.'

His head, which had drooped a little, jerked up. Luke said, struck by her suggestion, 'What exactly did you have in mind?'

'Why, seeing how much we enjoyed ourselves at the fair yesterday, and the rapport that you so obviously had, not only with the gypsies, but all the showmen and women present, you might use that rapport to write about them.

'Truthfully, of course, for it seems to me that I have never come across any really good prose which told of the lives of those who, after all, make up the greater number of the citizens of Britain. Do not the humble deserve to be celebrated as well as the great? And because you sympathise with them, who better than you to do it?'

Oh, how beautiful she looked, as well as clever and kind! What a splendid notion she had offered him. Luke's busy brain had already begun to see the possibilities of what she was saying.

Thinking by his silence that he was perhaps not impressed by her suggestion, Anne added in an encouraging tone, 'I believe you said that Mr Bayes was ready to hire someone like Mr Cruikshank to illustrate your work for you when you were writing scandal. If so, then could he not draw The Learned Pig, or the thimble-rigger in action instead?'

Luke could not contain himself. Mrs Britten or no Mrs Britten, duenna or no duenna, he was out of his chair at one bound, and was pulling Anne to her feet in order to kiss her vigorously on each cheek.

'Oh, my dear. What a splendid girl you are! There was my destiny staring me in the face, and I could not see it for looking, but you could. I can write about the gypsies and Mr Petulengro and try to make people understand their true nature, instead of believing myths about them! I do believe that if Bayes does not want me, then there are others who will.'

He whirled her around as though they were dancing

together – a vigorous kind of waltz, perhaps – before he tenderly settled her back in her chair again.

'Really, Mr Harcourt,' exclaimed Mrs Britten, scandalised. 'I would never have thought it of you, such a perfect young gentleman as you used to be. Mrs Cowper deserves more consideration from you.'

'And so she does.' Luke was jubilant. 'Let me do this in proper form!' He went down on one knee before the blushing Anne. 'Dear Mrs Cowper, allow me to thank you for your splendid suggestion. When I have made my fortune, I will offer you a suitable reward. There! Will that do?' He kissed her again: on the hand this time.

Anne was laughing. 'Oh, Luke,' she said, forgetting all decorum, all proper forms of address between a single young man and a young widow. 'Thank me when you have sold your first paper describing scenes from low life.'

'And that, too, is it,' declaimed Luke. 'My title. "Scenes from Low Life". Why, I do believe that there may be a book in it!'

Mrs Britten had never seen him behave so before. He had always been quietly courteous, so gentlemanly, so decorous. Whatever had got into him?

Anne Cowper had got into him. That, and his sudden understanding that she had just pointed out to him the way he ought to go. His first paper could be written almost from her point of view: that of someone who was seeing the fair for the first time.

He was on fire to begin at once. 'My dear Anne, you will forgive me, and Mrs Britten, you too. I must go upstairs immediately and begin to write before the muse deserts me. Tomorrow I shall visit Bayes, and if he doesn't want me, why, I know several other editors who I am sure will.'

The door closed behind him. Mrs Britten opened her mouth to remind Anne that she ought to go with care where Luke Harcourt was concerned, but the expression on her friend's face stopped her.

My dear Anne, he called me. And then he kissed me. That was all Anne Cowper knew, and all she needed to know.

Chapter Five

When had he fallen in love with her? Luke was in no doubt that what he felt for Anne was more than a mere passing fancy. It was both deep and true and had only been fully revealed to him when he had seen her innocent pleasure at Islington Fair – which did not mean that he had been struck down by his passion for her at that exact moment.

No, looking back, he could remember a hundred small things which should have told him that she was slowly turning into the one woman in the world whom Luke Harcourt wanted for a wife.

He remembered the night when he had seen Cressy at Lady Leominster's and had realised that he still loved her, but was no longer in love with her. Could Anne have been the reason for his change of heart? Surely not, for then he had scarcely known her. Was it conceivable that from the very first time that he met her she had begun to wind her way around his heart?

Luke was sure she was good: he also knew that she was both clever and kind. She was hardworking as well: stitching conscientiously away at gossamy baby clothes in order to earn a meagre living, and yet at the same time quietly and unobtrusively helping Mrs Britten about the house.

She was not at all the sort of young woman with whom he might have thought that he would fall in love. That woman would have been outgoing, perhaps a little racy in manner – in short, a woman like his stepmother Cressy.

But if Anne was quiet and retiring where Cressy was voluble and forthright, she possessed an integrity of character wholly admirable in one so frail and defence-less. Without either wealth or position she yet gave off an effortless aura of moral authority. Like Cressy, she was brave, but her bravery took a different form from that of his stepmother's, who had always lived in a protected world.

No, Anne was living at the margin where pennies were scarce and both men and women were exploited, but the influence which she was beginning to exert on him was a profound one. For the first time, Luke had begun to question his own life and to find it wanting.

Whose example but Anne's had made him determine to live as little as possible on his father's money, and instead try to carve out his own career? He had been a dilettante, idling his life away whilst pretending to be a writer; a typical younger son surviving on the edges of the great world of society, frittering away his talents.

If he had any, that was! Well he would soon find out. He had followed Anne's advice to write about the Fair and its people. He had worked far into the night, the words tumbling from his pen, his newly roused mind driving him on. Why had he never thought of writing about the life around him before?

He had been stuck in a rut where he poured out high-minded, moralising copy about the political world, or stale and perfumed gossip about the people he met in high society. And all the time he had possessed a talent for something quite different – and without Anne Cowper's prompting he would never have found it out!

By morning he was handing the newly written, unblotted sheets to Bayes, saying, 'I couldn't write scandal for you, sir, but here is something I *can* write, and which you might like to print. You could perhaps persuade Cruikshank – or someone like him – to illustrate them. If you approve of the idea, I would like to write a series about low life in London and the country and the gypsies who frequent the fairs.'

Bayes had begun to read Luke's work with a patronising smile on his face. He had always considered Harcourt promising as a writer, but held back by his being fundamentally unserious as a result of his class and his small, but dependable, income.

His smile faded. 'Good stuff, Harcourt!' he exclaimed. 'Damned lively. Didn't know you had it in you. There's a public for this you know. The people with money walk by this world and never see it. And you're right about an illustration. Yes, I'll take it, on the condition that you write me something like this for every number.'

The strength of his enthusiasm surprised Luke. Bayes was basically a cynical manipulator, but he had a keen eye for what people would pay to read. Here was an immediate source of income for him – and it was all owing to Anne Cowper's suggestion. Bayes picked up the first page again and began to read it more carefully.

'With this,' he enthused, 'we'll get our readers coming and going in every number. O'Hare can do the society stuff and you the low life.' He thought a moment, said, 'That's it, that's the title: "Scenes from Low Life"!'

Luke forbore to tell him that Anne Cowper had been

there before him. Let Bayes think that he was the originator. If the series was a success, he would doubtless soon be claiming the idea as his own. Well, let him, so long as he paid Luke Harcourt a good fee.

'You think that you can keep this up?' Bayes asked him anxiously.

Could he keep it up? Luke, who had resolved to go back to Islington and start writing immediately, now that inspiration had begun to flow, assured him that he could.

'My next will be about the tricksters at the fair, and then I'll probably write two about the gypsies – with your approval, of course.'

'Splendid, old feller. If Egan can have the public enthusing about boxers, then why not gypsies and tricksters from Harcourt, eh? Your name's a bit fancy, though, for someone writing about low life, ain't it? How about Solomon Grundy instead?'

The idea of being Solomon Grundy took Luke's fancy, if only because the name seemed to belong to someone vastly different from his own carefully dressed and well-mannered person.

'What a splendid notion,' he exclaimed approvingly. 'Solomon Grundy it shall be – so long as you don't address me as "Solly boy". I don't think that I could stomach that.'

'You'll stomach the money you're going to earn by using his name,' remarked Bayes shrewdly. 'Come to the ordinary with me and have a steak and kidney pie, and we'll agree terms while we eat. "Scenes from Low Life",' he repeated thoughtfully. 'I like it.'

On the way home, having decided that he must keep his expenses down, Luke stopped at the livery stables to order the proprietor to sell the horse he kept there, even though it hurt him to part with Tiger. Another problem was that he had agreed to have a night on the town with Pat O'Hare after he had dined with James and Cressy. It was too late for him to cancel it, but such self-indulgent treats must be a thing of the past until he had a steady income.

In the morning he would visit Jack Hatfield, who published a lighter magazine than Bayes, called *The Talk of the Town*, and offer him a little piece which was already running through his mind on fashionable slang and thieves' cant. It was just the kind of piece Hatfield was willing to pay for. He had a copy of Captain Robert Grose's elderly Dictionary of the Vulgar Tongue, and he could easily bring it up to date.

It was quite extraordinary how fertile his imagination had become since Anne Cowper had seeded it with her original suggestion. His gratitude would take the form of inviting her to visit Cremorne Gardens with him – Mrs Britten could act as their duenna. Alas, neither of them was at home so Luke left for dinner at Lyndale House without thanking her.

James and Cressy thought that he was rather less forthcoming at table than he usually was. Later that evening, after their last guest had left, dinner having been taken at the fashionable hour of four-thirty, Cressy chose to raise the subject of Luke with her husband.

'James, do you not consider it a trifle odd that Luke has scarcely been seen in society this season, has dined with us most infrequently, and tonight was very unlike his usual self? He can't be ill, surely? He didn't look ill,' she added doubtfully. 'What's more, he told Frank Belsize that he had sold Tiger when Frank asked him to ride with him in the Park on Saturday.'

'Sold Tiger!' exclaimed James, more struck by his son doing such an unlikely thing than by the fact that

Almacks, Devonshire House and other haunts of high life were being neglected by him. 'What an odd thing to do! I trust that he's not been extravagant lately and run into debt. I know his allowance isn't huge, but he's never done such a thing before. I would never have thought that he'd sell Tiger.'

'Well, that had occurred to me, too,' confessed Cressy, 'that he had run into debt – but when I asked him if he were strapped for cash, because if he were then I might be able to help him out, he was quite short with me. Short for Luke, that is,' she amended. 'You know how astonishingly polite he always is.

'He told me in no uncertain terms that, on the contrary, he was living well within his earnings, and intended to continue doing so. He did remember to thank me for my offer, though. As prettily as usual. Perhaps I'm being fanciful.'

James said slowly, 'I shan't reproach you for offering to bail him out if he were in trouble. And I don't think that you were being fanciful. He struck me as having changed in some way. . .'

'Perhaps he's fallen in love,' Cressy offered hopefully. 'But who can he have met to do so? Frank told me later that he has hardly seen him this year, either. If he's not going into society, he won't be meeting anyone suitable.'

She saw James's face change and, as usual, read it correctly, and said faintly, 'Oh, no, never say that he's fallen in love with someone *un*suitable!'

'It's possible. I know that he's always been steady, but very often it's the steady ones who kick over the traces when they do at last fall in love with someone.'

They stood silent for a moment before James took Cressy into his arms 'Do not fret, my love. He's a grown man, and in some ways he's been too chained to the pair of us for too long. He's going his own way now, and we mustn't stop him. Trust in his basic goodness, Cress, as I do.'

He rarely called her Cress, and she knew that, for all his brave words, James was worried about his son – who had never before given them the slightest occasion to think that he might kick over the traces.

'Very well, James. So long as he knows that there's always a haven for him with us.'

'Our home has an appropriate name. Haven's End, my love. It's his refuge as well as ours if ever he needs one – which I pray that he never will.'

Having a night on the town in company with Pat O'Hare and a crowd of other young bucks was not half so much fun as taking Anne to the fair, Luke was discovering.

They had begun by visiting a silver hell off the Haymarket, so called because it was not so expensive as some of the gaming halls where the top-notch swells went. Luke had never been a great gambler; that night he didn't want to gamble at all.

'Oh, come on, Harcourt,' grumbled Pat. 'You're a regular wet blanket these days. Risk a penny if you can't risk anything else.'

'Don't want to risk anything,' returned Luke equably while watching Pat in some surprise. Pat had already gambled a considerable sum, and for the moment luck appeared to be with him, since he had managed to double it. Idly, Luke wondered where Pat was getting his money from. He was usually short of the ready, but tonight he was flush with it. He certainly wasn't selling enough of his writing to Bayes, or anyone else, to have so much cash at his disposal.

'You're not as jolly as you used to be, Harcourt.' Pat

was already half-cut. 'And you ain't drinking, either. The drink's free, you know.'

Cynically, Luke thought that the free drink was there to fuddle the few wits of the committed gamesters who always believed that a really big win was waiting for them just around the corner.

Another thing just around the corner was Laura Knight's, which Pat wished to visit, although the rest of the party wanted to patronise The Coal Hole.

They ended by wrangling at the entrance to a dirty alley off the Haymarket, Luke wishing himself anywhere but where he was. He was wondering at the enthusiasm with which he had, in the past, joined in this type of excursion. Some wanted to go one way, some another, Luke was just about to perform his own judgment of Solomon by suggesting that the party cut itself in two when he heard a woman's wailing cry coming from halfway down the alley.

'Help me, oh, help, please.' The last word was cut off in mid-shout.

'What's that?' Luke turned towards the direction of the cry.

'That? Oh, some doxy complaining that her client is being a little too enthusiastic. Come on, Harcourt. Where do you want to go? Oh, the devil, he's gone to rescue the ladybird!'

There had been something so desperate in the woman's cry that Luke felt that he could not ignore it. He ran down the alley towards a pair of open gates before a large courtyard.

A small group of men were gathered there, watching another man, a large one, who had a woman pinned against the wall, his fell purpose quite plain. His watchers were so lost in their concentration on him, cheering the woman's attacker on, that Luke was through them, his companions streaming after him, before they realised that he was there.

He took the man by the shoulder in order to pull him away, which allowed his victim to scream at Luke, 'Oh, Gawd, mister, save me! Oh, I wants me Ma!' Except that it was not a woman who was the subject of public rape, but a girl who was little more than a child, her clothes torn, her face streaked with tears, her thin arms held up to protect herself.

It was fortunate for Luke that his friends had followed him. The girl's attacker was large, but no larger than his companions, who looked like a group of bruisers on holiday: they would have made short work of Luke had he been alone.

Instead, Luke's party got between them and the man he had swung towards him. Pat O'Hare took the child by the hand to pull her away from where Luke and the girl's attacker were struggling. Another of Luke's friends shouted, 'I'll fetch the Watch,' and ran back up the alley.

By now the man Luke held twisted almost free, sufficiently so to turn to confront him so that for a moment they were eye to eye. Luke almost let go of him in shocked surprise at discovering that the man whom he was holding on to so grimly was none other than the Marquess of Clairval. Clairval was equally shocked on recognising Luke.

'Damn you!' he gritted between his teeth. 'Loose your hold on me, Harcourt. I'll let no man's bastard interfere with my pleasure, even if Lyndale is his father.'

'And damn you, too,' retorted Luke, all his usual mild and courteous charm missing at the sight of a man publicly violating a child for the amusement of himself and his companions. 'I'll hand you over to the Watch

to deal with when they come. You'll face the magistrates in the morning, I'll make sure of that.'

Clairval was almost spitting with thwarted rage. He
tried to strike Luke in the face, but failed. His men
were fighting and struggling with Luke's party until one
of them saw that in the excitement of the fracas the
child had disappeared after wrenching herself free from
Pat.

He grasped Clairval by the arm and shouted, 'Stop,
m'lord, stop. The doxy has scarpered. Neither the
Watch nor the magistrates can do anything to you
without anyone to snitch on you!'

His voice was loud enough to end the struggle.
Clairval stood back, laughing at Luke, just as the Watch
arrived, a gross fat man, self-importance personified.

'What's this, then? A girl child attacked and like to
be ravished? Let me see her – and the man accused.'

Still laughing and now the picture of aristocratic
arrogance, Clairval strolled languidly forward, pulling
a guinea from his breeches pocket, he pressed it into
the watchman's hand.

'A misunderstanding, look you. Take this for your
wasted errand. I am Clairval, as my companions will
testify. Those who have drunk too deep, like our friend
here – ' and he waved a contemptuous hand at Luke
' – often see what isn't there. Look around you, there
is no child, there never was a child, as again my men
will testify.'

Which they did, surrounding the Watch and loudly
informing him that their master was the Marquess of
Clairval, a friend of the King, who would not stoop to
attack anyone or anything publicly – least of all a
woman.

'You lie, damn you,' cried Luke, seething with rage.
He looked reproachfully at Pat, who had carelessly

allowed the girl to run off. 'We all saw her – and you, as *my* friends will testify.'

'I don't know, nor do I wish to, what bees are buzzing in your bonnet, Harcourt. I am supposing that you are usually light in the attic, but I would advise you and your friends not to make reckless charges which you cannot substantiate,' drawled Clairval, now quite at his ease. He saw that, the excitement of the moment over, none of Luke's companions, who had not seen the worst of the attack on her, was willing to accuse him without the girl child being present.

They were only too well aware that the Marquess of Clairval was a great and powerful man whom a bench of magistrates might find it difficult to accuse without an overwhelming reason. Worse, they might also fear his revenge if they persisted in their accusation and it proved to be groundless.

Luke looked around him to see that Clairval had judged the matter correctly, and that his friends were hanging their heads and looking away from him.

He controlled with difficulty the red rage which was rapidly overcoming him, and said as coolly as he could, 'Both you and I know exactly what you were doing, Clairval. You may fool the Watch by your lies and intimidate my friends with your rank so that they will not testify against you, but it doesn't alter the fact that you were violating a girl child in public.'

Pat O'Hare pulled at Luke, before Clairval could reply. 'Leave it, Harcourt. Why make an unnecessary enemy? You've no hope of proving anything against such as Clairval without a cast-iron case.'

It seemed that Clairval had won, as Luke suspected that he always did and always would. Armoured by his rank and the deference paid to it by those below him, he might do as he pleased – short of murder. He must accept that it was his turn to be thwarted and that to betray his anger at Clairval's escape would only serve to add to Clairval's pleasure at having done so.

Clairval, indeed, was openly laughing at him, only waiting to throw a final triumphant sentence at Luke as soon as the Watch had walked away, apologising profusely and humbly to m'lord for taking the liberty of troubling him.

Once he had disappeared, Clairval thrust his ugly face in Luke's. 'I'll not forget this, Harcourt. I always make sure that any man who seeks to injure me subsequently pays a heavy price. Walk carefully, keep out of my way as much as you will, you will not escape me.'

'Perhaps not,' replied Luke hardily. 'But "the pitcher may go too often to the well" is a saying you might remember next time you attack a child.'

'Not if the man's name is Clairval,' replied the Marquess arrogantly.

Pat was pulling at Luke's arm again, 'Come away, Harcourt. You do no good bandying words with him.'

Clairval gave Pat a knowing nod. 'Well said, sir. It's a pity that your friend is not as wise as you are. I bid you both goodnight,' and he strolled off laughing, his lackeys behind him, guffawing their amusement.

Luke turned angrily on Pat. 'No need for you to say anything to placate him, O'Hare. If you had kept tight hold of the child, he would be singing a different song by now. Whatever possessed you to let her go?'

'Come now, Harcourt, no need to rail at me. She did you a good turn by disappearing. Nothing but trouble could have come of it, if you had succeeded in getting us all involved in a public fracas in court with Clairval. He would have demanded to be tried in the House of Lords by his peers, if it was decided that there was a

case against him. As it is, you've made a bad enemy of
him for life.'

'Well, I don't want him as a friend, that's for sure: an
enemy's better,' retorted Luke, who was finding depths
of anger and determination in himself which he had
never known existed. He was still annoyed with Pat,
whose carelessness had allowed Clairval to escape
punishment for his brutality.

Luke now believed that all the whispered stories
about Clairval's mistreatment of his young wife were
true, and he pitied any woman who found herself in his
power. All desire to make a night of it, never very
strong, had completely vanished. He felt only a desperate weariness of spirit.

Clapping him on the back, Pat said cheerfully, 'Leave
it that you did the right thing, Harcourt. Let's forget
Laura Knight's and go to The Coal Hole instead, and
drown our sorrows, eh?'

Luke shook his head at him and his fellows, who
obviously agreed with Pat that visiting a brothel after
what had passed was not quite the thing. 'Sorry,
O'Hare, I can't forget that child's face so easily. I'm for
home.'

Home? Where was that? he thought, as he hailed a
Hackney cab to take him back to Islington. Mrs
Britten's, like Haven's End, was simply a temporary
place where he might lay his head. The truth was that
he had no home. For the first time in his carefree life
he thought longingly of a different kind of haven where
a woman waited for him, and children, perhaps.

As for Pat, he didn't feel very proud of himself for
having saved Clairval's bacon by allowing the child to
run away. Not to have done so, however, would have
brought immediate vengeance down on his head from
Clairval who, notoriously, never forgave a slight, an

insult or an enemy. He had successfully diverted Clairval's anger from himself to Luke, but afterwards he drank himself senseless at The Coal Hole, in an effort to forget his treachery towards a good friend.

Chapter Six

'Let me take your bag from you, mam. It looks a little heavy.' Mary put out a willing hand to help Anne by carrying the bag full of linen and fine cotton that she had just collected from the drapers as part of her next commission. It was the material for a layette for a baby who was expected in the autumn, and making it would be a welcome addition to Anne's small income.

Smiling, she shook her head. 'Thank you, Mary, but no, I can easily manage to carry it up to my room these days.'

'Not surprising,' said Mary boldly, 'seeing as how you look so much better now.'

Privately she put this improvement down to Mr Luke Harcourt's influence. Why, she remembered how ill and weak Mrs Cowper had been when she had first arrived in Islington; so pale and listless that she didn't seem likely to be long for this world. And now, look at her! Cheeks rosy, eyes shining, her step lively, and looking as sleek and rounded as a well-fed kitten!

All this since Mr Harcourt had arrived back in the spring. Well, who could be surprised at that? A nicer, kinder gentleman never existed. Hard-working, too, these days.

Mary was not to know that if Mr Harcourt had improved Mrs Cowper, Mrs Cowper had done the same for Luke. Even Anne did not know how potent her influence had been. It was true that, on the morning after Luke had sold 'Scenes from Low Life' to Mr Bayes, he had come down to breakfast just as Anne and Mrs Britten had been finishing theirs and told them the good news and had also thanked Anne most heartily for her suggestion.

'And,' he had added, tucking into Mrs Britten's good porridge with a will, 'I shall take you both to Cremorne Gardens, if you will so allow. You, my dear Mrs Cowper, for providing me with inspiration, and you, Mrs Britten, for having taken Mrs Cowper in as a lodger. Now, ladies, thank me, as I have thanked you.'

Of course, she and Mrs Britten had thanked him vigorously, and agreed to accept his kind invitation. As with Islington Fair, Anne had never been allowed to visit anywhere as cheerfully doubtful as Cremorne was reputed to be, and for that very reason was all agog to go there.

For all his easiness of manner, Anne had thought that there was something troubling him. He had a bruise on his cheek and his left hand appeared to pain him a little. On neither of these small injuries had she seen fit to remark, although Mrs Britten had asked anxiously, 'I trust, Mr Harcourt, that nothing went amiss with you last night. You are carrying a nasty bruise on the face and I see that you favour your wrist. Perhaps a visit to an apothecary is called for.'

'By no means.' Luke was firm. 'A trifle, nothing else.' He seemed to think a moment before he had added, 'I met a most unpleasant fellow last night, and the fact that he was a Marquess, the Marquess of Clairval, in fact, did not exactly endear him to me. A man of his

station should know better than to act like a common
bully.'

He had been a little surprised, Anne had not been
able to help noticing, at her and Mrs Britten's strong
reaction to this statement which had been as far as he
had been prepared to go in explanation. What Clairval
had been interrupted in doing was no fit subject for
ladies' ears.

Anne had turned pale and looked down at her empty
plate. Mrs Britten had put a protective hand on her
arm, and at the same time had tried to divert Luke's
attention from her sudden malaise, and the possibility
that it might have been caused by his remark.

'I have heard nothing but ill of the Marquess,' she
had said. 'I am not all surprised if you witnessed him
behaving badly. Anne, my dear, I thought you looked
rather pale this morning. Would you care to lie down
for a little in order to recover? I am sure that Mr
Harcourt would not object if you were to leave the
table.'

If Luke had thought that up to the moment when he
had mentioned Clairval's name Mrs Anne Cowper had
looked in singularly glowing health, he had not said so.
Anne, herself, had thought that it was the most feeble
excuse for her sudden faintness and pallor which she
could ever hope to hear. What had surprised her the
most was the fact that even to have Clairval's name
spoken in her presence should have caused her such
distress. To learn that he was in London and trouble-
making had been even more shocking.

'Thank you, no,' she had said. 'It is a passing fit only,
Mr Harcourt. It would be a poor reward for your
kindness if I fled your company at the first opportunity.
Yes, I will go with you to Cremorne.'

And so it had been arranged.

'Do you think it wise to visit such a public place, Anne?' Mrs Britten had asked her when Luke had gone up to his room to write.

Wise? What was wise? Having had her life ruined by the arrangements of all those who had thought that they were being wise on her behalf, Anne had not been sure what being wise consisted of. Besides, she could not live her whole life paralysed by fear. Her youth and her regrown strength were all drawing her towards Luke, and she had the feeling that he was, equally, being drawn towards her.

Now, all things being as they were, this was perhaps the most unwise situation in which she could find herself. But the notion of living her life in a kind of purdah, like the poor ladies in the Sultan's *harem*, who were forbidden to go out of doors, had filled Anne with horror.

'No, it is not wise to go to Cremorne Gardens with Luke,' she had said with a firmness which Mrs Britten had never seen her exhibit before. 'But I cannot live on my knees, and oh, my dear friend, I have never in my life enjoyed those pleasures which most young women of my age have always taken for granted. Do not deny me this one!'

Neither had Mrs Britten ever heard her call Mr Harcourt Luke before, but he had been Luke in Anne's thoughts for some weeks now. If she had betrayed herself, and she had known that she had, then Mrs Britten had been tactful enough to say nothing – although she obviously had thought a great deal!

She had put her arms around Anne and drew her to her ample bosom. 'Oh, my poor girl. Of course you shall go to the Gardens. And you are right not to wish to hide yourself away in constant fear. But you heard what he said about Clairval. . .'

'No,' Anne had drawn away, her eyes aflame. 'Do not mention his name to me. I shall go to Cremorne, and I shall be friendly with Luke, and if this is wilful and dangerous of me, then in the past I have always lived an exemplary life – and you well know what that has earned me!'

After such a brave declaration, Mrs Britten could have denied her nothing, although it had been a great relief when they had gone to Cremorne Gardens and the only person who had accosted them had been Luke's friend, Pat O'Hare, who had had a lady of dubious virtue on his arm in the waltz, and who had waved to them from afar. So her own and Mrs Britten's fears had been all in vain. . .

Which had only served to add to Anne's pleasure when Luke had asked her to waltz with him. This had been so delightfully daring that Anne had almost turned him down as he had stood before her, his handsome head bent low, though not so low that she had not been able to see the light of admiration in his strange amber eyes.

After that, refusal of him had been impossible, and spinning around the dance floor, in the gathering dusk of a warm summer's evening, had been paradise enough for anyone, and Anne had been able to ask for nothing more of life.

She came back to the present. Mary was saying, a little timidly, 'I am sure, Mrs Cowper, that the missis would wish me to bring the tea board in for you, once you have put your work away.'

'I can't gainsay you, Mary. I must admit that a cup of tea would be most welcome.'

'And muffins,' offered Mary, as Anne made for the stairs. And Mr Luke Harcourt to eat and drink with, she added to herself, matchmaking. I'll go and knock on his door at once.

So it was that when Anne entered the drawing-room, she found Luke already there, the sofa table before him already laid for two, only awaiting the tray carrying the tea pot, hot water jug and Mrs Britten's silver muffin basket.

He rose to his feet immediately and bowed. His punctiliousness, his whole charming person, enchanted Anne even more than it usually did. She noticed that he was more casually dressed than she had recently seen him – several stages up, perhaps, from the yeoman's clothing he had worn to Islington Fair, but a stage or two down from his young gentleman-about-town's outfit. He was sporting a sober black coat and trousers, light boots and an unassuming cravat.

It didn't really matter what he wore, Anne concluded happily. He would be attractive in the clothes of a labourer or a London clerk.

'Mary tells me that she doesn't expect Mrs Britten back for some time, and has orders to see that we were looked after when you came in. She was so firm that I hardly dared to deny her. She also told me that Ben, the odd-job boy, has already fed Dizzy for you, so that you are not to put yourself out by going out to look after him. Ah, here come the tea and muffins. Allow me.'

He had walked over to take the big silver tea tray from Mary, who was staggering under its weight. 'Oh, you shouldn't, Mr Harcourt,' she told him reproachfully. 'It's no task for a gentleman.'

'Oh, but I'm not a gentleman any more, Mary,' he informed her. 'I'm that new-fangled thing, a journalist – or so Mr Bayes tells me.' He looked at Anne as he set the tray down in front of her. 'He's sending me to the House of Commons tomorrow to report on one of the debates there.'

So that was the reason for his quiet attire – and his ink-stained fingers – he was taking his writing more seriously. It occurred to Anne that when he had first arrived in London he had spent most of his time enjoying himself, going 'up West' as the saying had it. Not so, recently. Perhaps he had lost money? No matter.

'We seem to spend much of our time together eating muffins,' Anne ventured, only to reproach herself inwardly for offering an observation which might be taken in two ways.

'I can think of worse ways of passing the time,' said Luke, before biting carefully into his warm and well-buttered muffin. 'And few better. There! I have manoeuvred my muffin successfully today – a feat I do not always accomplish.'

This mild attempt at a joke set Anne laughing. Jokes had rarely come her way, Luke concluded, since she found so much pleasure in even the weakest of them. He could offer to take her to the theatre and enjoy himself watching her reactions to the farce, which always preceded the tragedy.

He suggested such an excursion immediately. Anne's reaction surprised him.

Almost before he had managed to get the words out, she was shaking her head vigorously. Go to the theatre! No, that was far too public a place, and plenty of the quality were sure to be there – and she might be seen.

'Oh, it's very kind of you, Mr Harcourt, and I thank you for the invitation, but no.' She sought for a reasonable explanation of her refusal. 'I find being in a crowd such as the one at a theatre very trying. It's weak of me, I know. . .'

How charming she looked! Every time Luke saw her he found her more enchanting. Her modesty pleased him the most of all. He was not used to such gratitude from the young ladies he met in society. Privately, he considered that even if Mrs Anne Cowper had been one of the well-dowered young women who took him for granted her manner to him would have been the same as it was in Mrs Britten's humble drawing-room.

Enchantment had him leaning forward to offer her another muffin, and saying, 'Not weak at all. It is something over which you can have little control. Would it be too great a hardship, or a breach of manners, for you to address me as Luke?'

Anne considered him with her great grave eyes after she had refused the muffin. 'I think that perhaps we ought not to be so familiar – ' for she rightly judged that he dearly wished to call her Anne ' – but we must consider Mrs Britten's feelings concerning propriety, as well as our own. After all, I am so recently widowed. . .'

She let the sentence hang in the air, and saw with what grace and tact he accepted her refusal.

'You are right, of course. We may not always please ourselves. When we have known one another a little longer, perhaps?'

'Perhaps.' And if she had admired his tact, it was now his turn to admire hers. She put up a finger. 'I think that I hear Mrs Britten arriving. We must not give her cause for worry.'

'Indeed, not. Especially since she has no cause to.' And that, Luke privately thought, was a matter for regret. How he had refrained from taking her in his arms once they were alone together, he would never know.

But it was not Mrs Britten at the door, it was Mary, bringing more hot water and more muffins. She looked at them, bright-eyed, hoping that they would take full advantage of being left alone together, but something which she rather doubted. The gentry were queer folk and, for all her poverty and working as a sempstress, Mrs Cowper was plainly a gentlewoman – and one who needed a husband, poor love. What on earth was Mr Harcourt holding back for?

A question which Mr Harcourt was asking himself. He appreciated the opportunity which Mary had offered him, but instinct, rather than reason, told him that he must go carefully with Anne, or risk losing her altogether.

And then something occurred which drove reason and prudence out of his head. Her tea and muffins consumed, Anne remembered that work awaited her, rose, excused herself and walked to the door. Ever the courteous gentleman, Luke leapt to his feet to reach the door before she did and open it for her. By ill luck – or was it good luck? – after he had done so he turned too quickly and his hand brushed hers.

Such a small contact, to have such a sudden and remarkable result. As though they were a pair of Signor Galvani's frogs subjected to an electric current, a powerful impulse passed between them.

Anne looked at Luke; her eyes were luminous with love for him, and Luke could not resist leaning down to kiss her. As he did so her eyes closed, and he kissed her on the lids as gently as a butterfly alighting. To his surprise, he found that this delicate caress gave him a sensation more erotic than the most passionate kiss on the lips.

He shuddered.

She shuddered.

Anne opened her eyes and looked at him again as he released her and that look told him everything. But what she said also told him that she was not quite ready to accept what was happening to her.

'No,' she said, 'no, we mustn't. . . I mustn't. Oh, Luke. . .'

'Why not?' he could not help asking. 'You must know how I feel about you.'

'So sudden,' she said, 'so sudden,' and he could sense her withdrawal from him. She was a shy bird, caught in a thicket, and perhaps he had gone a little fast for her. But he could not, must not lose her, and if she required him to be patient, so be it. At least he now knew that his love for her was reciprocated; for the moment, that must be enough.

The Marquess of Clairval paced around his study: a tiger confined. He had the unpleasant feeling that those who disliked or feared him were laughing behind his back. What more foolish and silly fellow, he imagined them saying, was there than a husband who could not control his wife? A man, moreover, whose wife had disappeared so successfully that, despite all his wealth and power, he had not been able to find her.

There were times when he hoped that she was lying dead beneath some hedge or in a ditch – except that, if that were so, her wealth would be lost to him.

No, dead or alive he needed her body. So far, not even the small fortune which he had promised to give to anyone who brought word of her whereabouts to him had succeeded in flushing her from her bolt hole. In the meantime he was also paying a noted thief taker to look for her – another waste of money, no doubt.

There was a timid knock on the door. 'Come in,' he roared, his roar being all the louder for the fact that he was feeling so much at odds with the world.

His secretary, a harried-looking man – all Clairval's

servants except the bruisers who did his dirty work for him looked harried – entered.

'Jenkinson to see you, m'lord.'

'Then send him in, man. Why are you delaying? There are times when I believe that no one was ever served by such a pack of fools as I am.'

The man waiting outside could hear Clairval's upraised, railing voice even through the massive oak double doors which the secretary had carefully fastened behind him. He grinned to himself, and was not surprised when the secretary emerged from m'lord's study looking more harried than ever.

'His lordship will see you now,' Browne said distastefully to the foxy-faced fellow who sat on the edge of his chair, visibly pricing everything in the vast anteroom, from the painting of Jove on the ceiling to the Aubusson carpet which graced the floor.

M'lord's study was equally grand. It could have served as a chamber of state instead of a room where a brutal nobleman bandied words with an ex-Bow Street Runner who had been dismissed on suspicion of bribery and corruption.

'Well, d'you have any news for me?'

'Not yet, m'lord, but soon. I am on a hot trail. I can tell you that you were right about one thing – it *was* your steward who helped your wife to escape.'

'As I thought. I hope he's rotting in the hell to which I have consigned him. And that's all? Something I'd already guessed and have seen to myself!'

'Not quite, m'lord. Did your wife ever speak to you of a Miss Latimer, who married a parson, Eli Britten? She was m'lady's governess before her marriage to you. I found that he had a living at Moorcroft in Surrey. I visited the parsonage there, only to discover that he had died prematurely some years ago.

'Their neighbours told me that he had left his wife but a small competence so she had decided to move to London and open a lodging house for the gentry – to make ends meet, they said. They also told me something else. Apparently she had received regular letters from one of her old charges and the local postmaster said that the letters came from Yorkshire.'

Clairval uttered an oath. 'What, in the devil's name, has all this to do with my wife? She never prated about governesses to me. She hardly ever spoke at all, damn her!'

'Only that, so far as I can discover, she had no other person to whom she might go for help. Her relatives have taken your part in this matter – so she would not go to them.

'I made further enquiries. She and this Mrs Britten were very close. Her father refused to allow her friends of her own age – he was a recluse himself, and intended that she should be one. He approved of her friendship with the governess, though. I should like to follow this up, but the thing is that I've run out of blunt. If I'm to trace the governess, I need some more of the ready.'

Clairval stared at him. 'And that's it? Some whim wham about a governess, and maunderings about letters from Yorkshire? Half England lives in Yorkshire! Dammit, man, you came highly recommended, and this is all you can offer me? And you have the gall to demand more money from me! Be damned to that for a tale. I've a good mind to tell you to take your Friday-face away!'

Jenkinson surveyed the unsavoury swine before him. What a bastard! No wonder his missis had run away from him. He pitied any poor bitch in his power – wife or what-have-you. It was almost enough to make him give up the job – but he needed the money.

'I told you, m'lord. It's the only lead I can find: a last resort, you might say. If it's a dead end, then I'll give up – and someone else may have a go. The neighbours said her rooms would be highly respectable – she hoped to take in the gentry. The name's uncommon and I can enquire among all the fly young fellows wanting lodgings who might have heard of her. I ain't hopeful – m'lady might be lying in a ditch somewhere, dead soon after she scarpered.'

Clairval sighed. A last resort. Yes, it was very much a last resort. And this fellow was supposed to be one of the best in his unsavoury profession. What, in God's name, could the worst be like? Incompetent idiots, all of them, no doubt.

'Tell my secretary to give you five guineas. But that's the last you'll get from me, mark you. If you do turn up trumps; then I'll see you well rewarded. Be off with you. I seem to have done nothing but throw guineas at you and get nothing back.'

'Short of the ready, is he?' Jenkinson asked the secretary as he was handed his guineas. 'Never met a fellow so bound and determined to get his money's worth. The fly word is that that's why he wants his missis back. She's the one with the blunt and without her he can't get at any more of it.'

If the secretary agreed with him, he did not say so. M'lord's temper was so uncertain these days that a still tongue in one's head was the best attribute any of his servants had – and even that might not save them from trouble.

Jenkinson took the money. As he reached the door he turned to say casually to Browne, 'M'lord had a steward, did he not? Name of Leethwaite or so I was told. If he helped m'lady escape, he might have something useful to tell me. Except that I can't find him.

Left m'lord's employ and disappeared – just like m'lady. Not the same day, but soon after. Know where he might have gone?'

'No, I do not.' The secretary was brief.

'No, nor wouldn't tell me if you did. Frightened of him, I dare say. Oh well. Never mind. He might turn up – like m'lady.'

'He didn't run off with her, if that's what you mean,' said the secretary shortly. 'He was fifty, had a doxy in Wakefield about as unlike m'lady as a woman could be. He's probably taken himself as far from m'lord as he could go. M' lord put the blame on him, but I have no notion of the truth of the matter.'

'Aye, happen so,' agreed Jenkinson, 'as they say in Yorkshire. Odd, though. But then, the whole business is odd.'

'You will excuse me, but I have work to do. I can't stay gossiping with you.'

Jenkinson forbore to say that gossip was the life's blood of a man on the trail of those missing. He had once thought that the secretary might have helped m'lady to run off but, looking at him, knew that was another dead end. A right desiccated cold fish, concerned only with himself.

So it was with considerable surprise that he heard the secretary, looking away from him, murmur in a distant voice as he finally walked through the door, 'The steward may have taken himself off, but all I can tell you is this: that no one saw him again after m'lord found that m'lady had gone.'

Chapter Seven

All that golden summer Luke did two things: he worked diligently at his writing and patiently, oh, so patiently, courted Anne Cowper.

After his first two papers had appeared in *The Pall Mall Gazette* which Bayes had transformed into a weekly on the strength of the work with which Luke and Pat and some other young men were providing him, the publishers, Chapman and Hall, approached Luke to suggest that he wrote either a book about gypsy life, or a novel based on his knowledge of it. Mr Chapman had been impressed by the paper which Luke had written about the gypsies at Islington Fair.

'But I've never even tried to write a novel,' Luke protested faintly. 'I'm sure that I shouldn't know how to.'

'Nothing to it, young man,' Chapman told him severely. 'My partner and I consider that your work shows great promise in that line. Your account of your conversations with the gypsy king told us all that we needed to know.'

Luke wanted to say that Jasper wasn't a gypsy king, but held his tongue. The terms that Chapman was offering him if he liked the novel were attractive ones. Chapman saw him hesitate.

'Come, young fellow,' he said, 'at least try. What can you lose?'

'Nothing,' exclaimed Luke, almost laughing aloud and, without meaning to, giving the publisher the benefit of all his famous charm. 'Nothing at all. Yes, I'll rough out a few chapters for you, and you can tell me if they're what you want.'

'Famous,' said Chapman warmly. 'I can see we shall deal well together. Let's shake hands on it.'

So they did, and Luke rushed straight back to Islington to tell Anne the good news. After all, she had started him on this road and who knew where it would end? He said nothing about his new career to his father or Cressy. Best to keep quiet until he had achieved something substantial. But Anne, oh, Anne was different – she was his muse, his inspiration, his *alter ego* – so he informed her, pouring out his hopes and aspirations about the novel which Chapman had suggested to him.

'Oh, Luke, I'm so pleased for you!' Anne's face was aglow.

They were alone in the drawing-room, for Mrs Britten had not expected him to be back so early. Had she known, she would have made a third and acted as duenna, but she did not, and had gone for a walk, leaving Anne to get on with her sewing.

Luke determined to take full advantage of the situation.

'How shall I reward you?' he asked her, his amber eyes glowing. He had never looked so handsome, never looked more like his unacknowledged father.

'Oh, it's not necessary to reward me,' Anne said. 'You have done this yourself.'

'Not so,' replied Luke energetically. 'Surely you know that you are my inspiration. Oh, Anne, ever since

I first met you my whole life has changed. I was so aimless, so careless, but your example, your encouragement have served to transform me. I feel that I could move mountains, never mind write a novel for Mr Chapman. You have given me a purpose in life.'

Anne had never been so moved, so touched. Looking at him, she knew that he was speaking the truth. Almost without meaning to, she had reached out and influenced another human being, and that human being was someone she had come to love.

Luke's essential goodness shone out of him. To some extent it had held him back, since the hint of steel, of resolute determination, which all men and women need if they are to succeed in this life, was missing because of it. But loving Anne, wanting to feel that he was worthy of her, and would be able to ask her to marry him once he had succeeded in the career on which he had embarked as a result of her encouragement, had roused in him the desire to excel.

'If that is so,' Anne said at last, 'then you have made me very happy. And I am as sure as Mr Chapman that you will succeed in your new venture. Having met the gypsies, I can't wait to read your novel about them.'

She dare not say more. Oh, if only her circumstances were different, she could have made the answer that would have had her in his arms. She sighed at the thought, which frightened as well as attracted her.

Luke mistook her slight hesitation. He thought that it sprang wholly from fear of him; that he was going too quickly. 'My dear,' he said gently, 'I did not mean to be so enthusiastic that I overwhelmed you. But I felt compelled to tell you how much you have come to mean to me. I haven't been overbold, I trust.'

'Oh, no, not at all,' exclaimed Anne, who was torn by two contrary desires. For while she did not wish to encourage Luke, for their case was hopeless, she also didn't want to lose his love; the sweetest thing which she had ever experienced was to hear him tell her how much he loved her. After all, that must have been what he meant by his recent declaration to her.

If only she could reciprocate by telling him how much she loved him! Tears sprang into her eyes. She bent over her work so that he should not see them. He mistook her again.

'I have overset you, and I will leave you. What's more I must justify both your and Mr Chapman's faith in me, and start work as soon as possible.'

No, no! He must not think her so weak a creature. 'Indeed, not, Mr Harcourt. Far from being overset, I am delighted by your success, and honoured that you think that I have a share in it.'

Impulsively, not thinking what she was doing, and forgetting what had occurred on the last occasion on which they had touched: Anne put out her hand to lay it on his in a spontaneous gesture of encouragement.

Again! It had happened again! As they touched, that strong electric current passed through them both. It was of such magnitude that, before he knew what he was doing, Luke had cupped her face in his hands and was giving Anne the kiss which he had been longing to bestow on her all afternoon.

And she was responding to it. Like a flower bud responding to the touch of rain, her mouth gently opened to receive and give back his offering. Of the two of them, Anne was the more surprised. First, because the shock which her whole body had received at his touch was something which she had never experienced before. Second, because before Luke kissed her on the lips she had always thought that she would reject any form of lovemaking, however slight, because not only would her reason forbid it, but her body would reject it vigorously too, as a consequence of her husband's brutal mistreatment of her.

Far from it! Far from rejecting him, Anne's arms, of their own volition, wound themselves around Luke's neck, and she was stroking his face as he was stroking hers: the kiss went on and on, growing ever more powerful and passionate. What brought the whole unexpected and delightful business to an end was the sound of footsteps – Mrs Britten's this time – advancing down the corridor towards the drawing-room door.

Neither of them was so far gone that they did not instantly spring apart. Anne's face was flushed, her mouth had softened and her whole body glowed as a result of her first experience of true love.

Luke's face had also changed. It was that of a man who had been given a most unexpected present. Knowing Anne's delicacy, her shrinking from any form of physical contact with anyone or anything except poor Dizzy, her timid response the last time he had kissed her, he had been half-expecting her to fight him off. Instead, he had met delighted co-operation. Regrettably, from his point of view, Mrs Britten's coming through the door to discover them now decently apart, and Anne on the point of leaving, meant that he had no opportunity to extend her co-operation further.

No matter. The ice having been broken, as it were, the winter would end and spring must surely follow. The only thing which remained was for him to assure her that his intentions were purely honourable, and this he would do as soon as decently possible.

He had no desire to hurry matters overmuch. Anne's kiss had told him more than she could know. Married she might have been, but her response had been that of an unawakened woman. Which begged a question which had been puzzling him for some time. What kind of marriage had Mrs Anne Cowper experienced? Again, no matter. This – and other problems – could wait until their better acquaintance had made it easy for them to talk of such intimate affairs.

Mrs Britten surveyed him suspiciously after she had poured out her tea. Mr Luke Harcourt looked like the cat which had just swallowed the canary. She was not to know that he was contemplating wooing Mrs Anne Cowper with just the kind of innocent courtship which his fly friends who visited Laura Knight, and others like her, would have laughed at him for proposing.

He might have laughed at himself, too, before he had met Anne. Instead, all that he could think of was that Anne loved him, and knowing that he went at once to his room and to win her he began to write. . . Exactly as Chapman had prophesied, the words flowed easily from his pen as he told of Jasper, his followers and the open road which was their home.

Later, Anne sat on her bed, her work unregarded, her hands held to her hot cheeks, her whole body vibrating after its first experience of passion. Whatever had she been thinking of? Instead of pushing Luke away as she ought to have done, she had encouraged him. But, oh, how sweet it had been to be held in a man's arms and kissed so gently and lovingly on the lips. Nothing in her marriage had led her to believe that love-making could be other than a torment for the woman, however much it seemed to please the man.

Whatever might have happened if Mrs Britten had not arrived to disturb them? No words had been exchanged between them afterwards, so Anne had no means of knowing whether Luke was toying with her; whether the kiss meant anything – or nothing.

This was all so new to her. She had never had a friend of her own age to talk and giggle with about young men and what they meant by sly glances and stolen kisses. One minute she had been barely out of childhood and the next she had been chained to a ruthless, cruel and selfish man who saw her as merely the means to get him an heir.

The worst thing of all was that she knew that she was falling in love with Luke.

No! Amend that. She *had* fallen in love with Luke and had some reason to believe that he might be in love with her. Which was hopeless, quite hopeless. There could be no future for them which embraced marriage, and so she must not encourage him, not tempt him to. . .to. . .

For the first time something which had always been abhorrent to Anne – the bodily union of a man and a woman – no longer seemed so.

It was to Anne that Luke brought home in triumph each copy of *The Pall Mall Gazette* that contained his articles and each part of the novel that he was writing as it came out every month. Chapman had been so pleased with the first chapters of *Lords of the Road* – the title Luke had given his novel – that he had taken the risk of issuing it in parts. If this put pressure on Luke, it was welcome, and he rapidly found that he was running ahead of publication.

More, the sales of the first part were so good that Chapman had raised the amount he was paying him for it. He had taken the pseudonym of James Linley for the work he was doing for Chapman and for Jack Hatfield. Solomon Grundy was reserved for his work for Bayes.

Hatfield had enthusiastically taken up his suggestion

for a series of light articles on fashionable and thieves' slang and cant, thus providing him with another source of income. If this continued, he would be able to offer marriage to Anne with a good conscience. This happy thought made him work the harder.

The one thing which he found difficult to understand was Mrs Britten's lacklustre reaction to the growing rapport between himself and Anne. He would have thought that she would welcome any chance of a marriage for her young protégée that would rescue her from grinding poverty. Luke knew that Anne sewed and embroidered into the night watches to make enough to keep herself from starving.

Mrs Britten stopped him one day after he had left the drawing-room where Anne was working in the good light of the large bow window. He had just given her the latest copy of 'Scenes from Low Life'. She said to him, without preamble, 'I hope you are remembering what I said to you earlier. About Mrs Cowper, I mean.'

'Oh, indeed.' Luke was a trifle stiff. 'You may rest assured that my intentions towards her are strictly honourable.'

'I have no doubt of that, Mr Harcourt. What worries me is Mrs Cowper's position. After all, you are the son of a member of the *haut ton* and Anne is but a sempstress.'

'I am a working writer, a journalist. I no longer wish to live on my father's bounty.' Luke was uncharacteristically blunt. 'I see little to choose between us.'

Mrs Britten stared at him helplessly. She could not, dare not, say more. To do so might put Anne in jeopardy. On the other hand, if Luke knew the truth about Anne, he would at once realise how hopeless his dreams were. Which was a sad pity, because he was

just the sort of young man who would have made Anne
a good husband. . .

She could not tell him that earlier that day, when she
had been escorting Anne to the shop that commissioned her work, Anne had pulled her arm free and
said in a distressed voice, 'Someone is staring after me.
I am sure of it. Someone who means me ill, I fear.'

Her face had turned quite white, and she had been
shivering. Mrs Britten had said, 'Where? I see no
one.'

'Nor I, either.' Anne's agitation had been extreme. 'I
cannot see him, but I know that he is somewhere
hereabouts. A foxy-faced man with red hair. He has
been watching and following me.'

'Not seen him?' had queried her protectress
dubiously. 'How then do you know that he is following
you?'

Anne had hung her head a little and had looked
away. 'I have not chosen to tell you – or Luke – but
ever since I visited the gypsy fortune teller I seem to
have developed an odd sense, something which I can't
explain. I can tell people's true thoughts, their true
characters, and I know when they are thinking about
me, even when they are not present. Oh, not every-
body, not everything all the time, but in odd flashes,
which come and go. It is a most inconvenient gift – for
gift it was – from the fortune teller. She told me so.'

She had looked up at her friend. 'You see, I know
for sure that you and Luke are both good people, and
that neither of you would ever harm me. This man who
has been watching me is not evil, but his watching me
is dangerous and can only do me harm.'

'My poor girl. Do you know what you are saying?'

Anne's smile had been melancholy. 'I dare say that
you think me mad. Stricken mad with suffering, I

suppose. But it is not so. I should not have spoken of it.'

She had shivered again. 'He is nearer to me now than he was. Not very far away.'

Even as she had spoken a man had walked out of the shop next to the one for which they had been making. He had been dressed in reasonably good clothing, similar to that of a superior clerk. He had worn a broad-crowned beaver hat, beneath which his reddish hair could be seen escaping in tight curls. His face had been undeniably foxy. He had walked by them without looking at them.

Mrs Britten had looked helplessly at Anne. She had thought a moment before exclaiming, 'Now, I know what caused *that*! You must have seen him out of the corner of your eye and he was sufficiently odd-looking for you to be frightened of him. And no wonder. In your case I should be running mad with worry.'

'But I am not mad,' Anne had answered with the gentle firmness which was her trademark. 'Please, we will talk of it no more. I wish you will say nothing to Mr Harcourt of this. I would not for the world have him think that I am turning simple-minded!'

Mr Harcourt! Mr Harcourt! He was all that Anne could think of when she ought to be thinking of her safety. No doubt of it at all, was Mrs Britten's sad reflection, she had forgotten all prudence from the moment she had met him. If only she could be frank with Mr Harcourt, but she dare not. She sighed helplessly as she watched him bound upstairs to his room – to start work again, she supposed. She would warn Anne not to encourage him, but that, too, would probably be useless

Even more useless than Mrs Britten might have imagined. As Anne stitched happily away, foremost in her mind was Luke's face when he had given her the latest copy of *The Pall Mall Gazette*. Mrs Britten's gentle admonitions went unheeded. Except that later that night Anne started up from sleep, crying out, the tears running down her face. ·

Her dream had begun as a happy one. She had been walking along Islington High Street, Dizzy trotting along in front of her, her hand on Luke's arm. She had looked up at him and he had been smiling down at her, his face so loving that in her dream her heart had given a little skip of delight. And then. . .and then. . .the foxy-faced man had come out of the shop, just as he had done that morning and walked towards her.

But instead of passing by, as he had done that morning, he had put out a hand, caught her by the wrist and pulled her towards him. . .and as he had done so, Luke, Dizzy, and Islington High Street had all disappeared. The foxy man disappeared, too, and all that was left in the world was – HIM. She was in a wood with HIM, and she could not tell whether it was night or day, only that she was alone with her doom.

Helplessly she awaited it, and as HE advanced towards her she found herself screaming. . .and she was back in her bed in Islington, and Mrs Britten was seated on it beside her, holding her to her broad bosom and trying to stop the hiccuping sobs which had succeeded the screams. Luke stood in the doorway, a candle in his hand. He was wearing a brocaded dressing-gown, just like a Chinese mandarin's. His hair was awry and the look on his face was so agonised at the sight of her distress that Anne felt for him, not for herself.

'There, there, my pet,' soothed Mrs Britten. 'A bad dream, was it?'

'Yes,' whispered Anne, recovering herself. 'Oh, I'm

so sorry. I did not mean to wake the house, but the dream was so real. . .'

'Never mind, my darling, never mind.' Mrs Britten began to rock her so that Anne closed her eyes, leaned against her friend, and surrendered herself to the maternal love which surrounded her. She had never known anything like it before, just as she had never known what it was to be truly loved by a man. She turned her head into Mrs Britten's bosom, her eyelids fluttered and after a little time, exhausted, she slept.

Mrs Britten laid her gently back on the pillows, and Anne stirred a little, smiling in her sleep. Neither Mrs Britten, nor Luke, knew that in her dreams Luke was with her again, and another presence was also there, the *chovihani* who, unseen and unheard by Luke, whispered in her ear, 'Never fear, I shall be with you both, even in the darkest hour of the night.'

Then the dream disappeared, and Anne slept, but the smile remained.

Luke walked to her bedside, disregarding his land-lady's disapproving stare. He looked down at Anne and his heart was filled with such protective love that he thought that it would burst. Mrs Britten took him by the hand, whispered, 'Come, let her sleep,' and led him to the landing so that he might return to his rooms.

But he resisted her, saying with the look of agony still on his face at the memory of Anne's terror, 'Tell me, Mrs Britten, does this happen often?'

'I will not lie to you, Mr Harcourt. When she first came here these fits occurred every night, but of late, no, she has not suffered from them.' She did not think that it was wise to tell him that Anne's terrible night-mares had ceased when he had returned to Islington.

'And the cause,' Luke said urgently. 'What is the cause? Do you know why she should suffer so?'

'Again I will not lie to you. Yes, I know the cause, but I cannot tell you of it. I cannot break Anne's confidence.' She hesitated. 'But I fear that this episode may have been caused by Anne's believing this morning that she was being followed by someone who wishes her ill.'

It was as much as she dare say to him, and perhaps it was too much, but Mr Harcourt was a good young man. If he thought that Anne was in danger, then he might be prepared to protect her.

'And was she being followed?'

'That I do not know. I saw nothing which might lead me to believe that she was, but Anne is not normally fanciful, you understand. Now I think that we ought to return to our beds.'

Luke wanted to ask her more questions, for he was beginning to think that there was something strange about Mrs Anne Cowper, more than met the eye. He could see, however, that Mrs Britten looked nearly as exhausted as Anne had done, so that, although he thought that she was being evasive, he said no more.

If Mrs Anne Cowper needed protection, then making her Mrs Luke Harcourt was the best protection he could offer her, and soon.

'I think, m'lord, that I may have tracked down your missis – beg pardon, her ladyship.' Jenkinson paused, smiling.

Clairval sprang to his feet. Jenkinson had arrived some time ago and had been made to wait to see him as a punishment for his failure so far. He knew at once that Jenkinson was playing cat and mouse with him to pay him back.

'Go on, man.' His voice dangerous. 'You cannot afford to palter with me.'

'No paltering, m'lord. I am not yet completely certain, you understand. Another day's work will doubtless do it. I have found the governess, Mrs Britten. She lives in Islington and keeps a respectable lodging house in Duke Street. Some months ago, according to local gossip, a poor young woman, alone and penniless, arrived at her address, seeking shelter. She was granted it and is living there, earning her keep as a sempstress. The young woman is uncommon like the miniature you showed me when you hired me some months ago – though badly dressed.'

'In that case,' Clairval bit back at him savagely, 'why are we waiting? Why cannot we go there immediately?'

Jenkinson managed to look more foxy-faced than ever. 'Because, begging your pardon, m'lord, I do not think that you ought to go off half-cock like, if she proves to be the wrong young woman, seeing the scandal as would follow, Mrs Britten being a most respectable party.'

Clairval turned his eyes to heaven. 'What next?' he declaimed nastily. 'Am I to be taught etiquette by a dirty hireling who does not know his place?'

Forelock touching from Jenkinson managed to convey neither suitable penance nor respect for his betters. 'Tomorrow,' he promised. 'I am taking out the other young woman who lives in the house, Mary by name, a servant, and will winkle out of her the exact date when our young woman arrived. If it matches the date you gave me for m'lady's flight, why, then you may storm Duke Street and claim your lady back.'

'And about time, too. However, if you have found m'lady and I recover her person, I shall pay you the reward I promised you.'

Aye, you will that, thought Jenkinson nastily, as he tugged his forelock again, especially since I have found something out about you, milord Marquess, which you would not want the world to know. Bilk me, and the whole world will know of it, this I promise you.

All this whilst he appeared to be listening to Clairval make arrangements for him to accompany the party that would visit Duke Street, if the young woman proved likely to be his missing wife.

Clairval could hardly wait to get his hands on her. He would teach her a lesson that would keep her from straying from home again. The thing which touched him most on the raw was to learn that m'lady Clairval was earning her living as a sempstress.

Chapter Eight

'Keep this up and you're a made man,' Chapman had told Luke after the roaring success of the second part of his novel, and after he had passed on to him the fourth part. He had read the third and was convinced that the praise – and consequent sales – which had accompanied the first two parts would be redoubled. Luke had discovered his true profession at last. The cleverness which was so essential a part of him had never before found an outlet: now it had.

He could hardly wait to rush home to Islington. He was compelled to accompany Chapman to a chop house – as with Bayes, a sure sign that he was valued – but he was chafing inside all the time, and refused the porter which Chapman tried to press on him. He would not propose to Anne with drink on his breath, that was for sure.

All the way home in the cab he prayed that she would be in her usual place on the sofa in the bow window, and lo, to his delight, there she was, head bent and stitching away. Well, once she was Mrs Harcourt she would no longer need to spend all her days working. He was already visualising a little cottage Chelsea way, where he might have a room overlooking the river to work in, and Anne somewhere in it, his love and his helpmeet.

Washed, his shirt changed, his hair brushed, his fingers and nails free of ink, he took himself to the drawing-room with a further prayer that, it being Wednesday, Mrs Britten might be out shopping at the market, Mary in attendance on her. She had been a little short with Mary lately.

It seemed that Mary had found an admirer and had become less diligent in her duties. Her mind was on her lover, no doubt. The foxy-faced man had been careful never to meet her at her place of work in case he was seen or recognised, preferring instead a rendez-vous in a small park nearby.

Luck was with Luke again. Fortune favours the brave, as the saying went, and it certainly appeared to be favouring him. Anne looked up from her work when he entered the drawing-room, and if he thought that she had never looked so pretty and desirable, she thought that he had never looked so handsome.

'I had hoped to find you alone.' He had decided that he had better not be too roundabout in his approach to her, for he wished to make his proposal before Mrs Britten returned. 'May I inform you that you look more lovely than ever.' So saying, he dropped on to one knee before her and took her small hand in his large one.

Anne did not repel him. She allowed the hand to rest there, but said in a voice which neither encouraged nor discouraged him, 'You did not ask me if you might do that.'

Positioned as they were, his face was on a level with hers so that he could look straight at her. Amber eyes and dark blue eyes met and meshed. 'And would you have refused permission if I had asked?'

'I should not have done,' was her reply, 'but I ought to have done.'

'Then,' said Luke gaily, 'what a good thing I did not ask,' and he bent his head in first to kiss her hand before he lifted it to kiss her cheek.

'You should not have done that, either,' said Anne slowly, lifting her own hand to touch her cheek exactly where his lips had brushed it.

Luke decided to be naughty, since he was greatly enjoying the game he was playing with her. 'Ah, I see that rather than being too bold I was not bold enough. Does this please you more?' This was a kiss directly on her lips, which she resisted a little at first before she surrendered to the delight that it induced, responding to him as freely and frankly as he could have wished.

The kiss went on and on. It changed in character, became wildly passionate, so that all the pent-up longing for her which Luke had kept inside him during the long weeks in which he had first known, and then loved Anne, found at last its true expression.

Dropping his head, he kissed her neck and then the tiny shadow which showed above the neck of her dress. Oh, such delight! So much so that he delved further as he pulled the dress down, using his hands as well as his mouth to stroke and caress her.

And she was with him all the way! She made no resistance. Her fear of him, and of all men, had vanished under the tenderness of his caresses, for he was careful not to distress her by allowing his passion to overcome him to the point where he no longer considered her feelings, but only his own. He willed himself to go slowly as she quivered and gasped her response to each delicate caress. Even when he pulled her dress further down still, gently, gently, until his mouth enclosed her right breast, she still shuddered with joy against him, her own hand rising to stroke his neck and head.

He must not frighten her! Whatever her dead husband had done to her had, Luke was sure, destroyed her ability to respond easily to an openly passionate assault on her senses, however much she might love the man who made it. If he could persuade her that she might join him in joy, and not in terror, then his battle was won. He could make his offer secure in the knowledge that she would not shrink away from him.

Far from shrinking away, she had begun to caress him, murmuring his name as he murmured hers, so that when his hands moved again to stroke her everywhere she still made no resistance. He lifted himself on to the sofa to lie beside her, to make their love-making the more easy, and still she did not resist him. Eyes blind, Anne was lost to the passion that was beginning to consume her and that she had never felt before.

Suddenly, how Anne never knew, she was on her back and Luke was above her. He was now lost to everything but the need to consummate fully the passion which they were sharing, and he began to fumble with the buttons on his breeches flap, desire making his hands clumsy.

He was never to know exactly what particular caress, what murmured endearment, or perhaps the direct evidence of his arousal, caused his love's sudden change of heart. One moment she was panting and sighing beneath him, the next she was pushing him away, pulling her bodice up and her skirts down, exclaiming wildly, 'No, no. I can't. I shouldn't. I mustn't. This is wrong of me. I shouldn't allow you. . .'

'No, not wrong,' cried Luke, 'never wrong,' and he tried to pull her down into the circle of his arms again. 'I love you. I want to marry you. I never meant to go so far so soon, but once I began to make love to you I was lost. Oh, Anne, marry me as soon as possible. Be my wife and make me the happiest man in England.'

This declaration, which was so patently, so vividly truthful, had quite the opposite effect from the one which Luke had expected. Anne sprang to her feet, retreated across the room to lean against the wall facing him, both hands in front of her mouth. Great tears began to rain down her face. Sobs shook her body.

'No, no! Do not ask me! It's impossible,' and now she held both her hands out in front of her as though warding off an enemy, not a man whose one desire was to make her his wife, and whose passion for her was as great as hers had so plainly been for him.

Luke, his hair awry, his dignity gone, unable even to stand until he had pulled up and fastened his wretched breeches, gasped at her, 'Oh, my darling, don't reject me now. Not now, when you have proved that our love is mutual.'

'Oh, Luke. I love you so – ' and this declaration came out through a hail of sobs ' – but I cannot marry you. You must not ask me why, for both our sakes. Oh, I cannot be your wife and I should never have fallen in love with you, but I have. . . I have. . . God help me. . . God help us both. Oh, I cannot stay here now. I cannot. We can't. . .we can't. . .'

Her pain and distress were so strong that Luke was quite unmanned at the sight. All the pleasant equability and charming self-control with which he had previously faced life had gone. He was across the room and by her side, trying to take her into his arms.

'Why cannot you marry me? Why? You are a widow. Why should we not marry. . .?'

Anne did not, could not, allow him to finish, saying

again, through her agony, 'Do not ask me. Please, I beg you.'

The very power of her passion, of her newly awakened senses, added to and compounded her distress. To see his beloved face before her, to want him and his love so desperately, and at the same time to know that she could not have him, must not have him, was like the torture of the damned. She threw herself face down in the nearest armchair to wail into the cushions. Luke knelt down beside her, alarmed by the strength of her misery.

'Oh, my love, my dearest love, only tell me what is wrong. You know how much I love you. I can't bear to see you in such despair, it is almost worse than suffering myself.'

Even as he spoke, Luke suddenly knew that the years of love which he had felt for Cressy were as nothing to the depth of the passion which he felt for Anne. So strong was it that her pain was his. Never before had he experienced the sensations which were overwhelming him now. That other love had been a mirage, something which, because of its hopelessness, had allowed him to distance himself from true feeling and true commitment to anyone else.

'Only tell me what is wrong,' was wrenched from him at last, 'and we can meet and overcome it together.'

But all that that produced, despite the tenderness with which he held her, was a shake of the head, before she buried it in the cushions again, until she raised herself once more to show him a face now tearless.

'I must be brave,' she said, her composure as great as it had always previously been. 'I must not behave like a hysterical fool, however deep and desperate my feelings are. Believe me, Luke, I love you to distraction, and because of that I cannot tell you of the burden which I carry round with me. I cannot, must not, share it with you – ever. You must let me go and try to forget me. I should never have allowed myself to fall in love with you, never have accepted your love-making.

'Once we began I should have stopped you, for I was being unfair to you to allow you to continue. But oh, my dearest love, you, and all the love which you have offered me, have overwhelmed me quite, have made me forget what I am, and what I must do. I will leave Mrs Britten's and you must try to forget me, as I must try to forget you.'

She turned her head away from him so that she might not see his suffering face.

'Forget you!' Luke's voice was a mixture of agony and disbelief. 'Look at me, Anne. How can you ask such a thing of me?'

But she only murmured, her head hung low, her voice calm – except that he could feel the pain beneath her outward composure – 'No, no, Luke. You must do as I ask you, please.'

It was hopeless. She was adamant. The strength of her will impressed Luke even as it distressed him, because it left him no hope. He rose slowly to his feet, his whole body still throbbing with the misery of passion rejected, and the equal misery of the knowledge that his suit was doomed to failure. Anne had become his guiding star. She had given him the spur to change his life so that he had begun to achieve what he ought to achieve, but at the very moment when success was in his grasp, he was about to lose her.

'You mean this, Anne, knowing that you have been my saviour, that you have given my life the point and purpose which it lacked until your encouragement? Can you not trust me with the reason why you are rejecting me?'

She shook her head. 'Believe me, Luke, it is for your benefit even more than mine, that I must remain silent. And yes, oh, yes, I must not be tempted to give way to your persuasions. Oh, if only I could speak, but I cannot. Please go, Luke. My heart is broken – as I can see that yours is. Be brave for me, Luke, if you truly love me. Think only that I have helped you.'

Be brave! How right she was. To rail at the fate which was keeping them apart – whatever that was – was to play a coward's part. If she could face him, her face white with pain, and endure what she must, then he would be less than a man if he gave way to the misery which was consuming him. If at one bound he had passed from heaven to hell, then so be it, he must live with it on his feet like a man and not on his knees, wailing.

Luke walked to the door.

His hand on the knob, he turned for one last look at her. She had not moved. Her face had resumed its usual stoic passivity. She was silent, her longing eyes fixed on him, only him. He must be silent, too.

But he could not stay at Mrs Britten's, for to do so would be to drive her away from what had plainly become her haven. More, to face her daily would be, as Anne had already seen, simply to compound their misery so he must play the man and leave as soon as could be arranged.

'Goodbye, my love,' he whispered to himself as he left her, and accepted the gift of courage which she had conferred on him.

He had lost her. Except that he had never possessed her. He knew now that, as he had sometimes suspected, there was a mystery attached to her presence, here as a humble sempstress in Mrs Britten's home. What could it be that held her in such terrible thrall, that made her reject him and his honourable proposal so decisively? He would ask Mrs Britten when she returned, but he knew, even as he made this decision, that she would tell him nothing.

All the warnings which she had uttered, her evident unhappiness at the sight of him and Anne falling in love with one another, made a terrible kind of sense if she knew that there were some strange circumstances which must keep them forever apart.

Nevertheless, when he heard Mrs Britten return, he ran down the stairs to confront her, to tell her that he had made an offer to Anne and that she had refused it in terror and distress. If she knew that, for some unexplained reason, his case was hopeless, she could at least assure him of that, if nothing else, and that it was not mere shrinking nervousness which held Anne back.

He caught her before she had a chance to speak with Anne, who had fled to her room as he had fled to his. He told her an edited version of what had just occurred and she heard him out in silence, although the face she turned on him was a compassionate one.

'Oh, Mr Harcourt, I did try to warn you not to become too involved with Anne, or she with you, but I could see by the behaviour of you both that it was not answering. I cannot tell you why she has refused you, and is right to do so, for I am bound to secrecy. If, as you say, she has told you to forget her, then you must try to do so. That is all I can say, and it is little enough.'

'But I cannot forget her,' Luke cried passionately, and then a suspicion, which the nature of her refusal had created in him, had him saying, 'She calls herself a widow, but is she truly one?'

He thought a shadow passed across Mrs Britten's face, but her answer was firm. 'I cannot tell you more than she has told you herself, Mr Harcourt. You must understand that.'

'Which is nothing,' Luke murmured sorrowfully. He could not badger the good woman before him any more. 'She says she will leave here,' were his last words, 'but it is I who must leave, for I can see that this is the only refuge which she has, whereas I can afford to leave – and must – even though it will break my heart to do so.'

The pity on Mrs Britten's face almost unmanned him, but if Anne were brave, then he must be, too. 'I will look for new rooms tomorrow, although I cannot hope to find a kinder landlady or a happier place to live.'

Mrs Britten did not say him nay, but sorrowfully watched him mount the stairs. He was bereft of hope, who had recently been so hopeful.

Once in his room, Luke thought that he might not be able to write, but to his surprise the words poured from his overful heart as he described the miseries of his gypsy hero, who had seen the girl he loved married to another. It was himself of whom he wrote. Later in the year when the part he was writing was published, his audience grieved and suffered with him, so powerful were the emotions which his own sorrow had enabled him to put on paper.

He did as he had promised Mrs Britten and began to look for another home, far from Islington so that he might not accidentally see Anne. He knew only too well that he could not bear the pain of knowing her near and being unable to approach her. As for Anne, on Mrs Britten telling her that he was about to leave, she almost lost her stoic poise.

'I am driving him from the home he has come to love,' she wailed. 'It is I who ought to leave.'

'Nonsense, child,' returned Mrs Britten briskly, 'for he has money – even if he has renounced the income from his father – and he has homes to go to, apart from his rooms, whereas you, you have only me, and I am sure that he knows that is the case. He is a good young man, and more's the pity that it is not possible for you to marry him.'

I will not cry, Anne thought, and held her head proudly high while she waited each day for Luke to leave the house before she came downstairs, and retreated to her room before he returned in the evening.

'The day after tomorrow,' Luke told Mrs Britten one morning, 'I shall leave. I have found a snug little cottage in Chelsea, near the river, and I shall say goodbye to you with a heavy heart.'

'You have the consolation of doing the right thing, Mr Harcourt.'

'But it isn't enough,' Luke said sadly, 'as you well know. You will tell Mrs Cowper from me how sorry I am to go, and that I wish her well. I think that it would harrow us both too much if I were to try to bid her a formal farewell.'

He walked painfully upstairs to his room. His writing had become a consolation for him, and a means of escape. He was not aware of how ill he looked, or of the pity with which Mrs Britten looked after him.

Later, she said to Anne who sat in her usual place on the drawing-room sofa, sewing, 'Mr Harcourt leaves us tomorrow. He asked me to say goodbye to you, and that he is sorry to go. He thought it wise not to try to see you before he leaves.'

Anne did not immediately reply, but kept her head

bent over her work before saying in a stifled voice, 'It is better so.'

The two women sat in silence. Mrs Britten did not wish to leave Anne on her own. Despite Anne's bent head, she could see the slow tears falling down Anne's face, and sighed a deep sigh over the wicked vagaries of an unkind fate which had brought Anne and Luke together, knowing that the love which would follow could never come to fruition.

The morning dragged on. Mrs Britten had, most unusually for her, taken up a novel – she never normally read before noon, that was for the afternoon's leisure – and her book did not capture her whole attention. Consequently, the sound of a coach, a grand affair, drawing up outside, and the bustle which accompanied it, had her rising and walking to the window.

To turn, her face pale with shock, to hiss at Anne, 'Up with you, my dear. It is he, your husband. He has tracked you here, but he must not find you.'

'Never say that it is Clairval!' Anne sprang to her feet, her sewing dropping unheeded on to the carpet as she ran to join Mrs Britten at the window, just as the Marquess of Clairval helped by a footman and followed by the foxy-faced, red-haired man whom she had seen and feared a fortnight earlier, stepped down from his coach.

'Oh, I am lost just when I thought that I was safe.'

Mrs Britten seized her by the hand. 'No! He shall not have you, but we must be quick. He will be in the house in a few moments, for Mary will undoubtedly let him in, such a grand personage as he is to come a-visiting here. Up the backstairs with you, at once.'

She ran to the door, dragging Anne with her, and the two women dashed along the corridor to the kitchen, fortunately missing Mary, who was already on her way to the front door to answer the peremptory ringing of the bell as well as the banging of m'lord Marquess's gold-topped cane on the front door!

Through the kitchen they ran like the wind, and up the narrow uncarpeted stairs, which were the back way to the first floor and then to the servants' quarters at the top of the house.

'Where are we going?' gasped Anne, as Mrs Britten's route took them across the first-floor landing to knock on Luke's door.

'Oh, no,' she cried, trying to drag her hand free. 'We cannot involve Luke. Think what Clairval would do to him if he found out that he had helped me, that he loved me.'

'Think rather of what Clairval will do you if he captures you here,' retorted Mrs Britten practically before knocking on Luke's door, and pushing Anne into his room. Luke started up from his work to stare at them, so wild and sudden was their arrival.

'There is no time to explain now,' gasped Mrs Britten at him, too distressed to straighten her widow's cap which had fallen awry in the violence of her dash upstairs.

'You must take Anne away from here as quickly as possible, lest a further great wrong be done to her. Go down the backstairs, out through the kitchen door, to a place as far away from here, and as secret as you can find. She can explain to you later. Now, you must go at once,' she almost roared at him, 'for I must leave you. I shall say that Anne is not here, gone a-marketing, and is not his wife. Anything to prevent Lord Clairval from taking her away.'

'Clairval!' Luke stared at Anne as Mrs Britten shot out of the door. All was suddenly plain to him, but there was no time to think of that. 'Of course, I shall help you, Anne.' Like Mrs Britten he, too, took her by the hand and began to urge her out of the door. 'Quick now, before he demands to search the house.'

'This is not my wish,' began Anne, 'Believe me, I never meant to involve you in my troubles, Luke. . .'

'No time for that, now,' replied Luke briskly. 'Explanations later.' He had not stayed to put on his coat, and together, he in his shirt sleeves rolled up to the elbow, Anne in her shabby morning gown, ran through Mrs Britten's garden towards safety – wherever that was to be found.

Mary smiled confusedly at her recent suitor, the foxy-faced man, who had followed m'lord Clairval into the house and ushered them both into Mrs Britten's drawing-room. Her mistress, her cap restored to its proper dignity, rose from the armchair in which she had apparently been reading. She placed her book on a side-table and curtsied profoundly to the great man before her.

'I believe that you wish to speak to me, m'lord. How may I be of service to you?'

So this was Anne's husband. He was staring around her room, a look of utter and complete contempt on his face. Mrs Britten could plainly see through its ruin the good looks that he had once possessed. She could also see his cruel mouth, and even crueller eyes.

He fixed them on her and said without preamble, as though he were speaking to the veriest serf, 'You may fetch my faithless and disobedient wife to me, woman, so that I may take her home – to the punishment which rightly awaits her.'

Inwardly quaking, Mrs Britten yet decided to be bold. 'Your wife, sir? I think that you must be mistaken. I have no Lady Clairval lodging with me here.'

For a moment she thought that he was going to strike her with the gold-topped cane which he was carrying. Instead, he banged it on the floor, and ground out, 'Do not lie to me, woman. I know that you were her governess. I also know that you have been harbouring her here under the name of – ' and he snapped his fingers at the man standing behind him ' – which is, Jenkinson?'

'Cowper, m'lord. Mrs Anne Cowper, who has been lodging here these many months,' his minion dutifully supplied.

'You heard him, woman! Summon her here immediately from whichever room she is hiding in before I send Jenkinson to fetch the authorities to remove her for me. I do not want a scandal, nor should you. Do you hear me? Or do you add deafness to your other incapacities?'

His voice had risen to a bellow on his last words.

Mrs Britten, fearful of him though she was, yet held her ground. 'She is not here, m'lord. She has gone to the shop where she collects her work as a sempstress. I cannot believe that Mrs Cowper is your wife.'

'So, woman. You are a double liar. You know quite well that she is my wife, and Jenkinson's man, who has been watching your house this morning, informed us that no one has left it.' Clairval's expression was baleful, mixed with grotesque triumph as he came out with this.

'Nevertheless, m'lord, I fear that you are mistaken. Mrs Cowper is not here.'

His face uglier still, Clairval swung round to address his henchman, who stood there silent, considering the brave defiance of the valiant woman before them. 'Search the house, Jenkinson. Spare no pains, and do not consider the feelings or possessions of the lying bitch before you. She is aiding and abetting a felony by keeping my wife from me.'

Not quite a felony, thought Jenkinson but he sped to do m'lord's bidding, Mrs Britten crying after him as he left the room, 'She is not here. You run a wasted errand.'

'Be quiet,' thundered Clairval. He flung himself into the armchair which Mrs Britten had earlier vacated, mannerlessly leaving her to stand, the better to inform her how little she – or any woman – mattered in the Marquess of Clairval's scheme of things.

Silence followed.

Mary could be heard crying in the distance. Was Jenkinson bullying her? Mrs Britten comforted herself with the knowledge that Mary knew nothing, and so could betray nothing. She hugged that thought to her when Jenkinson at last entered, his face glum.

'M'lady is not here, m'lord. I have searched the house. The maid says that to her knowledge she has not left it – but I cannot find her.'

'Then where the devil is she? She could not have escaped by the chimney.' He rose and roared at Mrs Britten with such ferocity that she retreated before him. 'Where has she gone?'

Jenkinson did not like to admit that he might have been careless, but honesty compelled him to say, 'Through the kitchen, perhaps, while the maid answered the door. There is a back way through the garden by which m'lady may have fled.'

'Oh, a back way, you say? Remind me of that when the time for settlement comes. The bird has flown and all is to do again. As for you, woman, your house will be watched, back and front, night and day, and if my wife so much as shows her face here, I'll have the pair of you before the magistrates.'

It was over. Mrs Britten, her legs failing her, sank into the armchair so lately occupied by m'lord. For the time being Anne was safe. She had no idea where Luke might have taken her, which was as well, for Clairval might yet return to try to drag the truth from her. But so far he had failed to find the lady!

She could hear him thundering his thwarted wrath at Jenkinson. Whatever he was saying was not pleasant, she was sure. Presently the front door opened and closed. They were gone.

She ran to the window. The coach was being driven at breakneck speed along the road towards London, but Jenkinson was not in it. He was standing on the pavement, gazing after it with a most malignant stare. M'lord had just turned him away without a penny, shouting that he had been light in the attic to trust such a fool to do his work for him.

'Not a penny,' he had bellowed at Jenkinson. 'Not a penny. You have spent my time and my money and all for nothing! The woman's loose again, leaving me like a gaby haring after her. You may find your own way back to town. Do not show me your curst face again.'

Oh, but I *shall* show you my curst face again, m'lord, and a sorry day it will be for you when I do, was Jenkinson's inward litany as the coach and Clairval disappeared round the corner.

Once he was well away from Mrs Britten's, Luke slowed down and tried to think where he might safely take Anne; whose hand lay so trustingly in his. He was struck by a sudden inspiration.

Josette! he thought, as they finally reached the road which led towards London. Josette will help me, I am sure. She is a good girl, and if she is not still in her rooms, then her friends will. Clairval will not be able to find us there, for Mrs Britten does not even know that Josette exists, let alone what her address is.

They walked briskly along the road, regardless of the stares which their inadequate dress attracted. Luke had just enough money in his breeches pocket to pay a hackney cab to take them to Josette's. He bundled Anne into it after he had paid the cab driver, who had demanded to see the colour of Luke's money before he consented to take them to the lodgings in a back street behind the Haymarket to which Josette had returned after she had broken with Luke.

Luck was with them. Josette's landlady was out, and it was she who answered the door.

'Luke Harcourt!' she exclaimed, looking from him to Anne. 'What are you doing here?'

'I shall explain in a minute,' Luke said gravely. 'I am well aware that I have no right to do so, but I have come to ask of you one last favour. This is my friend, Mrs Anne. . .Gordon, who is in need of a safe place to live. She is being pursued by her husband from whom she has fled, and who has treated her abominably.

'He can have no idea that she is here, but we shall both understand if you feel that you cannot help us – at least for one night, until I find somewhere safe to hide her.'

Josette looked doubtfully at them both. Something in the quiet desperation written on Anne's face touched her heart. That, and the tender way in which Luke was looking at her. Josette bore Luke no malice; he had been a kind and considerate lover, and very soon she would be back in the village where she had been born and Luke and his doings would have no part in his life.

'Of course, your friend may stay with me overnight Luke and longer, if it proves necessary. Pray sit down,

Mrs Gordon,' she added kindly. 'You look as though you are about to faint.'

'It is most good of you to help me,' Anne replied. 'Particularly as I have been unable to bring anything with me. No money and no clothes.'

'You may forget them both,' returned Josette. 'I am sure that I can find Mrs Gordon some night rail and something to eat. You may safely leave her with me, Luke, and if it is so necessary for her to disappear, then you must be off to find help for her as soon as possible.'

Anne did not wish Luke to leave. He was her sole remaining link with Islington and Mrs Britten, where for a short space she had been happy. Josette saw that she was distressed and, when Luke had gone, came over to sit by her.

'You are not just a friend, are you?' she asked. 'That is a tale he told to protect you. Luke loves you, does he not? Truly loves you.' Her voice was wistful.

From some depth of knowledge, never before fished in, Anne found words to answer her. 'He cares for you, too. A different form of love. He would not have brought me here, otherwise.'

Josette nodded. 'You were fortunate to find me here. I am going home this weekend, into the country, to marry my true love. I will be honest with you. I once thought that. . .someone else. . .was my true love. I was wrong.'

Anne had known from the moment that she had first seen Josette that she and Luke had been lovers. . . But what he did before he met me is past and gone – as is what happened to me before I met him at Mrs Britten's.

She trembled a little again as she thought of Clairval and what she must say of him when she next met Luke, and also at the thought of what might be happening to her good friend in Islington once Clairval found that his prey had eluded him again. . .

Once he had left Josette's' Luke tried to assemble his muddled thoughts and decide on a sensible plan of action. He could not leave Anne with Josette for very long. It would not be fair to Josette since, if Clairval found that she was sheltering his runaway wife, Luke had no doubt that he would wreak vengeance on her.

That might sound as though they were all living in a Drury Lane melodrama, but Clairval's reputation was so suspect that nothing must be left to chance. But where could he take her where she might not be found? He was so distracted that he did not hear his name being called until a hand touched his shoulder.

He looked up. Of all people, it was Tawno Chikno, as raffishly handsome as ever, and leading a prime horse.

'Luke, my brother, what's amiss?' He seemed to have acquired a little of the *chovihani's* second sight, for he added, 'I sense that something is wrong with you. May an old friend help?'

May an old friend help? Luke gaped at him. Had providence sent Tawno on his journey especially to help him? Now, that was demanding too much of life, but a thought, daring in its simplicity, struck him like a thunderbolt from Jove's hand reaching earth.

'Tawno, my beauty! Where are you all encamped?'

'Nigh to Greenwich. We shall be at the Fair.'

'And then, Tawno? Where do you go, then?'

'Why do you ask, friend Luke? You know as well as I do that after Greenwich we wend west, towards Bristol. Was it not near Haven's End that you and I learned to trust the horse so that it might, in return, trust us?'

Salvation! Salvation was before them – for now Luke knew that his destiny and Anne's were inextricably intertwined.

'A week, then? You leave in a week?'

'Indeed, friend.' Tawno stared at him. Like Pat, he had never seen Luke Harcourt so frantic, so unlike his usual controlled self.

Luke collected himself. 'If I asked a favour of Jasper, friend Tawno, would he be likely to grant it?'

'You know he would, Luke. You are almost one of us.'

'Then take me to him, Tawno. For I must ask it of him immediately.'

Chapter Nine

'Luke!' Josette had been waiting for his return, not in her room, but in the drawing-room of her landlady – a concession grudgingly granted to her. 'I have something to say to you. I have decided to return to Kent on the night coach today instead of waiting until the end of the week. Anne can rent my room until you find somewhere safer for her to hide – the landlady has already agreed that she may take it over.'

He had, after all, done the right thing in asking Josette to help him. Luke's new, and less selfish, attitude to life told him that he hardly deserved her generosity, and so he informed her in no uncertain terms.

'Pooh!' Josette waved his thanks away. 'We are still friends, I hope. It is the least that I can do for you both. I have given her a nightgown and a change of clothes – they are not those which I shall be taking back to Kent. They belong to my...different...life here and are unsuitable for country wear.'

How could he thank her? He bent down and kissed her cheek. A brotherly kiss. The look which she gave him in return told him that she had no regrets but was looking forward to her new life. They could wish each other well in perfect amity.

He let himself into what was now Anne's room – to find her asleep in her armchair. He did not disturb her but stood looking down at the picture which she presented. In sleep, as when awake, she possessed a lovely calm, a composure which he found astonishing when he tried to imagine what her life with Clairval must have been.

He didn't deserve Anne, as he hadn't deserved Josette, but he would try to make himself worthy of her. So thinking, he bent down and stroked her cheek. She awoke, to smile at him.

'You are back. I hadn't expected you until tomorrow. You know that Josette is leaving?'

'Yes, and I have said my farewells to her.' Luke sat down beside her and took her hand in his. 'I have good news for you. I have found a way for us to leave London secretly. First, though, let me assure you that Mrs Britten has not suffered as the result of your husband's visit although her house is being watched in case you try to return.'

'Mrs Britten! How ungrateful of me to fall asleep so easily, forgetting that she might be in danger. She has been so kind, and has now saved me, not once, but twice. First when she took me in, and today when she helped me to escape.'

'Hush,' said Luke. 'You must not reproach yourself. She sends you her love and the hope that you may escape from Clairval again.'

'And you?' asked Anne anxiously. 'He does not know that you helped me to get away from him?'

'No, indeed. And that is our greatest strength. I may not stay with you tonight, but tomorrow I shall come to you, and put my plan into action. I shall tell Mrs Britten that I am going into town to see my publisher, which will not be a total lie, seeing that I have the last part of my novel to deliver to him before I come to you. And then we shall leave London, but I shall not tell her where we are going.'

'Yes. Best that she knows nothing. Clairval is a pitiless man, as I well know,' and she shivered.

'Oh, Luke, I feel that it is only fair that I tell you my story before you commit yourself to trying to rescue me. It is not only that I wish to explain myself, I must inform you of the danger in which you stand if you help me.'

Luke was keenly aware that, as usual, Anne pitied everyone but herself – who needed it the most.

'Think nothing of that. Think only, that with my help, you may escape him again. And, if it pains you to tell me your story, then you need not do so. I have only to know Clairval to understand what your life with him must have been.'

It was Anne's turn to put out her hand to take Luke's. 'No, in a strange way I believe that it may help me. The plain truth is that Mrs Britten and I have been deceiving you all these months – for the best of reasons, it is true. But I have always been painfully conscious that I was not being honest with you. Now I must be, as I hope always to be in the future.'

'But I fully understand why you could not be,' protested Luke.

'True, and that is all the more reason why I should be open with you now. I was not always a rich heiress. Until I was sixteen years old I was simple Miss Anticleia Temple, although I was always known as Anne. My father was a poor scholar, a parson with a living near Oxford. My mother died when I was born, and my father did not remarry.

'We were very happy together until a distant cousin died and left my father a large fortune and a gloomy neglected house in Yorkshire. He felt it his duty to give up his living and look after his new estate, but I think that the move may have killed him. In six months he was dead and I was his heiress, left to the guardianship of relatives I hardly knew and who were determined to use my wealth to marry the family into the aristocracy.'

Anne stopped and shivered. 'This was how I came to meet Lord Clairval. I was not yet eighteen, and he came to visit my cousins at their express invitation. They saw only his title, his old and honoured name, not the man he really was. You must remember that this was nearly five years ago and he was still handsome. . .'

In telling Luke her sad story, Anne found herself back in the past again. She could remember quite plainly the first time she had met Clairval. He had been charm itself, and had spoken to her of the things which interested her, of books and music. He was always dressed in black – her cousins had told her that after his first wife had died suddenly he had gone into perpetual mourning, so stricken was he by her death.

He had made no secret of his relative poverty, so that he might not be accused of being a fortune hunter because he had concealed it. He had even laughed over it a little sadly, and she had felt sorry for him. Tears were in his eyes when he spoke to her of his late wife, even though she had died two years earlier. She had honoured him for his devotion to her, and told him so, not in words, but in the kind sympathy which she showed to him.

Even so, she had at first been a little shocked when he had, through her cousin and guardian, John Temple Masters, proposed to her. After all, he was over twenty-five years older than she was.

'But you like him,' John Masters had protested when she had demurred a little. 'And think what you are gaining. A man, not a boy, and one of England's oldest titles. His estates are a little encumbered, true, but your settlement will take care of that. We can arrange things so that your fortune is not swallowed up by his debts. Sufficient of an income can be assured to him so that a steady recovery will see Clairval's lands solvent again.'

That Clairval might not see matters in exactly the same light did not occur to her guardian, nor to Anne herself. She had lived a life far removed from the world which Clairval inhabited, and could not be aware of the deep and passionate tides which lay beneath the easy carelessness with which Clairval faced her relatives and her.

The true carelessness in the matter lay with her guardian, who should have heeded gossip more. The gossip which told of Clairval's darker side; the gossip about his conduct to his first wife; but the man and his name bedazzled him. Nor did he pause to think that if he made Anticleia's money really safe from Clairval's depredations, then the person who might suffer the most from this might be Anticleia herself.

As for Clairval, he told himself that however tightly her guardian might tie up Miss Temple's estates before her marriage, what might happen to them afterwards would be a very different thing!

The girl seemed young and biddable, and a little awed by him and his title, so he concentrated on pouring his charm over her, and her bedazzled connections. Consequently, the marriage, which took place at York Minster under the aegis of the Archbishop himself was arranged as a glorious pageant, ushering in a golden age for Clairval and his estates.

At this point in her story Anne stopped, and looked at Luke, her great eyes filling with tears.

'I was stupid enough to think that he truly was my

fairy prince or, better still, the older man who was going to take the place in my life which my father had always filled. And he, he had not the common sense to go slowly with me at first. I suppose that he thought that I was an obedient fool to whom he might do as he pleased.

'He made the mistake of drinking too much on our wedding night, and it was a disaster. Oh, I cannot speak of it. One moment we were in the Minster, looking like figures in a fairy story, and the next. . .

'The next I was finding that I had married a man who could only gain pleasure from another's pain. That first night I told myself that it was the drink which had done the damage, except that I soon discovered that, sober, he was more vile than when drunk. There was a coldness about him then. He told me once that the sooner I was with child the more I should please him, for then he could be off to find better entertainment elsewhere, and I might sleep alone.'

She looked away from Luke when she told him her carefully edited tale, for it was beyond her to reveal the true story of the brutality with which Clairval had treated her from the very first. She felt Luke stir, heard the oaths he muttered below his breath, and knew that he guessed much of what she was not telling him, what she could not tell him – for very shame – for Clairval's cruelty seemed to demean her as well as he who had inflicted it.

'My dear,' Luke said, 'if it pains you too much, you must stop.' He was remembering her broken wrist, her slight limp and the manner in which she had flinched away from him when she had first known him, before she had discovered that she could trust him.

She shook her head. 'No, for you do not yet understand the total of his brutality, what he might do to you, or cause to be done to you if he discovered not only that you had helped me, but that we love one another. After a time, some months in all, when no child came, he began to find trying to create one... difficult.

'It was then that his brutality became worse, made the more so because only the birth of a child to me would bring him the extra money which he claimed to need for his estates but which, I think, he meant to spend on debauchery. He became so careless in his treatment of me that he had to excuse my appearance by my clumsiness, making fun in company of what he called "my wife's inability to walk downstairs without falling over".

'And still a child eluded him, so one day he brought me a paper to sign which would give him control of my money without the birth of an heir. When I refused to sign it, for by now I was finding the strength to defy him, he threatened me with worse than I had already endured.

'He had, it seems, begun a whispering campaign about my sanity, and was telling the world that I had run mad and needed to be confined to my room. A man as powerful as Clairval can always find tools to do his bidding, and two of his hirelings solemnly examined me and pronounced me out of my wits. Only, what the world did not know, was that my room was a cell in one of Clairval Castle's towers, with the promise of imprisonment in a madhouse if I did not do his bidding.

'He vowed that he would beat me into submission, and the more I defied him, the crueller he grew. He could not believe that one poor woman would defy him so constantly. Where I gained the strength to oppose him, I shall never know. Oh, I prayed to God to help me or, failing that, to release me through death from a life which had become hateful, but all seemed in vain.

'Shortly before he had had me certified mad, I had written to my late guardian, John Masters, begging him to rescue me from the hell in which I was living. Alas, Clairval convinced him of my madness, and he, and others to whom I appealed, wrote to me, telling me to listen to my husband, take the medicine his doctors prescribed and behave myself. It seemed hopeless to try to escape him.

'Until one day, the steward who had been my gaoler came to me and said that he could see me mistreated no longer. He feared that what had happened to Clairval's first wife would happen to me, and his conscience would not let him bear the double dose of guilt which my death would bring him.

'He said that he would release me, find me sanctuary, delay the news of my flight and would then fly himself and take me to wherever I wished to go. The only person I could think of was my dear Mrs Britten, and so it was arranged.

'Except that, although he released me, he never joined me afterwards. I was hidden away in a poor cottage on the Nottinghamshire border where his brother and mother lived. One day his brother went to Clairval Castle to discover why he had not left Clairval's employment as he had promised.

'When he returned, he gave me just enough money to pay my coach fare to London. He told me that the steward had disappeared, and that the rumour in the servants' hall was that Clairval had likely killed him for freeing me. I was to leave as soon as possible, lest Clairval discover my whereabouts and punish them for harbouring me. The sooner I was gone, the safer they would be.

'So now you see the danger which you run by trying to save me. I already have one man's death on my conscience, and, oh, Luke, I would not have yours. If you love me, leave me.'

This plea was so wild, so impassioned, that it almost unmanned Luke.

He took his beloved girl in his arms, and whispered in her ear, 'No, never, my darling. What sort of cur should I be to compel you to bear this dreadful load on your own? I would have suggested that we go to your relatives and ask for help, but everything which you have told me, and the *on dits* about Clairval which are already circulating in society, have served only to convince me that that would be a hopeless cause.

'Years ago, only the fact that Lady Strathmore's relatives were rich and powerful, and were on her side, was able to save her from the similar wickedness of Stony Bowes. But your relatives have already refused to help you, and my father is a member of the government and a magistrate sworn to uphold the wicked law which condemns you to be treated as a chattel. You have no one but me to protect you, and what a poor insignificant prop I am, my darling heart, even if I love you truly.'

Without further touching, stroking or lovemaking they lay in one another's arms. It was not so much that their passion was spent, but that in the light of Anne's dreadful story it seemed inappropriate.

Presently Luke whispered, 'After what you just have told me, my dearest, it is all the more imperative that we leave London in secret as soon as possible. Today I visited Jasper Petulengro and the gypsies who are at present camped at Greenwich Fair, and they have promised us sanctuary. To rescue you, I must propose something which I at first thought a trifle melodramatic, but since hearing your story I am convinced is a necessity.

'Jasper and the Romanies are on their way west to Bristol – slowly – for they stop at country fairs and horse shows in order to earn their living. Once we reach Bristol, we can take a ship for the Americas under false names. Jasper will marry us according to the custom of the Romanies – he says that by their laws a marriage such as yours to Clairval cannot stand. Even Clairval would find it difficult to find us if we cross the broad Atlantic.

'It means leaving behind everything that we know, and making a new life overseas, but a man may use his ability to write in order to earn a living wherever he settles, and our life could hardly be harder than the one which you have endured since your marriage.'

Anne did not immediately answer him. She wriggled away from his arms to look him full in the eye, her own eyes glowing. 'Oh, Luke, I will go with you anywhere, and although once I would have thought it a sin to live with you as your wife when I am married to another, I no longer do so. If Ruth in the Bible could follow Naomi into a new country, then so can I follow you! But it is not I who should make this decision, for it is you who are the greater loser if we do as you propose.'

'Oh, brave,' said Luke softly, taking her ardent face between his two hands and kissing it gently. 'You shame me when I think of what you have suffered and endured whilst I was leading my idle, careless life. And even now, you think of me before you think of yourself.'

'Dear Luke.' Anne had responded to his caresses by taking one of his hands, turning it towards her mouth and kissing it on the palm. 'When I see what thinking only of one's self has done to Clairval, how can I put my own wishes and desires first? That would be to be as poor and shameful a thing as he is.'

What could Luke say to that, except to kiss her again? He might have wished to love the afternoon away, only there was much to be done if they were to join the gypsies on the morrow. There was Clairval to deceive.

And if he had once thought to involve his father and Cressy in Anne's troubles, he no longer wished to do so – for he dare not risk Clairval using the law to claim Anne back. And once he had done so, possession being nine points of the law, then even James, Lord Lyndale's name and power might not be sufficient to free her again.

For the law saw the wife's obedience to her husband as absolute. If he loved Anne, and were to save her – or try to – he must be prepared to give up everything, and make a new life where Marquesses had little power, and where a man was respected for what he was, not for the bedroom in which he had been born.

'You will be safe here tonight,' he said. 'And I shall come for you tomorrow afternoon, without fail. Mrs Britten shall not know that I am disappearing, nor anyone else – safer so. Tomorrow we shall be Mr and Mrs Gordon, on their way to set sail for a new life.'

'You are sure, Luke,' Anne asked him anxiously 'that this is what you want?'

He gave her one last kiss before he left her. 'It is what we must both want, Anne. For you cannot return to a monster who, at best, would consign you permanently to a madhouse, and at worse would kill you.'

'Welcome, friend Luke, and your woman, too. But if you are to ride and live with us, then you must look like us. You are both far too sleek to be Romanies as you are.'

Everything had gone according to plan. Luke had even spent part of the previous evening at the last great reception which James and Cressy were giving before they left London for Haven's End. Clairval had been there, giving Luke one of his most ferocious stares. Luke had no notion whether or not Clairval knew that he had been living in the same house as his wife, but he thought not. He was sure that Clairval would have accosted him otherwise.

He overheard him telling one of his friends that he hoped to recover his missing wife soon. 'The sooner the better,' he declared piously. 'The poor creature must be in dire need of medical help and careful nursing by now. Those who had charge of her are of the opinion that the longer she is out of their care, the worse she will grow.'

Luke did not know how he contained himself. The memory of Anne's story, and of her suffering face as she told it, was still strong in him. His father, who also overheard Clairval, growled something short about 'not believing people who protested too much,' but added, 'It is to be hoped that she continues to elude him, because once discovered, there is nothing that could be done for her, other than to hand her back to him.'

'A cruel law, that,' exclaimed Luke indignantly, 'which treats a man's wife as less than a serf, no more than a horse or a senseless thing like a chair or a table, for him to dispose of as he pleases.'

His father looked at him curiously, so strong was his son's indignation. There was some emotion in Luke's voice which he had never heard before. 'Most men treat their wives decently,' he said, a trifle defensively.

'Not all men are like you,' Luke proclaimed, and

then changed the subject. It was imperative that no one, absolutely no one, should be aware that Luke Harcourt and the missing wife of the Marquess of Clairval had anything to do with one another.

Without revealing his plans to Mrs Britten, he had left her a farewell letter and enough money to pay for his rooms until the quarter ended so that she should not be out of pocket. He had no need to tell her why he was disappearing – she knew that Anne's safety was paramount with him.

As for Anne, she had so little in the way of possessions that a large shawl, its ends knotted together, contained the few items of clothing which Josette had given her. She had fled from Clairval Castle with nothing, and now had fled from Islington after the same fashion.

Luke collected her from her rooms, gave the landlady a tip for her kindness, and then hired the cab which would take them to Greenwich Fair – and the gypsies.

For the first time in his life he was being careful with his money. He had been to Coutts Bank, had withdrawn most of his holdings there, and had hidden his guineas about his person. He thought that he would give Anne part of his small horde of wealth so that if, by chance, anything happened to him, she would have something of her own.

It was a strange feeling for him to be quite alone in the world without the cushion of his father's name and wealth to support him. He was not even Luke Harcourt – which was a made-up name in any case – but once they took ship for the Americas he would become a fictitious Mr Gordon, travelling with his wife to God knew where. For she was his wife, in the eyes of God, if not in the eyes of man, and he would cherish and protect her and bring her at last out of the shadows and into the sunlight.

Perhaps it was as well that Anne had so little with her, for the *chovihani* came to welcome her, to take her by the hand and say, 'We meet again, as I thought that we would, and you will be my companion for a little while – but first, if we are to hide you, we must arrange it so that you appear to be one of us. Come.'

Luke watched Anne walk away with the *chovihani*. She turned at the tent's flap to give him a smile, and he found himself smiling back. Long afterwards he was to remember everything about that golden late August afternoon; the friendship of the gypsies, Tawno Chikno riding by with a troop of horses, and raising a hand in greeting.

He would never forget the warmth of the welcome which they all gave him, and Jasper's praise for the story which he had written of their life and work.

'For you have not betrayed us, friend Luke,' Jasper told him, 'as so many have done before, but you have told the truth about us as far as in you lies, since as you well know, no man is ever completely truthful about anything!'

This was Jasper all over. Inside his tent Luke pulled on the clothes which were to make him one of the Rom: worn blue velveteen breeches, a heavy linen shirt, and a leather jacket decorated with arcane patterns burned on it with a hot poker. His fine boots were packed away with the rest of his gentleman's clothing. Instead he was given a pair of soft half-boots such as Tawno and his riders wore. The elegant gentleman which he had once been had disappeared quite.

'And you must allow your hair to grow,' Jasper commanded, 'for you will be part of Tawno's troop. He knows that you can haggle over horses, but the wretch has a passion to see you try to learn some of the more difficult tricks with which we entertain the mob.'

'Not the one where he rides at full gallop, then twists and turns to lie beneath the horse's belly, I hope,' riposted Luke with a grin.

'Even that,' smiled Jasper, 'if he so commands. You wish to be one with us, you and your woman, so you shall be one with us, and defy the devil and all his works. The *chovihani* says that the omens are good. Look where she comes, and your woman with her.'

He would scarcely have known that it was Anne who held the *chovihani*'s hand. She was wearing a dress which only reached to her mid-calf, deep blue in colour, matching her eyes, and trimmed with saffron-coloured lace. Her feet were bare and her lustrous dark hair had been loosened and fell about her shoulders. Around her neck was a chain of some base metal, and from it depended a star whose centre was a cluster of small pearls.

'Stella,' pronounced the *chovihani* solemnly as she presented Anne to Luke. 'That will be her name among us. Star because her vision will guide not only you, but us.'

Anne smiled and hung her head a little shyly, but the *chovihani* would have none of that. She seized her by the chin and lifted it up so that Anne faced the world full on, eyes high. 'Nay, child, be not abashed. Courage is yours, and courage is never shamed.'

'Truer words were never spoken,' Luke told them both, 'and what shall be my name? For I, too, must have a name to go among you.'

'Oh, that you shall have,' proclaimed a new, harsh voice. It was Tawno Chikno who had come among them unawares. 'Scribe you are, and lowly Scribe you shall be, until I have taught you a better, worthier trade and you have earned another name. Come, Scribe, it is time for you to learn that trade.'

So soon! Luke had imagined himself being slowly inaugurated into the gypsies' way of life, but he avowed ruefully that he should have known better. He had called on them for help and they were helping him but as with everything in this life, as Jasper was to emphasise to him later, there is always a price to pay.

He was Luke Harcourt no longer: that fine, easy young gentleman who had lived among the fleshpots all his life, accepting the service of others as his due. Instead he was Scribe, the lowliest and least accomplished of the horsemen over whom Tawno reigned – as he was soon to learn. Tawno took him by the shoulder and pushed him roughly towards the group of waiting riders, one of whom was holding a horse ready for him to mount.

Once he was in the saddle, Tawno shouted a hoarse word of command and the riders began to wheel and turn under his directions, performing intricate manoeuvres. The only way in which Anne could distinguish Luke from the others was by his clumsiness, as he tried to keep in line and do what they did.

Tawno seemed to take a delight in taunting him every time he made a mistake, and once, as he shot by him, struck Luke's horse with his whip so sharply that it reared suddenly and Luke found himself on the ground, with his horse trying to make its way into the next county.

Jasper and the rest of the gypsies laughed and cheered as Luke rose slowly to his feet to chase and try to catch his errant steed. Tawno's cries of derision accompanied him on his quest, before hot, sore and dusty, he finally cornered him. It had become very apparent to Anne that Luke had deliberately been given a mettlesome animal which he would have had difficulty in controlling even if he had ridden him before. She thought this rather unfair, and said so.

'Yes,' agreed the *chovihani*. 'You have the right of it, Stella. But consider what Tawno is doing. He is teaching Scribe that he is no longer the lord of his world, but the least-considered performer in a troop; every one of whom is a better rider than he is.

'Only by being made aware of his shortcomings will he ever improve – and if he does not try to improve, or gives up through false pride, then he will never be a Rom, but must remain Scribe, a *gorgio* and a servant. To be a complete man he must learn true pride, and that will only come through humility and the determination to overcome one's faults.'

She looked Anne full in the eye. 'You have learned that lesson, Stella. Scribe has yet to learn it.'

Oh, Luke was already learning something valuable. If he had not actively patronised the gypsies before he came to live among them, he had himself during his time with them easily proving that he could live their life as well as he had lived his own. He and Anne were to be a kind of prince and princess dwelling among the lowly. Instead he was being made to understand that if he were to live among the Rom and pass as one of them, then he must be a Rom in every way which counted.

Once the group riding had ended, Tawno handed a hot and tired Luke over to his chief lieutenant to be taught the basics of what the Rom believed riding to be. His horse's saddle was removed and he was made to ride barebacked, so that he could learn to control his mount without it.

The little crowd that had been watching the fun melted away when this routine grind began. The *cho-*

vihani touched Anne on the shoulder, saying, 'Come. You must help us to prepare the evening meal. Also, I understand from Scribe that you are a skilful sempstress. That being so, you must join Eliza, who looks after the sewing, and she will find work for you to do. No one eats who does not work, you understand. That is why Scribe must learn to be a good rider.'

Thus, when Luke had ended his first lesson, it was Anne who served him from the cauldron of hot rabbit stew which she had helped to prepare, handing him baked potatoes from the embers of the bonfire above which the cauldron had hung. He was trembling slightly from his exertions, ached all over and not even eating the hot food could restore his tired limbs.

Anne saw that he was hiding his weariness beneath his usual charming mask as he laughed and bantered with the riders who had put him through the hardest lesson of his life. She came to sit beside him on the grass, and said quietly, so that none should overhear them, 'Are you very tired, Luke? That looked like hard work.'

He shrugged his shoulders. Not even to Anne could Luke admit how difficult the last few hours had been. To do so would take the edge off his determination not to be beat. So, they thought him a soft *gorgio* did they? One who needed to be taught a stiff lesson. Well, be damned to that! If it killed him, he would learn to ride as well as they did – better, if possible.

Luke was discovering inside himself a hard core of resolution that he had not known he possessed. He had first become aware of it when Anne had spurred him on to write seriously of what he knew. Now it was telling him to prove himself a man whom the Rom could respect. It made him put an arm around Anne's shoulders and hug her reassuringly.

'You mustn't mind if I make a fool of myself at first, Anne. Nothing which is worth the doing comes easily. I shall try not to let you down.'

She rested her head on his shoulder and, remembering what the *chovihani* had said to her of the necessity for Luke to learn the harder lessons of life, said no more.

Later that night, though, when, unable to sleep, she left the tent she was sharing with the *chovihani* to walk towards the River Thames, which ran broad and silver in the moonlight not far from their camp, she passed Luke where he lay in the open, wrapped in a blanket, and heard him moaning in his sleep.

He was tossing, and trying to throw his blanket off. One hand was clenched beside his head, and she thought that he not only looked, but sounded, feverish. She went down on her hands and knees beside him, and called his name softly. 'Luke, what is it?'

He came awake immediately and grasped at the hand which she had laid on his damp brow. 'Anne! What are you doing here? Where are we?'

'At Greenwich, Luke, with the gypsies. Remember?'

His face cleared. He sat up, and said, 'Of course. But I had a bad dream. I had lost you, and Clairval was there. He was laughing.' He was obviously finding it painful to move, and said ruefully, 'So much unaccustomed exercise has done me in a little. Riding a pen is hardly a preparation for riding a horse!' A statement which had Anne laughing gently at him.

'And I am not used to paring potatoes and hauling cauldrons of stew about,' and she showed him her damaged hands. 'But if it means that we shall escape my husband, then I think that I would walk through hot coals to do so.'

Luke kissed her scarred and burned fingers. 'My

darling Stella, for I must remember to call you that, if you can turn yourself into a maid of all work, then for sure I can turn myself into one of Tawno's riders. I had a friend once who served in the cavalry during the late wars as an ordinary trooper, and he was always scornful of the gentleman riders who took their ease in Hyde Park. I am beginning to understand how he felt.'

He stifled a yawn. 'We must try to sleep and not waken the camp – but you will give me a kiss before you go?' He held out his arms to her.

'Gladly,' and for a moment she lowered herself to the grass beside him, so that they lay entwined – chastely, he under the blanket and she on top of it.

'Oh, Scribe, my Scribe, I wish so much that we might truly be husband and wife. The *chovihani* says that we must not touch one another until Jasper decides whether he is able to make us man and wife according to their rites. I do so wish that he would hurry up. I am beginning to understand what the poets meant when they spoke of lovers burning for one another.'

For a moment or two they lay in each other's arms, exchanging the most innocent of kisses. Neither of them wished to go against Jasper's order that they were not to make love until he had made his decision, but oh, it was sweet torment to know that they were restricted to the most innocent of kisses and strokings.

Presently Luke felt Anne's body change as sleep began to claim her and, agony though it was to see her leave, he sent her on her way. They must not abuse the gypsies' trust – and here was another hard lesson he was learning.

What did surprise him though was although his aching for Anne joined the pain of his overused body to torment him, it was not long before exhaustion claimed him and he also slept.

Chapter Ten

'A fortnight,' raged Clairval. 'It is a fortnight since she escaped me in Islington, and you say that you have no news of her. I am beginning to wish that I had not thrown Jenkinson off – he seems to have had more about him than you have.'

The ex-Runner, Greene, who had taken Jenkinson's place, was beginning to wish that he had never met his moody patron. Had he known the half of it, he would never have become involved with such an unreasonable monster – but so unreasonable was Clairval that he dare not resign his post. Best to wait until his capricious master tired of him and dismissed him in one of his tempers.

Whilst he made his latest report, two of Clairval's bruisers were present and stood there grinning at his discomfiture. He was saved from further reproach by a footman entering to tell m'lord that the writer, O'Hare, whom he had sent for, was waiting in the ante-room.

'Then bring him in, dolt,' Clairval snarled. Here was another underling upon whom he could vent his rage. Despite the good money he was paying O'Hare to write favourable pieces about him in the public prints, the public appeared to be singularly unimpressed by O'Hare's panegyrics.

'Well, man,' he greeted O'Hare as he entered, turning his back on his previous victim who stood there, uncertain whether it was more politic to go or to stay. 'You have another few pages on my mad wife with you, I hope, to persuade the fools who read your vapourings to turn her over to me if they come across her.'

He held out his hand, and Pat who, like Greene, was wishing that he had never become involved with such a patent madman even though the pay was good, said ruefully, 'I am sorry, m'lord, but after this one is printed I cannot place any further articles about your missing wife until I can offer some solid news. There are other, newer, scandals which editors wish to dwell on.'

Clairval's face purpled. 'What! I am paying you good money and this is all that you have to tell me? Suppose I were to give you details of where my mad wife was living before she ran away – would that interest them? I have not done so before because it is no business of the public's to be aware that the Marchioness of Clairval preferred to live in a back street in Islington among the scum rather than with her lawful husband. . .' He paused, his tongue having run out of its ability to keep up with his anger.

If both Pat and Greene were of the opinion that Clairval's pride of birth had overcome his good sense to the degree that it was hampering his discovery of his missing wife, neither of them dared to say so.

Pat, indeed, driven to say something, anything, to appease the monster before him, came out with a sentence whose utterance he was bitterly to regret.

'Islington is it? I know Islington well. Pray, m'lord, what part of Islington?'

'Duke Street, in a lodging house kept by her old

governess, now a widow. She was taking in sewing, by Gad! A sempstress, the Marchioness of Clairval earning her living as a sempstress! That alone should convince everyone that she has taken leave of her senses.'

Pat was carelessly unwise again. 'Duke Street, Mrs Britten's? Why, my fellow writer Luke Harcourt lodges there. Come to think of it, I met him at Islington Fair with Mrs Britten and a damned pretty girl on his arm, who was also a lodger there. . .'

He stopped. There was a ghastly silence. Clairval's face, now almost black with an infusion of rage-fed blood, was thrust into his. He seized Pat by his cravat and began to strangle him – slowly.

'Repeat that again,' he howled, 'about Luke Harcourt and the woman he was with. How long have you known that he was a lodger at Mrs Britten's? Answer me!'

'I can't,' gasped Pat, 'until you release me.' She couldn't have been his wife. . .could she?

Oh, but she could. And dancing around London with that upstart Luke Harcourt, who had humiliated him so publicly! What more likely?

Clairval half-threw Pat towards his two bruisers. Greene standing stolidly by, again inwardly cursed his bad luck in becoming involved with such a dangerous madman. Clairval was now instructing his men to 'knock the truth out of this Irish scribbler who doesn't possess the wits he was born with'.

'But I don't know anything,' cried Pat, now well and truly frightened for the first time in his comfortable life. 'Only that he was squiring a girl around the Fair. He called her Anne and Mrs Cowper. He seemed sweet on her, apart from that, nothing.'

'Sweet on her, and called her Anne and Mrs

Cowper – which was the name she was going under.'
Clairval was foaming at the mouth, spraying spittle
over Pat. 'He's almost certainly taking her to his
father's home – where else could they go?'

He swung on Greene. 'Are you listening, man?
Harcourt's natural father is the Earl of Lyndale, who
has a seat at Haven's End in Wiltshire. What more
likely than that they've disappeared in that direction?
He might even have taken her to Lyndale's home in
Piccadilly. Start making enquiries at once and report
back to me first thing tomorrow morning. Be off with
you.'

The door had scarcely closed behind Greene before
Clairval gave a wolfish grin in the direction of Pat, who
was being held in a cruel grip by Fernando, the larger
of the two bruisers. 'Teach that fool a lesson he won't
forget,' he ordered, 'and throw him into the street
when you've done with him. You've had your last
guinea from me, O'Hare.'

Before Pat lost consciousness under Fernando's
unkind ministrations he had one last spasm of regret:
that his loose tongue had put not only himself, but
Luke Harcourt and the pretty woman he had been
squiring at Islington Fair, at risk. Whatever the cost, he
must find some way of warning him.

The Romanies had arrived at a nameless heath some
forty miles out of London. Nameless to Anne, that was.
Bad weather had set in before they left Greenwich, but
by the time that they had spent two days at a small
horsefair at Staines it had turned again and had
remained gloriously fine and sunny.

A fortnight had passed. The only drawback in using
the gypsies to help him and Anne escape Luke found,
was that he had to travel at their pace. But the

unlikelihood that Clairval would guess what they were doing more than cancelled out the slowness of their progress.

Most of the women and some of the men were sitting outside the tents watching the riders perform. Today they were all, one after another, to gallop across the heath whilst performing the trick of which Luke had spoken to Jasper: the twist under the horse's belly. And Luke was to perform it, too.

The fortnight had seen a vast improvement in his equestrian ability, but even so Anne's heart was in her mouth, her sewing in her hand unheeded, as she watched the riders line up. Luke was to be the last one to go, followed only by Tawno, who gave each rider the signal to begin. Jasper Petulengro, as befitted the Pharaoh, was at the end of the run to salute each rider, whether successful, or unsuccessful, as he arrived.

The *chovihani* placed a calming hand on Anne's wrist. She felt her pulse – which was galloping as hard as the horses were like to do – and said, 'Fear not, I prophesy that today Scribe will gain a new name as a reward for his hard work.'

It began. The first three riders were successful, but the fourth failed to swing his body round correctly and regain his seat. His horse went careering away with him dangling upside down under its belly, before he ended on the ground. He lay quite still and a couple of the gypsies went over to him and helped him to his feet. He had broken his arm.

And he was one who had often done the trick before! Anne's fears for Luke grew, but as one rider after another reached Jasper, the trick accomplished, they diminished a little – until Tawno gave Luke the signal to begin his run.

Now he was thundering towards them, and halfway

along the run she saw him prepare to turn and swivel to lie safely tucked beneath his horse's belly, only righting himself shortly before he reached Jasper.

She could not bear to watch him! Even as Luke had begun the trick Anne dropped her sewing to the ground, her head between her knees, and prayed. . .

For her prayer to be disturbed by applause and cries of triumph from the watching riders who had finished their run. Luke had done it, and was swinging upright again even as he reached Jasper to greet him with his right hand held high and a look of triumph on his face such as Anne had never seen before.

And then it was Tawno's turn, and he swivelled under his horse not once, but twice, to show that he was master.

Once arrived in front of Jasper he gave the signal for the troop to dismount. Then he turned to Luke to hold his hand high. 'Not Scribe,' he proclaimed, 'but Orion is your name. Hunter you shall be, and so shall the Romanies know you. You may join Stella in the heavens.'

Luke had never known such a sense of accomplishment. A fortnight's gruelling training had transformed him in both mind and body. He saw Anne coming towards him, her hands held out, her face full of joy on hearing Tawno baptise him, for baptism it was.

He caught her by the waist and swung her round and round. 'Oh, Anne, Stella, my star, did you see me?'

When she shook her head at him, saying, 'Oh, Luke, I couldn't. . . I didn't see a thing. . . I was so frightened for you,' he took that as a testimony of her love for him, and kissed her full on the lips before them all.

'Oh, Anne, you must watch me. Only then will my day be complete.'

Luke bowed to Tawno, and asked 'May I?' of his

master, who gave him permission so that he remounted and galloped again in the opposite direction, this time with Anne watching. Love and triumph combined saw him perform the trick even more gracefully than before, for on his first run he had almost lost his balance as he had begun to turn under his horse.

Stars! Her eyes were stars to greet him with when he dismounted, still full of his triumph. There on the heath under Apollo's golden chariot, the sun, which was now running towards September's scents and fruitfulness, Luke and Anne embraced again.

Nothing was left of the fine lady and gentleman whom they had once been. They were as one with the Romanies who surrounded them. Orion and Stella, fallen from the heavens to spend a little time on earth before they took their place among the stars again. . .

Oh, it was glorious to be young and in love, to know that one's mind and body did one's bidding. One thing, and one thing only was lacking, and that was for the two bodies to become one, and surely the time for that was almost upon them before summer fled and winter arrived.

After Tawno and the horsemen had performed a galaxy of simpler tricks and team manoeuvres in which Luke doggedly played his part, he dismissed them for the day after the rest of the Rom had applauded them for their virtuosity.

'Next week,' Tawno announced, 'when we visit Aldershot, we shall try out our new tricks – and our new rider. Orion, my brother, now that you are truly one of us, the Pharaoh – ' he meant Jasper Petulengro ' – wishes to speak to you concerning your woman. Go to his tent where he awaits you.'

Now what could this mean? Luke was full of excitement. That very morning Jasper had said something to him, which indicated that he approved of the fact that he and Anne had obeyed his orders and refrained from becoming lovers until he had decided whether he could give them authority to marry according to the laws of the Rom.

Luke could hardly contain himself as he unsaddled his horse, fed and watered it, and saw that it was comfortable in the pen where he and his fellow steeds were kept once their work was over. After that, he ran down to the brook at the corner where the heath met the wood, washed himself, and made sure that everything about him was proper for an audience with the king. For king Jasper was and so conducted himself and, in calling on the Rom for help Luke had given them the right to demand that he follow their way of life.

Clean, refreshed, his sweaty shirt changed for a sweet-smelling one, his boots removed and a pair of soft-soled shoes exchanged for them, Luke made his way into the presence. Tawno was already there, and a group of the older gypsies. Anne, also in clean clothing, stood to one side, the *chovihani* and a group of older women, including Tawno's wife, at her back.

Jasper was seated on a highbacked chair, almost like a throne. On seeing Luke he called, 'Come, Orion, my brother, for now you are so named, for I have a judgment to make concerning yourself and Stella. Come forward also, Stella. For your supporters, I appoint Tawno and the *chovihani* my wife – if supporters you need.'

Neither Luke nor Anne needed a second bidding. They moved forward to stand before Jasper, their supporters behind them. Jasper said in a voice as stern as any Luke had yet heard from him, ' Join your right hand to Stella's left, Orion, and swear that you will speak true. After you have finished, Stella must so swear, too. If either of you should lie, then may the great author of the Universe strike you down.'

Luke took Anne's hand and, before he could stop himself, kissed it. He had no idea of what was to come, or what further ordeals might await them both, but he was ready and willing to obey his master. George IV might sit on the throne of England, but here on the heath, the sun shining down on them, a small wind blowing, his writ no longer ran. The law of the Rom was all.

They both swore to tell true, and when they had done, Jasper said, 'Stella, our sister, it is reported that you had a husband who treated you cruelly until you fled from the terror he wrought upon you. Is this story true? Swear!'

Anne's voice was low but firm. 'I swear that this is true.'

'Stella, my sister, when did your husband last lie with you in a true fashion, as a man lies with a woman to make a child? Tell true, now.'

For a moment Anne did not answer him, but hung her head. She began to shiver, and Luke pressed her hand in sympathy to let her know that she was not alone, that his love went with her.

Finally she raised her head. 'For the last year before I fled him over six months ago, we did not lie together as man and wife, and before that he was only able to do so after inflicting great cruelties on me. At the end he wished to put me in a madhouse, to live there for the rest of my days. This I swear before you – and before God.'

Rage, red and fierce, ran through Luke. The new strength, the new fortitude which he had gained from living and working among the gypsies had also had the effect of making his desire to protect Anne so strong that he now knew that he would kill for her – or suffer for her, if that was required of him. Now it was he who shivered and Anne who pressed his hand lovingly.

'And, Orion, my brother. You knew that Stella, who wishes to be your wife, had suffered greatly at the hands of the man who called himself husband?'

'Yes, this I swear,' replied Luke firmly. 'Not as to the details, for these are for Stella to know, and no one else, but that she had been treated with great cruelty is a matter of common knowledge.'

Jasper rose from his chair, and walked to where they stood.

He placed both his hands on their clasped ones, and said in a loud voice. 'May all the Rom hear what I have to say,' for while they had been talking the whole camp, men, women and children had arrived to stand in a circle around them, 'By heath and by hearth, by my will and rule as Pharaoh, I say that Stella's marriage was, by the law of the Rom, no marriage, and is thus ended. Let all who hear me acknowledge this.' He paused, and the assembled crowd cried with one voice, 'Aye'.

'And do you, Orion and Stella, together promise that you will remain faithful to one another and the marriage bond until death shall claim you?'

Facing one another, hands still clasped, and speaking together, they both said with the utmost solemnity, 'This we swear.'

'And now hear this. By heath and by hearth, by the law of the Rom, I declare Orion and Stella to be man and wife. That none shall come between them, or part them. This is my will, that of the Pharaoh. More, their supporters, Tawno and the tribe's *chovihani*, shall lead them to the spot before the brook where a broom has been placed on the ground, and as token of their becoming one, not two, they shall jump over the broom and become one forever. Tawno! Lead the way!'

It was as impressive a ceremony as either Luke or Anne had ever seen. Out in the open, walking together, still hand in hand behind Tawno and the *chovihani*, they led a small procession. At the head of it several of the younger children marched, carrying boughs of beech and willow, magic symbols of the Rom's long past. Behind them streamed Jasper's entire tribe, with him bringing up the rear, alone and majestic, his wife a little before him.

Solemnly Anne and Luke jumped over the broom, but there was one final rite yet to come. Jasper moved forward saying, 'And now the exchange of blood.' Whilst they held their hands out towards him he made, with the utmost ceremony, a small nick on each of their wrists with a silver knife, and mixed together the resulting blood which flowed from them.

'Thus I proclaim you truly one, in blood and in love.' He swung round to face the procession, crying, 'Fiddlers, I bid you play a merry song to send Orion and Stella happily on their marriage way. And if Stella's one-time husband shall dare to try to come between them, then the curse of the Rom be upon him and may he choke on his own blood. This is the word of me, Jasper Petulengro, your Pharaoh!'

They were married.

Anne was free of Clairval. And whether the marriage was legal or not, neither of them cared. For were they not part of the Rom now? And even if one day, they were to leave the Rom behind, then what they could not leave behind was the authority which had joined them together.

Oblivious of the crowd around them, of the music of

the fiddlers, of the chatter of the monkeys on their sticks which some of the Rom had brought with them to see Orion and Stella married, they embraced.

'Tonight,' cried Luke fiercely, and 'Tonight,' echoed Anne, for there was a tent prepared for their use alone, as ordered by Jasper, now their protector as well as their leader.

Until then there was music and dancing and feasting. Nor could either of them have thought that on the day that Luke had arrived back in Islington, a train of events had been set in motion which would end with them in one another's arms, under a clear sky, about to become man and wife.

Chapter Eleven

At last they were alone. The dancing, the feasting and the drinking were over. They had been led to the tent by all the Rom, the children at the front of the procession: the same children who had earlier made wreaths of late summer daisies and had crowned Orion and Stella with them.

The noise of the camp slowly died away. Silence fell. Outside the tent as well as in. Luke had taken Anne in his arms the moment that they were alone and had laid her down on a bed of the Rom's finest blankets given to them for this night, before he carefully removed their crowns of daisies. Tomorrow they would wear them again for a brief space as witness to the marriage's consummation.

He knelt down beside Anne – to discover that she was trembling, and that slow tears were running down her face. All her gaiety of the past hours had disappeared, and Luke knew quite well what was wrong. Throughout her short married life she had experienced what should have been an act of love as an act of terror where pain was inflicted, not pleasure given.

During their marriage ceremony, and after, she had been buoyed up by the sheer delight of knowing that

Luke was hers at last, but now that they were alone came the other knowledge – that being his she must give him her body, and that was sufficient to revive all her fears. Oh, she was not afraid that Luke would hurt her, she knew that he would not, but she was fearful that she might not be able to respond to him as she ought.

What if she were to turn away from him in fear when he began to make love to her, as she had tried to turn away from Clairval during those dreadful nights of torment, long endured? She had told Luke only a few days ago that she burned for him – but that was when he was forbidden to her, and lovemaking was a distant thing. Now that the moment of consummation was upon her, all her fears were revived again.

'What is it, my love?' Luke asked her tenderly, putting out a gentle finger to brush away the betraying tears.

'Oh Luke, I'm frightened. Not of you, but that I might not be able to love you as I ought.' She shuddered beneath his ardent gaze.

Clairval! Clairval had done this to her. Luke wished on him the death to which Jasper had doomed him to for what he had already done, let alone what he might do to Anne if he were fortunate enough to recapture her.

'You know that I shall not hurt you,' he told her, without further touching her.

'Oh, yes, Luke. I know that you are not at all like *him*. It is myself I am frightened of, not you.'

'Then we shall go slowly, my darling. For much though I wish to make you my wife, I do not want you to be truly mine until we are united in shared joy. For me to do otherwise to you would make me nothing but a brute beast.'

He did not say, 'Like Clairval.' He did not need to.

Anne knew full well what he meant. She held out her arms to him, whispering, 'Lie by me, Luke. I want to feel you near me.'

So, she was welcoming him. Which was promising, but did not mean that he could fall upon her. He must do nothing to remind her of *him* and his wicked demands. Slowly, slowly, Luke lay beside her. She turned towards him, rested her head on his chest, and he put an arm under her body around her shoulders so that they lay entwined.

'There,' and his voice was so gentle that she could hardly hear it. 'That was an easy beginning, was it not? And at your invitation, I may add, Mrs Harcourt. What would you wish me to do next?'

She spoke into his chest so softly that he had to strain to hear what she said, 'You could kiss me, Luke, on the cheek. I think that I should like that. That was the first kiss you ever gave me, at Mrs Britten's. Remember?'

Remember?

Of course he remembered, and he also remembered that in a mood of joyous spontaneity she had almost given herself to him then. So yes, he would do her bidding, even though to hold her so intimately was becoming a sweet torment to him, for his body was free of his mind and wished to do more with Anne than exchange simple kisses. But, if he were to gain her confidence and bring her safely through the gates of passion into the wide lands beyond them; he must subdue himself – or be like Clairval, unconsidering of another.

'Oh, I think that I could manage that,' he said at last.

This brought a ghostly chuckle from her as he kissed the warm cheek so near to his. And having done so he added, in as light a voice as he could, 'Kisses have no meaning between true lovers unless they are exchanged. Mr Harcourt would like a similar caress from Mrs Harcourt.'

So she kissed him, mimicking him before she did so! 'Oh, I think that I could manage that!'

'The next step,' Luke announced in an important voice, as though about to embark on a sermon, 'is to kiss together. The mouth is the usual spot chosen – at least to begin with. Shall we try it?'

Her answer was to turn her face so trustingly towards his that a strong spasm of desire ran through him. He restrained himself, put his mouth to hers, in a child's kiss first, with closed lips, and then, as she did not resist him, but put up her right hand to stroke his face, he deepened and strengthened it, pushing her lips apart so that his roving tongue might enter her mouth, and caress hers.

The effect on Anne was electric: Signor Galvani's frogs all over again. A thrill of pleasure shot through her so strongly that she sat up, tore her mouth from Luke's and exclaimed breathlessly, 'Oh, Luke, whatever did you do to me?'

He lay there looking at her. Her eyes were wide, like stars, her face was flushed, her lips were swollen.

'I kissed you,' he told her, 'and kisses are supposed to be exciting and pleasurable. I take it that you were thoroughly pleasured?' Her innocence enchanted, but at the same time saddened him, because it told him of the mistreatment which she had suffered, so that the simple early pleasures of loving had passed her by.

'Shall we try it again?' he offered.

'Oh, yes, please,' breathed Anne fervently, falling back into his arms, and offering him her mouth, which he took, more urgently this time. Next he set his hands awandering around her body, so that after the first shock of discovering the delights of kissing, Anne found that being stroked whilst being kissed heightened her pleasure immensely.

So much so that she began to kiss and stroke him in return, so that *she* might give *him* delight. Which she did, for after a moment or two he gave a little groan and rolled away from her. His desire for her was so strong that for him to be stroked so intimately by her was almost enough to send him over the edge of pleasure, he had been continent for so long.

'My darling,' he told her, 'we have begun in proper form, and as a child learns to walk, step by slow step, as he advances from crawling, so shall we too, this night, advance to where we may ourselves be lovers, as well as husband and wife. And for your next lesson you must allow me to see you, all of you.'

'All of me? You would like that, Luke?' So strong was the delight that Anne was already feeling, that it had her sitting up, and beginning to pull off her dress to please him.

'Dear girl,' Luke was laughing in joy at her eagerness, 'I know that you wish to please me, but one of a man's truest delights is undressing his love for the first time – and being undressed by her.'

'It is?'

Anne's eyes were full of wonderment. She remembered Clairval tearing at her clothed body on their wedding night, and entering her, with oh, such pain, that the memory of it set her shivering again. Nevertheless, she stilled herself, and when Luke gently drew her down again, and began to remove her clothing from her, piece by piece, she felt her fears beginning to recede. So much so that she joined in the game by unbuttoning his shirt, to reveal the dark and curling hairs on his chest.

Instinctively, without thinking, she buried her face in them to smell the essential Luke, man touched with horse, and the strong yellow soap which all the Rom used, including herself.

Luke stroked her dark head, realising what a major step she had taken in the game of love. He lifted her head back to kiss her on the lips, deeper and stronger than ever, before he helped her to pull off his velveteen breeches, until at last they were naked together, and Luke could see for the first time the lovely lines of Anne's beautiful body.

Even then, although Anne drank in the strength of Luke's chest and shoulders, the flatness of his stomach, all his muscles strengthened and hardened by the past few weeks of forced exercise, she dare not look at him, nor touch him, *there*. For *there* was what Clairval had used so often to hurt her in his thwarted attempts to pleasure himself or make a child.

Luke saw her fear, and inwardly cursed Clairval yet again. He was a third presence in their marriage bed, but he was determined to exorcise his ghost, to teach Anne that love could be joy, even though his task might be long and hard. He pulled her to him and began to stroke her all over until, when he reached her breasts, the points of her desire, she gave a little cry of joy achieved. But he dare not yet go near her dark and curling fleece, which hid what might, he hoped, yet give her her truest pleasure.

So gentle was he, so sweetly loving, that Anne sighed, and felt sleep beginning to claim her as she lay so trustingly in her lover's arms.

Which would not do at all, so that Luke deepened his caresses, until all desire to sleep fled and Anne found herself again full of strange flutterings and a strong wish to be nearer, ever nearer to the man who was loving her so considerately.

Time passed, and slowly, slowly, Luke led Anne towards the consummation which they both desired. How she came to be beneath him was a mystery. How it was that the most intimate caresses, which she had previously feared, came to be sources of such pleasure that she begged him for more. . .and more, Anne never knew.

Except that at some point it seemed the most natural thing in the world for her to caress Luke there, feeling him warm and velvet in her hand, so that she had no fear that inside her he would feel any different.

After such a major step, the knowledge that he would be part of her was simply an extension of the joy that love-making was already bringing to her. So much so that, when they were finally one, the ugly spectre of Clairval flew away for good and all, and she was shaking with ecstasy in Luke's arms, all fears forgotten.

At the last, ecstasy over, the tears running down Anne's face were those of joy, not pain, and she was clutching her dear love as though she never meant to let him go, crying, 'Oh, Luke, my love, my love, I had not known. . .'

She did not say what she had not known, but shortly after Luke had made love to her for the second time, and she was nearing the sweet sleep of its aftermath, she murmured drowsily, 'Poor Clairval. . .'

'Poor Clairval!' Luke jerked erect in surprise and shock at such an unlikely statement from Clairval's late victim. 'How so?'

'Because he never experienced the joy that you and I have just shared, for he thought only of himself and never of his partner.'

It was Clairval's epitaph. Their marriage might now go ahead without his shadow marring it. One final thing that Anne said before sleep claimed them both was, 'Oh, Luke, I hope that you do not think me wicked to forget the teachings of the church and enjoy my union with you when, surely, no parson would think our marriage legal.

'I remember once, I went to the Rector of Clairval church to ask him for sanctuary from Clairval's mistreatment, and he told me to be a good woman and return to him, for I must be very sinful if my husband thought it necessary to correct me so sternly!'

Luke kissed her. 'Dear Anne. He was wrong, and I know that not all parsons are like him. He was probably frightened of Clairval, too. And no, I don't think that either of us are wicked. Only the law that makes a woman like you a victim of a man like Clairval.'

After that reassurance they both slept – to wake with the dawn and love again.

The world did not cease to turn as the lovers made their slow way westwards to what they hoped would be salvation. In his rooms in London, Pat O'Hare nursed his broken wrist and his black eye and regretted his betrayal of Luke Harcourt to a man who wished him harm. He had tried to make amends by sending for his friend, George Jackson, who had stared in astonishment at Pat's battered body.

'An accident merely,' lied Pat, pre-empting George's demands for an explanation. 'As you see, I cannot write. You would do me a great favour if you would act as my secretary and write a letter to Luke Harcourt on my behalf.'

If George thought that there was more to Pat's injuries than Pat cared to confess, he did not say so.

Instead, he carefully penned a cryptic letter to Luke in which Pat said that a mutual enemy, of whom Luke was aware, was on his trail, following him to the west country, intending to do him harm. A word to the wise, was his last sentence.

'Now what the devil is all this about?' wondered George aloud, for Pat to say,

'Best for you not to know. Oh, George, I've been a damned careless fool and put Luke in danger. Seal the letter for me and take it to Lyndale's place in Piccadilly. If he and the Countess have gone to Haven's End, then ask the housekeeper – or whoever you speak to – to send it on to Wiltshire immediately. I can only pray that somehow it reaches Luke before danger does.'

After George had gone, promising to do everything which was asked of him, Pat sank back, his heart a little lighter. At least he had done *something* to try to warn Luke, even if that something might be too little and too late. He tried not to think of what would happen to him if Clairval ever found out what he had done.

Clairval was on his way to Haven's End.

Like George Jackson, he had gone to Piccadilly to find that Lyndale and his wife had already left town. The housekeeper had said quite categorically, in response to his enquiries, that Mr Luke was not with them, indeed, had scarcely visited them all summer.

Too busy seducing my wife, was Clairval's inward furious response before returning to plan his journey to the west. He would travel with as much speed as possible, stopping at inns and hostelries on the way to try to discover whether the guilty pair had stayed there for the night. Finding no such evidence as he drove towards that damned swine Lyndale's place was not calculated to improve his temper, nor did it. Luke

Harcourt and Anticleia, Lady Clairval, seemed to have disappeared from the face of the earth.

Clairval was not the only traveller pursuing a westward path towards Haven's End. In a private room in a set of offices in Whitehall, a Very Grand Personage indeed gave an audience to the Runner, Jenkinson. They had met before when Jenkinson had done this Grand Personage – and the State – some favours of which none but he and the Grand Personage knew.

'Well, what is it that you have discovered this time – and how much do you want for it?' demanded the Personage, who no more wished to waste words than Jenkinson did. It was a pleasure to deal with him after Clairval.

'Something which I think will please you, seeing that the party in question never votes with the government in the Lords.'

'Who is. . .?'

'Clairval, m'lord. The Marquess of. Ah, I see by your expression that you and he are scarcely bosom bows.'

'Indeed not,' replied the Personage frostily. 'Out with it, man. What do you know to his discredit?'

Jenkinson told him.

'Murder and planned murder, aye. That is a juicy titbit for an evil-minded cat to devour at leisure. I have a wish to be evil-minded where Clairval is concerned. His day of reckoning is long overdue. One more gross scandal in high life and those who plot revolution here will have a field day. You are sure that our man has committed, or intends to commit, both these crimes?'

Jenkinson nodded. 'Quite sure. I have the depositions as to the murder of his steward. Many who were frightened of him have now become willing to shop him so that they may not be the next target for his murderous temper.'

'Quite so. And his intention to murder his wife – when he catches her and imprisons her again – how do you hope to prove that?'

'Because I have depositions as to the death of his first wife, and to his declared intention before witnesses of his determination to dispose of the second – to secure her estate.'

The Grand Personage paced the room in silence, pausing to stare at a flattering portrait of King George IV which transformed the gross elderly man he was to something like the handsome young man he had once been.

He turned to face Jenkinson. 'So! I would like this business solved without scandal – you understand me. When you catch up with him – please God before he reaches his wife – you will use your discretion as to what action to take. You understand me,' he repeated.

'I will see that you are re-instated as a Runner, given proper warrants – including a blank one – which will allow you to arrest him and take him to the nearest gaol, to be brought to London to be tried before his peers in the House of Lords – if that is what you think will answer. But I would prefer the matter settled by other means.'

He repeated the last words again, adding, 'I do not need to tell you that I want this disposed of without scandal and a great noise being made. I shall thus support whatever measure you see fit to take to ensure that end – on condition that, if you make a mistake and are caught out in it, I shall disclaim all knowledge of you if you try to involve me. On the other hand, your reward will be great if all goes well. You have my word on that – as you have had in the past.'

It would have to do. Jenkinson did not intend to be caught, and had more sense than to try to involve the Grand Personage before him if things did go wrong – which they wouldn't.

'You may depend upon me, m'lord,' he said, bowing, 'to dispose of this affair in as discreet and satisfactory a manner as possible.'

He told the Grand Personage nothing of the details of his search: that Greene, who had been dismissed by Clairval for incompetence, had told him that Clairval believed that Luke Harcourt, the natural son of Lord Lyndale, had made away with Lady Clairval and hidden her. It was assumed that he would take her to his father's home in the west country.

Greene's reward had been that Jenkinson had hired him as an aide. 'To do exactly what you're told mind, and not go off on your own. Disobey me, and I'll have your guts for garters.'

So an agreement was struck. Greene knew that Jenkinson was a swine, but he was a fair swine, unlike Clairval. He would not swindle you unless you had swindled him first. It would be a pleasure to join forces with him and try to put one over on Clairval – who deserved all the bad luck which the two Runners could arrange for him.

'Thing is, though,' said Greene, 'I couldn't find any trace of where Harcourt and the woman had gone – and nor could my haughty m'lord. Disappeared off the face of the earth, they have, and me turned away because I'd lost their trail. Truth is, I never found it.

'But I've been thinking. Harcourt had a friend, Pat O'Hare, who was one of Clairval's toadies. He fell foul of m'lord and m'lord had him given a beating for his pains. What say we interview Master O'Hare? I'll be bound he'd tell us what he knows of Harcourt, if only to do Clairval a bad turn. After all, they must have gone somewhere.'

'True,' Jenkinson agreed. 'Always better to try something rather than nothing. At the moment we're chasing moonbeams.'

So it was that Pat O'Hare, still nursing his injuries, and a bitter hate in his heart for Clairval, was surprised to find the two Runners on his doorstep.

At first he refused to let them in. 'How the devil do I know that you're both not still working for Clairval – tell me that?'

'Working against him, more like,' grinned Jenkinson. 'He's turned us off, as he turned you off. Only he thought it best not to have us ill-treated. If you'd like to pay him back for your broken wrist, now's your only chance. Tell us what you know of Luke Harcourt. We're after Clairval, not him, but find Harcourt and sooner or later we shall find Clairval.'

'Luke's my friend,' grunted Pat, reluctantly letting them in. 'I've already done him one ill turn, I don't want to do him another.'

'Nor will you.' Jenkinson was looking about him. 'He's disappeared, and apparently the lady with him. Now, what do you know of his haunts – where might he have gone? Talk freely, you may not know that you are already aware of something which might help us, only you don't know of its importance.'

The two men grilled Pat mercilessly once he was convinced that they truly did not mean Luke harm.

He appeared to know nothing useful until Jenkinson said, desperate to try anything. 'Did you ever meet the lady?'

'Yes,' said Pat. 'Once. At Islington Fair. She was there with him. She and Luke's landlady.' He smiled reminiscently. 'I thought that they were sweet on one another then. I saw him take her over to meet the gypsies.'

'Meet the gypsies?' Jenkinson took Pat up smartly. 'Harcourt is friendly with the gypsies?'

'Yes,' said Pat, puzzled, and wondering what that had got to do with anything. 'Always has been. Writes about them. Been friendly with them since he was a little lad.'

Jenkinson jumped to his feet. 'That's it! That's how they could have disappeared off the face of the earth. There were gypsies at Greenwich Fair the week they disappeared. What's the odds he took her there, and they're travelling westward with them?'

'To Haven's End, his father, Lord Lyndale's home in Wiltshire,' Pat ventured.

'Oh, I think Master Luke's cleverer than that,' returned Jenkinson. 'He's a writer. That means he can work anywhere. He can't safely live with m'lady here, Clairval being so powerful. Nor can he marry her, either. What price he's making for a seaport? Bristol, mayhap. Somewhere where he could take ship for the Americas.'

Pat looked doubtful, but Greene, who knew Jenkinson and his successful long shots of old, said slowly, 'Aye, that makes sense. They could take off their fine lady and gent's clothes, and melt into the gypsy band... Who would think to find them there? Or identify them easily?'

Jenkinson shook the bemused Pat's hand. 'Thank you for that, sir. It can't hurt to track the gypsy band down and try to find out if they're with them. Better than running round the west country like a headless hen as Clairval is doing.'

'But why follow Luke? Why not follow Clairval if it's

him you want to catch?' Pat asked, just before they left.

'Oh, the more we have on him and his villainy, before we catch him, the better,' remarked Jenkinson, looking mysterious.

It was not for such as Pat O'Hare, or even his colleague Greene, to know anything of his collaboration with the Grand Personage, and the real end of his quest.

Now that he had mastered all the equestrian tricks and become a trusted member of Tawno's troop, Luke found that he had time in the early evening to sit at leisure under the shadiest and most secluded tree he could find, and begin to write the novel had been fermenting at the back of his mind ever since he had left London.

Anne sat by him, sewing, until both of them, tiring of their work at the same time, turned into each other's arms to celebrate as nymph and shepherd should on a bed of grass with the birds calling above them.

Still slowly the gypsies wended their way westward, stopping at fairs and horse fairs to earn their living against the coming winter when all such junketing would stop – until spring returned.

Late one afternoon after they had left a small town not far from Salisbury, with their goal of Bristol drawing ever nearer, Anne arrived to sit by Luke with the strangest expression on her face. He was sensitive to all her moods these days and said at once, 'My love, what is it?'

'Oh, Luke, you will think me fanciful, but I have just remembered the dream I had last night – or rather, nightmare. And I know that it came to me because for the last few days I have had the feeling that we are being watched and followed.'

Ever since the *chovihani* had bestowed the gifts of empathy and prescience on Anne, she had been subject to strange visions and what she liked to think of as understandings. Luke had learned not to dismiss them.

'No, I don't think that you are being fanciful. You were right about the red-headed man you thought was following you – he was. Tell me, what did the dream say?'

'Nothing directly. Only I learned from it that we *are* being followed – and by more than one party. They are not yet near us, and I am not sure that they know that we are with the gypsies, only that we are travelling westwards. One of them is the red-headed man, but it's rather strange. I have the feeling that this time he does not mean me harm, although I cannot be sure of that. Our other follower is Clairval.'

She did not tell Luke that in her dream the vision of Clairval had been a horrible one. Not only had he been following her at some distance, but in the dream he had caught her up and, having done so, had leaned forward to clutch at her, his face evil and triumphant. But at the very moment in which he had laid his hands on her, a tide of blood had appeared from nowhere and swept him away.

Awake again, Anne could only think that she had been remembering Jasper's curse – that if Clairval tried to harm her again he would choke in his own blood. The vision had been so horrible that she had found her whole body running in sweat and she had been compelled to rise from her bed and towel herself dry. After that, she dare not sleep again, for fear that the vision might return.

Sitting by Luke, though, on a sunny afternoon, the vision seemed far away. On the other hand, her sense of being followed was so strong that she had felt compelled to warn him so that he might speak to Jasper and with his, and the Roms' help, keep watch both when they camped on the heaths and when they travelled the roads.

Luke had heard her out in silence. He was sure that she was not telling him everything which she had experienced, but he did not badger her for further information.

He said slowly, 'If Clairval has discovered that it was I who rescued you when he came to Islington, then it is possible that he thinks that I am taking you to my father's home at Haven's End. Since we are not going there, that should sidetrack him long enough for us to get clean away. As for your red-headed man, that is a mystery. You're sure that he is following us?'

Anne nodded. 'Quite sure, but it comes to me, as from a distance, that it is Clairval he is following, not us – or rather us and Clairval, but Clairval is his true target.'

She paused, before saying, 'There is another odd thing. I see you and him together – or rather, I don't exactly see you, but I know that you and the red-headed man are strangely interlinked – and that I am not with you when you meet.'

For a moment she looked so frustrated that Luke was afraid that she might be going to cry – and that would never do. Before he could reassure her, she added a rider to what she had been saying. 'This gift makes me fearful, Luke, for it never speaks quite plainly. I have to make sense of it, and I can never know whether I have succeeded until what it tells me is upon me – and then it is often too late to do anything about it.'

Oh, but that was the trouble with magic, both black and white, was it not? Luke thought of what a greater writer than he was had once written, the devil 'palters with us in a double sense...' On the other hand, his reason told him that it was not good for mankind to know too much about its future fate.

In that case, he thought robustly, best not to know anything at all! But he could not say so to Anne, who had a burden to bear and one which she had not chosen. The *chovihani* had called it a gift, but the gift was two-edged and both gave and took away.

He put a friendly arm around Anne's shoulders, not a loving one, for Anne was not in the mood to enjoy the wilder passions. 'Let it pass,' he said. 'Do not brood, my darling. What will happen, will happen, and there's an end of it.'

But, as so often happens, life would not let them treat the matter so easily.

The next morning, Jasper came to him as he was about to mount his horse, and said curtly, 'A word, Brother Orion. Come where we may be private.'

They strode away from the rest, out of earshot. Jasper spoke bluntly and to the point. 'We are being followed – or rather, I suspect, you and Stella are being followed.'

Luke's reaction was instantaneous. 'Clairval!' he exclaimed. 'But how did he discover that we are with you?'

Jasper shook his head. 'Not Clairval. Tawno knows them. He has seen them several times over the past few days. He knows one of them, a one-time Bow Street

Runner called Jenkinson. A red-haired man. Another of his kidney is with him.'

'But they are Clairval's men,' said Luke, despair in his voice. 'Jenkinson led Clairval to Anne's refuge in Islington. No doubt he is still doing Clairval's dirty work for him.'

'Not so, Orion. The *chovihani* has read him. He is after Clairval, not you, but thinks to find Clairval by waiting until he discovers you. Why, she cannot *scry*.'

By *scry* Jasper meant foretell or read the future. 'What she does know is that Clairval is not far away, and him she can read and his near future, for his wickedness is strong. He will find you, Orion, but not Stella or us. You understand what this means?'

His face was so dour, so foreboding, that Luke was filled with a nameless dread.

'You think that the *chovihani* tells true, Jasper?'

'I am sure of it. She says the omens are among the strongest that she has ever experienced. She thinks that Stella is reading them, too, but will not face their meaning because she does not wish to.'

That would explain the distress which Anne was suffering. It was bound up with him – although he was sure that, unlike the *chovihani*, whose powers were so much stronger, Anne knew none of the details of the future which she feared.

He nodded agreement. 'The only thing I understand from what you tell me is that I must leave you – and Stella – and that for her safety.'

'To act as decoy, Orion, with all that that implies. Not immediately, but in a few days when the moon is full and Clairval, and the red-headed man, are nearer to us. And, Orion, I have hard words for you. You face a testing time, and how you come through it will determine not only your fate, but Stella's. If you hold the faith, and play the man, as Tawno has taught you, then all will be well. But weaken, and even the *chovihani*, Pharaoh's wife, cannot save you.'

To leave Anne behind, to travel alone, away from the Rom to draw Clairval and the red-headed man away, so that both he and Anne might be saved, was in itself a hard task for Luke. But Jasper was hinting at something more.

'You said that I was to be tested, Jasper. In what way? I would be prepared.'

'Alas, I cannot tell you. All that the *chovihani* knows is that there will be a test and that you must pass it. She does not know its nature. Believe me, if she did, we would tell you.'

That was that. He looked away from Jasper and saw that his wife was talking to Anne most earnestly. By the expression on Anne's face, she was undoubtedly telling her of their coming parting. Oh, how hard it would be to leave her, so soon, so soon. Particularly since, for all Jasper's promises, he knew that the end which they both desired would not necessarily be ensured.

Their safety was conditional on his behaviour during a difficult and unknown test. Almost Luke wavered. But the hard core at the centre of his being, which his days with the Romanies had enlarged and strengthened, had him accepting the doom which lay before him.

From the moment he had met Anne, this time of trial and trouble had been waiting for him and he would be but a poor thing if he took the easy path because salvation lay along a difficult one.

Almost at once he began to plan what he would do, and his next words drew strong approval from Jasper.

'So be it,' he said. 'Amen. And, Jasper, if I am not to

betray where I have been, I must turn myself into Luke Harcourt, a fine young gentleman, and forget Orion who rides with Tawno and the troop.'

'Indeed and indeed. We shall advise you on what route to take to draw them away from us. They will be delighted once they find you, and think that Stella cannot be far away, so you must be far away from us.'

'And if I succeed, Jasper, and pass the test, what then?'

'Why, fate and circumstance will tell you what to do, Orion, and in order to prove yourself worthy, you will do it.'

Well, you could hardly get more cryptic than that, was Luke's sardonic inward response, but it would have to do.

Chapter Twelve

'James, I am troubled in my mind over Luke. Not only did we not see him in town this summer, but we have not heard a word from him in months. Since we arrived here I have written to him at his lodgings in Islington, but have received no answer. Such conduct is most unlike him. It is almost as though he has disappeared off the face of the earth.'

Cressy was on the terrace overlooking the park at Haven's End. James had just arrived to sit with her, after spending the morning with his agent. He frowned a little, and said, 'I agree with you, my love. Earlier, back in town, I thought that you might be repining overmuch on his absence, but this prolonged lack of news from him worries me more than a little.'

His answer relieved his wife. Cressy had begun to think that she might be making overmuch of Luke's change of habit, but if James, that model of steadiness and applied reason, was beginning to be troubled by his son's untoward behaviour, then it was likely that something might be wrong.

'I suppose,' she said slowly, 'it is feeling so helpless that exaggerates the worry. I know that he is a grown man, but he has always been so considerate of us before. . .'

'Over-considerate, perhaps,' added James, as his wife's voice trailed off. 'I will promise you this. If yet another month goes by without word of him, then I will travel to London and try to track him down. Will that do?'

Before Cressy could answer, the butler came through the glass doors which led to the terrace. 'There is a person to see you, m'lord. It is the Marquess of Clairval and he says that his business with you is most urgent.'

James rose, a look of surprise on his face. 'Clairval here? On urgent business with me? What the deuce can it be? Where have you put him?'

'In the drawing-room, m'lord.' He hesitated, then added, 'I should perhaps say that he appears to be in somewhat of a high temper, m'lord.' He said no more, but James knew at once that if his trusted servant felt it necessary to make such a personal remark about a superior then it would be as well to take heed of what he was being told.

He found Clairval in the drawing-room, pacing up and down like a caged tiger. He advanced on James, saying in an angry voice, 'Ah, Lyndale, at last. I have somewhat of a bone to pick with you!'

James, Lord Lyndale, had a high temper of his own, usually kept under restraint. He held himself in check with difficulty, so menacing was Clairval's manner.

'Indeed, Clairval. And what bone is that? Not politics, I hope. I thought that I had done with them when I reached Wiltshire.'

'Politics!' sneered Clairval. 'I am not interested in politics! No, I have reason to believe that you are harbouring your bastard, Luke Harcourt, and my wife, Lady Clairval, with whom he has eloped, or abducted, or run away with, call it what you will.'

'Luke! Run away with your wife!' James could hardly

have been, or sounded, more flabbergasted. 'Run away with your missing wife? I was not aware that he was even acquainted with her.'

'Oh, don't try to flim-flam me, Lyndale! I know for certain that he is my wife's paramour and has made off with her. And what more likely than that he has brought her here?'

James held his temper in check with difficulty.

'Then your idea of what is more likely, Clairval, differs completely from mine. I have not seen my son for several months, and he is certainly not here, my word upon it.'

'I think nothing of any man's word, Lyndale. Least of all yours, seeing that you represent a party for which I feel no respect, and have spawned a son whose honour is as low as his birth. No! I demand that you allow me to have Haven's End searched before I accept that the guilty pair are not here.'

'Demand, Clairval? Demand? By what right do you demand anything of me, here, in my own home?'

'By the right of a man whose wife has been reft from him. Suppose it were your wife who was missing, Lyndale, what then?'

This had James reining in his fury. What could he lose – except dignity – by allowing Clairval to conduct a search? Nothing, and since he knew that Luke was not at Haven's End, then he would have the pleasure of seeing Clairval thwarted – and of demanding an apology from him.

'Very well,' he said grudgingly. 'Go ahead, but I warn you that you will find nothing – nor, I may add, has my son been here recently. I repeat, I have not seen him for some months now.'

James was quite unsurprised when the two bruisers for whom Clairval sent found nothing, whilst their

master sprawled gracelessly in an armchair in James's
drawing-room. Halfway through the wretched business,
Cressy, warned by the housekeeper of what was going
on, walked in to where James and Clairval sat, glaring
at one another.

'Ah, m'lord,' she said sweetly, as Clairval rose slowly
to his feet. 'I cannot say that I am honoured by your
presence, seeing that you only remain here because
you refuse to accept my husband's word of honour.
Nevertheless, you are a guest in this house. You will
accept a little refreshment, perhaps.'

She was aware of James's fury that she was offering
Clairval anything, but Cressy had a mind of her own.
She wished to see Clairval wrong-footed a little, and
was, up to a point, succeeding.

'Thank you, no,' he said a little more gracefully.
Only to revert to savagery again as he went on, 'Any
food you could serve me would choke me – in view of
the reason I have visited Haven's End at all – the
misconduct of your husband's bastard.'

'See here,' began James hotly, his face like thunder,
'you are not to speak so before my wife. . .' only for
Cressy to interrupt him.

'Oh, do be quiet, James. M'lord Marquess is only
speaking as he does to bait you. For you and I to retain
our perfect manners in the face of his insults is to win
a small battle. You do understand that, m'lord, I trust,'
she added, turning towards Clairval, who was wishing
that he could give Cressy, Lady Lyndale, a taste of the
stick which he had used upon his wife before she had
disappeared.

Cressy, well aware of the thoughts which were written so plainly on Clairval's face, waved a hand at
Fernando and his minion, who had returned empty-
handed from a lengthy search of Haven's End from

cellar to attics in company with servants who constantly informed him that Master Luke had not been part of the household since early spring.

'You come empty-handed, I see,' she proclaimed brightly as Fernando shook his head at his master. 'I think that a few apologies are in order, don't you, m'lord? You can breach protocol and begin by doing so to James, since it is he whom you have insulted the most by refusing to accept his word, and then you may pass on to me.'

James was openly smiling. He knew his wife and how little the behaviour of such as Clairval disturbed her. She was the last member of a family noted for its pride and its *savoir faire* and he was amused at Clairval's inability to dent her armour. He knew that armour of old.

Clairval, unable to attack Cressy physically in order to punish her insolence towards him, rounded on James. 'I wonder at you, Lyndale, I really do, for allowing your termagant of a wife to speak for you. She needs a strong hand to control her, I see, and I advise you to use that strong hand on her as soon as possible – unless you are unmanned quite. Of course, I shall not apologise. I have nothing to apologise for.'

James walked to the door and flung it open. 'I think, Clairval, that it is time that you left, before I order my servants to throw you out of doors. I am beginning to understand why your wife ran away from you. Good day, m'lord. You are not welcome here.'

Whether or not Clairval wished to do more than leave in impotent fury, and without having apologised, James neither knew nor cared, so long as he went.

Their unwanted guest gone, the face he turned on Cressy was a serious one. 'Clairval was wrong in assuming that Luke was here, but I fear that we may now have an explanation for his behaviour. How or why it has happened, how he met her, or what he has done with her, I do not know, but I strongly suspect that Luke *has* run off with Lady Clairval.'

'In that case,' said Cressy sadly, 'we are no wiser than we were. We have no idea of his – or their – whereabouts. But you said one true thing, James, which makes me fear a little for them both. You said that you understood why his wife left him – as I do – for a harsher, more cruel, man I do not wish to meet. It is plain to me that he is capable of anything.

'But, oh, I do wish that we knew where Luke might be found. I am sorry that he did not see fit to come here if he needed a refuge. And I am sorrier still that the law gives a man like Clairval such complete power over his unfortunate wife.'

He put an arm around Cressy. 'I fear that Luke has made a powerful enemy. But one thing Clairval has done by his conduct towards both you and myself today: he has ensured that if Luke does bring Lady Clairval here, I shall certainly not hand her over to her husband if it prove that he has been as cruel to her as rumour says. Haven's End shall be true to its name, if a haven is what she needs.'

Cressy had never loved him so much. The sense of honour which had driven her husband all his life was as strong as ever. She had never suspected otherwise, but to witness him demonstrate it comforted her.

'I cannot believe that Luke would ever do anything wrong, and so I must believe that he thinks the lady persecuted. I am with you on this, James, if Luke has run off with her. But, as yet, we have no confirmation of this, only Clairval's suppositions.'

'And the fact that they both seem to have disappeared at the same time. No use in worrying, my dear, but we must be ready for anything.'

Luke and Anne spent their last night together in each other's arms. Earlier, after Luke had told her that he was leaving the Romanies to draw Clairval away from her, she had protested long and tearfully that he must do no such thing. She would take her chances with him.

When he had proved adamant, saying that Jasper and the *chovihani* were agreed upon the matter, Anne had left him to go and argue with the *chovihani*. She found her sitting in the open, looking out across the heath, her eyes blank, in deep meditation.

Anne waited for her to return safely to the mundane world of every day before she spoke to her.

'I don't want Luke to leave us,' she announced bluntly, all her usual tactful charm gone. 'I don't understand why he should put himself into danger.'

'Nor do I,' agreed the *chovihani* 'except that he must. All the signs are that, by doing so, he will prevent your enemy from finding you until shortly before his doom is upon him. For him to find you earlier than that means that he will capture you and take you into eternal imprisonment and death.'

She added after a moment. 'I can tell you nothing more than that, for more than that I cannot see.'

'That is not sufficient.' Anne was firm. 'All the signs, you said. What of the tarot cards? What do they say?' She had seen the *chovihani* use the cards to tell the future more than once.

'They say the same.'

'Then show me.'

Anne's tone was peremptory, that of Lady Clairval. It was a tone which she had never used before to anyone.

The *chovihani* sighed. 'Child, child,' she said reprovingly, 'you lack trust. Nevertheless, come with me, and you shall shuffle the cards and I shall read them, and if they tell a different story today, then Orion need not leave us.'

So it was agreed. The *chovihani* went to the tent which she shared with her husband, Jasper, the Pharaoh, and came out carrying a small wooden box containing a pack of tarot cards wrapped in a square of purple silk. No one but their owner was allowed to touch them, apart from the person asking a question of them, who was always known as the querent and who was allowed to shuffle them.

'One question,' said the *chovihani* firmly, 'and a horseshoe spread to answer it.'

'This is my question,' said Anne equally firmly, as she accepted the cards and began to shuffle them. 'Must Luke leave me tomorrow in order to ensure our safety?'

'That is plain enough, Stella. Now hand me back the cards and watch.'

The *chovihani* began to lay out, face down on the grass before her, seven cards in the shape of a horseshoe: the traditional pattern for answering a single question. Each card had a specific part to play in the answer after it was turned over.

Anne had already been taught how to use the cards and had decided to acquire a pack of her own. Now she watched as the *chovihani* turned the cards over, one by one, and began to read them. The last card of all was the one which would tell Anne whether or not Luke would achieve success for her if he left.

Anxiously, Anne watched as the cards began to foretell the future. Danger was all around them, they said. There had been great danger in the past, and there would be in the future. It was essential that Luke make the right choice when his testing time came, or they were doomed to be lost to one another. Death stalked the pair of them.

Finally, the *chovihani* turned over the last card of all, and Anne trembled as she did so, for on this card all her hopes for a happy future lay. It was The Sun, and it was the right way up so that Anne clapped her hands together in joy, even though it meant that Luke must leave her. A reversed card meant failure and despair, but The Sun, glowing in all its splendour, predicted a happy outcome for her and Luke.

'But only after much suffering and tribulation,' prophesied the *chovihani*, her face grave. 'But do not despair, Stella. The cards are in your favour. See, there are The Lovers, Justice, The Tower, The Hanged Man and The Chariot, and most of them are the right way up. I also see that help for you will arrive from a strange quarter – the cards rarely speak plainly to us, although their intent is plain.'

She had her answer. Luke must leave her. To gain something that one wanted, one often had to surrender something. One had to give as well as take, a lesson which the *chovihani* had hinted to her, more than once, all mankind had to learn.

Thus, when at daybreak Luke rose to go to Jasper to be transformed from Orion back into the young gentleman of fashion he had so lately been, both the lovers were submitting to the fate which the magic of the gypsies was forecasting for them.

'Happiness after sorrow,' Luke whispered to Anne before he kissed her goodbye, 'is better than no happiness at all. I hope it will not be long before we meet again.'

He had not told her of the cruel test which Jasper

had said awaited him whilst he was gone from her, although he knew that in a guarded fashion the *chovihani* had warned Anne that trials for him lay ahead before they met again.

They clung together for a long moment, unwilling to part, not even knowing whether they would ever meet again, for who could be sure that the *chovihani's* prophecies were true ones. Until, growing impatient, Luke's horse, Cassius, one of Tawno's finer animals, gently nudged at him. He released Anne reluctantly. Tawno, who had been standing by, lent him his linked hands so that he might the more easily mount Cassius.

Once aboard him, he was again Mr Luke Harcourt, Lord Lyndale's freely acknowledged son, in a bottle-green jacket, fine linen shirt and cravat, cream breeches, highly polished boots, and a hat as unlike the battered trophies worn by Tawno and company as possible. His hair, which had been allowed to grow a little whilst he was with the Romanies, had been cut short. Only his amber eyes remained to betray that Luke was Orion – or that Orion was Luke.

His saddle bags contained food and other supplies. Jasper had given him a horse pistol, and altogether he looked well equipped to ride the autumn roads. September was king now in all its fruitful lushness.

'Northwards,' said Jasper, who had come to see him off, as had most of the camp, 'always northwards, the magic says.'

'Towards Haven's End, then,' remarked Luke, frowning.

'Aye. Haven's End is where your doom lies – and perhaps your salvation. Goodbye, young gentleman, brother Luke, no longer brother Orion. One day, perhaps, we may see Orion again. Perhaps.'

It was his farewell.

Never look back, Orpheus had been told before he returned from the Underworld. Luke was returning to the Overworld and, unlike Orpheus, he did not look over his shoulder at what he was leaving behind, precious though it was, and Jasper and the Romanies honoured him for it.

As they honoured Anne who, tearless on the outside, although crying inside, watched him until the pathway turned and he was hidden from her sight.

Chapter Thirteen

'So, where's he off to, then?' remarked Greene to Jenkinson. They had been trailing the Romanies for several days, keeping at a discreet distance. Long-sighted Jenkinson had been given a lengthy description of Luke by Pat O'Hare, who was eager to make up for his treachery towards him. Jenkinson already knew what Anne looked like from his surveillance of Mrs Britten's.

He had lain in the undergrowth the whole of the morning when Luke was preparing to leave watching the gypsies come and go. He had recognised Anne, changed though she was, and guessed that the gypsyish-looking young fellow in a blue velveteen suit with an arm around her was the young man with whom she had run off. He was sure of it when, some time later, the same young man disappeared into a tent with the Pharaoh, only to emerge later dressed as a fine young gent.

The affecting farewells between the fine young gent and the supposed gypsy woman who was actually Lady Clairval merely served to convince Jenkinson that he had found the missing lovers. Any surmise he was making about why Luke Harcourt should resume his town clothes was confirmed for him when he rode off northwards. For whatever reason, he and the Romanies had decided that he was to act as a decoy, drawing Clairval away from his prey.

And if Clairval was after Master Luke, then to follow him would mean that the two Runners could find Clairval without them alerting the whole of the south-west as to what they were doing – which was to their – and the Grand Personage's – advantage.

'Decoy,' he said briefly to Greene. 'They're trying to draw Clairval away from her. I suppose that they hope that when they reach their destination, which by my guess is Bristol, Master Luke will try to elude Clairval and rejoin them.'

'Why Bristol?' queried Greene, a trifle aggressively. 'Since you seem able to guess so much, perhaps you can tell me that.'

'Bristol's a port where you may leave for the Americas, you gaby,' said Jenkinson unkindly.

'But he's going in the wrong direction for Bristol,' objected Greene triumphantly. 'I think he's heading for Papa's place at Haven's End.'

'That, too,' said Jenkinson cryptically, and said no more, motioning Greene to take to his horse again and follow Master Luke – at a discreet distance. Following would be easy since there were few byways in this part of the world, and if Master Luke wished to be found, as seemed likely, he would make for a posthouse on the road to the west leading to Bristol, via Bath, and try to discover whether Clairval had gone through or was expected.

It all depended on whether Clairval had already visited Haven's End and that Jenkinson did not know. He had no wish to become entangled in any way with Lord Lyndale, who had a reputation for being upright,

but a bit of a tough, unless he had to. He supposed that
Master Luke had no idea where Clairval was, and was
trusting in luck to find him – or be found.

All unknowing that he was being carefully tracked,
Luke was doing exactly what Jenkinson supposed and
riding slightly northward to the turnpike to Bath. It
was an even bet that Clairval might be making for Bath
to hire lodgings there and use it as a centre to try to
discover where his missing wife and her lover were. He
might, of course, have turned back towards London,
but Luke didn't think so.

Like Jenkinson, Luke wished that he knew whether
Clairval had already visited Haven's End. He was still
wishing it when he reached Marlborough in the early
evening, and stopped at the inn there to rest his horse
and himself. Ostlers rushed forward to help the fine
young gentleman whom he appeared to be, and he was
glad of the store of guineas which he had brought with
him from London, which enabled him to throw money
about with a happy abandon, even if he were travelling
on horseback and without a servant.

The innkeeper was duly subservient when Luke, in
lordly fashion, demanded the best room in the house.

'I don't suppose,' he remarked casually later on,
when the landlord brought him a dish of roast beef to
eat by the fire, for the evening had turned chilly, 'that
you have seen my friend, the Marquess of Clairval,
pass through lately?'

'Indeed, young sir, but we have,' answered the
landlord eagerly, always ready to assist apparent
wealth. 'He was here but a few days ago, and I expect
him back tomorrow. He has been a-visiting at Haven's
End, but he thought it unlikely that he would stay with

m'lord – he being of the opposite political persuasion
from m'lord Clairval, you understand.'

'Oh, aye, indeed,' returned Luke cryptically, giving
nothing away. Finding Clairval so quickly was a piece
of luck which he had not expected.

'I trust that you will not object to passing on to him
my good wishes. I suppose that I shall miss him, unless
we meet on the road tomorrow, for I am making for
Haven's End myself.'

This last was, of course, untrue, since Luke had no
intention of visiting his father, although he had every
intention of wandering around the country in which his
father's home stood, waiting for Clairval to find him –
and discover that Anne was not with him. After that,
he would try to convince him that he had no idea where
Anne was, and that their leaving Mrs Britten's at
roughly the same time was an unfortunate coincidence.

If he were successful in deceiving Clairval, he might
then make for Haven's End to put Clairval even further
off the scent, and persuade him that he ought to renew
his search for his lost wife in London.

In the taproom at the back, with the servants and the
lowly men of the road, Jenkinson and Greene ate bread
and cheese for supper, and drank their ale. They, too,
had made enquiries about m'lord Clairval, but more
discreetly than Luke, since they did not wish to be
discovered.

One of the men drinking with them had been turned
off by Clairval and had secured a job as a groom at the
inn. Several pints of ale, bought for him by the apparently generous Jenkinson, had him telling the two
Runners as much of Clairval's business as he knew,
so that, like Luke, they were made aware of
m'lord's plans.

'Do we take him tomorrow, if we find him?' Greene asked. 'I know you've got a warrant to do so.'

Jenkinson shook his head. 'No. I don't want to arrest him – if I have to arrest him, that is – until he catches up with m'lady. If he does catch up with her, that is. I think that when he does, he will give us an opportunity to deal with him ourselves.'

'Meaning?'

'Don't ask, Greene. Don't ask. There's them as wants this business cleared up quietly, no questions asked then, or later. We do what we wants, when we wants. M'lord Marquess has a nasty temper, as well I know. I suspicion that that temper – if he can be provoked – may work in our favour. Until then, mum's the word.'

He said no more and, like Luke, went to bed conscious of a day's work well done.

'Haven's End, landlord,' exclaimed Clairval. 'You're sure that this flash young gentleman said that he was going to Haven's End, and that his name was Mr Luke Harcourt?'

'Aye, m'lord, that is so. Wished me to pay you his compliments, and say how sorry he was to miss you, so he did.'

'Never mind that, you fool. Was there anyone travelling with him? A lady, perhaps.'

'Nay, m'lord. He was alone, came on a good horse, so he did, left on it, said as how he was making for Haven's End.'

'And I've just come from there, after a night at a dam'd poor local inn,' swore Clairval. 'Took the main road, did he?'

'No, m'lord. The byway, the one which goes towards Haven's End direct. Your chaises might just manage it if you wish to follow him.' Although Clairval was

travelling in some state, it was not as much as he was
accustomed to – another cause for grievance against
the upstart Harcourt and his faithless wife – and he had
only two chaises with him instead of his usual large
train.

He swung round, bellowing for Fernando. 'More
horses for the chaises, man, and we take the byway for
Haven's End. At least we're on the track of one of our
quarry. But what the devil has he done with my wife?
Tell me that!' he abjured the heavens, for he had no
doubt that Luke Harcourt had run off with her and,
where he was, m'lady Clairval could not be far away.

Luke dawdled along the byway which would ultimately
lead him to his father's home in the hope that he might
meet Clairval on his way back to Marlborough. He had
no wish to meet him near Haven's End, for what might
happen then could possibly embarrass his father.

After a time, he decided that Clairval might have
returned to Marlborough by the main road, which was
longer, but easier and speedier to travel on, but having
settled on this route he decided to follow it. If unsuccessful, he could always return to Marlborough in the
hope of finding Clairval there. Jasper had half-hinted
that it would not be long before he found Clairval – or
Clairval found him.

Finally, some time after noon, Luke slid from the
saddle, tethered his horse to a tree, pulled the luncheon
which the landlady had packed for him from his saddle
bags, and sat down in the shade of some trees, well in
sight of the road, to eat it.

After that he leaned against the bole of one of the
trees, and rested for a little. He was missing Anne
cruelly, had slept little the night before and soon found

himself drowsy. Before he fell asleep, he tried to pretend that she was resting by him, her hand in his.

He was still half-asleep when he heard Clairval arrive. He debated whether or not to leap to his feet when the chaise with Clairval's ornate coat of arms on its door came to a stop at the sight of him. He decided that a lazy surveyal of Clairval's equipage, rather than showing a great deal of excitement at his arrival, might serve to convince Clairval of his innocence.

It was not until Fernando leaped out of Clairval's chaise bellowing his name and demanding his attention that he rose to his feet and strolled slowly towards the chaise. So slowly, that by the time he had reached it, Clairval was already waiting for him, his gold-topped cane in his hand.

'Mr Harcourt, I believe,' Clairval drawled. 'I cannot say that we are well met, except, of course, for the trifling fact that now we *have* met you will do me the goodness of telling me where you have hidden my mad wife!'

'Charmed to do so,' returned Luke, giving Clairval a bow of exactly the right strength, 'if only I knew where she is – or was. I believe that you mistake your man.'

He was neither insolent nor servile, merely a young gentleman of good birth offering a man of higher rank the deference and attention which that rank deserved.

Clairval was neither deceived nor placated. 'Come, come, sir,' he said, 'do not palter with me. I am well aware that you spirited my poor mad wife away when I traced her to Islington. You will save yourself a deal of trouble if you cease your futile pretence and tell me what I need to know. The poor thing urgently needs the attention of the best mad doctor I can hire. You, being a bastard required to earn your own living, can hardly do that.'

Luke resisted the temptation to deny Anne's madness. Even as Clairval had spoken of it, he had a sudden memory of her on the heath, among the gypsies, one happy hand in his, watching the man who owned the educated pig putting it through its paces, her eyes alight with mirth.

'M'lord,' he said. 'I have told you that you are mistook. As you see, I am all alone, travelling towards my father's place at Haven's End. You will have the goodness to allow me to pass on my way. If your wife is lost, then you waste time dallying with me.'

Clairval's patience snapped. 'Damn you for an ill-gotten bastard, Master Luke Harcourt,' he roared. 'I know that you have stolen my wife, and hidden her, God knows where. I warn you, for the last time, that if you do not answer me fair straight away then it will go ill with you. I shall hand you over to Fernando and his friends so that they may beat out of you the name of the place where you have left her.'

He snapped his fingers at Fernando and at two more bruisers who had climbed out of the second chaise and were waiting for his orders.

'I do not palter with you,' he added. 'You may ask Fernando what he did to your Irish friend when I found out that he had not been telling me all he knew. And I warn you again, that was child's play to what I will have him – and his companions – do to you.'

If Luke quailed inwardly, which he did, there was no sign of it on his face. So, the monster before him had had poor Pat beaten – and doubtless it was Pat who had unwittingly betrayed him to Clairval. Jasper had said that he would face a severe test and now that test was upon him. All that concerned him was that God would grant him the power to hold true and that pain and fear did not have him blabbing of where Anne and the Romanies might be found.

No, he told himself firmly. I must behave as though what I have said is the truth. I have no idea where Anticleia, Lady Clairval is, and so I cannot help him.

Even as he thought this, he said it, at the same time looking around him. The two new bruisers were moving to cut off his escape into the wood at his rear, while Fernando was preparing to attack him from the front.

'Liar,' screamed Clairval – which was true enough, but not to the point. 'Teach him to tell the truth, Fernando.'

Luke bunched his hands into fists and tried to remember what the Romany boxers with whom he had playfully sparred, had taught him. But this was not sparring, and here were three fully trained pugilists attacking him in fierce reality, not in play.

He landed one blow to Fernando's midriff before he was seized from the rear and held by his two henchmen so that Fernando might strike him at will – which he did. Through failing consciousness and increasing pain he could see Clairval laughing at the sight of his agony. Presently, when Fernando stopped hitting him, the two lesser men held him up before Clairval so that he might question him again.

'Now, Master Luke, you know that I meant what I said. Tell me where my wife is and save yourself further punishment.'

'Go to Hell,' gasped Luke, pain riding him. 'If I knew, I would not tell you.' He could only hope that the strength of his will would stop him from confessing everything to save his ill-treated body from further pain.

'No, Master Luke. That is where you are going.

Persuade him a little further, Fernando, but leave him conscious.'

This time, when Clairval ordered Fernando to stop, Luke was on his hands and knees on the ground, and Clairval had to bend down to question him again.

'Come, man, don't be a fool. Tell me what I wish to know. The trull isn't worth what you are suffering for her.'

From where he found the strength and resolution to do what he did, Luke never knew. He would have said beforehand that he could not have withstood the brutal battering he had received from Fernando and his friends without confessing everything. The training in self-denial, resolution, and the enduring of pain, which Jasper and Tawno had put him through during his time as a Romany, had strengthened his will as well as his courage.

Thus, even through the mists of pain and suffering, he lifted his head and spat full in Clairval's face.

'That's for you for the insult you have offered to a good woman,' he mumbled.

He did not know whether Clairval heard or understood what he had said. What he did know was that, as he knelt there helpless, he suddenly saw Anne before him, the heath and the Romanies' tents behind her, her face a mask of pain – and then everything, including Anne, disappeared as he fell into a pit of blackness.

He didn't even feel the blow to the face which Clairval gave him in return, nor the further punishment which Fernando inflicted on him before he lost consciousness.

'Damn you,' shrieked Clairval at Fernando, his face scarlet with rage mixed with frustration. 'Lift him up, and bring him round so that I may question him again.'

Fernando shook his head regretfully. 'I'll not be

party to murder, m'lord. He can't take much more from me without risk of his dying on me. I would never have thought that such a pampered young gent would resist me so stubborn-like, and taken such punishment without talking. I'd have given odds that he'd have blabbed everything long ago.'

In exasperation, Clairval walked over to where Luke lay unconscious on the ground and kicked him in the ribs. 'A fine botch you've made of it,' he roared. 'What in Hell's name do we do now? The bitch is still missing, and all we have for our pains is a piece of almost carrion on our hands. . .'

If Fernando baulked at the notion of direct murder, indirect murder seemed a little more attractive to him.

'Leave him here,' he suggested. 'Not many pass down this byway. Let Nature take its course with him. I'll shove him among the bushes, cut his horse loose and let it run free. A young gent will have disappeared – and who's to know it's anything to do with us?'

'That'll have to do,' declared Clairval morosely. 'Everything seems to go ill with me these days. The devil's in it. Shove him in the bushes then, and we'll cut line. I'll have bills posted up for m'lady's recovery. At least she's not got Master Luke protecting her now. And you're right. Who's to know we've anything to do with this?' And he gave Luke one last kick before Fernando dragged him by the heels into the undergrowth.

But they were wrong. Lying out of sight in the scrub, watching everything, wincing at each blow which Luke received, were Jenkinson and Greene, who had been following Luke after he had left the inn at Marlborough. Useless to intervene, or try to help him, for they were outnumbered. They could only wait until Clairval and his murderous party were on their way

again before they emerged from the undergrowth to
pull Luke free and try to revive him.

'Damn that Fernando,' muttered Jenkinson, pouring
water from a bottle which had been strapped to his
saddle, and which Greene fetched from where their
horses were tethered in the wood, some distance away.
'I'll see him turned off for good on Tyburn Tree one of
these days, but not for this poor young fellow, I hope.
Give me a hand, man, I've no mind to have him die on
us, a splendid witness to m'lord Marquess's cruelty as
he is.'

'Can't imagine why you didn't use your warrant and
arrest him on the spot, and save the poor young fellow
from this,' complained Greene as he gently held Luke
so that Jenkinson could wipe his bruised face.

'Use your loaf, man. What d'you think that m'lord
would have done to any warrant I'd waved in his face
whilst his bruisers were cuffing up this poor young
feller and us here in this wilderness without any spec-
tators? Torn it up, he would have done, *and* had them
duff me up – and you – and sworn blind that *we'd*
attacked *him* on the road – with our bodies to prove it.
No, a mad dog is m'lord Clairval, and as a mad dog
he'll have to be muzzled – and soon. But we'll pick our
ground when we do it.'

In the middle of this diatribe Luke gave a groan,
clutched at the lapel of Jenkinson's coat and mumbled
through bruised and swollen lips, 'I didn't tell. Anne,
my darling, I didn't tell him where you are.'

'No more you did,' said Jenkinson, holding the water
bottle to Luke's mouth. 'And I promise you, that if it's
the last thing I do, m'lord shall pay dear for this day's
work.'

They tended Luke for a little while longer. He lapsed
in and out of consciousness, but the periods of con-

sciousness gradually grew longer. Jenkinson finally said to Greene as he helped Luke to sit up for the first time, 'We'll try to find help for him. That place where his father lives, Haven's End, ain't far from here.'

Luke muttered something unintelligible about Haven's End as Greene hoisted him up on Jenkinson's horse, tying him on, so that Jenkinson could walk him along the byway to a place which was truly a haven.

Earlier that day after helping the *chovihani* to teach some of the little children their letters, Anne had taken her work and sat down in the shade not far from where the older girls were busy learning a dance that they proposed to introduce into their small act.

They were carrying tambourines, which they held high above their heads, sounding them at intervals as they twisted and turned in time to a fiddler. Presently they put the tambourines down and a gypsy boy came forward carrying a silk scarf.

This was the signal for them to rehearse yet another dance, which Anne had not yet seen them perform. The girls formed a circle round the boy, who handed the scarf to a girl, who danced with it for a short time, twisting and twirling it, while the boy danced a jig before her.

After a time, she passed the scarf on to the girl on her right and the boy now danced before her. In this manner the scarf passed round the circle until it reached the first girl, who ceremoniously handed it to the boy, who bowed in turn to them all, the scarf held high, before the music stopped, and they all sank to the ground, in a grand curtsy.

Anne joined the older gypsies who had arrived to watch in clapping and applauding the children, who rose and waved to them. One of them ran to her and gave her the scarf to hold.

Even as she touched it, a wave of pain ran through Anne. The bright scene around her darkened and disappeared as the pain came again, stronger than ever. So strong was it that she sank on to her knees on the ground, her hands shielding her bent head, crying out she knew not what.

The *chovihani*, who was standing by, put her arms around her and tried to comfort her. Anne lifted an agonised face and wailed, 'Oh, it's Luke! It's Luke! Someone is hurting him cruelly. Oh, it's Clairval! Oh, I cannot bear the pain.'

As she spoke the scene around her vanished completely. She was with Luke, she almost was Luke, except that at the same time she could see his agonised face and feel the blows which were being rained upon him. Then, when it became almost unbearable, the pain disappeared, and Anne fell into a dark pit of nothingness. . . Even as she reached the bottom she was back on the heath again, in the *chovihani*'s arms.

'Luke!' she cried. 'He's killed him! Oh, why did I let him go?'

'No,' said the *chovihani*, gently. 'I saw him even as the pain stopped. He is hurt, but he is not dead. Death I would have recognised, and Death was not there. The spirits are merciful and bestowed freedom from pain on him, so that he might not be tormented further.'

But nothing that she could say consoled Anne. She still sat, crouched on the ground, sobbing for her lost love. Tawno's wife, who had left them on a nod from the *chovihani*, came running back carrying a cup full of a clear liquid.

'Come,' said the *chovihani*, putting the cup to Anne's lips. 'Drink of the poppy, and find rest. I can only see darkly, but what I see tells me that, for the moment, Orion has escaped his tormentor. Drink and rest, my sister. The gift I bestowed on you earlier this year is even more powerful than I intended it to be. The greater mysteries are not meant for a novice such as yourself to endure.'

Anne drank, and allowed the gypsies to lead her to the tent that she had shared with Luke, and there, his velveteen jacket clutched in her arms, sleep took her and, at the *chovihani*'s gift, all her dreams were pleasant.

What the Romanies did not tell Anne, for they did not wish to disturb her further, was that towards nightfall the horse on which Luke had been riding returned, covered with foam, with Luke's saddlebags, still unpacked. . .

Clairval's thoughts were not pleasant. By the time they had reached the end of the byway on which they had caught Luke and were about to turn towards Marlborough, he changed his mind and bade his coachman return to the spot where they had left him.

'I was a fool,' he told Fernando angrily, as though it were his fault. 'I should never have left him there. He would have been a valuable prize. We should have taken him with us to question him further when he recovered consciousness. The devil was in him to make him so obstinate. Who would have thought that he would take so much punishment?'

Fernando did not argue with a man who was growing more capricious by the hour. They sent the second chaise back to the inn at Marlborough to have rooms prepared for m'lord, whilst Clairval returned to pick up the injured Luke. The trouble was that, when they reached the small clearing where they had left him, they could see the marks which Fernando had made dragging him into the scrub, but there was no sign of him.

'Gone!' roared Clairval, now in a lather of rage and frustration at Fernando and life generally, when told this surprising news. 'How can he be gone? He was unconscious when we left him. Or were you mistaken?'

'I know a stunned man when I see one,' returned Fernando. 'I suppose,' he offered doubtfully, 'he might have come to and staggered away. Yes, that would be it.'

'Then the pair of you had better look for him. In the state he was in, he can't have gone far.'

But search though they might, they found no sign of the missing Luke. Fernando, on returning to tell his master the bad news, watched him turn purple with rage.

'Disappeared! How can he have disappeared? He was in no state to walk any distance.'

'A passer-by might have seen him.' Even Fernando thought this suggestion a lame one. He thought that the Marquess was about to choke on it.

'Seen him? Seen what? You left him so that he wasn't visible from the byway.'

'Well, m'lord,' the goaded Fernando replied, turning, like the proverbial worm, at last. 'What do *you* suggest?'

'Me? I pay you to think, man. But since you appear to be unable to do so, *I* think that we'll cut our losses, return to Marlborough, and make for Haven's End again on the morrow. I believe that Lord Lyndale knows a great deal more than he's telling.'

Which, like most of m'lord Marquess's suppositions was, as usual, a case of the dog barking up the wrong tree – but occasionally getting the right answer!

* * *

Unaware of what was going on behind them, Jenkinson and Greene plodded steadily towards Haven's End. The vast parkland surrounding the great house was in sight when a party from it came into view.

At the front of it was Cressy, Lady Lyndale, superbly turned out in deep blue, and wearing a man's top hat with a pale blue silk scarf swathed around it. She was driving a curricle picked out in blue and silver. Two grooms accompanied her.

Jenkinson knew the quality when he saw it. M'lady's small procession could be the salvation of Master Luke. To stop it, he put up a hand which wavered between the peremptory and the servile.

Cressy, curious at the sight of a man slumped in the saddle of a horse being led by another man, did not at first realise that the slumped man was Luke. Nevertheless, she slowed down, leaned forwards to speak to Jenkinson, and said, 'I am Lady Lyndale, at your service. Your companion appears to be injured. How may we help you?'

'By arranging, m'lady, that Mr Luke Harcourt, who is your stepson, I believe, is taken to his father's house and a doctor found for him as soon as possible. He has been most cruelly beaten.'

Cressy, her face white with shock, drove over to Luke. 'Who has been responsible for this?' she demanded fiercely, inexpressibly shocked by the sight of his bruised and swollen face and his torn clothing.

Jenkinson saw no point in evasion. 'M'lord Clairval ordered it done, m'lady.'

Cressy's hand turned into a clenched fist. 'Did he, indeed? I think that my husband will have something to say about this. Stephen,' she added, turning to the young groom who had also ridden up to inspect Luke, his face full of concern, 'you and Russell may lift Mr

Luke from this gentleman's horse, and carry him into my curricle. That will get him home double quick.

'You, sir,' she said, turning to Jenkinson as the two grooms sprang to do her bidding, 'may explain to me how this terrible thing came about when we reach the house. M'lord is sitting at the Quarter Sessions today and will not reach home until tomorrow morning, so I will have to act for him.'

Luke, transferred to the curricle where he regained consciousness sufficiently to recognise Cressy, although he did not speak to her, was driven at all speed to his father's home, Greene and Jenkinson, restored to his horse, riding behind him.

Chapter Fourteen

Clairval arrived at Haven's End, the next day, at almost exactly the same time as James, Lord Lyndale. James looked from his coach's window with some surprise at the sight of Clairval's chaise with its tell-tale coat of arms and the two smartly dressed grooms standing at the back. Fernando was already waiting on the gravel sweep, his arm out, ready to accommodate his master as he stepped from his carriage.

James raised his fine black brows. He had no wish to speak to Clairval again and could not understand what had brought him back to Haven's End. He sighed, allowed himself to be helped out of his own coach and watched Clairval advance on him, his face purple. He adopted an expression of resigned patience, which he was very far from feeling.

He was attacked without preamble by the furious man before him.

'I almost believed you the other day, Lyndale, when you assured me that you had no notion of the whereabouts of your bastard and my adulterous wife. I now have reason to know that you lied to me. I demand that you allow Fernando and his companion to search your house again.'

'Demand away, Clairval,' returned James coolly. 'I have no intention of allowing either you, or your bully boys, into my home again. You are not welcome here, sir. Pray leave. You have my word that I still have no notion where Mr Harcourt is. He is certainly not at Haven's End. You must remain content with that. I bid you good day.'

He bowed and swept on into the house. He could hear Clairval gibbering behind him, and see Cressy standing in the doorway, a wry expression on her face. She had heard every word which the two men had exchanged.

She thought that James looked his magnificent best in black. He always dressed soberly for the Assizes, both coming and going, in order to emphasise his respect for the law. Age – and a happy marriage – had served only to enhance his looks and bearing. He had scarcely reached her before Clairval was snapping at his heels again.

'See here, Lyndale. I insist that you pay heed to me.'

'Go into the house, my dear. I do not want you present whilst I dispose of this importunate fly,' James said coldly, before turning, and saying in his most scathing manner, 'Your insistence and the manner in which you express it, serve only to harden my determination to have as little as possible to do with you. I have no intention of allowing you, ever again, into my home. I despise a man who will not accept my word. You will oblige me by leaving.'

For a moment Clairval made as if to pull him back by main force – or order Fernando to do so – until he took one look at the array of footmen and lackeys who had assembled on the gravel sweep to attend James on his arrival. It was not likely that they would disobey any orders which Lyndale might give – such as bidding them to see Clairval's small party off the premises, by force, if necessary.

He contented himself with shrieking, 'This is not the end of the matter,' before he allowed Fernando to help him into the chaise. The great double doors at the front of Haven's End clanged to, and he was left to make his way down the drive, his tail between his legs.

Cressy was waiting for James in the hall. Her expression was still odd, he thought. He knew his Cressy well. There was no doubt that she was bursting to tell him something – but what?

'James,' she began a trifle breathlessly, and then, looking at the waiting servants, 'not here. In the drawing-room.'

'Very urgent, is it?'

'Very urgent,' repeated Cressy, after the drawing-room doors were closed behind them. 'Oh, James, I heard you tell Clairval that Luke is not here. It is true that you have no idea of where he is, and that was no lie, but since five o'clock yesterday he has been at Haven's End – in his old room.'

James's eyebrows arched upwards, and his mouth thinned after a fashion which Cressy had not seen since the days before their marriage when he and she had jousted verbally together.

'Luke? Here? With Lady Clairval?' He gave a half-laugh. 'So Clairval was right in his assumptions after all, and I was an unintended liar when I assured him that Luke was not here!'

Something odd about what Cressy had just said struck him. 'In his room? Why in his room, pray? Is he afraid to face me?' He started towards the door.

Cressy was after him in a flash. 'No, James. Don't fly into the boughs. Lady Clairval is not with him. He was carried here yesterday, semi-conscious, by two Bow

Street Runners who had found him abandoned after Clairval had him beaten to try to make him reveal where he had hidden Lady Clairval. Doctor Spence says that his life is not in danger, but he has suffered a light fever and is in great pain. His left arm is hurt and his ribs are badly bruised.'

James's anger was now directed towards Clairval. He started for the door again, and Cressy read him rightly. She caught him by the arm.

'No, James. You are not to do anything rash, like following Clairval and calling him out. Think! Luke would not want the scandal that would follow. Nor would you.'

James gave a short laugh, and turned back. 'My dear, it is something of an event, you must allow, when it is *you* who are cautioning *me* not to be over-hasty, and not me you. Punishing Clairval must wait. Is...' he hesitated '...is Luke well enough for me to talk to him?'

'He is now, I think. But he was not last night. The two Runners are still here and wish to speak to you – but only after you have spoken to Luke. Or so the leading one of the two said. You must understand that they probably saved Luke's life. They found him hidden away, off the road in the undergrowth, where he could not easily be seen. He could have died there.'

'Luke first, then,' was James's answer to that.

He found Luke awake, lying propped up against the pillows, his face bruised and swollen. Behind the bruises his pallor was extreme. Cressy had told James that before he had fully recovered his senses Luke had said over and over again, 'I didn't tell him, Anne. Believe me, I never told him where you are. I would die, rather.'

So far as James was concerned, what he had seen of

Clairval's recent conduct appeared to bear out the supposition that he might be prepared to go as far as murder. Luke's condition was a witness to the brutality with which he had been treated. James sat down on the bed, facing his son.

Luke stared steadily at him, his face guarded. He made no effort to speak until James remarked, as casually as he could, for rage at Clairval for what he had done to Luke was consuming him, 'You have a look of having been in the wars, old fellow. Care to tell me anything about it?'

Luke shook his head. Every movement hurt. Even speech hurt. 'No. Only that Clairval tried to make me tell him where Anne – Lady Clairval – is by having his bruisers thrash me, and I wouldn't. I suppose that is why he left me for dead.'

'So you did run away with Lady Clairval.'

'I ran away with Anne, yes. To save her from him, you understand – he would kill her if he recaptured her – and because we love one another.'

Speech was painful and his voice was husky, but Luke felt that he had to make his father understand that what had been done had not been done lightly.

'Oh, Luke, she is another man's wife. And you know how the law stands between man and wife. We talked on that earlier this summer.'

Luke turned his face away from his father. He was not about to be persuaded into betraying Anne so that she might be handed back to the monster who had tried to kill her.

'I regard her as my wife, not Clairval's. It is my duty to protect her.'

He spoke to his father as though to an enemy. Before he had left Haven's End in the spring, James had told Cressy that he feared that Luke might lack steel. He had been wrong. The face that his son turned on him as he spoke was implacable. Painful though it obviously was for him to speak, Luke was ready to do so to defend the woman he loved – even from his father. Or refuse to speak, if that was necessary.

James made up his mind. 'I have only recently met Clairval, but I have seen and heard enough of him to know that any woman unfortunate enough to be his wife would be in danger of the greatest persecution.

'I am prepared to back you – and the lady – in every possible way, legally and financially, so that she may divorce him, as the Countess of Strathmore divorced Stony Bowes in my father's day. But you must not be seen to be lovers. Only tell me where she is, and I will go and fetch her to give her sanctuary here – even if it costs me Government office. I cannot say fairer than that.'

Could he not! Luke saw Cressy's face glow with pleasure at this great concession from her husband. But Luke's face hardened still further.

He turned away again, closed his eyes, and said in a faraway voice, 'By no means. I have not the slightest intention of telling you where my dear Anne is. She has been betrayed by too many people who had previously called themselves her friends. It is not that I don't trust *you*, but I don't trust the law, and the pressures which would be put upon you. No, allow me to recover – and once I have done so, I shall leave as soon as possible, and go to her.'

He stopped. James was about to speak, to argue with him, but again Cressy acted as mediator. She shook her head, placed a finger on her lips, and put out her other hand to lie it on James's.

'Come, my dear. Let us leave Luke so that he may rest and recover himself. He is shortly due to have another draught of the poppy to give him relief from pain. Why not talk with him later when he may be feeling better?'

James looked from his wife to his son – the son who had always been a credit to him, and who, whatever else, had been prepared to protect the woman he loved at the risk of his life. The son who was so greatly changed, not merely as a consequence of the beating, but because of the new hard determination with which he had spoken, despite his pain.

'Yes,' he said. 'I will talk to the Runners. I am curious to know why they appeared to be following Luke. Or were they following Clairval? Why should they concern themselves with a quarrel between a man and his wife?'

He found Jenkinson and Greene waiting for him in his study. He recognised Jenkinson at once. He had seen him before, waiting in an ante-room, and for some reason the very oddness of seeing his fox face, his red hair and his square blunt body in the corridors of power at Whitehall had struck him forcibly.

It was plain that Jenkinson knew him. His manner was straightforward without being insolent. 'I suppose, m'lord, that you wish to learn something of how and why we came to find Mr Harcourt.'

'Indeed,' said James, 'and if it be possible, given your calling, how and why you came to be following him? Or was it m'lord Clairval who was your quarry?'

Jenkinson looked at the ceiling and then at Greene, whose honest, dull face showed how dazzled he was to be in such grand company.

'Why, as to that, m'lord, if it were possible to send my colleague here on a small errand concerning our horses, I might find it in me to be a little straighter with you in private.'

This Machiavellian answer from such a coarse-seeming brute almost had James laughing. It certainly confused Greene, who looked at Jenkinson with a dazed face. 'Eh?' he began, 'What?'

'The stables,' James said to him. 'I gather that your horses were a trifle weary when you arrived here with my son late yesterday. I should be pleased to offer you a sounder pair. You may tell my chief groom so, with my compliments.'

'Now,' said James, taking a seat behind his great desk in the window which overlooked Haven's End's park, 'you may tell me, Mr Jenkinson, exactly what your little game is, and who you are playing it with and for, and perhaps you will allow me a hand in it if I so wish – if it benefits my son, that is. You see, I am being frank with you.'

'Aye, m'lord, I quite see that. Now the way of it is this,' and confidentially, his finger beside his nose once or twice, Mr Jenkinson began to conspire with James Chavasse, the Most Noble the Earl of Lyndale, who was only too happy to conspire back, both of them being pragmatic men with an eye to the main chance.

It went without saying that neither of them was completely frank in their dealings with the other.

The Marquess of Clairval was so enraged that his common sense, never his strongest point, had almost deserted him.

He roared at Fernando all the way back to Marlborough. If he had not been paying Fernando right royally to do his dirty work for him, that gentleman would have planted a facer on the Marquess's jaw and fled the carriage. As it was, he took all that Clairval chose to throw at him, and when he had finally run down, merely said, 'And next, m'lord? What do we do next?'

'Stay at Marlborough for a time,' said Clairval, his face resuming its normal colour, a dirty yellow.

'I am convinced that Lyndale was lying and that his bastard was hidden somewhere near Haven's End. Where he is, my wife cannot be far away. That being so, you and your minions can do some reconnoitring for me. I don't think that even Lyndale has the gall to hide her at Haven's End itself, but in Hell's name, she must be *somewhere* near here.' His voice rose dangerously, and his expression of annoyance was back again.

It was even worse when he discovered that he had to share his dinner and the inn parlour with a gentleman who had arrived during his chase after Luke, and who insisted on treating Clairval, whom he had never seen before, as an old friend.

Except that, as they sat waiting for the landlord to bring them a loaf and some cheese with which to finish the meal, the gentleman flourished a magazine at m'lord and said confidentially, 'Some fine writing about these days, m'lord. Quite extraordinary. A tale about the gypsies and their life. Written by a young gentleman of consequence, I am told, who is a friend of theirs, and has lived among them. Although he does not use his true name on the title page.'

It took Clairval the remaining shred of his temper not to inform the fool opposite that he had no use for magazines, gypsies or fine young gentlemen who wrote about them.

All that he managed was a lofty grunt, which his tormentor took as a signal to continue his virtual monologue.

'Very true, m'lord,' he said, being of the opinion that any noise made by a lord was meaningful. 'It is to be supposed that you know him. His real name is Harcourt, Luke Harcourt.' He paused to look a trifle sly, and added, 'He is by way of being a very close relative of Lord Lyndale, whose seat is nearby, I believe. As also are the gypsies. They are camped on the outskirts of Bath, I am told.'

What he believed was suddenly immaterial. On hearing the words Luke Harcourt, gypsies and Bath, m'lord the Marquess of Clairval leaned forward and virtually snatched the magazine from the intrusive gentleman's hands.

He remembered his manners at the last moment, and gabbled, 'I would be much obliged, sir, if you allowed me to examine this work at my leisure,' before he rushed to the inn's parlour door and began to bawl for Fernando, who was eating his supper in the tap room.

The intrusive gentleman stared after him. He had heard much of the reserved and haughty manners of the aristocracy, but so far Clairval had displayed little of either. He stood helplessly by as Clairval, Fernando, and his magazine, all disappeared up the stairs to Clairval's bedroom.

'I have found my lost bird,' Clairval carolled exultantly at Fernando. 'What odds would you lay that she and Master Luke have been travelling with the gypsies, and that he has left her with them? That ass in the parlour said that they are camped near Bath. Tomorrow morning I shall go to Bath and enlist the services of the local magistrates and their officers in order to help me to recover her from the scum with whom she is travelling. By nightfall she shall be mine again.'

'Aye,' said Fernando. 'Tomorrow, you say? We are off to Bath tomorrow? I suppose it's as good a bet as any.'

He sounded more than a little dubious. Clairval was a man who constantly went off half-cock. He was like an unreliable cannon on a ship's gun deck, which fired its ball whether its gunner wished it to or no. On the other hand, no harm in visiting the gypsies, either.

Luke had refused to drink the poppy which Cressy had brought for him. He was still feeling bruised in every limb, but the worst of his sufferings, he hoped, were over. He wanted to be away from Haven's End, as much to save his father and his stepmother from Clairval, as to draw Clairval away from Anne. The physician had bound his ribs with stout canvas, had assured him that his left wrist was sprained, not broken, and that a few days rest – and the poppy – would improve him mightily.

By the early evening he was sitting up, looking belligerent, and assuring a worried Cressy that he would be gone as soon as he could climb on to a horse. Like James, she saw that she was dealing with a different person from the charming, rather easy young man whom she had always known.

Luke had always been clever, but until now he had shown little of the severity, amounting to sternness, which was such a feature of his father's character. So formidable did he look that Cressy was not entirely sure that James would find the new Luke as easy to control as the old one.

'You were never a naughty boy,' she told him, mock severe herself. 'I suppose that you are making up for lost time now by refusing to take your medicine.'

She was carrying a letter which she handed to Luke, saying, 'This came some little time ago. It was marked urgent, but as we had no notion where you were, we could not forward it. I shall leave you to read it in peace.'

To Luke's surprise, the letter was from Pat O'Hare,

although it was not in his hand, which Luke knew well. He read it with a wry smile on his lips. A word to the wise, indeed. Alas, Clairval had already done the damage to him that Pat had feared.

He had just finished reading the letter when James came in. There was an air of purpose about him which his son recognised immediately. A James who had made up his mind was a formidable person indeed.

'Now what is it?' said Luke, smiling at his father for the first time. 'What new persuasions have you come to try on me, father?'

'Powerful ones,' replied James briefly, drawing up a chair. 'I have been talking to the two Runners, or rather to the chief of them, Jenkinson, who appears to be a man of sense.'

'Oh, and did the man of sense inform you how he came to be following me about the countryside? I am aware that I owe him my life, but I cannot help but wonder what I have done to deserve such attention.'

'Oh, he wasn't following you. Or rather, he was doing so, hoping that you would lead him to Clairval. Why couldn't he simply follow Clairval, one may reasonably ask? He couldn't answer that other than to say "matters of state".'

'Matters of state, eh?' Luke began to laugh, looking and sounding like his old self for the first time since he had arrived at Haven's End. He was beginning to feel a little better, no doubt about it. 'What matters of state could involve Clairval? No, don't tell me – that was another secret!'

'Indeed,' said James, laughing in his turn. 'But he did give me some information which might persuade you to change your plans a little. But first, I must ask you another question. I take it that you do not intend to live permanently with the gypsies, and if so, what was your destination? How could you hope to keep your – and the lady's whereabouts – secret?'

There was colour in Luke's cheeks for the first time. 'I suppose that I had better tell you. We were making for Bristol to take ship to the Americas, where even Clairval might have found it difficult to track us down. I was going to send you a letter shortly before we boarded, informing you of my intentions. After all, as a writer, I follow a trade which I can practise anywhere, and the Yankees like writers, or so I am told.'

James said softly, 'You love one another so much, then?'

'Like Romeo and Juliet, or Orpheus and Eurydice, yes.'

'"The world well lost for love"?'

'What world for me,' retorted Luke hardily, 'without my dear Anne in it? What world if Clairval regained her? Tell me that. Do not try to talk me out of my intentions, Father. My mind is quite made up.'

'But if Clairval were disposed of, and Anne freed, you would not leave, I trust? There would be no need for you to cut yourself off forever from family and friends.'

'What hope of overcoming Clairval so easily? No, Anne and I must find somewhere where we can live together in peace.'

This came out with all Luke's new determination and hardihood. He was the cheerful dilettante no longer. If Lady Clairval had done this to him, thought James, then she would be a woman worth meeting.

'I think, Luke, from what the Runners have told me, that the secret of where you have hidden the lady is no secret. They seem to think that they know what you have done with her, and a secret, once breached, is a secret no longer.'

Luke threw off the bedclothes and made to rise from the bed, to leave Haven's End, to try to find her, to. . .

His father leaned forward and caught him by the wrist. 'No need for that. They tell me that you have left her with the gypsies. They believe that you were attempting to draw Clairval away from them and her. That you were acting as a decoy.' He could see by Luke's face that he was speaking the truth.

'How could they know? By what magic. . .?' He felt numb. He accepted that what his father had just said was true: a secret, once breached, is a secret no longer.

'No magic; something your friend Pat O'Hare told them when they interviewed him put them on the track.'

Pat, whose letter he had just read. Pat, who had betrayed him – and now, in a manner, had saved him. For if the Runners had not followed the gypsies – and then him – he would have lain rotting in the undergrowth, lost forever. Instead, they had found him and carried him to Haven's End.

'So,' he said, 'what follows? I suppose that, if chance could set the Runners on the right track, then it follows that chance might aid Clairval. . .'

'Indeed,' nodded his father. 'How long will it be before Clairval stops flailing about like a loose cannon on the gun deck of a crippled battleship, and stops to think?'

'But we may reach Bristol – and safety – before then.'

'And he will have driven you out of England. Listen to my proposition. I am prepared to use my standing and my wealth, to back you against Clairval. To take the lady into my care and do all that is necessary to gain her a divorce. Jenkinson assures me that he has enough evidence of Clairval's cruelties towards her to make that possible.

'Allow me to go to Bath tomorrow morning, for that is where Jenkinson says that the gypsies are encamped, and bring her to Haven's End, so that we may begin our campaign against him as soon as possible.'

Luke was throwing back the covers again. 'By no means. You shall not go without me, and if you insist on going to Bath, now that you know where she is, I shall go with you. For it is Anne, and Anne alone, who must make the decision regarding her future. After all, it is she who has borne the most unimaginable cruelties from him, and she who will suffer if your plan fails. That is as far as I am prepared to go to fall in with your wishes.'

He was standing up, shrugging off his nightwear, looking about for his clothes.

'You are not fit to get up now, or sit on a horse tomorrow,' protested his father.

'Nonsense. Where Anne is concerned I am fit enough for anything. A pretty fellow I should look to let a few bruises keep me from her.'

His head was swimming, but his will was strong. The glare he gave his father, who began to try to argue with him, was a powerful one. 'No, sir. I have always obeyed you in the past. I will not obey you in this. It touches both me, and the woman I love. Would you let another dictate your behaviour towards Cressy?'

That did it. James lay back in his chair and said with a resigned air, 'If you must, then, you may ride with me. But is it possible for you to ride so far? For we must ride. Jenkinson believes that time is of the essence.'

'Jenkinson? And what part do the Runners play in this, if I may be so bold as to ask?'

'They will not accompany us. They will go to Marlborough – for that was Clairval's destination yesterday, a decision made in their hearing – and they will start for there as soon as my plans are made, in order to follow him.'

'Our plans,' interjected Luke determinedly, '*our* plans, father.'

'Our plans, then,' agreed his father, coming at last to terms with a son whose will had become as stern and implacable as his own.

'And it is agreed that Anne shall decide as to our future plans, and that you will not seek to stop us if she wishes to leave for the Americas?'

'Agreed.'

Father and son faced one another on equal terms for the first time in their lives. Mutual respect now lay between them. The shadow of patronage in which Luke had always led his life had disappeared. To know that his father was with him, was his partner, and his friend was a happy feeling, which remained with Luke until he fell into a dreamless, poppyless sleep.

He could only hope that he would be strong enough by morning to allow him to ride to Bath, the gypsies – and Anne. . .

Chapter Fifteen

'Oh, they're beautiful, Mrs Chikno, quite beautiful! You're sure that you wish to give them to me?'

Mrs Chikno nodded shyly at Anne. 'The *chovihani* says that it is your birthday, that you have expressed a wish to possess a pack of tarot cards – and I possess two packs. This is an old one which belonged to my mother. Tawno gave me another, and it seems a shame that this should be hidden away unused. Take it with my blessing.'

Anne leaned forward and kissed Mrs Chikno on the cheek. It was her birthday and the gypsies had been bringing her small gifts all morning. They were encamped outside Bath and, in the distance, The Crescent shone white on the hillside above them.

She thought of all the grand parties and receptions to which Clairval had escorted her in the early days of their marriage. Parties attended by the whole of the fashionable world, and not once had she felt as happy and contented as she did today, sitting on the grass, her sewing in her hand among the unconsidered of the world in which she had once lived.

If only Luke were with her! The sun was shining, she was surrounded by love and friendship, her life satisfied

her, but without him. . . Oh, without him she was only
half a being. Nor did she even have the satisfaction of
knowing that he was safe from harm. But no one whom
Clairval thought of as an enemy was ever safe.

She bent her head and said a little prayer, asking
God to send him back to her soon. There had been
times when Anne's faith in God had faltered, but since
she had met Luke she had begun to recover it again.
Perhaps now that He had chastened her by allowing
her to marry Clairval, with all the dreadful consequences which had flown from that, God would allow
Luke a safe journey back to her.

She spread Mrs Chikno's cards on the grass, having
asked a question of them. The answer they gave
pleased her. Soon, they said, soon. Luke will return
soon.

Could she believe them? She knew that the gypsies
did. That they used them constantly, as they used the
divinatory powers of the *chovihani*. She sighed and
returned to her work. September it might be, but the
summer still seemed to be with them, and a perfect
peace had settled on the encampment.

Tawno and his fellow riders had gone into Bath so
that the gentry might inspect their cattle and possibly
buy some of them – although not the pride of Tawno's
troop. These he kept for himself and his better riders.

She was almost asleep when she heard the sound of
horses approaching; they were being ridden at speed.
Surely it could not be Tawno, back so soon? She sat
up, shaded her eyes from the sun and looked towards
them. It was not Tawno. It was a large party of
mounted men, followed at a distance by two chaises,
which stopped on the road when the riders left it in
order to gallop towards them.

'No!' cried Anne, jumping to her feet, her cry so

anguished that all the Romanies nearby turned to look at her and then at the approaching horsemen. 'Oh, no! It cannot be Clairval.'

But it was.

The *chovihani* was at her side in an instant. 'What is it, child? What do you fear?' And then, looking at the approaching horsemen, asked, 'Is it your husband?'

'Yes,' said Anne, despair engulfing her.

'Come, child, quickly. Let us hide you.'

She caught Anne by the hand and ran her towards a group of women who were preparing food outside one of the tents. She took a scarlet handkerchief from one of them, and twisted it around Anne's head. From another she took her gold necklaces and hung them around Anne's neck. There was a spent fire in the grass, she bent down, rubbed her hands in the ashes and smeared Anne's face with them.

'Off with your shoes and stockings.' The *chovihani* stood back to admire her handiwork. 'And now you are the very picture of a Rom. He will not know you, I am sure, even if you stood before him. Stay here among the women. Do nothing to draw attention to yourself. We shall deny all knowledge of Lady Clairval, and rightly so. You are Stella, Orion's mate. One of us.'

'But Luke?' cried Anne. 'What of Luke? Has he made Luke tell him where I am? Oh, what has he done to him?' She was shaking and shivering, once more the poor creature who had fled her prison at Clairval Castle, no longer Luke's happy and much-loved wife.

'Hush, child, hush. Luke would never have betrayed you. He is braver than that. No, your husband must have found out by some ill chance. But courage, we shall not surrender you. Get you in the middle of the women and you will be as one of them.'

Whilst they had been speaking, Jasper had walked

up to the leading riders to hold up a commanding hand as they sought to drive straight through the camp, disregarding women, children and the handiwork of the women spread out on the grass.

'Hold!' he shouted. 'What do you want with us?'

They stopped. Grudgingly.

The leading man dismounted. He was a portly gentleman, well turned out and he announced himself with all the customary arrogance of a minor jack-in-office.

'I am Sir Christopher Cave, magistrate, of the City of Bath, and I am come here with, and on behalf of, the Most Noble the Marquess of Clairval, to recover his wife, whom he has good reason to believe is hidden among you. These men with me are my officers.'

'So, then,' replied Jasper, equally arrogant, 'it is he with whom I will deal, and not you.'

'You mistake, you vagabond. It is I who am the law here, and m'lord Clairval has rightly called upon me to administer it.'

'No, *you* mistake. You are on the heath, and in the camp of the Romanies, and it is I who am the law. Nevertheless, I will speak to this man who has lost his wife, if he has the courage to face me and explain why and how he lost her – and why he thinks that she is here.'

Anne was near enough to them to hear what they were saying. She had also seen that several men had left the chaises parked on the road, had taken horse and were riding towards Jasper and Sir Christopher. One of them, she was sure, was Clairval.

She was not mistaken. He arrived at the gallop, surveyed the scene before him contemptuously, and barked at Sir Christopher, 'Well, man? Has he not surrendered my wife to you yet?'

'He refuses to speak to me at all, since I am not the

complainant,' returned Sir Christopher, somewhat plaintively, 'although I have assured him that I am the law. . .'

'Well, be damned to that,' roared Clairval. 'What the devil was the use of bringing you along if you were going to bleat at every dirty gypsy who chooses to bandy words with you! Fernando,' he bellowed at that gentleman who had carefully walked his way towards the centre of interest. 'Be ready for me, should I need you.

'Now, you piece of filth,' he bellowed unpleasantly at Jasper, who was still standing, face inscrutable, staring at him. 'I am Clairval. I believe that you are hiding my adulterous and runaway wife from me. The law says that she is mine to claim, and yours to surrender. Bring her out immediately, or it will be the worse for all of you.'

He had ridden his horse in front of Sir Christopher's and rose in the saddle to stare menacingly down at Jasper, his face even more purple than usual. His anger was a living thing, hanging in the air above Jasper.

But Jasper was in no wise daunted. He did not retreat so much as a step. He merely held his ground, stared up at m'lord Marquess, and said, his voice cool, 'I assure you, m'lord, that I harbour no Lady Clairval in this camp.'

This almost brought a hysterical choked laugh from the listening Anne. For was not Jasper's apparently massive untruth, a truth? For it was not many weeks since he had divorced her from the angry man in front of him and turned her into Luke's wife.

By the laws of the Rom, that was. Not by the laws of Sir Christopher and his kind.

Clairval was no fool. He was not deceived. He raised

his hand, and shouted, 'Do not palter with me, man. Give me back my wife, or it will be the worse for you.'

Jasper slowly turned around. He looked at the silent women, at the children, some of them whimpering a little as they felt the hostility which surrounded them, and then renewed his gaze on Clairval.

'Why, sir, I see no Lady Clairval among us. Nor, I think, do you.' For he was certain that the *chovihani* would have arranged matters so that Anne could not be identified.

'And what kind of an answer is that? Sir Christopher,' Clairval announced, turning his feral eyes on that shivering functionary who was rapidly seeing his authority draining away from him, usurped by Clairval. 'I shall order your constables and my men to raze this camp to the ground so that my wife may not be hidden from me, seeing that their leader – for so I suppose this clown to be – will not answer me straight and fair.'

'Oh, I only do that to those who speak to *me* straight and fair,' announced Jasper, still standing his ground despite Clairval's threats.

Clairval leaned forward, his face dark and ominous. 'Little man, little man, I do not make idle threats. That is not Clairval's way. If you do not hand my wife over, I shall destroy this encampment utterly. Tonight you will truly lay your heads on the bare earth and lament that you gave refuge to a lying bitch of an adulteress.'

He meant it. Anne, of all of them there present, knew that Clairval meant it, that he was uttering no idle threat. He would destroy the gypsies' means of living without a thought – for that had become his way.

She shuddered. There was only one thing left for her to do. She thought of the gypsies and their kindnesses to her. Of the tarot pack that Mrs Chikno had given to her that very morning, of the joy which she had felt over the past weeks since she and Luke had joined them. Of Luke's new-found strength of mind, and of body, which had been enhanced by the time he had spent with Tawno and his men. Of her own happiness.

She closed her eyes. The *chovihani* looked at her, and divined her purpose. She said softly, 'No, child, no. We shall not give way to him.'

Anne shook her head. She knew the man before them only too well. He would leave the gypsies nothing: he would destroy them utterly. And she would be the cause of it. At whatever cost, she must stop him.

She rose to her feet and walked towards him. As she passed Jasper, he too, said, 'No, Stella, no,' but she shook her head again before coming to a stop just below Clairval, where he towered above them in all his pride of caste.

He looked down at her, a trifle puzzled. Anne knew at once that what the *chovihani* had told her was true. He did not know her. He did not associate Anne's golden glory of face and figure, her lustrous black hair streaming down her back, and her proud carriage, with the hunted and beaten creature he had driven from his home by his cruelties.

'M'lord, for I cannot call you husband,' she said. His whole bulky body came to attention when she spoke, and he recognised her voice – although he did not recognise her proud defiance: that was new.

'M'lord, there is no need to threaten these good people with the loss of their homes and their livelihood. At whatever cost, I am surrendering myself to you in order to prevent that.'

His whole face changed. He threw his head back and laughed. 'So, madam, they have turned you into one of them, a randy gypsy bitch indeed, I'll be bound, as brazen as they are. I shall have the greatest pleasure in taming you. The game is won. Fernando,' he bawled, 'you may take m'lady Clairval to the chaise.'

But Fernando was not paying attention. He was watching another large party approach them, a party which was arriving unheeded since the attention of both the Romanies and their would-be invaders was concentrated on the three principals in the action: Jasper, Clairval and Anne.

The new riders were cutting off the route to Clairval's two chaises, were galloping across the heath and were upon them, before any saw them. What new players in the game were these?

'You have not yet won, m'lord,' Fernando told Clairval, for he had recognised one of the leading riders as Luke Harcourt, last seen left for dead on the road to Haven's End.

What Fernando had not seen was that two other riders were approaching from quite the opposite direction, and were equally intent on arriving at the heart of the Romany encampment where Clairval and the Earl of Lyndale's party were now facing one another.

Luke and James had left Haven's End early that morning.

Something, he knew not what, was driving Luke on. In the night he had dreamed of Anne. She was looking even more of a Romany than she had done when he left her, and her arms were held out to him. She was pleading with him to come to her. He knew at once that she was in some kind of trouble.

The dream was so strong that when Luke had risen and walked painfully down to breakfast, he had said to James, 'Father, I know I may sound childish and odd, but I have the strongest feeling that we ought to set out as soon as possible for Bath. If we don't, we may be too late.'

James did not argue with him, merely ordered the head groom to have the horses ready for them within the next half-hour. He had decided to take along with him a goodly contingent of Haven's End's grooms and stable lads. Who knew what might be needed when they caught up with Clairval?

As they pounded along the rough roads towards Bath, Luke was so troubled by the premonition which would not leave him, and which told him that Anne was in real danger, that he did not feel the full pain of his bruised body. He only had one idea in his head: that he must reach Anne before Clairval did. For he was sure that the danger Anne was in came from Clairval.

Thus it was that when they galloped towards the heath where Jasper and the Romanies were camped, he was not surprised to see two chaises, with Clairval's arms emblazoned on them, standing in the road which led to it.

He ground out an oath, and forgetting pain, forgetting everything, turned and shouted at his father, 'We are too late. He is here, and, oh, God, I swear that she is surrendering herself to him!'

Father and son spurred their way forward at full gallop across the heath to reach the spot where Luke's dear love was on the point of accepting hideous captivity again for the sake of those who had been kind to her. Like Fernando, they did not see the two Runners approaching from the opposite direction. They were concentrating too hard on reaching Clairval and Anne before he had time to snatch her away.

On seeing them, Clairval, his expression uglier than ever, swore at Luke and James with such force that his horse became agitated, and he had difficulty controlling it.

'So, Lyndale, I see that you are a proven liar. You were concealing your rogue of a son whilst prating to me that you knew nothing of him! Well, you may leave, and take your by-blow with you. You are too late. Lady Clairval is my wife, my chattel, and she will return with me to Clairval Castle, where my physicians will decide what treatment she needs to restore her to her senses.'

Luke, who had flung himself from his horse to run to Anne, who was staring at him as though he were the god in the old Greek plays who had descended from heaven in a chariot to save the beleaguered hero and heroine, said savagely, 'No, Clairval. It is you who are too late. Anne will return with me to Haven's End. She needs no physicians, and you lie when you tell the world that she is mad – as all the good people assembled here will testify.'

There was a murmur of consent from the Romanies. Jasper Petulengro, not in the least put out by the presence of the new actors in the drama, nor intimidated by the aristocrats around him, said in his most composed voice, 'I wish to say only to you, Sir Christopher, that Stella here is as sane a lady as I have ever met. She needs no physician – only love.'

James and Clairval spoke together. James to say, 'I have decided that I shall offer Lady Clairval sanctuary and that I am prepared to help her to argue her case against you in every court in the land, if need be.'

Clairval's bellow was, 'Stella' And who the devil is Stella? Oh, I suppose you mean my slut of a wife.'

Pandemonium suddenly reigned. Luke, angered by the slur put upon Anne, let go of her, and seized Clairval by the leg in order to pull him from the saddle. Clairval, taken by surprise, lost his balance and, before he knew it, was on the ground with Luke now attempting to grasp him by the throat. Clairval's horse, already excited as a result of his master's capricious treatment of him, threw back its head, showed its teeth and, neighing madly, galloped at speed across the heath, away from the noise of the wrangling men, to disappear from view among the trees on its boundary.

'No,' exclaimed Jasper, as Clairval and Luke rolled, fighting, on the ground before him, 'There is no need for this.' He gave an order to the Romany men about him to pull the two combatants apart.

James had also dismounted, and watched whilst Luke and Clairval were separated, both of them glaring their hate at the other. The *chovihani* had come up to support her husband. She put an arm around Anne's shoulders to comfort her.

'Truly spoken, husband,' she said, her voice mild. 'The parties are at a stand off,' for James's small army had now arrived and was facing Clairval and Sir Christopher's followers, who had thus lost their ability to do as they wished to Anne and the Romanies without let or hindrance.

'Truly spoken, wife. It is stalemate, since I assume that neither Lord Clairval nor Lord Lyndale wishes to fight a pitched battle on the heath,' announced Jasper, putting himself on the other side of Anne.

'I remind you again,' he continued, 'my law rules here on the heath. I order that Stella, or Lady Clairval, whichever you care to call her, shall choose with whom she leaves.'

'No,' cried Clairval, who had wrenched himself free from the men who had been holding him. 'She is my wife. The law of the land is here in the person of Sir Christopher Cave, and he has already ruled that she will return with me.'

Not quite stalemate then, was Luke's wry response. He knew that any court in the land would rule that, as the case stood, Anne had no option but to return to her husband – as a moment ago she had been so prepared. Besides that, his father was a magistrate, sworn to uphold the law which Clairval was constantly invoking. Had he and Luke arrived before Clairval they could have taken Anne away and thus created a whole new situation: but they had not.

Triumph rode on Clairval's face. Improbably, given all that he was, and all that he had done, he had the moral and legal advantage – for what that was worth. For like pieces on a chessboard, pinned in an impossible position, all the actors in the drama had no immediate move which they could make to enforce their will on the others – short of a public brawl.

Except that God, or Fate, or Providence, call it what you would, had placed a pair of new pieces on to the board. The two Runners who had been sitting their horses at a little distance, unconsidered, whilst the drama was being played out, now moved into action.

Jenkinson rode foward until he was immediately before Clairval, crying, 'Hold a moment. I have a duty to perform which may settle this matter once and for all.'

'You?' snarled Clairval, his face even more scarlet with fury than before. 'What the devil are *you* doing here, interfering with me and mine? Be off with you, before I have Sir Christopher whip you from the heath.'

'Oh, I think not,' said Jenkinson, smiling, his revenge for all the humiliations he had suffered at Clairval's hands, now ready to be taken and savoured. 'Mr Luke Harcourt, I see that you are sufficiently recovered from the beating which m'lord Clairval ordered to be inflicted on you, for you to be able to ride here today to care for your lady.'

'My lady,' bellowed Clairval, 'not his.'

Jenkinson was not to be deflected. He had heard Clairval name Sir Christopher Cave, knew who he was, and now spoke commandingly to that somewhat bewildered gentleman who had come on what had seemed to be a simple errand, but had found himself in the middle of an almost feudal war.

'Sir, I take it that you are the magistrate from Bath enlisted to do this criminal's dirty work,' and he waved at Clairval. 'Take note that I, a Bow Street Runner, carrying the commission of the Home Secretary, am serving a warrant on m'lord Clairval, and his servants George Fernando and Jem Haskins, and other person, or persons unknown, for assault and battery on the person of Mr Harcourt, done in the presence of myself and my companion here,' and now he waved at Greene.

'Also take further note that it is your duty to convey m'lord Clairval to the gaol in the precincts of Bath, there to await the arrival of officers of the law from London who will convey him to the capital to stand trial for that assault before his peers in the House of Lords. His servants will be dealt with in the appropriate court.'

He paused dramatically. Clairval, now almost black in the face, swung on Sir Christopher, shouting, 'The man's mad! How dare he speak thus to me? Take heed that, if you obey him, I shall make sure that you never hold office again.'

'I have not finished,' said Jenkinson. 'Take heed of *me*, Sir Christopher, for I am now serving a warrant on m'lord Clairval, which commands you to arrest him for the murder of his steward in the county of York some time during the summer of 1826. This warrant is to be added to the one concerning Mr Luke Harcourt, and thus it is your double duty to commit him at once to prison.

'Here are the warrants, signed by the Home Secretary and duly attested and sealed. Here also is a further warrant relating to m'lord's treatment of m'lady, but that I shall not read aloud for very decency's sake. Sir, do your duty.'

Dazed, Sir Christopher took from Jenkinson the three warrants which he was holding out. During the whole of Jenkinson's announcement there had been a deathly quiet. Every eye had been upon him.

Luke, who was by Anne's side again, an arm round her, felt that he wanted to cheer as Jenkinson threw his grenades, one by one, at Clairval's feet. He could see his father smiling in relief. Anne was whispering to him, 'I don't understand, Luke. How did they find out what he had done?'

Before Luke could try to answer her, Fernando was the first to break. He began to run across the heath at top speed, only to be tripped up, and then sat upon, by several of the Romanies. Clairval, his face working, swung on that broken reed, Sir Christopher Cave, again.

'You cannot believe this piece of scum. He has no authority to demand that you arrest me, and my servants. I defy him to do so.'

Sir Christopher, who had been reading the warrants, said unhappily, 'Alas, m'lord. These documents are all in proper form, and signed by the Home Secretary as the man has said. I have no alternative but to execute them, and convey you to the gaol at Bath. . .'

He got no further. Clairval, his face now almost black, so suffused was it with blood, his eyes wandering, his mouth twisted, and his voice almost unintelligible, cried out in a faltering voice, 'No, you cannot. . .' and he threw up his arms in supplication. In his despair, he appealed to James as a fellow peer to help him, even though he had so recently treated him as an enemy.

'Lyndale, I beg of you, you must assist me. . .' But before James could reply, as though his mind, like his eyes, was wandering, unable to fix itself on anything, Clairval turned his distorted face on Anne again.

'It is you who have done this to me, and you. . .' and he pointed at Jenkinson who leaned forward in the saddle to say softly to him.

'You should have treated me fair. . .but you did not.'

Clairval took no heed of him. For a moment he stood silent. He was now facing Anne and Luke, his hands outstretched towards them, foam on his lips, his eyes wild, his face working. He began to walk towards them, but before he reached them he gave a great cry and pitched to the ground at their feet. To lie there, unmoving, blood running slowly from his mouth.

Jasper's curse delivered on the day of Anne and Luke's wedding had been fulfilled. He who had tried to part them had been struck down. . .

Chapter Sixteen

Later, much later, both Anne and Luke would look back on what had become their deliverance and wonder at what followed it. Surprisingly, in the seconds after Clairval's fall, there was a great silence before everyone began to crowd around the body to issue instructions, each according to his own nature and his official position.

James, the nearest to person to the stricken man, was the first to move towards him, only for Anne to run from Luke's side to fall on her knees beside the man who had so mistreated her, and who had intended to kill her as soon as she was in his power again.

He had been her husband, and before he had married her he had treated her kindly. Even though she knew that this had been done to deceive her, the essential goodness of Anne's nature warred with her sense of relief that her tormentor was either dead, or so injured in mind and body that he no longer presented a threat to her.

His dying eyes looked into hers. He seemed to be trying to say something to her. His mouth quivered a little before slackening. His whole body shuddered and then stilled in the finality of death.

It was over.

The long years of fear and pain were behind Anne, and now would never be renewed in a further imprisonment. Luke had bent down to lift her up, to take her away, so that Clairval might be examined in order to establish that he was really dead, although none who saw him stretched out on the grass, his face livid, could believe otherwise.

'Come away,' he said gently. 'His race is run, and so is your suffering at his hands.'

Anne clutched at him for comfort. To the surprise of both of them, tears began to run down her face. Luke wiped them away with a gentle hand, and said, 'You are surely not weeping for him?'

She shook her head, 'Oh, no. But, Luke, what a wasted life. He was never happy during the whole time I knew him. He seemed to be so for a little before we married, but afterwards, never.'

Sir Christopher Cave had dismounted and was supervising his officials. He would be responsible for reporting Clairval's death, and for all the local arrangements which would flow from it.

'God struck him down in his wickedness, m'lady, and called him to judgement,' he felt impelled to say to Anne. He had read the warrants detailing all the dead man's crimes, and had seen on Luke's face and body the marks of the brutal beating for which the dead man had been responsible. He was regretting the ease with which he had allowed Clairval to deceive him as to his true nature – but who would have thought a Marquess to be such a wretch?

'Not God,' said Jenkinson, who had also left his horse, and needed to be present when Clairval was officially reported to be dead. 'Not God, but he, himself, was responsible for his death. His rages and his foul temper brought him daily nearer to it. I have seen such a fatality from apoplexy before when a man has allowed his rage to overcome him.'

Both James and Luke looked sharply at him. Neither said anything, although both thought of the glee with which Jenkinson had produced his warrants and how his taunting words had so fuelled Clairval's anger that they had brought about the final outburst which had killed him.

Luke had a duty of gratitude to perform. He held out his hand to Jenkinson and said, 'I understand from my father that I owe my life to you and your companion – and perhaps a little to Pat O'Hare, who put you on my trail. We – that is, Anne, the Romanies and I, thought that you were following us in order to arrest me for kidnapping Lady Clairval.'

'That weren't nohow, Master Luke. Once m'lord turned me off, he was always my target. I learned too much about his wicked ways when I was working for him. It is a blessing that he was struck down when he was. A blessing, indeed. His sudden death has saved us all a deal of trouble, expense and scandal – you and the lady most of all.'

'How much did my father know of this?' asked Luke shrewdly.

'Why, as to that, not much. Enough. Naught about the warrants. As for you, Master Luke, it was a pleasure to save a man who took his punishment so bravely and never said a word, or did aught to stop it by blabbing all. You and your lady should be happy together. You make a gallant pair, for she was ready to give herself up to the monster who was after her in order to save those who had given her a refuge.'

Anne hid her face in Luke's chest on hearing Jenkinson praise her. She lifted it to say, 'I deserve no thanks for trying to help those who had sheltered me and made me happy, but it is kind of you to say so. You are the one who is to be thanked, for pursuing my husband for his crimes when many would have allowed his rank to deter them.'

'My duty too, m'lady.' Jenkinson was thinking how well everything had gone for him. So far, that was. There was still Sir Christopher to square. He took that gentleman on one side, said, a confidential expression on his face, 'Very fortunate for you, sir, that m'lord dropped dead when he did.'

'Eh, what's that, man?'

Jenkinson sighed. So the ass wanted chapter and verse, did he, before common sense struck him on the head?

'Saved you and the nobility and gentry from another nasty scandal, sir, to excite the mob and have them howling for blood and the guillotine. I'll lay odds Lord Lyndale won't want a noise made about this.'

'True, yes, very true.' Sir Christopher struggled this out unwillingly. 'But the accusations of murder, and the warrants. . .' His voice died away.

'Never got to serve them, sir, did you? Dead of excitement at the pleasure of finding m'lady, wasn't he, before you had time. . .?' He would have winked at Sir Christopher had he dared.

'Best you hand them back to me. I can restore them to my master and tell him as how they was never properly served.'

Sir Christopher's sense of expediency warred with his sense of what were his dues to the law as a magistrate. But Jenkinson had tipped the balance for him.

'Oh, very well – but the constables. . .what of them?'

'You're not short of a guinea or two, are you, sir?

And they are, if you follow me. Mum's the word, you know.'

Yes, Sir Christopher followed him. And so it was arranged. M'lord had been struck down even as he had found m'lady and the brouhaha on the heath had never happened. The nation's peace and civil order were preserved until another scandal came along – and Jenkinson had earned his reward. . .

The milling about Clairval's body had now ceased. His death was certain and Lord Lyndale, the senior magnate there, had decided that his body should be conveyed to Bath in the chaise in which he had arrived.

Jasper and the Romanies had stood silently by whilst the great men around them carried out the due processes of the law. Fernando, who was busy telling all he knew of his master's doings in an effort to save himself from prosecution for what he had done to Luke, was to be allowed to go.

'For,' said Jenkinson to Lord Lyndale and to Sir Christopher Cave, 'we none of us want what happened here today to be brought up in a court of law. The man who set all in train is dead and Fernando and his friends were but poor tools hired to do his dirty work for him. Let them go with a warning, I say. If I know aught, it'll be back to London for them all. No pickings for 'em in Bath, Sir Christopher.'

Both Luke and his father thought that it was a pleasure to watch such a master of intrigue at work. Even Anne said to Luke, 'I am glad that the foxy-faced man was on our side at the end. I don't think we should have been so lucky if my late husband had had the sense to let him keep charge of his affairs!'

A statement which convinced James that his daughter-in-law was clever as well as good. He now said quietly to Luke and Anne as they stood side by side, hand in hand, 'You will both of you, of course, wish to return to Haven's End with me. There is no bar now on Lady Clairval going wherever she wishes. Sir Christopher assures me that he will not have need of her in Bath.

'Her lawyers will have to be written to, and her position *vis-à-vis* her personal wealth will have to be clarified, and it will be easier for her to do that from Haven's End, or even Lyndale House in Piccadilly, than from a gypsy encampment.'

Anne gave a great sigh. She was back in the busy world of consequence again, and she must leave the Arcadia in which she had so briefly lived with Luke and the Romanies. Common sense told her that her place, and Luke's, was in that world, however much she might wish to retain the freedom of the heath and the road.

So all that remained was for Luke and Anne to say goodbye to the Romanies and thank them for the sanctuary they had so freely offered. Tawno Chikno and his men had arrived back just as Clairval's body was being carried to his chaise. He had offered his opinion to Jasper that he and his men would have seen the lot of them off if he had been present when the various parties had arrived!

'Then it was as well you weren't,' was Jasper's quiet reply. 'For all's well that ends well, particularly without bloodshed.'

A statement which was echoed by his wife. The *chovihani* looked at Anne's unhappy face, and knew the reason for it.

'Child,' she said, 'you must go back to your own world, although you and Orion will always find a welcome with us should you need one. But the stars tell me that you will not, that after sailing a stormy sea you have at last reached harbour.'

'Oh, I wish that I could stay with you.' Anne's eyes were bright with unshed tears. 'I have been so happy.'

'But you have only lived the sunny days with us, my child, not the cold and storms of winter. And you were not born to this life. Remember, you take my gift with you. Use it well, for to be aware of the true nature of others when it is needful is a gift worth preserving. The gift of love you and your man already possess.'

Anne did not need to be told that with Luke's arm around her. Together they gathered up their few possessions. Mrs Chikno came to kiss her goodbye and to tell her to consult the tarot cards whenever she needed an answer to a difficult question. 'Do not quite forget us,' she finished.

'Never, never,' was Anne's passionate cry. She kissed all the little ones whom she had been teaching to read and write, and handed over her unfinished sewing to Mrs Chikno to complete it for her.

James, Lord Lyndale, watching the Romanies come, one by one, to say farewell to his son and the woman he loved, found himself strangely moved. He was a hard man in many ways, although tender to those whom he loved, but the gypsies' farewell to Anne impressed him, there was such affection in it. He had spent some time wondering what the woman was like who had obviously been such a profound influence on Luke, and now he knew that his son had chosen well.

Finally Jasper shook hands with Luke and Anne, repeating what the *chovihani* had told Luke: that they were both welcome to return to his tribe whenever they so wished.

'And do not forget the tricks which Tawno taught you,' were his final words to Luke. He had arranged that one of the gypsy wagons would drive Anne and Luke back to Bath where James, who would accompany them on horseback, would hire a chaise to take them to Haven's End.

Alone at last, in the chaise, Luke's arm around her, her head resting on his chest, Anne gave a little laugh. 'Oh, Luke, life is so strange. Do you remember what you told me about the thimble-rigger and the way he tricked us at Islington Fair? And then you said that there was a similar game called Find the Lady? Isn't that what everyone who arrived at the gypsy camp was trying to do? Find the Lady – whom you and Jasper and the rest had so cunningly hidden away? When you rode away from the camp you were diverting everyone's attention just like the thimble-rigger did – and in the end it saved me.'

'Yes,' replied Luke, his face thoughtful. 'I suppose that you could say that the tricks at the Fair all have their parallels in real life – what a splendid notion for an article for Bayes! What a girl you are, Anne, I shall never lack for ideas with you near me,' and he rewarded her with a kiss.

Somehow, with Anne in his arms the journey to his home seemed all too short, when previously it had seemed too long!

James and Cressy sat on the terrace above the park, where earlier in the spring they had entertained Luke before he had returned to London. It was autumn now, the trees burning with red and gold, not the delicate green of the reviving year. No one then could have foreseen the dramatic events which would follow, nor the fashion in which Luke would return to Haven's End.

They were waiting for Anne and Luke to join them

for an *al fresco* meal. 'For,' as Cressy said, 'an informal setting will make matters easier for Luke and his lady than if we assembled around a strictly ordered dining-table.'

It was the day after they had brought Luke and Anne back to Haven's End. Cressy had taken one look at Anne's white face when she had walked into the huge entrance hall where a fierce dog embedded in a mosaic pavement guarded the house from danger, and said, 'My dear, I have prepared a room for you, and you may go there immediately to rest and recover. Luke, you look as though a good rest would benefit you as well. You may tell me of your adventures later.'

'I think,' said Luke, leaning forward to kiss his stepmother on the cheek, 'we ought to inform you straightaway that Anne is in no danger of being dragged back to imprisonment, so we may all rest quiet in our beds.'

'No chance of m'lord Clairval appearing to act as turnkey and gaoler, then?' asked Cressy.

'No, indeed.' It was Anne speaking, before she allowed a footman and a lady's maid to escort her to her room. 'My husband dropped dead of an apoplectic fit earlier today. I am free at last, but the manner in which I achieved my freedom was hardly one which I would have wished. I think that I always harboured the foolish hope that he might allow me to part from him voluntarily. Everything that happened today proved exactly how foolish it was.'

'Oh, you poor thing.' Cressy, always impulsive, always frank in her approach to life, put her arms around Anne and hugged her. 'And now you are here, you must try to forget all that has passed. I shall send a *tisane* to your room, and you must promise me that you will drink it. And Luke, too.'

She stood back before adding in her forthright way, 'I cannot say that I feel much sorrow over your husband's death. I met him on only a few occasions and he always felt it incumbent on him to insult me. And James, too. I suppose I shouldn't say that, one is never allowed to speak ill of the dead – a most foolish maxim in my opinion, particularly when the dead man behaved as badly as your late husband did.'

This spirited comment had all parties present suppressing a smile, and Anne, who had been a little worried about what the nature of her reception by Lady Lyndale might be, went to her room greatly relieved. Luke had told her that his stepmother was a clever lady of decided views, and was not afraid to air them. As usual, he had been speaking the truth.

James said gravely to his wife, when all the arrangements had been made for the care of the lovers, 'I'm afraid that you spoke truer than you knew of Clairval's villainy. This information is to remain private between the two of us, although I fear that it may yet become public knowledge. It seems that he murdered both his first wife and the steward who helped Anne to escape from her prison.'

'No surprise to me,' returned Cressy briskly. 'And now we must do all we can for Luke and his lady. You are agreed?'

James did not need to answer her, but he also felt that there were matters in the sorry affair in which his son had become embroiled which needed to be cleared up. Tactfully, of course.

The tact was in evidence on the next day when Anne and Luke, both looking refreshed, joined them on the terrace to eat their lunch and to sit in the sun afterwards, talking, apparently idly. Anne said little, content to leave conversation to the three others.

Luke was telling James and Cressy of their time among the gypsies. 'It was all very odd,' he said thoughtfully, after he had spoken briefly of gypsy magic and their belief in their ability to foretell the future, 'how everything worked out as the Romany fortune teller prophesied. It was enough to make one believe in them.'

'Oh, come, Luke,' said his father, that stalwart inheritor of the eighteenth-century Age of Reason with its dismissal of all things supernatural. 'Fortune tellers and prophecies, forsooth!'

Luke, now seated at Anne's feet, her hand gently stroking his head, read James's thoughts.

'Oh, I know that you are a sceptic, father, and that tales of magic and divination amuse you. But consider this. Jasper and the *chovihani* his wife, were insistent in their demands that I leave their camp to draw Clairval away from it and Anne.

'Jasper told me that not only was I needed to be a decoy, but that whilst I was acting as one I should be required to pass a test to save both Anne and myself.'

He paused. 'I don't think that I believed him. I went – but solely to act as decoy, nothing else. But you must admit that events fell out as Jasper foretold. The consequence of my side-tracking Clairval and passing my test was that his arrival in Bath was delayed. Thus, when he finally found Anne, he did so only shortly before you and I, and the Runners arrived to spoil his plans. Had we not done so, he would have snatched Anne back again.

'And that caused the rage and fury which brought him his death.

'So, Jasper was right. I had to pass the test to save her. And he and Tawno Chikno, their equestrian *extraordinaire*, had prepared me for it by making my life as hard as they could – they thought that I was a soft cit, you see, and they were right.'

Luke smiled up at Anne again. 'Anne will tell you that I can now perform the most remarkable feats on a horse. I could gain work at Astley's Amphitheatre tomorrow, I am sure.'

'True,' said Anne. 'He – and they – frightened me to death. The *chovihani* told me that it was necessary, but I did not know why.'

'To conquer fear,' said Luke soberly.

But Anne could see that they had not quite convinced James.

'More than that, m'lord,' she said quietly. 'When he married us, Jasper put a curse on anyone who would try to separate Luke and me. He said that they would perish by drowning in their own blood. And that was exactly what happened to my husband – as you saw.'

'Married you!'

Both Cressy and James were almost more struck by this piece of information than by Jasper's ability to foretell the future over the manner of Clairval's death. They both spoke at once. James was incredulous, and Cressy amused – although she did not allow her amusement to show.

'Well, he did divorce us first,' said Anne reasonably, her face a little pink, but 'Speak the truth and shame the devil', her father had always said. 'By Romany law, of course, which allowed him to divorce me from Clairval because of his cruelty to me. And Clairval did try to separate us, and he did die choking on his own blood.'

'Married!' pursued James. 'And you lived together as man and wife?'

He addressed this question to the air between Luke and Anne, looking at neither of them. Cressy, unknown to the other three was giggling internally, although nothing showed. My poor conventional James! What a turn up! Nice Luke, previously as conventional as his father, living among the gypsies and marrying his runaway love! Oh, how I should have liked to have been present when he did.

'Yes,' said Luke, looking his father in the eye. 'Jasper married us as soon as he saw that we really loved one another, and that I was a fit person to look after her. He took some convincing of that, I can tell you. After all, they had given us sanctuary and we were living by their law.'

For some reason, Anne began to find this whole conversation amusing. The rules which governed the conduct of those who lived in the polite world seemed to be the silly ones, not those of the Rom. She was cautious enough not to say so, and careful not to catch Cressy's eye. She had the impression that Cressy's notions of commonsense living might be a little different from those of her husband.

'Of course,' Luke went on, 'now that Clairval is dead, Anne is free, and we are back in polite society again, we do intend to go through a formal marriage ceremony first – before we live together, that is.'

This offering was intended to placate his father, and assure him that he and Anne were serious in their love for one another, and were not engaging in a passing affair.

'No reflection on the Romanies and their marriage laws, you understand, merely an acknowledgement that our laws demand it,' he added. 'We must always remember that they helped to save Anne's life when they gave her refuge, and were willing to sacrifice themselves when Clairval arrived at their camp and demanded her back.'

'You haven't proposed to me formally since we left the gypsy camp, have you, Luke? But, seeing that I am already your wife, you hardly needed to. Of course, I shall remarry you, by English law this time – to satisfy the proprieties.'

If there was a touch of satire in this last statement, then Anne thought that she might be forgiven it. After all, the proprieties had done precious little for her whilst she had been undergoing Clairval's persecution!

'At once, if not sooner!' Luke replied, his eyes on her brimming with love. 'I shall travel to London tomorrow, haste, post haste, and obtain a special licence so that we may be married on my return. We shall attract less notice if we marry quietly, here at Haven's End.'

'She's but a new widow. . .' began James, and then faltered to a stop. He knew that it was his last attack on an impregnable position, and he was not sure that he wanted to win it.

'No one would expect my dear Anne to go into mourning for a husband who had repeatedly abused her and had tried to kill her. It would be eccentric in the extreme! Besides, I no longer have any respect for what our world considers *comme il faut*. It nearly condemned Anne to an early death.'

There was no denying that. Luke said into the silence of agreement, for he wished to be alone with his love a little before he left for London, 'Pray allow me, Cressy and you, sir, to take Anne on a tour of the grounds. I have told her more than once how beautiful they are.'

His father and stepmother watched them walk down the terrace steps and into the park.

'He has chosen well,' said James. 'What a fool her first husband was, to value her only for her money.'

'Neither the first nor the last,' returned Cressy.

'I am a little worried about how Luke will feel about marrying an heiress.'

'No need to worry,' said Cressy. 'Just trust Luke – and the lady. She seems to possess a deal of common-sense, which is surprising in one so young.'

James nodded his agreement.

'What is it, Luke?' Anne's voice was gently probing. She knew him well enough to be aware that, happy though he was that Clairval no longer stood as a barrier between them, something was troubling him a little.

It was. Earlier that day James had said to him, apparently casually, 'Coutts tells me that for the last three quarters you have not touched the allowance which I have settled on you. May I ask why?'

'You may, sir. I had been meaning to speak to you of this: but in all the brouhaha of the affair with Clairval it had slipped my mind. I have decided that I must live on what I earn, not on you. I have depended on your kindness and your generosity for too long. I must make my own way in the world. By my writing, which, as you must be aware, has grown increasingly more successful of late. Successful enough, I believe, to enable me to keep a wife.'

'Yes.' Cressy had handed him Luke's novel to read and its power had surprised and impressed him. Everything about Luke was surprising and impressing his father these days. He was a changed man, and the change was for the better.

'The thing is,' James had said gravely, 'that I would wish you to have the money. For my sake, not yours. I am only too aware that if in the past, matters had fallen out a trifle differently, you would have been my heir. Allow me to continue your allowance – you need not touch it, you may let the capital accumulate. It will be there for you should you ever need it.'

He had given a half-laugh. 'Not that you will. You are marrying an exceedingly rich woman, have you thought of that?'

'Yes,' Luke had said, looking away from his father. 'Not until Clairval dropped dead, that is – but his death did more than simply provide me with the opportunity to marry Anne.'

His father had been able to see that Luke had been troubled, but he had not pursued the matter further. Luke had cut himself free from his dependence on Haven's End and all that it stood for, and he must allow him to go his own way, and make his own decisions. . .

Luke was back in the present again. He was out in the open with his love, and, perhaps symbolically, they had reached the very limits of the park and the open country was before them. Beyond the boundary fence lay coarse grassland, scrub and a dark wood. Luke flung himself on the ground, and drew Anne down beside him to kiss her.

'And that is all we may allow ourselves to do for the present,' he told her regretfully. 'For, out of respect for James and Cressy's feelings, we must behave ourselves until we are married. Romany weddings and divorces forsooth, I can hear my father saying.'

Anne rearranged her dishevelled clothing. 'It won't be long,' she said practically. 'Although I think it a great nonsense, all the same. Jasper well and truly married us, but I suppose that we need the law to secure our children's futures.'

Luke kissed her again. 'So pleased to learn that you propose a family, madam. In a sense, that is what is troubling me. You are so filthy rich, and I really don't want your money.'

'Oh, that,' said Anne dismissively. She knew that he was speaking the truth, and loved him for it.

'Yes, that.' He paused and began to laugh at the determined expression on her small face. Behind her air of demure rectitude and inborn modesty Anne possessed a spirit and determination allied to a forth-rightness that had sustained her through Clairval's long persecution and its aftermath.

'You see, Luke, I have been thinking. There is so much to do, so much to think about. I want to visit Islington to thank kind Mrs Britten and to see poor Dizzy again. I hope that he hasn't missed me too much. I enjoyed our simple life together on the road and the heath, and I want to come to live with you in your little house in Chelsea and look after you while you earn our living. You will earn our living, won't you, Luke?'

'Yes,' he said, taking her hand and kissing it. 'Now that we are not off to the Americas, I can take up Chapman's offer for another novel, and start on all the articles I have been asked to write by Bayes and the others. You don't mind being a struggling author's wife?'

'The *chovihani* and the tarot cards say that you won't struggle long. But even so, I would sooner struggle with you than live in the grandest castle. You see, I have decided that, with your agreement, my wealth must be put into trusts for our children and for the maintenance of the estate that I inherited on my father's death, keeping only a small income for us. But there is also another problem, which we shall have to solve together.'

'And that is?'

'Oh, it's the oddest thing, Luke. You see, Clairval

was the last of his line, and there was no entail, so our marriage settlement said that, if he died before me without leaving an heir, it would all come to me. He did it to spite the Crown which otherwise would have taken all.

'It's a strange irony, isn't it? He never thought that I would inherit because he was so sure that once married, he would soon have an heir. Consequently, when he dropped dead, I inherited everything. So we shall need another trust – if you so agree.'

Luke looked at her in awe. 'Did you think of all that by yourself? It's a splendid way out of being too wealthy!'

Anne leaned over to kiss him on the nose. She loved him as much for his goodness as she hoped he loved her for her attempt to live an honest life. She put up her hand to stroke, as gently as she could, the bruises plain on his face, mute witnesses of his determination to protect her from harm.

'Oh, Luke, all the time that I was with the gypsies, I was thinking about what to do with my money if I ever gained my freedom from him. I didn't want it to come between us, you see.'

'Nor shall it,' returned Luke happily. 'But I am a little worried that you might regret not living the comfortable life which your wealth would give you.'

Anne was silent for a long moment.

'Never,' she said at last. 'I was married to conse-quence and a title. We had money and comfort in plenty, and all was dust and ashes. Oh, Luke, do but remember what the Bible says.'

She began to quote a text from it, but before she had reached the third word his voice had joined hers, and they were reciting it together.

'"Better a dinner of herbs where love is, than a stalled ox and hatred therewith".'

Whilst they were speaking, they had stood up and were face to face, hands clasped. Luke leaned forward to kiss her.

'Dear Mrs Harcourt, for you are already my wife, I love and worship you, and is it any wonder that I cannot wait for us to be alone together with none to come between us? We have earned our happiness, and we must not waste it. I loved you long before I knew who you were. It was the penniless sempstress I wanted to marry, not Lady Clairval. My love who was so happy with me in the Romany camp.'

'Dear Luke. There is something else I must tell you. I was fearful that I might be the barren one, not Clairval. But there is another reason for us to marry soon. I am already breeding, or so the *chovihani* says, and we must make our child legitimate by English, as well as by Romany, law.'

Joy on his face, as well as in his heart, Luke kissed her again. 'Our wedding night!' he exclaimed exultantly. 'Is it possible that our child was conceived on our wedding night?'

'Yes,' said Anne, 'we were doubly blessed.'

They stood for a moment, silent before they began to walk together into the future, where quiet contentment and fulfilment awaited them in the little house in Chelsea, not the alarums and excursions of the past year. . .

Above them, James and Cressy looked down on the lovers as they walked hand in hand across the grass towards the terrace steps.

'I wish them,' she said, 'all the happiness which you

and I have achieved. I cannot wish them more. I could bestow on them no greater blessing.'

'Amen to that,' James said.

So be it, and so it was.

The Passionate Friends
by
Meg Alexander

After living in southern Spain for many years, **Meg Alexander** now lives in East Sussex, although having been born in Lancashire, she feels that her roots are in the north of England. Meg's career has encompassed a wide variety of roles, from professional cook to assistant director of a conference centre. She has always been a voracious reader, and loves to write. Other loves include history, cats, gardening, cooking and travel. She has a son and two grandchildren.

Chapter One

1802

Elizabeth Wentworth gasped in dismay. "Judith, you can't mean it! Do you tell us that you have agreed to marry Truscott? I won't believe you!"

A slight cough from the third member of the trio of ladies seated in the salon of the house in Mount Street checked a further outburst for the moment.

Elizabeth looked at her sister-in-law in a mute appeal for support, but Lady Wentworth refused to catch her eye.

In the twelve years since her marriage, Prudence had mellowed, learning to control her temper. Hasty words could never be recalled, however much one might regret them later.

Now, heavily pregnant with her fourth child, she struggled to sit upright on the sofa, smiling at their visitor as she did so.

"When did this happen, Judith? How you have surprised us! We had no idea…'' Her voice was gentle, and the look she gave her friend was full of affection.

The effort to soften the impropriety of Elizabeth's reaction to Judith's news did not succeed. The younger girl jumped to her feet, and began to pace the room.

''Why did you accept him?'' she cried. ''Oh, Judith, he won't make you happy. Why, the man is a charlatan, a mountebank! I know that he is all the rage at present, with his fashionable sermons, but he doesn't believe a word of them. For all his talk of hellfire and damnation, he likes nothing better than to mix with the very society which he affects to despise.''

''Elizabeth, you go too far!'' Prudence said sternly. ''Pray allow Judith to speak at least one word. You might also pay her the compliment of believing that she knows her own mind.''

Elizabeth looked mutinous, but she held her tongue as she flung herself into a chair.

''Pru, don't scold,'' Judith said quietly. ''I knew that this must come as a shock to both of you. After all, the Reverend Truscott has never given me reason to believe that he had noticed me…that is, until these last few weeks.''

Elizabeth tensed, and seemed about to speak, but a glance from Prudence silenced her. Each knew what the other was thinking. It was less than a month since Judith had learned of her handsome inheritance from her mother's brother. Nothing had been expected from the elderly recluse, but he had surprised the Polite World by leaving his vast wealth to his only niece.

''I was surprised myself,'' Judith continued in her gentle way. She gave her listeners a faint smile. ''I am no beauty, as you know, and I don't shine in society. I find it hard to chat to people I don't know, and as for being witty…?'' She pulled a wry face at the thought of her own shortcomings.

''Dearest Judith, you underestimate yourself,'' Elizabeth exclaimed with warmth. ''Confess it! You have a wicked sense of humour. Why, on occasion have we not been helpless, all three of us, when you have been telling us your tales?''

''That's because I know you well, and I feel easy in your company. Your family has been so good to me… I still miss the Dowager Duchess dreadfully.''

''And she was fond of you.'' Elizabeth returned to the attack. ''What would she have said, I wonder, had she known of your decision?''

''She always wished me to marry,'' Judith said mildly. ''She was so happy for both her sons when they chose you and Prudence. She longed for the same joy for me.''

''That was different!'' Elizabeth said firmly. ''Judith, will you tell us that you have a *tendre* for this man?''

Judith coloured. ''Perhaps not everyone can hope to be as fortunate as you were yourselves…to find the one person in the world for whom you'd give your life.''

''Then wait!'' Elizabeth cried in an agony of mind. ''You are still young. There must be a dozen men more suitable than Truscott. Few could be less so. You haven't given yourself a chance.''

''I'm twenty-five, and I've had several Seasons. How many men have offered for me? No, don't bother to reply. You know that I didn't take, as the saying goes.''

''That's because you are so quiet. You don't give anyone a chance to know you. Dearest, we all love you. At one time we had hoped that you and Dan—''

"Elizabeth, that is quite enough!" At the mention of her adopted son, Prudence felt it wise to put an end to Elizabeth's incautious remarks.

Six years ago she too had hoped that Judith and Dan might make a match of it. She'd welcomed the growing friendship between the two young people, so different from her own fiery relationship with Sebastian, or Elizabeth and Perry's stormy wooing.

Judith and Dan would sit for hours, exchanging few words but evidently content in each other's company, as Dan drew his designs for improvements to the warships of the British Fleet, and Judith put her thoughts on paper.

Only with friends could she be persuaded to read her words aloud, but they were worth waiting for. Her pithy little vignettes describing the foibles of the world about her reduced her tiny audience to tears of laughter.

Now, at the mention of Dan's name, Judith started and turned her head. Naked emotion showed for an instant on her face, but it was quickly banished.

"How is Dan?" she asked in an even voice. Not for a second must she betray the wrenching agony of that final interview six years ago. These loving friends must never know how bitterly she regretted her decision to refuse the man she loved. They loved him too, and they would not forgive her.

"He's home at last," Elizabeth said with satisfaction. "He's changed, of course—quite the elegant man about town now that he is grown so tall and broad—but beneath it all he is still the same old Dan."

Judith felt a twinge of panic. She must not see him, especially now when she had steeled herself to wed the

Reverend Truscott. That would be a refinement of torture. She rose to take her leave.

"Do stay!" Elizabeth begged. "The men will be
home quite soon. Perry and Sebastian will be sorry to
miss you, and you haven't seen Dan for years—"

"Judith may have other appointments," Prudence
broke in swiftly. She was well aware of what had happened all those years ago. Had she not spent months
listening to an inconsolable Dan? How she'd struggled
to provide him with diversions, but nothing had served
to comfort him. In the end it was Sebastian who had
suggested a solution. Dan had been accepted as a chart-
maker on a trip to the Antipodes. To part with the boy
she'd first known as a terrified nine-year-old foundling
had been a wrench, but Dan had welcomed the suggestion, and therefore she'd agreed to it.

Judith would not be swayed. She drew on her gloves
with what she hoped was not unseemly haste. Then she
looked down at the anxious faces of her friends.

"My dears, you must not worry about me," she said
quietly. "I am persuaded that this is for the best. I shall
have my own home, and hopefully a family. That must
count for something…" Her smile wavered only a very
little.

Judith's expression cut Elizabeth to the heart. She
flung her arms about her friends.

"Promise me one thing," she cried. "Don't set your
wedding date just yet! Give yourself time to consider…"

"I have considered," Judith replied. "We are to wed
in four weeks' time…"

"Oh, no—!" Whatever Elizabeth had been about to
add to this unfortunate remark was stilled as the door

to the salon opened, and three gentlemen entered the room.

It was obvious at once that two of them were brothers. The family resemblance between Sebastian, Lord Wentworth, and the younger figure of Peregrine was strong. Both men were well above the middle height, and powerfully built, though Peregrine topped his brother by an inch or two. They had the same dark eyes, strong features, and a decided air of authority. Perhaps it was something in the clean lines of the jaw, or a certain firmness in the mobile lips which did not invite argument.

Now both men were smiling as they led their companion towards Judith.

"Here is an old friend come to greet you," Peregrine announced cheerfully. "He is grown so large that I shall not wonder if you do not recognise him."

Judith was forced to proffer a trembling hand, but she could not meet Dan's eyes. Then the familiar head, topped with a mass of red-gold curls, bent to salute her fingertips. Dan stopped just short of pressing his lips against her skin. The gesture was all that courtesy demanded, but the touch of his hand was enough to set her senses reeling.

She drew her own away as if she had been stung, but Dan did not appear to notice.

"I hope I find you well, Miss Aveton," he said with cool formality.

Elizabeth looked startled. "Great heavens, Dan, what is this? You are grown mighty high in the instep since you lived among the aborigines. This is our own dear Judith. Have you forgot?"

"I have forgotten nothing." He laid no stress upon

his words, but Judith understood. The wound had gone too deep. She would not be given an opportunity to explain, and perhaps it was better not to try. They must go their separate ways, though the thought of her own future filled her with despair.

Later she could not remember how she got herself out of the room and into her carriage. She had some vague recollections of promising another visit, but her head was spinning. It was all she could do to take her leave with an exchange of mechanical civilities, struggling for self-control until she could be alone.

As the door closed behind her, Peregrine looked at his wife.

"Well, my love, had you not best tell us all about it? I know that look of old. Something has happened to distress you—"

"Judith is going to be wed," Elizabeth said flatly.

Sebastian smiled at her. "That, surely, is a matter for congratulation, is it not?"

"No, it isn't!" Elizabeth cried. "Oh, Perry, you won't believe it! She is to marry that awful creature, the Reverend Truscott."

"My darling, I hope that you did not tell her of your views. It must have been her own decision, and hardly your concern."

"It *is* my concern. Judith is my friend. I can't bear to see her throw herself away on that…that snake!"

"These are strong words, Elizabeth." Sebastian's smile had vanished. "The man is a well-known preacher. Why have you taken him in such dislike?"

Elizabeth glanced at her husband, and knew that she must speak with caution. Perry's temper was as hasty as her own. She must not mention the leering looks with

which the preacher always greeted her, the silky mur-
murings in her ear with offers to counsel her alone, or
the fact that the Reverend Truscott always held her hand
for much longer than courtesy demanded.

"I don't quite know," she murmured. "I find him
sinister. There is something of the night about him."

"It must be your imagination, dearest." Perry took
Elizabeth's hand. "I suspect that you have no wish to
lose your friend to anyone."

Sebastian looked at Prudence. "You are very quiet,
my love. Have you no opinions on this matter?"

Prudence was struggling with her own emotions. She
knew Dan's heart almost as well as she knew her own.

Dan had stiffened for just a moment at Elizabeth's
news, but when she forced herself to glance at him his
expression was carefully neutral.

"Judith's announcement came as a shock to us," she
said lightly. "We had no idea, you see, that Mr Truscott
thought of Judith, or she of him. He gave no indication
of any special attachment to her."

"Until she became an heiress," Elizabeth cried
fiercely. "Can you be in any doubt of the reason for
this sudden offer?"

"My darling, that is unfair," Perry protested at once.
"We all love Judith for her special qualities. I wonder
only that she had not wed before."

It was at this point that Dan excused himself, with a
muttered explanation of a forgotten engagement. He had
grown so pale that the freckles stood out sharply against
his fair skin, and there was a strange, lost look in his
blue eyes.

"Everyone is behaving so strangely today," Elizabeth complained. "What ails Dan? Have I said something to upset him?"

"Perhaps he doesn't care to listen to gossip," Prudence soothed. "He is still out of things as yet. He doesn't know the people of whom we speak."

"He knows Judith. I should have thought that he'd like to know about the man whom she is to wed. Oh, Prudence, now that he is back, do you think that she will change her mind?"

"I doubt it. She seemed quite determined."

"Then something must have happened to persuade her. I'd lay odds that her frightful stepmother is behind all this. That woman should have been drowned at birth!"

Prudence felt unable to argue. She was well aware that it was Mrs Aveton's violet opposition to Dan's suit which had caused so much unhappiness between the two young lovers all those years ago. The woman had conducted a campaign of hate, telling all her acquaintances that Dan was naught but a penniless foundling, sprung from who knew what vile slum in the industrial north of England.

Her venomous tongue had done its work. Dan had been cut dead by certain members of the *ton* on more than one occasion. His friendships fell away, and Prudence had been surprised to find that he was no longer included in the invitations which reached her daily.

She had made it her business to find out why, and when she had discovered the truth she confronted Mrs Aveton. It had been an unpleasant interview, with protestations of innocence on the lady's part, and Prudence in such a towering rage that Mrs Aveton was forced to retract her slanderous remarks.

By then the damage was done, and Judith could bear it no longer. Though it broke her heart to do so, she had sent Dan away, vowing as she did so that no other man for whom she felt the least affection would be subjected to such inhuman treatment.

Dan had fought her decision with everything in his power, but she would not be swayed. His honour and his good name were at stake.

She placed no reliance on Mrs Aveton's promise not to return to the attack. Her stepmother's machinations might become more subtle, but they would not cease.

Now, as Judith was borne back to the house which she shared with her two half sisters and their mother, she regretted the impulse which had taken her to Mount Street that day. Prudence and Elizabeth had been shocked by the news of her betrothal. That much was clear. How could she explain the reasons which had led to her decision?

The news of her inheritance had caused uproar within the Aveton family, though the money was to be held in trust for her unless she married. True, she might use the income from it as she wished, but she might not touch the capital.

Mrs Aveton had spared no pains to discover if it was possible to break the terms of the old man's will. When Judith's lawyers explained that this could not be done, the girl had been subjected to a series of merciless attacks. They had continued until Judith began to fear for her own sanity.

There was nothing she could do. A woman of her age might not set up her own establishment, even had she the means to do so. The constant quarrelling caused her to retreat even further into her shell. Until today she believed that she'd succeeded in crushing her emotions to the point where nothing mattered any more.

Yet it wasn't entirely out of desperation that she'd accepted the Reverend Truscott's offer for her hand. She'd been moved by his kindly interest in her, and the way he took her part against her stepmother.

Mrs Aveton had seemed a little afraid of him. Certainly the preacher's tall cadaverous figure was imposing. Dressed always in funereal black, when he thundered forth his exhortations from the pulpit the deep-set eyes held all the fire of a fanatic.

Yet, to Judith's surprise, Mrs Aveton had welcomed his suit. Perhaps she welcomed the opportunity to be rid of a girl who was a constant irritation to her.

Judith walked across the hall, intending to seek the sanctuary of her own room. Her thoughts were in turmoil. The sight of Dan had brought the agony of her loss flooding back again. She had deceived herself into thinking that she had succeeded in forgetting him. Her present pain was as raw as it had been six years ago.

A footman stopped her before she reached the staircase.

"Madam has asked to see you, miss, as soon as you returned."

With lagging steps, Judith entered the salon, to find Mrs Aveton at her writing desk.

"There you are at last." There was no note of welcome in her stepmother's voice. "Selfish as always! Had you no thought of helping me to write these invitations?"

"I'm sorry, ma'am. Had you mentioned it, I would have stayed behind." Judith glanced at the pile of cards.

"So many? I thought we had agreed upon a quiet wedding."

"Nonsense! The Reverend Truscott is a man of note. His marriage cannot be seen as some hole-and-corner affair. It is to take place in his own church, and he tells me that you are to be married by the bishop."

"He called today?"

"He did, and he was not best pleased to miss you. One might have thought that you would wait for him. What an oddity you are, to be sure! You take no interest in arrangements for the reception, the food, the musicians, or even in your trousseau."

"I shall need very little," Judith told her quietly. "Ma'am, who is to pay for all this? I would not put you to so much expense."

An unbecoming flush stained Mrs Aveton's cheeks. "The expense must fall upon the bride and her family, naturally. When you are wed, your husband will control your fortune. The creditors will wait until then."

"I see." Judith realised that she herself was to pay. "Shall I finish the invitations for you?"

"You may continue. Dear me, there is so much to do. My girls, at least, are pleased with their new gowns."

Judith was silent, glancing down at the list of names upon the bureau. An exclamation escaped her lips.

"Well, what is it now?" her stepmother cried impatiently.

"The Wentworths, ma'am? Lady Wentworth is with child. She won't be able to accept."

"I know that well enough. It need not prevent us sending her an invitation. I detest the woman, and that uppish sister-in-law of hers, but we must not be lacking in our attentions to Lord Wentworth and his family. I have included the Earl and Countess of Brandon, of course. My dear Amelia will be certain to attend.'' With this pronouncement she swept from the room.

As Judith walked upstairs she permitted herself a wry smile, knowing full well that Amelia, Countess of Brandon, would be furious to hear herself described in such familiar terms. Mrs Aveton was her toady, tolerated only for her well-known propensity for gossip.

Judith sighed. She liked the Earl of Brandon. As head of the Wentworth family and a highly placed member of the Government she knew him only slightly, but he had always treated her with courtesy and kindness. His wife was a cross which he bore with fortitude.

She removed her coat and bonnet and then returned to the salon. There she sat dreaming for some time, the pile of invitations forgotten. Her life might have been so different had she and Dan been allowed to wed. Now it was all too late.

''Great heavens, Judith! You have not got on at all.''

The door opened to admit the Reverend Charles Truscott, with Mrs Aveton by his side.

''Now, ma'am, you shall not scold my little bride. If I forgive her, I am sure that you may do so too.'' The preacher rested a benevolent hand upon Judith's hair, as if in blessing.

It was all she could do not to jerk her head away. She rose to her feet and turned to face him, but she could not summon up a smile.

''So grave, my love? Well, it is to be expected. Marriage is a serious step, but given to us by the Lord especially for the procreation of children. Better to marry than to burn, as the saying goes.''

Judith had the odd impression that he was almost licking his lips. Revulsion overwhelmed her. How could she let him touch her? Her flesh crawled at the thought. For an instant she was tempted to cry out that it had all been a mistake, that she had changed her mind and no longer wished to wed him, but he and Mrs Aveton had moved away. Now they were deep in conversation by the window. She could not hear what they were saying.

"The arrangement stands?" Mrs Aveton asked in a low voice.

"I gave you my word, dear lady. When the money is in my hands, you will receive your share." The preacher glanced across at his bride-to-be. "I shall earn mine, I think. Your stepdaughter is the oddest creature. Half the time I have no idea what she is thinking."

"That need not concern you, sir. Give her enough children, and you will keep her occupied, but you must bear down hard upon her radical notions. She likes to read, and she even writes a little, I believe."

"Both most unsuitable occupations for a woman, but she will be taught to forget that nonsense."

The Reverend Truscott glanced at his betrothed. There was much else that he would teach her. Judith was no beauty. The brown hair, grave grey eyes, and delicate colouring were not to his taste at all, but her figure was spectacular. Tall and slender, he guessed that his hands would span her waist, but the swelling hips and splendid bosom promised untold pleasures.

His eyes kindled at the thought, but the prospect of controlling her inheritance gave him even greater joy. He banished his lascivious expression and looked down at the list of guests upon the bureau, noticing at once

that there were no ticks against the names of the Wentworth family.

"My dear child, you must not forget to invite your
friends," he chided. "I know how much you think of
them, and I must learn to know them better."

"I could well do without the ladies of the family,"
Mrs Aveton snapped. "Lady Wentworth is mighty free
with her opinions, and as for the Honourable Mrs Peregrine Wentworth…? Words fail me!"

"A little…er…sprightly, perhaps? The privilege of
rank, dear lady. After all, we must speak with charity
of our fellow-creatures. And, you are friendly with the
Countess of Brandon, are you not?"

"She thinks no better of them than I do myself…"

Judith made an unsuccessful attempt to hide her
amusement. The animosity was mutual.

"There now, we have made our dear Judith smile at
last! Believe me, my love, your friends will always be
welcome at our home."

Judith gave him a grateful look. Perhaps he would be
kind. It was fortunate that she could not read his mind.
The Reverend Truscott knew an enemy when he met
one, and Prudence, Lady Wentworth, had left him in no
doubt of her own opinion.

He'd seen her look of disgust as he moved about
among his congregation, fawning on the women, and
flattering the men. She had surprised him once, when
he'd cornered one of his young parishioners beside the
vestry. He'd gone too far on that occasion, and the girl
was looking distressed.

Her ladyship had not addressed him, but her dagger-
glance was enough to persuade him to hurry away, leaving the girl to rearrange her bodice as best she could.

Mrs Peregrine was quite another matter. She was a beauty, that one, and he'd sensed the fire beneath the Madonna-like appearance. She hated and despised him. That much was clear. He could not mistake the expression in her huge, dark eyes, but her dislike only served to whet his appetite. He'd conquered such women before, with his talk of love and salvation. It would be a pleasure to add her to his list of victims.

Looking up, he caught sight of his reflection in the mirror, and felt his usual sense of satisfaction. His looks were the only thing for which he had to thank his actress mother and his unknown father.

Was he growing too gaunt? He thought not. His tall, spare figure and the dark head with the deep-set eyes and narrow jaw had just a touch of the fanatic. It was no bad thing. A certain air of the vulpine had served him well in his chosen profession. Who could resist him when he thundered forth his message from the pulpit?

He sensed that Judith was watching him.

"Forgive me, my dear," he said easily. "I should not have come to you looking as I do. My duties with parishioners have kept me out all day. You must think me sadly dishevelled, but I could not resist the temptation to call upon you."

"Judith thinks nothing of the kind," Mrs Aveton interposed. "It is good of you to call again, when this foolish girl was not here to greet you earlier in the day."

"Perhaps she believes that absence makes the heart grow fonder," the preacher chuckled. With many protestations of devotion he took his leave of them.

"You had best get on with the invitations, Judith. There is little time to spare before your marriage, and

I suppose we must do something about your trousseau. Tomorrow we had best go into Bond Street.''

Judith nodded her agreement.

However, on the following day, her stepmother lost all patience with her lack of interest in the garments offered for her inspection.

''Do pay attention!'' she cried sharply. ''Nothing will make you into a beauty, but you owe it to your husband to appear respectable.''

''Miss has a perfect figure,'' the modiste encouraged. ''She would look well in any of these wedding gowns.''

''Hold your tongue!'' Mrs Aveton glared at her. Her own daughters were both short and dumpy. ''I will decide upon a suitable garment.'' She settled upon a dull lavender which did nothing for Judith's colouring.

''This will do! And now I have the headache, thanks to your stupidity. The rest of your things you may choose for yourself whenever you wish. I have no time to accompany you again.''

Judith said nothing, though she felt relieved. The excuse to complete her shopping alone would get her out of the house, and away from the constant carping and criticism. She must take her maid, of course, but the girl was her only friend within the household, and she understood her quiet mistress well.

This fact had not escaped Mrs Averton's notice. She had already spoken to the Reverend Truscott on the subject.

On the following day she confronted Judith.

''You are grown too familiar with that girl,'' she said. ''You had best make it clear that she should be looking for another position after you are married. Your husband will not care to find you being friendly with a servant.''

''I had hoped to take her with me. She is the daughter of my father's housekeeper, and I've known her all my life.''

''Your father has been dead these many years. I should have dismissed her long ago.''

A lump came into Judith's throat, but she did not argue further. Her husband-to-be might view the girl more kindly.

Mrs Aveton glanced through the window. ''It may be coming on to rain,'' she said. ''I shall need the carriage myself this morning. You may walk to Bond Street. There is plenty of shelter on the way.''

Judith didn't care if it poured. She could use a shower as an excuse to stay out for as long as possible. She left the house as quickly as possible, and walked along the street with Bessie beside her.

''Miss Judith, it's spitting already. You'll get drenched. Must you go out today?''

''I think so, Bessie. Have you got the list?''

''It's in my pocket, miss, but it's coming on heavier than ever. Won't you step into this doorway?''

The wind was already sweeping the rain into their faces, and both girls ran for shelter. Half-blinded by the shower, Judith did not notice the hackney carriage until it stopped beside them. Then a strong hand gripped her elbow.

''Get in!'' Dan said. ''I want to talk to you.''

Chapter Two

Judith was too startled to do other than obey him. It was only when she was seated in a corner of the carriage that she realised the folly of her action.

She glanced up, a protest ready on her lips, but Dan was smiling at Bessie.

"I hope I see you well," he said kindly. "It's Bessie, isn't it? Do you remember me?"

"You haven't changed, Mr Dan. I'd know you anywhere."

He grinned at that. "Once seen, never forgotten? It's my carroty top that gives me away."

"Dan, please! I'm sorry, but we have so much to do this morning. I am to go to Bond Street. Bessie has a list..." Judith felt that she was babbling inanities. What did her shopping matter?

"Then Bessie can do your shopping for you. Your credit is good, I take it? She may order your things to be delivered..."

"No, she can't! I mean, that would not do at all. I am to choose...at least..." Her voice tailed away.

"Bessie, will you do this for us? I must speak to your mistress."

"No, you must not! Bessie, I forbid you…"

Bessie took not the slightest notice of her pleas. She was beaming at Dan, who had always been a favourite with her.

"I'll be happy to do it, Mr Dan."

"Then we'll pick you up on the corner of Piccadilly. Shall we say in two hours' time?"

"Dan, I can't! Please set us down. We shall be missed, and then there will be trouble."

"Nonsense! Prudence informs me that shopping takes an age. Besides, I can't wait outside your door indefinitely, hoping to catch you on your own."

"We might have met again in Mount Street," she protested.

Dan gave her a quizzical look. "Yesterday I had the impression that you didn't plan to visit your friends for some little time."

They had reached Bond Street, and he rapped on the roof of the carriage to stop the driver. Bessie sprang down, but when Judith tried to follow her he barred the way.

"Hear me out!" he begged. "It is little enough to ask of you."

Sensing his determination, Judith sank back into the corner. She had no wish to create a scene in public, and if he followed them someone of her acquaintance might see them together, and draw the wrong conclusions.

"This is folly!" she told him quietly. "You should not have sought me out."

"Folly?" Dan's smile vanished. "What of your own? What do you know of the man you plan to marry?"

Judith turned her face away. "He has been kind to me, and he stands up to Mrs Aveton. In his presence she is not so cruel."

"And that is enough for you? You have not asked yourself why they deal so well together? What a pair! The man is a monster, Judith! He is a charlatan...a womaniser—"

"Stop!" Judith's nerves were at breaking point. "You must not...you have no right to say such things to me..."

"Long ago I thought I had a right to tell you all that was in my heart. That is past, I know. I can't deny that our feelings for each other must have changed, but I may still stand your friend, I hope?"

"You have a strange way of showing it. Did Prudence and Elizabeth send you to me? I may tell you that I don't care to have my affairs discussed behind my back."

"No one sent me. I came of my own accord. They spoke of you, of course..."

"And obviously of Mr Truscott too. They are both prejudiced against him, but why, I can't imagine."

"Perhaps they see another side to his character. You meet him at his best, but how long will that last? If you become his wife you will be powerless against him."

"Dan, you are making him out to be an ogre. Oh, I know you mean it for the best, and I am grateful..."

"I don't want your gratitude," he muttered. "Like all your friends, I wish only for your happiness."

"Then believe me, you must say no more. You are but recently returned to England. How can you judge a man of whom you have no knowledge?"

"I trust Prudence, and Elizabeth too. They love you

dearly, Judith. Would they stand in the way of your happiness? Both of them have hearts of gold. Neither would be so set against this man without some sound basis for their feelings.''

''I have made my choice.'' Her face was set.

''Have you? Or have others made it for you? Forgive me, I don't mean to suggest that you are easily swayed. I know you better than that. You will always do what you think right.''

''Then why won't you believe me?''

Dan leaned back and folded his arms. ''You haven't told me why you wish to marry Truscott. I am told that he is all the rage among the *ton,* but that won't weigh with you, I know. To capture him might be a feather in some other woman's cap, but not in yours.''

''At least you don't insult me by suggesting it.''

''Kindness then, and protection from your step-mother? It seems poor enough reason to accept him.''

For once Judith lost her temper. ''You don't know what my life has been! How could you? It was bad enough before, but my uncle's money has become a curse. You heard of my inheritance?''

Dan nodded.

''I thought I would go mad,'' she told him simply. ''I was allowed no rest until I agreed to try to break the trust. It couldn't be done. Then matters grew much worse. Marriage seemed to be the only answer.''

Dan laid a sympathetic hand upon her own, but she snatched it away at once.

''I don't want sympathy,'' she cried in anguish. ''That only makes things worse…''

''Oh, Judith, was there no one else? Someone who might have made you happy?''

Judith felt like screaming at him. Of course there was someone else. Why could he not see it? Her situation was so different now. Years ago, when they were both penniless they could have no hope of marriage. Now she could offer him her fortune. It was a vain hope. Knowing him as she did, the money would prove to be an even greater barrier, even if he loved her still.

He didn't. Had he not mentioned that their feelings must have changed during their years of separation? His present concern stemmed only from the memory of past friendship, urged on, no doubt, by Prudence and Elizabeth, in spite of his denials.

She could not know of the discussion which had taken place the previous evening in the Wentworth home. In her forthright way, Prudence had tackled Dan outright, sweeping away his initial refusal to seek out Judith.

"Don't try to gammon me," she'd said. "I know that you still love her. You gave yourself away this afternoon. Will you stand by and let her throw herself away upon a man who will condemn her to a life of misery?"

"Pru, I can't. She would see it as a piece of gross impertinence on my part, and she would be right."

"Stuff and nonsense! I think at least that you should try to persuade her to reconsider. Elizabeth and I can do no good with her. She seems bent on self-destruction."

"And you think that I will fare better?"

"She loves you, Dan. She always has. I know Judith well. Once given, her affections will not change. If you were to offer for her now, all might yet be well."

She was dismayed to see the bitterness in his normally cheerful face.

"Would you have me add to my tarnished reputation? Must I be considered a fortune-hunter too?"

"So you will sacrifice your love for pride? I had thought better of you. Mrs Aveton's evil words were forgotten long ago."

"They would be recalled if I did as you suggest. Judith suffered enough before. This time I doubt if she could bear more slurs. I did not think her looking well at all."

"She isn't happy, Dan. At least see her. If nothing more you might persuade her to delay the ceremony. Truscott may yet betray himself." Prudence rose to her feet, pressing her hands against her aching back, and Dan gave her an anxious look.

"You shall not worry," he said. "It can't be good for you, especially at this present time. I'll do as you say if it will comfort you, though I think you are mistaken in what you say. Judith no longer cares for me."

Prudence let that pass. No words of hers would convince him. Dan must find out for himself. She smiled at him in gratitude.

"I think I must be carrying twins," she joked. "By the start of the seventh month I was not as large as this with my other children."

"Then you must take extra care. Shall you stay in London for the birth?"

"I don't know yet. It can be very hot and noisy in the summer months. Sebastian thinks that we should go down to Hallwood." She reached out a hand to him. "Dearest Dan, I've missed you so. It is so good to have you home again. As for Judith, I knew that you wouldn't fail me."

"Don't expect too much," he warned. "My powers of persuasion aren't as great as yours."

He found that he was right. Judith would not be swayed.

"At least postpone the ceremony," he urged. "It would give us time to make enquiries."

Her voice grew cold. "Are you suggesting that you intend to spy on my betrothed?"

"Judith, the man appeared from nowhere. I can't find a soul who knows anything of his background or his antecedents—" He stopped, and looked at her set face. "Forgive me! I, of all people, have no right to say such things. My own background is sneered at by the *ton*."

Judith fired up at that. "I hope you are not suddenly ashamed of it. Your mother and father were good country folk, as Prudence and Sebastian soon discovered." For the first time she gave him a faint smile. "Your skills must have come from somewhere…"

"Sadly, they haven't yet made my fortune but, Judith, we were not discussing my affairs…"

"Believe me, I prefer that you say no more of mine. Dan, it must be late. Is it not time to pick up Bessie?"

"Not yet. We still have a few moments. Will you promise me one thing?"

"If I can."

"Don't cut yourself off from your friends for these next few weeks. Come to Mount Street. The change will do you good. It will be like old times."

Her lips began to tremble. "I'm tired," she said. "I can't fight my friends as well as Mrs Aveton."

"Then they shall say nothing to distress you. I'll guarantee it. Do you promise?"

"I'll try." With an effort she regained a little of her

self-control. "You've told me nothing of your own concerns. This voyage has been of some advantage to you?"

Wisely, Dan accepted the change of subject.

"I learned much about the operation of a sailing ship, and other vessels too, even to the handling of an outrigger canoe in the South Seas. All are designed to take advantage of certain conditions of wind and weather."

"And your own designs? You were always inventing something."

"I have a thick sheaf of them. Some I sent back to England for the attention of my Lords of the Admiralty, but I have heard nothing."

"Wouldn't the Earl of Brandon mention your work?" she suggested shyly. "If Lord Wentworth were to ask him…?"

"I don't want patronage. My work must stand on its own merit, or not at all."

"You'll get there one day," she encouraged. "You have plenty of time."

"Have I?" His lip curled. "I am twenty-six already."

"A very great age indeed," she twinkled.

"Pitt was younger when he first became a Member of Parliament…"

Judith gave him a droll look. "I didn't know that you had the ambition to become a politician."

She'd hoped to cheer him, and was rewarded with a grin.

"I haven't, and well you know it."

Judith smiled back at him. "That's a relief! I was beginning to tremble for the future of the country. Oh, there is Bessie! I must leave you now."

"Not yet!" he begged. He tried to take her hand but she shook her head. With a sigh he stopped the coachman, and prepared to take up Bessie.

"We shall walk," Judith told him hurriedly. "The rain has cleared—"

"I won't hear of it. Get in, Bessie!" He rapped on the roof of the carriage to tell the man to drive on. As they entered the street where he had found them, Judith turned to him.

"Pray set us down here," she said. "If I am seen in your company there may be trouble."

When Dan returned to Mount Street it was to report the failure of his mission.

"Well, I, for one, will not give up," Elizabeth cried at once. "Will Judith come to us today?"

"I doubt it. She fears you will return to the attack." Dan's smile robbed his words of all offence.

"And so I shall."

"No, you will not, my darling." Perry gave his wife an affectionate look. "Subtlety is needed here. You cannot gain your way with confrontation."

His words brought a roar of laughter from each member of his family.

"Subtlety, Perry? Since when are you a master of the art?"

Perry took Sebastian's teasing in good part.

"I can be devious when I choose," he replied in airy tones. "I may surprise you yet."

"You have already done so. I was never more astonished in my life. Tell me, how is this subtle approach to be accomplished?"

"I haven't decided yet, but I'll think of something."

"Perry, there is so little time." Elizabeth's eyes were anxious. "The days go by so quickly, and Judith's wedding will be upon us before we know it."

Sebastian's eyes were resting upon his wife's face, and when he began to speak he chose his words with care.

"Let us consider this matter sensibly. We have no proof that the Reverend Truscott is other than he claims to be."

"We could find out," Dan said quickly.

Sebastian held up a hand for silence. "Hear me out. Prudence and Elizabeth both dislike and distrust him. They may be right, but if they are mistaken I must point out to you that Judith's happiness is at stake. Any interference on our part would be a serious matter."

"Sebastian, we have no wish to injure her." Prudence gave him a pitiful look.

"Dearest, I know that well enough, but Judith has had an unhappy time since her father died. We must be careful not to make things worse."

"They would be much worse if she married that dreadful creature!" Elizabeth was unrepentant.

"Quiet! The oracle is speaking!" Perry laid a finger against his wife's lips.

Sebastian laughed at that. "I'm no oracle, but we must do nothing foolish."

"Then what *can* we do? She may be walking blindfold into a life of misery. I won't stand by and let that happen." Dan ran his fingers through his flaming hair. "I'll abduct her first."

"You will do no such thing!" Sebastian's tone was cutting. "Would you expose her to scandal? Her life would be ruined; she would be cut by society, unable to see her friends and received by none. Let us hear no more of such nonsense.''

''There's no need to cut up rough at Dan, old chap. What do you suggest?''

''There can be no harm in making a few enquiries. I'll see what I can do.''

''And I can ask around,'' Perry broke in cheerfully. ''I ain't much of a one for church-going, but I could mingle with the Reverend's congregation and question a few people.''

''With your well-known subtlety?'' His brother's tone was ironic. ''I can hear you now. Would it not be something on the following lines, 'We think your preacher is a rogue. What do you know against him?''

Even Perry was forced to join in the laughter.

''Perhaps you're right,'' he admitted. ''I'd best leave it to you.''

''I think you had. It should not take above a day or two.''

''Don't be too sure,'' Elizabeth warned. ''That snake will cover his tracks.''

''Yet even snakes may be trapped and destroyed, my dear.'' With these words from Sebastian the rest of the company had to be content.

Unwittingly, Elizabeth had hit upon the truth, but the past life which the preacher had been at such pains to conceal was, at that moment, in danger of being revealed to the world.

Truscott had, that very morning, been approached by a filthy urchin in his own church.

''Out!'' He'd eyed the ragged figure with distaste.

The child was little better than a scarecrow. "You'll get no charity here."

"Don't want none, mester. I been paid. I wuz to give you this." The child held out a grimy scrap of paper, but his eyes were wary. He kept his distance, as if ready to dodge a blow.

"What's it about?"

"Dunno. I was to fetch you with me."

A discreet cough drew the preacher's attention to a small group of ladies advancing down the nave towards him.

"My dear sir, do you never rest?" one of them asked tenderly. "We'd hoped that you'd take tea with us to-day. We are raising funds for the Foundling Hospital."

"God bless you! Sadly, this little chap is in some kind of trouble." The Reverend Truscott considered resting a benevolent hand upon the urchin's spiky hair, but he thought better of it.

"You ain't read the note," the child accused.

"My little man, you have given me no time to do so." With the eyes of the ladies upon him, he was forced to open the paper. Drat the child! Had they been alone he would have been well rewarded for his impertinence.

The words were ill-spelt, and formed in an illiterate hand, but the message was all too clear. As its full enormity sank into his consciousness the colour drained from his face. He swayed, and held himself upright only by clutching at the back of the nearest pew.

"Bad news? Mr Truscott, you must sit down. Let me get you a glass of water."

He could have struck the speaker. What he needed at that moment was a glass of brandy. If only these ridiculous old biddies would go away! He raised a hand to cover his eyes.

"Thank you, pray don't trouble yourself," he murmured. "This is but a momentary faintness."

"It is exhaustion, sir. You do too much. This child must not trouble you today." She tried to shoo the boy away. "Your bride-to-be will scold you."

"Let him be! The Lord will sustain me in his work. I will accompany the child. I fear it is to a deathbed."

If only it were, he thought savagely. So many of his problems would be solved. With a brave smile he ushered the ladies from the church. Then he returned to the vestry to draw on a voluminous cloak, and cram a wide-brimmed hat low on his brow.

The boy's eyes never left him. A child indeed! There was cynicism in that look, and a quick intelligence which, he knew well enough, stemmed from a life of survival on the streets.

He spared no sympathy for the lad. The strong survived, and the weak went under. He'd been lucky. No, that wasn't true! Luck had played no part in his rise to fame. Say rather that a ruthless streak had helped him climb the ladder to success.

And was he to lose it now? The words of the message burned in his brain like letters of fire.

"'My friend seen your notice in the paper, Charlie. Time yore pore old mother had a share. The boy will fetch you to me. Best come, or you'll be sorry.'"

It was unsigned, but no signature was needed. The letter was authentic. Only his mother had ever called him Charlie.

"Is it far?" He spat out the question to the boy.

"Not far. I allus walks it, rain or shine." The child

inspected him with critical eyes. "Best hide that ticker, guv'nor, and the chain. You'll lose it, certain sure."

The preacher said nothing. He never walked abroad without his knife, a long and narrow blade, honed to razor sharpness. As a child, he'd learned to take care of himself. His lips drew back in a snarl. He was more than a match for any ruffian.

Now anger threatened to choke him. It was sheer ill-luck that had revealed his whereabouts. The *Gazette,* which had carried the announcement of his betrothal, was unlikely to fall into his mother's hands. In any case, she could not read. He'd thought himself safe. Yet some cruel trick of fate had given her a friend who was sharper than herself.

He glanced about him, and was not surprised to find that he was being led towards the parish of St Giles. He knew the area well, but he had not thought to enter it again.

Preoccupied with the scarce-veiled threat contained in the message, he was unaware that he was being followed. Even so, he pulled his cloak close, sinking the lower part of his face deep within its folds. Then he glanced about him before he entered the maze of alleys which led far into that part of London known as "The Rookery."

Behind him, Dan prepared to follow, but his way was blocked by a thick-set individual wearing a slouch hat and a rough jacket out-at-elbows.

"Not in there, sir, if you please! You wouldn't come out alive."

Dan stared at the man. He was an unprepossessing individual. His broken nose and battered ears suggested a previous career as a pugilist. When he smiled his missing teeth confirmed it.

"Out of my way, man!" Dan snapped impatiently. The figure of the Reverend Truscott had already disappeared.

"Now, sir, you wouldn't want me to plant you a facer, as I must do if you intend to be a foolish gentleman? I has my orders from his lordship..."

"Who are you?"

"A Redbreast, sir."

"You mean you are a Bow Street Runner?"

The man threw his eyes to heaven, and dragged Dan into a doorway. "Not so loud!" he begged. "You'll get my throat slit."

"I'll go with you."

"No, you won't, young sir. You'll slow me down. This ain't the place for you. Now be a good gentleman, and leave this job to me." His tone was respectful, but extremely firm.

Dan thought of pushing past him, but the Runner was already on his toes, ready for any sudden move. "We're wasting time," he said significantly.

"Then I'll wait for you here."

"Best go back to Mount Street, sir. I may be some time." He turned quickly and disappeared into an alley way.

Wild with frustration, Dan retraced his steps. The delay had lost him his quarry.

Damn Sebastian! Why must he always be one step ahead? Then common sense returned. At least his lordship had wasted no time in setting enquiries afoot. The Runner had seemed competent enough. His very appearance would make him inconspicuous in that nefarious area.

Dan himself was unarmed. It hadn't occurred to him to carry a weapon. Now, on reflection, he knew that the Runner had been right to stop him.

Always a poor parish, in the previous century the Church Lane rookery had reached the depths of squalor with its population of hawkers, beggars and thieves. Every fourth building was a gin shop, where the verminous inhabitants could drink themselves into oblivion for a copper or two. Stupefied with liquor, they could forget the filthy decaying lodging houses in which they lived under wretched conditions.

The narrow warrens and dimly lit courts had always attracted a transient population. Overcrowding was rife, and it was easy enough for the worst of criminals to cover their tracks, hiding in perfect safety among the teeming masses. They issued forth only to rob the unwary, and murder was a commonplace.

Dan shuddered. He didn't lack courage, but, unarmed, he'd be no match for a mob. He'd been a fool to think of entering that slum alone. His very appearance made him a tempting target. An attack might, at best, have left him injured. He could be of no possible service to Judith then.

Meantime, the Reverend Charles Truscott had penetrated to the very heart of the thieves' den. As a child he'd grown accustomed to the sight of the tumbledown hovels, the piles of rotting garbage in the streets, and the all-pervading stench.

Now he had grown fastidious, and the smell which assailed his nostrils made him want to gag. Then his guide pushed open a door which swung drunkenly on its broken hinges, and beckoned him inside.

"Up there!" The boy jerked a thumb towards a rickety flight of stairs and vanished.

The preacher found that his stomach was churning, and he could taste bile in his throat. He was tempted to turn and flee, but he dared not risk the loss of all that had been so hard-won.

He schooled his features into an expression of smooth benevolence, mounted the stairs, and knocked at the door which faced him.

It swung open at his touch, and for a moment he thought the room was empty. He looked about him in disgust. He'd seen squalor in his time, but this was beyond all. Flies swarmed over a broken bowl of half-eaten food, and looking down, he saw that they had laid their eggs. The place was bare, except for a single chair without a back, and a battered wooden crate. A heap of rags lay upon the floor, but there was neither bed nor mattress.

"Well, Charlie, how do you like it? A regular palace, ain't it?" A face peered out at him from beneath the heap of rags.

The preacher stared at his mother without affection.

"What are you doing here?" he asked. "I thought you'd be long gone."

"In a wooden box? That would have suited you…"

He was in full agreement with this sentiment, but he must not antagonise her.

"I meant only that I thought you would have found a better place."

"Ho, yus? Look at me, Charlie!" With a swift movement she thrust aside the rags, and staggered to her feet. He was aware of the strong smell of gin.

"You're drunk," he accused.

"Drunk for a penny, dead drunk for twopence," she jeered. "Well, son, how would you like to see me on a stage?" She thrust her face so close to his that the stench was overpowering.

He hadn't seen her for years, and now the raddled features shocked him. Nellie Truscott had been a beauty. Her looks were all she had had to offer in the marketplace. Now she was painfully thin, her hair grey and unkempt, and her face bloated with excess.

He tried without success to hide his feelings, and his expression roused her to fury.

"Quite the fine gentleman, ain't you? Ashamed of your poor old mother? You done nothing to help me, Charlie. Now it's time to pay."

"Don't be a fool," he told her roughly. "I'm naught but a poor parson."

"And on the way to being a rich one. You was always smooth, my lad. Now your lady wife will help me."

His face grew dark and the look in his eyes was frightening. She cowered away from him.

"You'll stay away from her," he said softly. "Shall I remind you how I serve those who cross me?"

She made a feeble attempt to placate him. "I shan't do nothing you don't like, but I must have money, Charlie. Even the men round here don't want me now I'm sick…"

The preacher had been about to grip her wrist. A reminder of his capacity for inflicting pain would have done no harm, but now he shrank back. Thank God he hadn't touched her. He had no difficulty in guessing at the disease from which she suffered. It was a common cause of death in prostitutes.

"Here!" He threw a handful of coins on to the wooden chest. "This is all I have with me."

"It ain't much, Charlie. Can you come tomorrow?"

"No, I can't." He was about to say more when a man and a woman entered the room.

"It's no matter, Nellie. Tomorrow we'll all go up town to hear the Reverend preach. I hear it's a rare treat." The woman laughed, and even her companion smiled. They had him in their power and they knew it.

The preacher ground his teeth, but he knew when he was beaten. With a sudden access of native cunning his mother had used her newfound knowledge of his coming fortune to surround herself with friends. She must have promised them a share.

"I'll come at the same time," he said.

Chapter Three

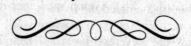

Judith was puzzled. She'd promised to accompany the Reverend Truscott to the charity tea in aid of the foundling children. When he didn't arrive she decided that she must have mistaken his instructions. Eventually, she went alone, only to discover that he had been called away on parish business.

The next day, at her stepmother's insistence, she stayed indoors to wait for his usual daily visit, but he did not arrive. That evening, a note was delivered to her, explaining that he would be away for several days in connection with a family matter. This did not trouble her unduly. In fact, it was something of a relief to be spared the need to agree with his sententious remarks.

She took herself to task for this unworthy thought. No one was perfect, least of all herself, and if her betrothed seemed, at times, to be a little pompous, it was easy to forgive his didactic manner. He was a good man. That she believed with all her heart.

She stayed in her sitting-room all morning, conscious of her own failings. She had not been entirely truthful with the man she was to marry. What would he say when he learned that she was actually writing a novel? It could not be considered a suitable occupation for a preacher's wife, but the story begged to be written. Throughout each day she found herself composing further snatches of dialogue, or planning yet another scene.

She was not destined to be left in peace for long. At nuncheon that day, Mrs Aveton made her displeasure clear.

"Must I tell you yet again?" she cried. "You have not bought above one half of the items on your list. You put me out of all patience, Judith. Peace will return to this household only when you are wed and gone from here."

Judith doubted the truth of this statement. Mrs Aveton's daughters were as ill-tempered as she was herself, and the servants were treated frequently to the sound of quarrelling, screams, and wild hysterics. Neither of the girls had yet been sought in marriage. They had neither fortunes, not a pleasant disposition to recommend them.

"Must I go back to Bond Street, ma'am?" she asked hopefully. She welcomed any excuse to get her out of the house.

"I see no other way of obtaining your necessary purchases," came the sarcastic reply.

"And I may take the carriage?"

"I suppose so. At least you will be there and back more quickly than you were the other day. You must watch this habit of dawdling, Judith. It cannot please your husband."

Judith felt a tiny spurt of rebellion. Was everything she did now to be directed to that desirable end? Her face grew wooden. She'd buy those last items as quickly as possible. Then she'd pay a visit to Mount Street. Perhaps it was folly. She suspected that it was, but at that moment she longed to be with those who loved her.

With Bessie in attendance, she hurried through her shopping, paying scant attention to the items on her list. It was done at last, and glancing at the clock in Bond Street she discovered that she had at least an hour of freedom before her absence would be remarked as being unduly long. It was a bitter disappointment to discover that Perry and Elizabeth were away from home, and that Prudence had been ordered to rest that day.

"Lord Wentworth will see you, ma'am. At present he is speaking to the doctor, but if you would care to wait…?"

The butler opened the door to the small salon, but Judith shook her head.

"I won't disturb him. Pray give my regards to Lady Wentworth. I will call again at a more convenient time."

She turned away, and was about to leave when Dan threw open the library door, and hurried towards her.

"I thought I heard your voice, Judith, don't run away. Come and talk to me!"

She hesitated, looking doubtful, but he gave her a reassuring smile.

"Don't worry! I intend to keep my word. I shall say nothing to distress you."

He had disturbing news, but at Sebastian's insistence he knew that he must keep it to himself.

The Bow Street Runner had followed the Reverend Truscott to his destination in "The Rookery". When the preacher left he'd knocked at the same door on the pretext of discovering the whereabouts of a well-known fence, but the man who opened it had sent him on his way.

"Best peddle your wares elsewhere," he'd snarled. "There's plenty as will buy your gew-gaws at the drinking shop, and no questions asked."

The Runner retired to consider his next move. It was soon decided when the man left the hovel with a woman on each arm. He followed them for several yards, and turned in behind them at the drinking shop.

They didn't suspect him, he was sure of it. After all, the man himself had suggested the place as the ideal spot to pursue his supposed nefarious activities.

Smiling pleasantly, he settled himself close by the tattered trio, and received a slight nod of acknowledgement in reply.

He'd been hoping to engage them in conversation, but the older woman was already quarrelling with the owner.

"No more credit, Nellie. If you ain't got blunt you'll get no drink from me—"

"Shut your face!" The woman slammed a coin down on the counter. "There's plenty more where that came from. Now give me a bottle!"

The man bit the coin, and whistled in surprise.

"Come into money, have you? Where's the body?"

The woman ignored him. Picking up the bottle, she returned to her companions. The three of them soon emptied it, and bought another.

The Runner waited. At the rate they were drinking they would soon begin to talk more freely. He had underestimated their capacity, though the older woman had been far from sober when she'd entered the place.

Even so, a third bottle was half-empty before she set it down, wiped her lips, and subsided into helpless giggles.

"It wuz 'is face!" she explained to her companions. "Proud as Lucifer, 'e is, but we've got 'im now."

"And not before time!" the man agreed. "That devil done you wrong, my lass."

The Runner was puzzled. Had the woman been younger he'd have drawn the obvious conclusion, but this raddled creature must be in her sixties. He eyed her closely. There was something about her features which struck a chord...the nose, perhaps, or the sunken eyes?

From what little he'd seen of the Reverend Truscott's face he couldn't be sure, but his suspicions grew.

"You'll know us next time," the younger woman snapped. "Wot you starin at?"

"Just looking about me. I'll move on. Ain't nobody here who's likely to be of use to me..." He scowled and left them.

His report to Sebastian had been succinct, and it roused fresh hope in Dan.

"It does seem that he gave them money," he said eagerly. "Why would he do that?"

"There could be a number of reasons...charity among them."

"But it isn't his parish," Dan protested. "Why would he go so far? He seemed to know the place well, or so the Runner said. And how was he able to walk there unmolested? Your man warned me against attempting it."

"You forget that the Reverend Truscott is a man of the cloth. That alone is sufficient to protect him."

Dan sniffed. "He was so heavily muffled that he might have been anyone."

"Perhaps he's known in the district," Sebastian said gravely.

"Perhaps he is." Dan's voice was full of meaning. "Well, I'm not satisfied, for one. Your own man thought there was something strange. Did he not mention a certain resemblance in the woman?"

"And what of that? Even supposing that it's true, we have no proof. It was merely an impression…"

"It ain't very savoury, though." Perry had been listening with interest. "St Giles is the worst sink in London. It wouldn't be the place I'd want to find my relatives…"

"The man can't be blamed for his connections," Sebastian said firmly.

"But, Seb, only thieves and vagabonds live in 'The Rookery'. You know its reputation. As for the women…"

"Again, I say we have no proof. The Runner may be mistaken. Truscott's visit may have been no more than a simple act of Christian charity."

"You sound more like Frederick every day," Perry told him in disgust. "Next thing you'll be following our elder brother into Government."

"Not so!" Sebastian laughed and shook his head. "And, Perry, he did well enough for you. Without his help you might have lost Elizabeth."

"I know it. I have much to thank him for. He surprised me then, you know. I thought him a model of rectitude, but he moved fast when there was danger."

"And I shall do the same."

Dan's face cleared. "Then you won't let it go?"

"No! I won't let it go." Sebastian looked at his adopted son. "Prudence and Elizabeth are troubled and I won't have my wife upset at a time like this."

"Shall you tell them anything?"

"Only that our enquiries are going forward."

"Then I may not tell Elizabeth of the Runner's findings."

"Certainly not. We have discovered only that the Reverend Truscott paid a visit to a squalid part of London. All the rest is merely surmise. Would that satisfy Elizabeth?"

Perry smiled at his brother. "How well you know her! She is afraid of nothing. Not even your famous Runner would stop her if she set her mind upon entering that infamous district."

"Exactly!" Sebastian looked at his companions. "This information must go no further than the three of us. I'll let you know when, and if, I have further news."

With this his listeners had to be content, though Dan had grave misgivings. Of the three of them he alone had seen the preacher's furtive manner, which was not that of a man of God bent upon some charitable enterprise.

Now he led Judith into the library with the air of a man who had no other thought in mind than welcoming an old friend.

She glanced at the sheets of paper which covered a large table.

"But I'm disturbing you," she protested.

"I'm glad of the interruption." Dan gave her a mischievous smile. "Now I shall be able to bore you with some of my ideas…"

"You won't do that." She glanced down at the drawings. "Warships, Dan? Surely the war with the French is at an end? Did not the Peace of Amiens come into effect only last month?"

"The Earl of Brandon thinks it but a cessation in hostilities. Perry and Sebastian agree with him."

"And what do you think?"

"I think we shall be at war quite soon. Napoleon has lost none of his ambition to make himself the master of Europe and beyond. Our Fleet is all that has stopped him until now."

"But this present Treaty?"

"Will give him time to build up his reserves, and to commission new ships. He has suffered heavy defeats at sea. That is where he must destroy us first."

"And are the French ships better than ours?"

"They are faster, and lighter too. Our own are built for strength. The first essential role of a warship is to carry armaments into battle, and the gun decks must be able to take the weight of the artillery."

"I see. It must be difficult to strike the right balance between strength and speed." Her attention was engaged at once.

"That's it exactly. I knew you'd understand. Too many guns and too much weight reduce the sailing qualities of a vessel. There's so much to consider."

"Such as?"

"Seaworthiness, maintenance, manoeuvrability, stability, different weather conditions, and accommodation."

"Such a list!" She began to smile.

"What is it, Judith?"

"Oh, I don't know. I thought you might have

changed in these past years, but I see that you have not."

He raised an eyebrow in enquiry, but she laughed and shook her head. "I meant only that you are still intrigued by technical problems. It is the thing I remember most about you."

"Is it?" His voice was heavy with meaning.

Aware that she was treading on dangerous ground, Judith tried again. "Of course!" she told him lightly. "I recall the day we met when you hung upside down on a small craft by the river at Kew. We all thought you were about to dive beneath it to examine the hull."

He chuckled. "I remember. Perry gave me a roasting later. You stayed behind when the others moved away. Why did you do that?"

"You didn't worry me!" she murmured. "You left me to my thoughts. I didn't feel obliged to talk to you."

Dan grimaced. "You must have thought me a boor, busy only with my own concerns. Perry informed me that I might, at least, have engaged you in conversation."

"There was no need," she told him briefly. "The silence was so comfortable." She held out her hand. "I think I must go now."

"Not yet!" He took her hand, but he did not release it. "May I not show you what I'm working on at present?"

Judith was tempted. There was plenty of time before she need return home and when he drew out a chair for her she sat beside him to examine the drawings. There was much she didn't understand, but her questions were both pertinent and sensible. Spurred on by her interest, Dan was soon well launched upon his favourite subject.

Apparently absorbed, he was quick to sense her growing ease of manner, and pleased to see that her somewhat strained expression had disappeared.

Then, as the clock struck five, she jumped.

"Great heavens! I have been gone this age," she cried. "Will you give my kind regards to Prudence and Elizabeth?" She rose as if to take her leave. Then her heart turned over as he gave her a dazzling smile.

"You have encouraged me to be selfish," he accused. "I've spent the last hour speaking of my own affairs, and you have told me nothing of your own."

Judith returned his smile. "I couldn't get a word in," she teased gently.

"But you are still writing? Are they still short pieces?"

Judith hesitated. "No…"

"Then what?" Dan looked at her averted face, and his eyes began to sparkle. "Judith, have you started on a book at last? You always meant to write one."

She blushed. "I don't know how good it is. It is just that…well…I was trying to make sense of the world, and it helps to put my thoughts on paper."

"But that is splendid!"

"It is probably quite trivial."

"No, I won't have that. You haven't got a trivial mind. How much have you done?"

"Just a few chapters," she murmured. "Perhaps I'm wasting my time. I'm not the best judge of my own work, I fear."

"Then I'll indulge in a great impertinence. Will you let me see it?"

She flushed with pleasure. "I'd be glad of another

opinion,'' she confessed. ''You always used to read my things, and I found your comments helpful.''

''Then it's settled. When can you bring the manuscript?''

''I don't know.'' Judith's eyes grew shadowed. ''I...I have other commitments...''

''Ah, yes, I understand.'' Dan's manner became formal, and for the first time a silence fell between them, though the forbidden subject of her marriage occupied each of their minds.

Judith found the tense atmosphere unbearable. She thrust out her hand and prepared to take her leave.

''Too late!'' a merry voice cried. ''We've caught you and we won't let you go.'' Elizabeth swept into the room accompanied by a chattering group of children.

Judith smiled in spite of herself as Sebastian's three boys bowed politely to her. They were clearly impatient to reach Dan's side.

Then Perry walked in, holding his elder daughter by the hand, and carrying his younger girl. He was quick to dismiss an anxious tutor, and a hovering nursemaid.

''No, leave them be!'' he ordered. ''Here is a lady who will be glad to see them. Judith, shall you object to a nursery invasion?''

''Of course not!'' Judith smiled warmly at the children, and took Perry's eldest girl upon her knee.

''We met them as they were coming from the park,'' Elizabeth explained. ''As Judith is here we must have a treat. Tea in the salon, do you think?''

This suggestion was greeted with whoops of delight from the boys, and Perry laughed.

''As you wish, my love.'' He rang the bell and gave

his orders. "You spoil them, dearest. Prudence will have your blood! Think of her carpets…"

"We'll be careful, Uncle Perry." Eleven-year-old Thomas stood upon his dignity, clearly affronted by Peregrine's reference to the nursery. "Henry doesn't drop things."

"And I don't drop things either." The youngest boy glared at his eldest brother.

"Yes, you do, and they always land with the butter side down." Thomas directed a quelling glance at Crispin.

"He won't do so today." Judith reached out a hand to Crispin. "Have you had an exciting day?"

"We went to the Tower to see the wild animals." The little boy's eyes grew round. "There were lions, you know…"

"And were they very fierce?"

"I didn't like it when they roared."

"He put his hands over his ears," said Thomas in disgust.

"I expect I'd have done the same myself," Judith announced mildly. "An unexpected noise can be frightening…" She looked at Henry. "What did you like best about today?"

Henry was dear to her heart. Less ebullient than his brothers, he had a retiring nature. She and he had struck up a friendship based upon long silences, trust, and occasional conversations when the boy had opened up his innermost feelings to her.

"I liked it all," he said. "I made some drawings of the animals. They were all so strange and new. Would you like to see them?"

"I'd love to, Henry, but I must go home. Next time, perhaps?"

"No, Judith, I won't have it." Elizabeth sprang to her feet. "We see so little of you nowadays. You must stay and dine with us—"

"But, my dear, I can't. I am expected. In any case, I am not dressed for dinner."

"Then I won't change. After all, we are dining *en famille*. Dearest Judith, may we not send a message to your home?"

"Oh, please!" The three boys stood in a semi-circle round her. "We haven't shown you the presents which Dan brought for us."

"Judith may be expecting her betrothed," Dan said stiffly.

"No! He is away at present." Judith spoke without thinking.

"Then there can't be the least objection."

"Objection to what?" Sebastian had come to join them.

"To Judith dining with us. Sebastian, how is Prudence?" Elizabeth gazed at him with anxious eyes.

"Perfectly well, and all the better for her rest. She will come down for dinner."

"There, you see!" Elizabeth turned to Judith. "Now you can't refuse. Prudence will be so glad to see you."

Judith wavered. The temptation to enjoy the warmth of this happy family circle was almost irresistible, if only for a little longer. Still she hesitated.

"Mrs Aveton dines from home this evening," she murmured. "She will require the carriage…"

"Then let us send it back with your message." Elizabeth clapped her hands. "We shall see you home, and since Mrs Aveton will be out you won't be missed."

The circle of pleading faces was too much for Judith.

"Very well," she agreed. "I shall be happy to stay."

Elizabeth beamed at her. "I'll write a note myself," she insisted. "Then there can be no objection."

"Of course not," Perry said dryly. "Who will stand in the way of a *force majeure?*" He turned to Judith. "Eight years of marriage and two children have not yet reduced my wife to the shrinking violet whom I'd hoped to wed."

Elizabeth laughed up at him. "You gave no sign of it when we first met, my love."

His look of affection was disarming. "No!" he agreed. "I like a challenge and I haven't been disappointed. You continue to surprise me."

Judith looked down as a small hand stole into hers.

"I'm glad you're staying," Henry told her. "Now we can show you the things which Dan brought back for us."

Thomas came to join his brother. "Mine is a dagger from India. It has a jewelled hilt. I can't carry it yet, of course, but when I'm older I shall do so."

"And yours?" Judith turned to Henry.

"It is a wooden mask. Dan says that it will ward off evil spirits."

"A useful item." Perry twinkled at his nephew. "And certainly a thing which no gentleman's household is complete without."

"Perry, I believe you're jealous!" Judith began to smile.

"Of course I am. I was tempted to send Dan away again to fetch a similar thing for me."

Two small fat hands reached up to touch his face. "Papa, you won't do that, will you? I love Dan. I don't want him to go away…"

Perry hugged his daughter. "I'm teasing, Puss. Dan won't go away again."

"I should think not, after such an unsolicited testimonial." Sebastian looked amused. "Now, boys, off you go. Judith will call in upon you later, but your mother wishes to see you."

Sebastian settled himself in the great wing-chair and Judith lost her charge as the little girl struggled from her lap and ran to climb upon her uncle's knee.

"A daughter next, Sebastian?" Perry asked with a grin.

"Only if she is as pretty as our little Kate here." His brother dropped a kiss upon the child's head. Then his face grew grave. "I shall not mind, as long as Prudence and the babe are well."

Judith was quick to sense his concern. "Are you worried about her? The doctor gave you a good report, I hope?"

"Prudence is well enough at present, though I can't persuade her to rest. Judith, I'd be grateful if you'd have a word with her. She is accustomed to be so active, but you are always a calming influence."

"I'll do my best," she promised.

"Then come and see her now." Elizabeth jumped to her feet. "Oh, I had forgot. We've ordered tea in the salon. The boys will be starving…" She held out her hands to her daughter, and led the way across the hall.

Under their father's watchful eye, the boys were on their best behaviour, and to Elizabeth's evident relief, the carpets suffered no disaster. Her own girls ate little, and were clearly flagging after their walk in the park.

"Time for bed, I think," their mother said firmly. "Come, Judith, shall you care to see them bathed?"

Her pride in her children was evident, and Perry smiled as the little party left the room.

"Judith is such a dear," he said warmly. "She's looking better today, I think, don't you?"

"She's at her best with children," Sebastian agreed. "I was surprised to see her here this afternoon. When did she arrive?"

"It must have been a couple of hours ago." Dan's attempt at a casual reply was unconvincing.

"Why, you sly dog, you've been keeping her to yourself. What will the dreaded Truscott say to that, I wonder?"

"She tells me that he's gone away…"

"For good, I hope?"

"No such luck." Dan's glance at his companions was filled with meaning. "He is attending to some family business, so I hear."

"I wonder if we've flushed him out?" Perry's eyes began to sparkle. "Odd behaviour…I mean, to leave so suddenly. Don't you agree, Sebastian?"

His brother frowned. "There may be a good reason. Why must you insist on jumping to the worst conclusions?"

"Don't like the look of the chap."

"I didn't know you'd seen him. You don't accompany Elizabeth to his sermons, do you?"

"Just thought I'd take a look at him on the night we heard the news."

"Perry, you are the outside of enough! Did I not warn you not to make enquiries in his parish?"

"I didn't." Perry looked injured. "I stood at the back of the church and watched him ranting from the pulpit."

"Then you'll oblige me by leaving it at that."

"You've heard nothing more?" Dan intervened.

"No, but he is being followed." Sebastian gazed at the ceiling. "I agree that his disappearance is a little strange, especially at this time, but we must take great care not to alarm him."

"Why so?" Dan was unconvinced.

"Must I explain to you young hot-heads? If the man's dealings are above-board we shall be guilty of unwarranted interference in his affairs."

"And if not?"

Sebastian hesitated, considering his words with care. "Our quarry may take fright and disappear."

"Good riddance!" Dan insisted warmly. "So much the better for Judith!"

"No, Dan, think! If he is the villain you believe him to be, will he give up the chance to get his hands upon a fortune?"

Dan paled. "You mean…you mean that we may be putting Judith in great danger?"

"That is possible. Girls have been seized before and forced into marriage with unscrupulous men. Once wed, and with the money in his hands, he would leave no trace behind him."

Perry sprang from his seat and began to pace the room. "We can't have that!"

"Agreed!" His brother's face was calm. "You both see now that we must proceed with caution?" Sebastian leaned back in his chair, satisfied that he had made his point.

Still doubtful, he'd have been concerned to learn that he had hit upon the truth.

The threat of blackmail had caused the Reverend Truscott to spend a sleepless night. Then, as his initial panic subsided he began to pull himself together. Still unaware that he was being followed, he paid a second visit to "The Rookery", carrying with him the contents of the collection box. This was irritating. Such funds had previously found their way into his private account, but no matter. He had begun to lay his plans.

As he had expected, the money was regarded simply as a down payment. His mother and her friends intended to bleed him white. He permitted himself a grim smile. They did not know him.

With a promise of a further payment before the week was out he explained that he was called away on parish work for the next day or two. He didn't intend to waste this brief respite. Judith must be satisfied with a note explaining his absence. He had other matters to attend.

His next journey took him into the pauper colony of Seven Dials. His destination was a brick-built dwelling, apparently no better than any of the others. He let himself in with his own key, and looked about him with a grunt of satisfaction. This was one in the eye for his high-principled parishioners. He'd lavished money on the place, delighted to be putting it to better use than throwing it away on a bunch of ragged urchins.

The place was empty, and his face grew dark with rage. Where the devil was the wench? She was supposed to be here when he wanted her.

When he heard her footstep on the stair he waited

behind the door, seizing her from behind as she entered the room. Twisting his fingers in her hair he dragged her round to face him, smiling as she whimpered with pain.

"You're hurting me!" she cried.

"I'll hurt you even more, you slut, if you don't obey my orders. Didn't I say that you weren't to leave the house? Been playing me false, have you?" He tightened his grip, forcing her to her knees.

"I wunna do that." Her eyes were watering with agony. "I went out for bread…" She pointed to her basket. "I weren't expecting you. You didn't let me know."

"I'm not likely to do that," he said softly. "Will I give you the chance to get up to some trick?" He dragged her to her feet.

The sight of her pain had roused him. With one swift movement he ripped her gown from neck to hem, flung her on the bed, and threw himself upon her like an animal.

It was growing dark before he was fully satiated. With a growl he kicked her away from him.

"Fetch your brothers!" he ordered. "I have work for them."

Chapter Four

Next morning, in a part of London far from the slums of Seven Dials, Judith was summoned to an interview with her stepmother.

"At this hour?" she asked Bessie in surprise. Mrs Aveton was not normally an early riser.

"She said at once, Miss Judith. She's in her bed-chamber."

Judith entered the room to find Mrs Aveton sitting up in bed, sipping at her chocolate.

"Well, miss, did you enjoy your evening with your friends?"

The enquiry startled Judith. Her own enjoyment had not previously been a subject of any interest to her step-mother.

"Why, yes, ma'am, I thank you. I hoped you would not mind, since you were dining out yourself. The carriage was returned in plenty of time, I believe."

A short laugh greeted her words. "Most certainly, together with a most insulting note from Mrs Peregrine Wentworth." She tossed a letter towards Judith.

"Insulting, ma'am?" Judith scanned the note. "This

merely explains the invitation, with a promise to see me safely home.''

"You see nothing strange in the fact that Mrs Peregrine sends no compliments to me, or enquiries about my health?''

"She was not aware that you were sick, and nor was I. I'm sorry. Were you unable to visit your friends?''

"I dined with them, and I thank heavens that I did so. I learned more disturbing news.''

"Ma'am?''

"Come, don't play the innocent with me! You were always a sly, secretive creature, but now I know the truth…''

"I don't understand.''

"Don't you? Perhaps you will explain why you didn't tell me that the pauper, Ashburn, is returned to the Wentworth household?''

Judith went cold, but her voice was calm when she replied, "I did not think that it would interest you.''

"If I'm not mistaken, it interests you, my girl. Such deceit! You knew quite well that had I known I should have forbidden you to go there.''

Judith's hands were shaking. She hid them in the pockets of her gown. "Must I remind you, ma'am, that I am betrothed to Mr Truscott?''

"I wonder that you remember it. To cheapen yourself in the company of that creature is the outside of enough. Have you not learned your lesson yet?''

Judith's anger threatened to consume her. "I have learned much in these past few years,'' she said quietly. "I think you have forgotten that Mr Ashburn is Lord Wentworth's adopted son.''

A sniff greeted her reply. "And that is enough to

transform a slum child into a member of the *ton?* What a fool you are! The aristocracy may be allowed their eccentricities. Must you try to ape them?''

''I had no thought of doing so. Mr Ashburn is an old friend. I intend to be civil to him.'' Judith was surprised at her own temerity. In the usual way she did not argue with her formidable stepmother.

Mrs Aveton's head went up, and her small black eyes began to glitter.

''Impudence! You are grown mighty high in the in-step in these last few weeks. Your husband will knock that nonsense out of you...'' She caught herself in time. Judith must not be allowed to guess at the darker side of the Reverend Truscott's nature.

This quiet-looking girl had a streak of iron in her character. Mrs Aveton had seen it only seldom, but her attempts to crush that stubborn will had failed. If Judith should change her mind and put an end to her engage-ment, she herself might say goodbye to the sum of money soon to be in her hands.

Her malevolent expression vanished. ''I mean, of course, that the Reverend Truscott has a position to up-hold. His wife must not be seen to gather about her friends who are...er...unsuitable.''

''He seems happy enough to think that I am friendly with the Wentworth family. He tells me that they will always be welcome in our home.''

''That is quite another matter. Judith, you are placing yourself in a most invidious position. You may have forgotten that unfortunate nonsense of six years ago. The same may not be true of Ashburn. You are an heir-ess now, and a fine catch for him. Has he made further advances to you?''

"He has not!" Judith ground her teeth. The temptation to strike her questioner was strong.

"Doubtless he will do so. You must not see him again before your marriage."

Judith drew herself to her full height. "I have promised to return," she said stiffly. "Do you think me so ill-behaved that I won't conduct myself with propriety?"

"You are headstrong, miss. I have never been deceived by your milk-and-water ways. In this you will obey me. You may not leave this house again before I speak to Mr Truscott."

Dismissed without ceremony, Judith returned to her room. She was seething with rage. If she'd ever had any doubts of the need to escape from Mrs Aveton's clutches, they vanished now. She'd thought long and hard before she had accepted the preacher's offer for her hand, fearing that she was cheating both herself and him. She didn't love him, but in the materialistic circles in which she moved, love seldom played a part in settling a marriage contract.

And she was no longer the timid nineteen-year-old who had given up her love in the face of calumnies and opposition. The years had changed her. Unless she was to wither away in the Aveton household, she could see no alternative to marriage. What else could she do? She might have taught in some small dame school, or become a governess, had she not inherited her fortune. Now it was out of the question.

And she would not cheat Charles Truscott. In her heart she had vowed to make him a good wife. She could help him in his parish work, run his household, and bear his children.

She buried her face in her hands, knowing now that it would never be enough.

Why had Dan come back at just this time? In another month she would be safely wed, and could put him out of her mind for ever. She would not think of him. She mustn't. She pulled down the central flap of her writing desk, and pressed a small knob just behind the hinges. A hidden drawer slid out, revealing a pile of manuscript. Listlessly, she scanned the pages, noting an expression here and there which might possibly be improved to make her meaning more exact. With pen in hand she scored out several lines, and began to write.

When the Reverend Truscott was announced, Judith was not informed immediately. Mrs Aveton received him in her salon.

As always, he was quick to sense trouble.

"What is it, ma'am?" he murmured.

"You may well ask, sir. Your bride-to-be is behaving ill, I fear."

"How so, dear lady?"

She was quick to put him in possession of the facts.

"Judith was besotted with the creature, and he with her. Now he is returned, and I fear that she may change her mind."

It was only with the greatest difficulty that he forced a smile. He had drunk deep the night before at the house in Seven Dials, and his head was pounding. A day of debauchery had done nothing for his temper, but a man had to have some relief. The strain of leading an apparently blameless life could be borne for just so long, and the intervals between his visits to his trollop were growing shorter.

It was unfortunate that he'd had to go away, but on this occasion he'd had a purpose other than bedding the wench. His mission had been successful, though her brothers were not, at first, as easily persuaded as he'd hoped.

"Not murder?" the younger one had pleaded. "Won't a beating serve?"

"No! That won't make an end of it!" He'd indicated the pile of gold upon the table.

"It might make an end of us. I've no wish to dance on air at Newgate…" The elder of the two had shaken his head.

"You aren't thinking straight," the preacher snarled. "I'm speaking of an accident."

"To three people?"

"Three drunken sots. They might be run down by a cart or, better still, fall into the river."

"What do they want you for, Josh?"

"Mr Ferris to you, my lad. And my quarrel with them is none of your concern. Haven't I always paid you well?"

"Aye, Mr Ferris, if that's your name, which I take leave to doubt. But it were for smaller jobs. This gelt ain't enough for what you're asking us to do."

"Of course not! There will be more."

"How much more?"

The preacher named a figure which brought an avaricious sparkle to both pairs of eyes. Then he leaned back, smiling easily, prepared to discuss the details of his plan. He was safe enough. He was known to them only under an assumed name, and they could not trace him.

Now his look was bland as he confronted Mrs Aveton. They'd understood each other from the first, but even she had no idea of the lengths to which he was prepared to go to gain his objective. Inwardly, he was cursing his own ill luck. The fates themselves seemed determined to thwart him, but Judith should not escape. He'd have her and her fortune one way or another.

"I must hope that you haven't distressed our little Judith, ma'am," he said mildly. "Nothing could be more fatal to our plans than to set up opposition."

"She'll do as she is bidden," came the sharp reply. "Now, as you may guess, she is sulking in her room. I have forbidden her to go out."

"Utter folly!" His voice was harsher than he had intended. "You have no notion of how to handle her."

"You think you will do better?" A snort of disbelief accompanied Mrs Aveton's words.

"Pray allow me to try. Won't you send for her?"

His glance followed his companion as she rose to ring the bell. He detested her. Aside from anything else, the woman was a fool. His lips twisted in amusement. Did she really believe that she would get her share of Judith's fortune?

An unpleasant surprise awaited her. She might storm and rage to her heart's content, but she would have no redress. She could not force him to pay. Would she sue him in the courts? He thought not.

He turned as Judith came to join them; walking across the room, he took her hand.

"I hope I find you well, my love?" he murmured. "Are you, perhaps, a little low in spirits? You seem to have no smile for me..."

She looked at him uncertainly.

"Now let us sit down together," he suggested.

"Your mama has been telling me of her worries about your peace of mind. I have assured her that she is mistaken."

"Thank you!" she said briefly.

"Come, you shall not be so stiff and formal. Mrs Aveton thinks only of your happiness and my own, my dear. I hope I have convinced her that nothing in your conduct could ever fail to please me."

Judith gave him a grateful look. "Then I may visit my friends?"

"Of course! I would not have you consider me an ogre. Why should I object when these visits give you so much pleasure? There can be no possible harm in your going about just as you would wish."

Judith smiled at him then, feeling that she had never liked him quite so much before.

"You are very good," she whispered.

"Nonsense! A woman of honour must be the best judge of her own actions. Now, dearest, I have some boring details to discuss with your mama. Will you excuse us? I am somewhat pressed for time today, but I'll call on you tomorrow."

"I shall look forward to your visit." With another charming smile Judith left them. Once again he had smoothed over an ugly quarrel. She sighed, wondering why she found so little pleasure in his company. It must be a fault of her own character.

"Well, ma'am?" The Reverend Truscott glanced at his companion. "Was I right?"

"I suppose so." The admission was made with some reluctance. "You are mighty clever, sir, but the girl puts me out of all patience. She will bear watching. I wonder that you allow her so much freedom. Pray heaven that you won't regret it.''

''It won't be for long,'' he promised. ''Meantime, Mrs Aveton, you will oblige me by avoiding these unpleasant confrontations. Where shall we be if Judith takes against me? Very much out of pocket, I believe.''

''She needs ruling with an iron hand.''

''Agreed! But not just yet. This is the time to walk more softly. I know these stubborn natures…fight them and you won't succeed. Now, a gentle appeal to honour and a sense of duty, and the game is yours.''

Mrs Aveton felt a first twinge of misgiving. This man was too clever by half. She must keep on the right side of him if she hoped to keep him to their agreement.

She nodded. ''You may be right. I hope so.''

''I am sure of it.'' With an ironic bow he took his leave of her.

As promised, Mrs Aveton followed his instructions, and when Judith announced her intention to go out that afternoon she made no objection, though she eyed her stepdaughter with some misgiving.

Judith, who normally took so little interest in her own appearance, had chosen on this occasion to wear a new toilette, chosen as part of her trousseau. The soft blue of her woollen redingote became her well, as did her matching bonnet with its pleated ribbon trim.

The sparkle in her huge grey eyes filled Mrs Aveton with foreboding. She had never before seen the girl so animated. With a faint flush of colour in her cheeks she looked almost pretty.

She herself was in no doubt of the reason for this sudden change in Judith, and all her fears returned.

Truscott might believe that his bride-to-be was tied handfast to him, but he was an arrogant creature, too sure of himself to think that he might fail in his objective. She lost no time in sending him a note.

Judith alone rejoiced in her good fortune. Free for once to come and go as she wished, she'd crammed the pages of her manuscript into her largest reticule. Dan would give his honest opinion of her work, giving praise where it was due, but quick to detect any weakness in her story.

Mrs Aveton's surprising change of heart had not extended to the offer of the carriage, but Judith didn't care. The day was fine, with a slight breeze blowing, but she wouldn't have cared if the rain had pelted down. She hurried along, oblivious of the other pedestrians, and deaf to Bessie's chatter.

''Why, miss, I don't believe you've heard a word I said! You'll have me out of breath if you go at this pace!''

Judith slowed, but clearly she was impatient to reach her destination, and Bessie said no more. Her young mistress was in the best of spirits, and it was a pleasure to see her looking so happy.

That Mr Dan should never have gone away. If only he'd returned a year ago the young couple might have made a match of it. She chuckled to herself. They might still do so. With a fine disregard for the conventions she dismissed the Reverend Truscott's offer out of hand. She'd always distrusted him, for all his smarmy ways. If she had the chance she'd see him off, and good riddance.

Judith heard the chuckle. ''What is it, Bess?''

''Nothing, miss.'' The girl was too wise to voice her

thoughts. "It's my belief I'm getting fat. I'm out of puff already."

"We're almost there." Judith turned the corner of Mount Street and ran up the steps of the Wentworth mansion. Then, as she lifted the knocker, doubts assailed her.

Dan might be out. She hadn't promised to come today; in fact, she hadn't given him any idea of when she might return. She'd scarcely hoped that it would be so soon. Then the door opened and Dan came hurrying towards her, both hands outstretched in welcome. She placed her own in his and he grasped them warmly.

"What luck!" he told her. "I've been waiting for you since this morning. Truscott is still away?"

"No, he is returned, but he has given permission for me to call upon my friends."

"Good of him!" Dan's tone was sardonic.

"Indeed it was! Without his intervention I should not have been allowed to leave the house. Mrs Aveton has learned of your return."

"Then should you be here?" he asked stiffly. "You won't tell me that my old enemy has lost any of her loathing for me?"

"Oh, Dan, may we not forget about her just for once?" Judith pleaded. "I've brought my manuscript. I hoped that you would read it…"

"Forgive me!" he said quickly. "I should know better than to remind you of that harridan. Come into the library. Then we may be comfortable."

He settled her into a chair, handing her book he'd been reading. "Tell me what you think of this. Scott is all the rage, I hear. Have you read his poems?"

She shook her head. Then she opened her reticule and handed him a sheaf of closely written pages.

Dan took the opposite chair, and began to read with total concentration. He was soon absorbed in the book, and as she looked at the red-gold head, bent over work which was hers alone, a surge of affection filled her heart. She longed to throw her arms about him, and to hear again those words of love which had meant so much to her all those years ago.

Now her own decision to send him away filled her with bitter regret. She and Dan should have faced the storm which broke about their heads. He would have done so, and gladly. She had been the weaker partner. She hadn't thought so at the time, believing that she must protect him from Mrs Aveton's insinuations. She'd been a fool, but she and Dan had been so young. Even so, she should have listened to his pleadings.

Better by far to have faced the world beside him than to find herself in her present situation, loving Dan as she did, and promised in marriage to another. She could cry off, even at this late stage, but it would avail her nothing.

Dan had changed. She'd tried to deny it both to herself and to him, but it was true. He was no longer the eager lad who'd believed the world well lost for love. It was only to be expected. Their parting had been bitter, and even now she could not bear to think of his reproaches. The look of agony on his face had cut her to the heart, but she had held to her decision, believing it in his best interests.

Perhaps it was. She glanced at him again. She would have known him anywhere, but there was a certain maturity about his manner which was new to her. Not by a word or a gesture had he indicated that he now thought of her as anyone other than an old friend. Indeed, on occasion his formality had startled her.

What did she expect? She was promised to another man. If Dan had loved her still, his own sense of honour would have prevented him from telling her so. He didn't, and for that she must be grateful. He, at least, had found peace of mind in these last few years. She could only wish him happiness. Then she heard a chuckle, and raised an eyebrow in enquiry.

"Judith, this is very good! I can't put it down. You haven't lost your sense of fun, I see. How cleverly you seize upon the foibles of our world."

"Perhaps I haven't been very kind…"

"At least you have been honest. Your insight frightens me. I shall have to watch my *p*'s and *q*'s."

Judith laughed. "Not you!" she protested. "I don't intend to ridicule my friends—"

"No, no, I didn't mean that! Your characters are not recognisable, but I'm much amused by your comments on some of our present follies. You are a dangerous woman!" His smile robbed his words of all offence.

"Then you must keep my secret. No one else has seen the book."

"But, Judith, you must publish it! It would be a great success."

"No, I can't do that. Think of the scandal!"

"What scandal? Other women have been successful authors. It's more than a hundred years since Mrs Aphra Behn published her plays and novels, and what of Fanny Burney?"

"Madame d'Arblay? That was different. Her father

was an author and he encouraged her. Besides, did she not publish anonymously at first?"

"You might do the same."

Judith shook her head. "Suppose the truth came out? You forget, I think, that I am to marry a parson. It would be considered unsuitable."

"I have not forgotten," he told her savagely. "That is but one more reason why you should not wed him."

"Oh, Dan, you promised that we should not speak of it. Give me the manuscript. I wrote it for my own pleasure, but I'm glad you think it entertaining."

"It's more than that, my dear. May I not keep it for a day or two?" Dan was anxious to chase away the frown which had appeared between her brows. "I want to know what happens next."

"Very well, but it must be our secret. Now tell me, how does your own work go on?"

"I keep busy." He gave her a rueful look. "Sometimes I wonder if my plans will ever get a hearing."

"They will," she comforted him. "You are still determined that you won't use your connections?"

"I don't want charity."

"But it wouldn't be that. If your ideas are sound, and I'm sure they are, they should be put to use. After all, even the most willing of acquaintance would not support a scheme to build an unseaworthy vessel."

"Doubtless my Lords of the Admiralty have no plans to build at all. After all, we are at peace…"

"But not for long, or so you believe. Dan, there must be other men who think as you do. Perry and Sebastian are of the same mind," Judith paused for a moment. "Shall you think me interfering if I suggest another scheme?"

"I'll try anything."

"Then why not write direct to Admiral Nelson? Perry met him but the once, yet he is Nelson's man for life."

"Another connection?"

"Not at all. The Admiral is unlikely to remember a lowly first lieutenant. In any case, you need not mention it. Why not send him your drawings, and leave them to his judgment?"

The look of affection in Dan's eyes made her heart turn over.

"How like you to think of others rather than yourself," he murmured. "When did you decide on this idea?"

"It just came into my head," she told him hurriedly. She could not explain that he had been constantly in her thoughts since the day he had returned.

Dan rose to his feet and held out his hands to her, drawing her up to face him. His eyes were sparkling.

"Clever Judith!" he said tenderly. "Why could I not have thought of that myself?"

"Then you will do it?" Her words were almost inaudible. He was much too close, and she found that she was trembling. How well she remembered the touch of those loving hands, and the way the small pulse beat in his throat. She swayed, and he slipped an arm about her waist.

"Judith?" Whatever he had been about to say was lost when the door flew open and Elizabeth hurried into the room.

After a first quick glance she gave no indication of her surprise at finding Judith in Dan's arms.

"Why, there you are, my love!" she cried. "This is

an unexpected pleasure. We hadn't hoped that you would be able to escape again so soon."

Judith grew scarlet with embarrassment, but Elizabeth was apparently blind to her discomfiture.

"Won't you join us in the salon?" she coaxed. "We are but this instant back from driving in the Park. Prudence is not so tired today. She will be glad to see you."

In silence Dan and Judith followed her. Whatever lingering confusion remained in Judith's breast was soon dispelled as she was greeted with delight.

Prudence, she thought, was looking better, and she said so.

"I am obeying orders," came the dry reply. "Between Sebastian and Dr Wilton, I find myself wrapped in swansdown. As for you, my dear, I think you have no need of any doctor. How well that shade of blue becomes you!"

Judith blushed at the compliment, and her colour deepened when she found Dan's eyes upon her. He seemed to be in full agreement.

Elizabeth was quick to break the silence which followed. She tugged sharply at the bell-rope.

"Judith, you shall not go away without a visit from your godchild. Kate has learned a poem…"

Perry groaned in mock dismay. "Again? Judith, would you care to hear my version? I can repeat it word for word."

"What nonsense!" Elizabeth beamed upon her husband. "Don't allow Perry to deceive you, my dear. He is so proud of her."

"And don't forget our little Caroline," Perry teased. "I'm sure her chatter must mean something."

"Of course it does. Did she not say 'Papa' this week?"

Sebastian looked at Prudence. "In a little while we shall be in competition with these proud parents," he joked.

"And high time too." Prudence returned his smile. "They are getting above themselves."

Elizabeth ignored this gibe as her elder daughter stood upon the hearth rug and entertained the assembled company.

As the burst of clapping died away, Judith held out her arms and the little girl ran to her.

"What a lovely poem," she said. "Do you know any more?"

"Don't encourage her," Perry groaned. "Kat's latest pleasure lies in jokes. Some of them are more ancient than my own."

"Serves him right!" his wife announced. "Who taught them to her in the first place?"

This brought a ripple of amusement from the assembled company.

"Do they not call it 'hoist with your own petard'?" his brother enquired unsympathetically. "Be sure your sins will find you out!"

"Not so!" Perry sat down upon the rug. "Come, Kate. Let us play at spillikins. Judith will like that."

"Not in her new gown." Prudence protested faintly. "Judith, you must not allow Perry to persuade you—"

"I don't mind at all." Judith tossed aside her bonnet, and slipped out of her redingote. "There, I am quite ready, but I think we need another player."

Dan was more than ready to oblige. He took his place

by Judith. "Watch out!" he warned. "I shan't care to be beaten."

At the height of the game, none of them noticed when the door to the salon opened. Then a hush descended at the butler's words.

"The Reverend Charles Truscott," he announced.

Chapter Five

Judith sprang to her feet at once, scattering the spillikins in all directions.

Beside her Dan rose to his full height, as the Reverend Charles advanced towards them. With punctilious courtesy he bowed first to Prudence, and then to Elizabeth, not forgetting a proprietorial smile for Judith.

"Lord Wentworth, will you forgive me for intruding upon such a happy family scene? I am come to escort my little Judith to her home."

"I...I thought you were much occupied today," Judith muttered wildly.

"But never too occupied to consider my beloved."

Beside her, Judith felt Dan stir. Unconsciously, she drew a little closer to him.

Sebastian rose to greet his visitor. "Why, sir, you are welcome," he said smoothly. "We have been wishing for some time to make your better acquaintance. You are already known, I think, to Lady Wentworth and to my brother's wife, Mrs Peregrine Wentworth?"

The preacher bowed his acknowledgment.

"Pray allow me to present her husband. And this, my dear sir, is my adopted son, Daniel Ashburn."

"And this pretty little miss?" Truscott bent a benevolent eye on Kate, but the child darted behind her mother's skirts.

"My niece. She is somewhat shy with strangers."

This assurance was belied when a childish voice piped up. "I don't like that man. He looks like a black stick."

Perry made a choking sound, attempting unsuccessfully to turn it into a cough, but Elizabeth was equal to the occasion.

"Forgive my daughter, Mr Truscott. She is but a babe as yet." Her expression indicated that she was uninterested in his forgiveness.

Truscott gave a hearty laugh. "Pray don't apologise, ma'am. We hear the truth from the mouths of babes and sucklings. In my clerical garb I must appear formidable to a little one."

Elizabeth gave him a perfunctory smile. She was undeceived. Left to his own devices the child would have received a beating. She rang quickly for the nurse.

"Such forbearance!" Sebastian said lightly. "My dear sir, pray sit down. You must allow me to offer you refreshment. A glass of wine, perhaps?"

Any thought of protesting that liquor never touched his lips died away as the preacher saw Sebastian's bland expression. He understood at once. These people hoped to trap him in some way. He smiled inwardly. It would not be with a simple lie.

"Thank you, my lord," he said. "A glass of wine would be most welcome. Then, I fear, that we must trespass no longer on your hospitality."

It was a test of sorts and it succeeded. Perry drew forward a chair.

''Nonsense!'' he uttered in jovial tones. ''Now that you are here, we shall not allow you to escape.''

A glance from his brother silenced him, but the Reverend Charles appeared to have read no sinister meaning into his words. He glanced about him at the assembled company.

From the moment he'd entered the room he'd been aware that this aristocratic family had closed ranks against him. A quick assessment of any situation had always been essential to his survival. He wondered if they had the least idea how much he despised them and their kind. How he resented that inborn air of self-assurance, and their calm assumption of authority.

What gave them the right to think themselves superior? In his experience most members of the *ton* led lives which were notable only for folly and extravagance, protected by their wealth and their positions.

Could *any* of them have matched his own achievements? He'd dragged himself from the depths of squalor to the point where he was at least on speaking terms with the leaders of Polite Society. Given one half of their advantages it would not have taken him so long.

And even now, what was he, after all? A preacher, however fashionable, would not receive the invitations for which he craved. Not for him was membership of White's, or any of the other gentlemen's clubs which lined St James's Street. He would receive no cards for routs and balls, nor be asked to make up a party for the Vauxhall Gardens.

Envy welled up in his heart as he looked at the Wentworth brothers, noting the perfect fit of their attire, and the fashionable haircuts. They seemed unconscious of the splendour of their surroundings.

Truscott himself was not. He'd never entered a more magnificent room, with its pastel-coloured walls, fine pictures and elegant furniture. The house in Seven Dials, of which he'd been so proud, now seemed to him to be furnished in tawdry fashion. All that would change, he vowed, once he was in possession of Judith's fortune.

Now he leaned back, apparently at ease, and sipped at a glass of wine which was most certainly of excellent vintage.

Sebastian took a seat beside him. "We are most anxious to get to know you better, Mr Truscott," he said pleasantly. "Your reputation has preceded you. You have blazed like a comet across the London scene."

"And so unexpectedly," Perry intervened. "With your gifts I wonder that we had not heard of you until a year ago."

The preacher bowed his thanks for the compliment, but he was tempted to laugh aloud. So that was to be their game? Did they not realise that they were fencing with a master of deception?

"My early years were spent among the heathen," he replied. "Alas, it was poor health alone which caused me to return to England."

"How interesting! You must tell us more about your travels…" Prudence was moved to engage their unexpected visitor in conversation. She'd sensed that Judith was struggling to regain some semblance of composure after the shock of Truscott's sudden appearance. Now the girl was on pins, knowing the family's opinion of him.

Truscott himself was equal to the occasion. A fluent command of language was part of his stock in trade, and he'd taken good care to verse himself to perfection in every detail of his story.

Elizabeth could only marvel as his tales of distant lands poured out. She didn't believe a word of them, but she kept her opinion to herself.

Dan was of the same mind. Aware of Judith's pleading look, his bow to the preacher had been courteous, but he had taken no part in the conversation, and nor had she.

Truscott glanced at his betrothed. He favoured her with a loving smile, though briefly. Then he turned back to Lady Wentworth. He'd taken great care not to stare at the man who stood so close to Judith. There was little need. He'd taken in every aspect of the fellow's appearance at first sight.

His inward amusement grew. How like the stupid girl to give her heart to this nonentity! And given it she had. He'd known it from the moment that he'd seen her sitting on the rug, her face alight with pleasure. No childish game had caused the change in her.

The fellow was a blockhead. He hadn't uttered a word for the past hour. Handsome, perhaps, in a fresh-faced guileless way, but that flaming head was an offence to any man of taste. So Mrs Aveton had been right in her suspicions. He'd determined to find out for himself, and when her note arrived he'd made it his business to pay a visit to Mount Street.

Well, they were certainly well-matched, those two, with not an ounce of character between them. If he'd needed any further confirmation of their feelings for each other, he saw it now in Judith's face. She looked as guilty as if she had spent the afternoon locked in her lover's arms.

Upon reflection, he thought it unlikely. Judith was far too much the lady to allow the fellow any liberties. In any case, he doubted if she had any notion of the passions which were his own besetting sin. Cold as ice, he thought gleefully, but he would melt her.

For just a second his expression was unguarded, and he felt Dan's gaze upon him. Looking up, he felt the full glare of those bright blue eyes, and was shaken out of his composure. He rose to his feet.

"My lord, you have been most kind." He bowed to Sebastian. "Will you forgive me if I take my little Judith back to her mama? At this present time Mrs Aveton is much in need of her assistance." He couldn't resist a parting shot. "Wedding preparations, you understand?" He sensed Dan stiffen, and was satisfied.

With one of the Wentworth carriages placed at their disposal he handed Judith up, and waved a farewell greeting to his host.

"Such condescension!" he murmured as they drove way. "My love, I don't know when I've spent a happier afternoon. Your friends are charming."

"Sir, I hope that you were not offended by my god-daughter—"

"The little Kate? Great heavens, no! I confess I was surprised to find her allowed so much latitude."

He was quick to notice the frown on Judith's face.

"Mr Truscott, she is just a child…"

"Of course, my dear. I meant only that it is not usual to find the young in adult company at that time of day. Perhaps these are the latest ideas. Do you approve of them?"

"Perry and Elizabeth love their children, as do Prudence and Sebastian—"

"Naturally, Judith. That is not in dispute. I understand, however, that it is more usual to have one's offspring brought down by their nurse at a certain time each day, both for correction and chastisement."

Judith was silent as a strong sense of rebellion seized her.

Truscott knew that he had said too much. Incautiously, he had exposed the iron hand beneath the velvet glove. Immediately, he sought to reassure her.

"Those were the bad old days," he said cheerfully. "Now we must move with the times. I cannot fault your friends as parents. What a happy family they are!"

Back in Mount Street, the Wentworth family was looking far from happy.

"What a creature!" Perry said with feeling. "He's much worse than we thought, Sebastian, you must agree?"

"I found his conversation interesting," Sebastian said slowly.

Elizabeth looked ready to explode. "You won't say that you believed him?"

"I used the word interesting, rather than believable, my dear. Some of his stories were familiar. He seemed to be quoting word for word from some of the travel books I've read."

"The man is a villain," Dan said savagely. "My God! Did you see the way he looked at Judith?"

"I did. It confirms my belief that we must go carefully." Sebastian looked across at his wife. "My dear, you should rest before we dine tonight. Then we shall spend a quiet evening on our own.''

''Shall you mind?'' Elizabeth asked anxiously. ''Darling Prudence, we seem to be having all the fun, whilst you are tied indoors.''

''I am content, my love. A Government reception would not be my chosen entertainment at the present time.'' Prudence stretched out her hand towards her husband and he kissed it tenderly.

Elizabeth nodded. She had decided upon a certain plan of her own.

Later that evening she left Perry's side to go in search of his formidable eldest brother.

The Earl of Brandon greeted her with a show of affection which he reserved for her alone. Elizabeth held a special place within his heart, and had done so since the time when she had so nearly been lost to them.

''Well, Puss?'' he said kindly. ''I hadn't thought it possible that you could grow more lovely, but you succeed in doing so.''

Elizabeth brushed aside the compliment. She wasn't vain, regarding her startling beauty as an accident of birth, for which she could take no credit.

''Frederick, will you spare me a few moments for a private conversation?'' she murmured.

''Certainly, my dear.'' He led the way into a small anteroom. ''How may I serve you?''

''It isn't for me,'' she told him quickly. ''You remember Judith Aveton?''

''Indeed I do. A quiet girl, with a beautiful speaking voice, as I recall... So different from that Aveton creature who is never out of my home.''

"Quite! Frederick, we fear she is in trouble. You have heard of her betrothal?"

"It has been brought to my attention," he said drily. "Why are you so concerned?"

"It is this man, this so-called Reverend Truscott."

"The preacher? I know of nothing against him."

"You would not," she told him bitterly. "He has all the cunning of the devil which I believe him to be."

"Strong words, my dear! Have you any proof?"

Elizabeth hesitated. The Earl had always stood her friend. Now she must trust him. "I can't tell Perry," she murmured in a low voice. "But the loathsome creature has made advances to me…"

The Earl's face changed. "A man of the cloth?" he said in disbelief.

"It's hard to credit," she agreed. "But if you don't believe me you should speak to Prudence. She caught him out in his own church."

Frederick laid a hand upon her arm. "I do believe you," he said quietly. "Have you told Judith?"

"Not in so many words. She knows, of course, that we dislike the man, but we cannot sway her. It is hardly to be wondered at. Marriage must seem to her to be the only alternative to a life of misery with Mrs Aveton."

"Scarce a fate which one would wish upon one's worst enemy. Judith may be right, my dear. Men have strong passions. Marriage may prove to be the cure for those."

Frederick was a man of the world. He was well aware of the adulation which a fervent orator could arouse in the female breast. Possibly this Truscott had allowed his admiration for the ladies to go too far upon occasion, but doubtless it was no more than a foolish attempt to cling to a hand for longer than propriety allowed, or to indulge in a few glowing words.

"Frederick, you disappoint me!" his tiny sister-in-law said sharply. "Truscott did not pay me idle compliments. He was importunate. Perry would have killed him had he known of it."

"And who, my dear one, is to be the object of my retribution?" Perry strolled towards them. "What mischief are you planning now?"

Elizabeth coloured and looked confused, wondering how much of the conversation he had heard. Perry was not the mildest of men, and any insult to his wife would not be overlooked.

"We were speaking of Charles Truscott," Frederick replied easily. "Not one of Elizabeth's favourites, I hear."

"Nor mine. He is a shabby fellow, with an unknown background. Do *you* know anything about him?"

"No more than is common knowledge. He has enjoyed a sudden rise to fame, I believe."

"Too sudden!" Perry stepped upon the hem of his wife's gown, and then looked down in horror. "Damme! Now I've torn your dress. I'm so sorry, dearest. Shall you be able to pin it up? Blest if I ain't grown clumsier than ever!"

Elizabeth looked at him in mock reproach, and then she gave him a rueful grin. Gathering up her skirt, she departed in search of a maid.

"Clumsy indeed, my dear chap! Sometimes I wonder that your wife does not see through you."

"Most of the time she does…"

"Well, then, since you wish to speak to me alone, you'd best tell me what is on your mind."

"It's this Truscott creature. I tell you, Frederick, there is something smoky there. Sebastian had him followed into the stews, and again to Seven Dials. We haven't told Prudence and Elizabeth."

"I should hope not, Perry. Knowing your wife, I believe she is more than likely to tackle him direct when he might simply be abroad on errands of mercy."

"Mercy? You don't know him," Perry said darkly. "I, for one, trust Elizabeth's judgment."

"Quite right!" The Earl gave his youngest brother a slight smile. "It was always better than your own."

Perry ignored the gibe. "Call it feminine intuition if you like, but the girls were appalled when they heard of the betrothal. We...I mean Sebastian...thought they were being fanciful at first, but now even he is worried."

The Earl of Brandon made a steeple of his fingertips. "You both believe you are right to interfere?"

"Frederick, you know old Seb. He ain't one to tilt at windmills."

"Unlike yourself?" came the mocking answer. "Well, what would you have me do?"

"You have sources which aren't available to the rest of us. Will you not ask around? Discretion will be necessary, of course."

The Earl was not often heard to laugh aloud, but now he did so. "I think I can promise you that," he said. His discretion was a byword in Government circles.

"Yes, I know it," Perry said earnestly. "I wouldn't ask except that Judith is a friend of ours. We can't have her made into a human sacrifice."

"Dear me! You are growing quite poetic. Now tell me, is the lady herself happy with her choice?"

"She is, but, you see, she is an innocent. This clever scoundrel has deceived her."

"You seem very sure of that. Let us hope that you are mistaken. Leave it with me, Perry. You will forgive me, but I must rejoin my guests."

Perry was not entirely satisfied, but was forced to be content with his brother's promise of discretion. He decided to add a last clincher to his argument.

"We ain't mistaken," he muttered. "Never think that Truscott visits the stews for charitable work. He spent the night at Seven Dials."

The Earl raised a quizzical eyebrow. "As a well-known parson, would you expect him to visit the more fashionable ladies of the town?"

He moved away, leaving Perry feeling like a foolish schoolboy. His brother might be right. It was possible that Truscott visited the slums simply to slake his lusts. In a man of the cloth it was not admirable, but it was understandable.

Perry himself had had high-flyers in his keeping before his marriage. Since then, he hadn't even been tempted. Compared with his ravishing Elizabeth, all other women were pale shadows.

Now she returned to join him with a smile upon her lips.

"Need you have sacrificed my gown?" she teased.

"Is it ruined? I'm sorry, love—"

"Sorry about the gown, or sorry for attempting to deceive me?"

He gave a reluctant laugh as he tucked her arm through his. "Shall I ever be able to do that?"

"I doubt it. You need only have asked me to go away if you wished to speak to Frederick alone."

"And would you have gone?"

"Only with the greatest reluctance." The lovely flower-face smiled up at him. "I wanted to hear your secrets."

"Secrets, my darling?"

"Yes, my darling. You have been big with news for at least two days. I think it time you shared it."

"Trust me! You'll hear the whole quite soon, I hope." Taking her arm, he led her back into the ball-room to take part in a quadrille.

From across the room Elizabeth was soon aware that she was under scrutiny. She nodded pleasantly to her sister-in-law, who was sitting with Mrs Aveton.

Elizabeth looked for Judith, but the girl was nowhere to be seen. As the dance ended, she drew Perry towards the two ladies. Perry was surprised. Neither he nor his wife were favourites with these malicious gossips, although it was clear that they had both been under discussion.

Even as he bowed to the Countess and her friend, he found himself wondering at Elizabeth's object. She was more than capable of issuing a crushing set-down, but to his astonishment she favoured Mrs Aveton with a dazzling smile.

"Are we not to have the pleasure of Judith's company this evening?" she asked sweetly.

"Madam, you saw her earlier today, I believe. Did she not explain that she isn't well?"

"On the contrary, we thought her looking better than in recent months."

"Quite possibly. Her forthcoming marriage must be a source of joy to her. However, the dear child has been overtaxing her strength with all her visiting, which I consider quite unnecessary. Tonight she has the headache…''

Elizabeth murmured a brief expression of sympathy to which Mrs Aveton paid no attention. Instead, she turned to the Countess.

''It is no bad thing that Judith was unable to be here this evening, your ladyship. Her way of life will be very different after she is wed.''

Perry was quick to remove his wife before she could speak the words which he guessed were already upon her lips.

''Let's find Dan,'' he suggested as they moved away. ''He knows few people here. He must be feeling out of things…''

As he expected, Dan was looking disconsolate.

''I thought she'd be here tonight,'' he murmured. ''Did that creature forbid her to attend?''

''Nothing of the kind,'' Elizabeth said briskly. ''Judith has the headache, that is all.''

''Is it serious?'' His voice quickened with alarm. ''Could it be a fever, or worse?''

''Great heavens, Dan, you saw Judith yourself today. Was she not looking positively blooming?''

''She was…at least until Truscott arrived. Perhaps he has upset her.'' Dan's face grew dark with anger.

''Unlikely! He'll take good care to keep on good terms with her.''

Perry's prediction wasn't much consolation, and for the rest of the evening Dan's thoughts were with his stricken love.

* * *

Judith herself was feeling wretched. The Reverend Truscott's visit to her friends had not been a success in spite of his assurance otherwise.

Always sensitive to tension, she was well aware that the atmosphere at the house in Mount Street had changed with his arrival. Until then it had been the happiest of gatherings, and in playing that childish game she had forgotten all her present worries.

The next hour had been an agony, and she'd been on pins in case the volatile Elizabeth should be tempted to speak her mind. Beside her, Dan too had been bristling with antagonism. Only a promise not to distress her had ensured their civility.

She would not put them in that position again. Her visits to Mount Street must stop. They were naught but self-indulgence, although to be in Dan's company again was rather an exquisite torture.

In accepting Charles Truscott's offer she had sealed her own fate, believing that her decision was for the best. Now she felt ashamed, suspecting that she herself was playing with fire. Was she guilty of deceit and double-dealing? He did not deserve such treatment.

Tomorrow she would go to him, and ask to be given some useful work.

The decision cost her a sleepless night and many bitter tears. She couldn't even be sure of the purity of her own motives. Had she made it simply because she knew beyond all doubt that Dan was lost to her for ever?

How cold he'd looked when he'd spoken of refusing charity, even when that charity might consist only of a recommendation from his highly placed connections to the unapproachable Lords of the Admiralty.

Judith had known then that even had he loved her,

her fortune would have proved a far more insurmountable barrier to his pride than any previous opposition. He was lost to her, and she must face the truth.

With a heavy heart she rose next day and announced her intention to visit her betrothed.

"Well, miss, I'm glad to see that you are come to your senses at the last," Mrs Aveton snapped. "As I told your precious friends last night, it is high time that you gave up all this gadding about. Most unsuitable for the wife of a man in holy orders—"

"Which friends were those, ma'am?"

"Have you so many? I refer to the Honourable Peregrine Wentworth and his wife...pert baggage that she is! I declare that I was ashamed to see the exhibition which they make of themselves. Why, the man never takes his eyes off her. He must be always holding her hand, or dancing with her..."

"She is very lovely. She is also his wife," Judith observed quietly.

"One might hope that they would observe the proprieties. Amelia has no patience with them. She thinks it affectation."

Judith was silent. There was little point in arguing.

"I must hope that you will not follow their example. I should not care to see you always hanging about your husband's neck. Mr Truscott will not care for that, or to see you gazing at him like a mooncalf."

"There is little danger of that," Judith replied more sharply than she had intended.

Mrs Aveton stared at her. The girl was not improving. In these last few days there had been more than a hint of rebellion in her tone. She recalled Charles Truscott's words, and did not pursue the matter, though she longed to do so.

Judith would soon be taught a lesson, if she was any judge of men. Her days of balls, reviews and picnics were now over. She could hardly restrain her glee. Now Judith's pride would take a tumble, and that cool reserve which she had always found so trying would be shattered for ever by the worthy Truscott.

Worthy? Her lip curled. He was little better than a common thief. She despised him, having taken his measure from their first meeting. What other man would have agreed to pay for her own good offices in helping to win his bride? She knew that her antagonism was returned, but it did not worry her. The preacher was useful. She would keep him to his part of their bargain.

Unaware that he was the object of her thoughts, Charles Truscott had awakened in a better frame of mind. His plans were going well. No strangers to violence, his henchmen at Seven Dials would serve him as they had done before. After all, there was no greater incentive than the sight of gold.

As for Judith? Let her torture herself and her young lover for these next few weeks. It would make his conquest all the sweeter when it came. When the time was right, he would pluck her from the circle of her friends as easily as one might seize a ripening fruit.

He spared no more than a passing thought for Dan. The man was a nobody, unworthy of his consideration, and possessed of neither birth nor fortune. He might dream of winning Judith and her wealth, but he should never have her.

As always, his morning service was well attended,

and the sermon held his congregation enthralled. Quite one of his best, he considered with satisfaction, combining as it did the threat of hellfire with the promise of salvation.

When the service ended he followed his usual practice, standing in the porch and smiling gravely at his departing parishioners. A word or two to the wealthier among them brought congratulations and fervent promises of help with his good works.

As he re-entered the empty church he rubbed his hands. That tiresome task was over for another day. It was a small price to pay for what must be a handsome sum, in the collection boxes. He was looking forward to counting it.

Then he saw the child behind the pillar. He hurried forward, anxious to hear the news for which he had been waiting.

''Well?'' he asked impatiently.

The boy stepped back, keeping a heavy pew between them. ''You're wanted, mester. There's a couple of stiff 'uns as needs getting rid of.''

The preacher froze. His hirelings must have botched the affair. Had he not suggested the river, where the bodies would have been carried downstream? But just two corpses? He had to know.

''Who…who is dead?'' His throat was dry.

''Friends of yourn, so Nellie says.'' The urchin gave him a knowing smile.

Truscott staggered back. He could hardly breathe. A red mist swam before his eyes as an uncontrollable rage consumed him.

At the sight of his contorted face the child began to

run, but the preacher was too quick for him. He twisted the stick-like arm behind the urchin's back.

"I won't go," he hissed.

Tears of agony rolled down the starveling's face.

"It ain't my fault," he sobbed. "If you ain't there by nightfall they'll come to you..."

It was then that his tormentor lost the last vestiges of his self-control. Something inside him snapped. He wanted to strike out...to injure those who were responsible for the ruin of his plans. Someone must suffer. He began to punch the boy about the head, splitting the thin lips and closing one terrified eye.

"Stop!" The horrified surprise in Judith's voice reached him even through that bout of murderous anger.

He looked up to see her standing in the open doorway, but this was a Judith whom he did not recognise. Gone was the timid girl who had so little to say. Now she ran towards him with blazing eyes, and caught at his upraised arm.

"Stop, I say! Don't you see that the child is bleeding?"

Truscott released his victim, but his look was terrible. For a moment Judith thought that he would strike her too. She faced him squarely, fully prepared to stand her ground as she pushed the boy behind her.

Chapter Six

Truscott thought fast. His eyes grew blank as he sank into the nearest pew, covering them with a trembling hand.

Judith ignored him. She looked about her for some means of reviving his battered victim. The boy lay half-unconscious at her feet, and he was still bleeding. Water! She must have water! She took out her handkerchief, thrust aside the cover of the christening font, and soaked it thoroughly. Then she knelt down, supporting the child's head upon her arm, whilst she dabbed gently at his lips.

He gazed at her dully for a moment. Then he began to struggle.

"Let me go!" he shrieked.

"You may go when you can stand," she soothed. "Would you like to try?"

His face was a fearful sight, but he twisted like a cat as he sprang upright. Then he pointed at the preacher as he backed away.

"He'll pay for this!" he cried.

Judith pretended to misunderstand him. "Were you

to be paid?'' She reached into her reticule and handed him some coins. ''You are so thin,'' she said. ''Won't you use it to buy food?''

The money disappeared with astonishing speed, but the cracked lips attempted a weak smile.

''You ain't so bad,'' the child offered. ''He won't beat you, will he?''

''Most certainly he will not,'' Judith told him firmly. ''Off you go, and don't forget the food.''

She watched as he limped painfully to the open door. Then she turned her attention to his tormentor.

''Well, sir, what have you to say?'' she asked in icy tones. ''There can be no possible excuse for such a disgraceful attack upon a child.''

Truscott had been watching her through his fingers. Who did she think she was? She'd flown at him like some avenging angel, ready to strike at him herself if he had not obeyed her. She'd pay for her interference, but not just yet.

He dropped his hands, staring at her with a blank expression.

''Where am I?'' he murmured. ''What has happened? I have no recollection of anything since the service ended.''

Judith was unimpressed. She suspected him of lying. Was this some ploy to persuade her to excuse the inexcusable? She had been deeply shocked by his behaviour. That a grown man should use such violence to a child was unbelievable.

''You are in your own church, sir. Hardly the place for the scene which I have just witnessed.''

''The boy?'' he whispered vaguely. ''Was there a boy? I seem to recall a child approaching me…''

"How could you forget it? You left him stunned and bleeding—"

"No, no! That can't be true! It is unthinkable!"

"Then look at the blood upon the ground, and on my handkerchief." Judith pointed to the sodden scrap of fabric.

Truscott gave a cry and clutched his head. "I am going mad! Why would I attack a child? Oh, Judith, help me! I am beset with horrors…" He buried his face in his hands once more and began to sob as if his heart would break.

Judith was both startled and embarrassed. Men did not cry, if her own experience was anything to go by. She hesitated, looking at the heaving shoulders, and felt a twinge of pity. The Reverend Charles had broken down completely. For that to happen there must be something sadly wrong.

"I'm ready to listen, if you wish to speak of it," she said more kindly.

"I…I can't! You are an angel. Why should I burden you with my troubles?"

"I thought we had promised to share them." She sat down beside him.

"My dearest, I'd hoped to spare you all distress."

"Not all, I hope. Charles, you can't protect me from life itself. Please tell me what is troubling you. I'll try to understand."

The preacher raised a tearstained face to hers. His capacity for histrionics, which included the ability to weep at will, had often caused him to wonder if he should have followed his mother's example, and sought his fortune on the stage. A precarious profession, he'd decided. His present career was much to be preferred.

"So noble!" he whispered in broken tones. "It shall be as you wish." He stopped then as if to gather his thoughts. "It is my mother, dearest one. I remember now...the boy brought me news of her. Oh, Judith, she is dying! The shock destroyed my reason."

"We must go to her at once." Judith took his hand. "You must be strong, my dear. If we delay we may be too late."

"I won't allow you to put yourself in danger. She has been suffering from the smallpox. Judith, you knew that I was called away on family business. Now you know the truth of it."

"But, Charles, she must be cared for. We cannot let her die alone."

"She is in the best of hands. That was my first consideration. We had hopes of a recovery, but now those hopes are shattered. It is all too much to bear..." Apparently crushed, he bent his head.

"I'm not afraid of sickness," she protested.

"Sickness?" He managed a ghastly smile. "This is not sickness as you know it, Judith. You can have no idea..."

With sly relish he began to describe the headaches, the agonising muscle pains, the vomiting and the delirium suffered by the victims of the scourge before the appearance of the pustules which often covered the whole body.

Judith's hand flew to her mouth and she gazed at him in horror. He was watching her closely. Had he frightened her enough?

"The disease is highly contagious," he continued sadly. "My dear, would you bring such a fate upon your family, let alone yourself? That would be a wicked thing to do.''

"You are right," she told him earnestly. "But, Charles, what of you? You must also be in danger."

"No, no! I had a slight attack in India some years ago. The experience was unpleasant, but it is considered to be a form of vaccination, so I understand. For me, there is no danger of infection."

"Then go to your mother. I must not delay you."

"How good you are!" He was wise enough not to attempt to take her hand. Possibly he had regained some standing in her eyes, but he couldn't be quite sure in spite of her expressions of sympathy.

Judith's reaction to his attack upon the child had astounded him. In his murderous rage he had lost all self-control, but she hadn't flinched. Though she had expressed it in a different way, her anger had matched his own.

Had he convinced her of his reason for the outburst? For the first time he sensed that he was on shifting ground. He'd been so sure of his ability to bend her to his will, but today he'd seen another side to her character. He had misjudged her, that was all too clear. It was an unnerving thought.

The ability to assess the nature of his fellow-creatures was all-important to his survival. Today this quiet girl, with her softly spoken ways, had caused him to doubt it. There was unsuspected strength beneath that modest exterior.

"I may be away for several days," he murmured, as he gave her a covert glance. Was it his imagination, or did he detect a fleeting look of relief?

He'd never come closer to losing her, and he knew

it. He must give her time to recover from the shock she'd suffered that day. His mother's fictitious illness gave him the perfect excuse. In any case, the little matter of Nellie and her friends must be dealt with at once.

They'd keep their word. He was in no doubt of it, and he dared not risk a visit from the unsavoury trio.

Judith refused his offer to escort her to her home, urging him to hurry to his mother's side. He wasn't sorry to leave her. There was something in her expression, beyond her usual reserve, which made him feel uncomfortable.

She herself was deeply troubled, feeling that for the first time in her life she had gazed into the pit. She'd accepted Charles Truscott's explanation for his outburst of fury, and even offered her sympathy, but were his words enough? She could not dismiss the memory of the child's small figure, lying insensible on the ground. Charles must have had some kind of fit...some brainstorm to cause him to act in such a way.

A little worm of doubt stirred in her mind. Suppose that her friends were right about him? It didn't bear thinking about, but she must face it.

Suddenly she longed for Dan. She'd settle for his friendship, if for nothing else, but even that would be lost to her if she married the Reverend Charles.

Yet she'd vowed that she wouldn't return to Mount Street.

Judith's thoughts were churning as she went up to her room. Thank heavens that Bessie had stayed outside the church. She hadn't witnessed the ugly scene, which was a blessing. The sight would have sent her in search of help for her young mistress, and her first thought would

have been to summon Dan, or another member of the
Wentworth household.

Judith took off her coat and bonnet, and sank down
upon the window-seat, resting her forehead against the
cool glass. She must think. Had Charles been lying to
her? It didn't seém possible. Only a consummate actor
would have broken down and wept real tears as he had
done. Perhaps she herself was lacking in human charity.
If he'd been telling the truth she owed him her support.

And if not? The prospect made her shudder. Life in
the Aveton household must be preferable to marriage to
a liar and a bully. If only she might discover the truth
with certainty. She cast about in her mind for some way
of doing so, but she could think of nothing. An appeal
to her friends was out of the question. Prudence was in
no condition to be worried at this time. In any case, she
had no right to place the burden on their shoulders.

She must watch and wait. For the next few days, at
least, she would have time to think back and consider,
but it was difficult to recall in detail the events of these
past few months. She must have been living in some
kind of trance.

Now all that must change. Her very survival was at
stake. She knew it, and her determination hardened.
With a strong sense of purpose, she pulled out her papers and began to write. This was one gift which no
one could take away from her.

For the next two days she worked on steadily, thankful
to be left to her own devices, and pausing only to take
her meals with Mrs Aveton and her daughters.

That lady intended to make full use of the remaining
weeks before Judith's marriage to order all the gowns

and scarves, bonnets, gloves and underwear which she and her children might require for the coming Season. Judith, she imagined, would not examine the bills too closely, and the forthcoming wedding gave her an excellent excuse.

It was Bessie who noticed Judith's pallor.

"Miss, you'll ruin your eyes with all this scribbling," she announced. "I don't know how you see at night with just the one candle."

"I'm all right, Bessie." Judith smiled up at her.

"No, you ain't! Why, you ain't been out for days. See, miss, the sun is shining. Won't you walk in the Park today?"

Judith hesitated, but at last she allowed herself to be persuaded.

It was pleasant to stretch her legs again, and to feel the sun upon her back. She was pacing slowly beside the press of carriages and horsemen, listening in amusement to Bessie's pithy comments upon the more outrageous toilettes of certain members of the *ton,* when Dan fell into step beside her.

Bessie moved a few steps to the rear, ignoring Judith's look of reproach.

"I think you have an ally, sir," she said.

"Don't be cross with Bessie! How else was I to see you? You haven't left the house for days…"

"That was my own choice."

"It was a mistake. You are looking positively hagged!"

"Thank you!" There was a suspicious sparkle in Judith's eyes. She was close to tears. She was plain enough, heaven knew. It was hard to be told that any claim to looks had quite deserted her.

"Don't be foolish!" Dan took her arm and led her down a side path. "To me you are always beautiful. What is wrong, my dear?"

The tenderness in his voice was her undoing.

"I don't know," she said unsteadily. "I wish I did."

"Something has happened?" His hands rested lightly on her shoulders, holding her away from him as he gazed into her eyes. "Can you tell me?"

Judith longed to pour out the full story of that ugly scene in the church, but her own uncertainty held her back. Dan had disliked Charles Truscott from the first. How could he give her an unbiased opinion! What she needed most was facts.

"Dan, what do you know about smallpox?" she asked.

"A little, Judith, but why do you ask?"

"I just wondered. Is there an epidemic in the city at the present time? It is infectious, I believe…"

"Most certainly! Dearest Judith, you have not been exposed to it, I hope?"

She managed a faint smile. "Of course not, but someone told me that there are cases in the city."

"I have not heard of it," he frowned. "In the usual way, you know, the very mention of the word is enough to cause a general exodus."

"Even if it happened in some outlying part?" Charles Truscott hadn't mentioned his mother's whereabouts.

"It isn't easy to keep the news of an outbreak quiet," Dan assured her. "It spreads so quickly."

This information did nothing to ease Judith's mind. Her uneasiness increased. On the day of the attack upon the child she'd been too shocked and confused to question her betrothed. He'd given her no opportunity to ask why he'd made no previous mention of his mother. She'd taken it for granted that neither of his parents were alive, otherwise she would have been asked to meet them.

It had to be admitted that she knew very little about him. Upon reflection, she realized that they had had few private conversations. Apart from the moment of his proposal, their meetings had always taken place in the presence of Mrs Aveton.

She hadn't found it strange. Propriety dictated that young ladies did not spend time alone with unmarried men. As a parson, Charles was allowed more latitude, but he'd never sought private interviews with her. She'd put it down to a strict regard for the conventions, and she'd been glad of his forbearance. She could never think of anything to say to him.

Now she began to wonder. Had he been afraid that she might ply him with awkward questions?

"So you are sure that even isolated cases could not be concealed?" she asked.

"One can't be sure. There are parts of the city where sickness is rife, and the first symptoms of smallpox resemble those of a chill, with shivering and a headache. My dear, this isn't a cheerful subject. Why are you so concerned?"

"It was just that Charles mentioned—" Her words stuck in her throat. She could not explain her suspicions to Dan.

He was on the alert at once. This was the opening for which he had been waiting.

"He would, of course, be the first aware of it...that is, if he ever ventures into the slums...?" He glanced sideways at her face, but noticed no reaction. It was clear that Truscott had mentioned neither his visit to "The Rookery", nor to the house in Seven Dials.

"His duties bring him into contact with the poor," she admitted. "But he says that he is in no danger, as he had a mild attack of the disease some years ago. I wanted to go with him, but he wouldn't hear of it."

Dan stopped, appalled. "You must not consider entering those places!" he ordered roughly. "It isn't just the smallpox, Judith. They are the closest thing to hell that anyone might see."

She looked at him then, and the huge grey eyes were sad. "I know about the poverty and the overcrowding. Prudence and Sebastian take an interest in these matters."

"And do you know about the filth, the stench, the drunken beggars, the ragged children, the thieves, and the murderers?"

Judith's face grew pale. "Then Charles must be in danger every day of his life?"

"Not he! You speak of accompanying him. Did he say where he was going?"

"Not into the slums, my dear." Her anxiety could no longer be contained. "He is gone to visit his mama. He fears she has the smallpox."

Suddenly everything fell into place for Dan. He knew now why Truscott had mentioned the disease.

"Have you met her?" he asked quietly. "I have not heard her spoken of before."

"Nor I." Judith was aware of his startled expression. "You will think me foolish, but I had not thought to ask."

"Nor he to tell you?" All the old antagonism was

back in his tone, and she laid a gentle hand upon his arm.

"Don't let us quarrel," she pleaded. "We have little time, and I am so very glad to see you." She looked up at him with an expression of perfect trust.

Dan's heart turned over. He longed to take her in his arms and to swear that he would care for her forever, but he restrained himself.

What could he offer her? He had neither fortune nor position. The idea of living on her money sickened him, though the winning of an heiress was the stated aim of most of the young bachelors of his acquaintance. Let them do so if they could.

He believed that a man should be able to provide for his own family. His face grew dark. Would he ever reach the point where he could do so?

"Dan? What is it?" Judith slipped her hand in his, but he drew it away as if he could not bear her touch.

"Don't!" he said savagely.

"I'm sorry!" Her lips were trembling. "I didn't mean to offend you."

"Offend me? Don't you know that I...?" He bit back the words he'd been about to say. "Excuse me!" he continued. "I have no wish to quarrel with you."

They had wandered further from Rotten Row, and the pathway between the bushes was almost deserted.

"We should go back," she murmured. If any of their acquaintance should see them together in this place it would be construed as an assignation.

"Why?" he demanded. "Shall we be accused of skulking through the undergrowth?"

Judith smiled at that. "Skulking is not your style, I

think, or mine, but to be found here must give rise to comment.''

He slipped his arm through hers. ''There is no danger of that. It's too early for the beaux. Brummell, you know, is said to spend a full five hours at his toilette each morning…''

''Is that true? I've met him, and I liked him. There's nothing dandified in his appearance, and he is not forever worrying about the set of his coat, or the fall of his cravat.''

''Once dressed, he doesn't give his clothing another thought. One cannot improve on perfection, Judith.''

Dan's blue eyes were twinkling, and Judith felt relieved. This hour with him was a precious time which must not be wasted.

''Have you taken my advice?'' she asked eagerly.

''About the drawings? Yes, I did. Lord Nelson is returned to England, as you know. He is staying at Merton with…er…with the Hamiltons. It isn't far from London…''

''And you have written to him?''

''I heard that at the Battle of the Nile, and again at Copenhagen, he was short of frigates. I sent him my designs for a fast vessel, which is easy to manoeuvre.''

Judith clapped her hands. Her eyes were shining.

''Then if you can supply his needs, you must hear something…?''

''I don't wish to raise your hopes. He may not find the time to study my ideas…''

''He will, I know it! Oh, Dan, he is a wonderful man…a genius! Nothing escapes his attention.''

Dan smiled at her enthusiasm. ''You, too, are an admirer of the hero of the hour?''

"Isn't everyone? This present Peace is due to him. Had he not defeated the French and their allies the war would not have ended."

"Agreed! But enough of my affairs. I've finished reading the chapters which you left with me. Bessie has them in her pocket. She tells me that you have continued with the book."

Judith nodded.

"Then may I see the next part? It is so entertaining. I love the way it flows. You have a way with words, my dear."

"Only on paper," she protested shyly.

"Nonsense! With us there was never time enough to finish our discussions. Am I not right?"

Blushing with pleasure at his praise, Judith failed to notice the approach of a gentleman who strolled towards them from the opposite direction.

It was only when Dan bowed and uttered a word of greeting that she was aware of him.

Significantly, the man did not stop, but looking up, she saw his surprised expression, and wished that the ground might open up and swallow her.

"Take me back to Rotten Row!" she said quickly.

Dan gave her arm a little shake. "I know what you are thinking, but there is no need for alarm. Chessington isn't a rattle."

"That isn't the point. We shouldn't be here alone. I feel like a criminal."

"A sweet criminal," he murmured tenderly. "Must we go back? It is too early for the Grand Strut…"

His teasing served to remove her troubled frown. He knew as well as she that Judith had no interest in admiring the exquisites who strolled among the rank and fashion, quizzing the ladies, indulging in gossip, and speculating upon the likely cost of the newest and most dashing turn-outs of both carriages and horses. This daily event took place between the hours of five o'clock and six.

She gave him a reluctant smile. "Don't make game of me! You know that I am right."

"Very well, if you will have it so." He turned and began to retrace his steps along the path which they had taken from the Row. "But promise me one thing? You will go on…you will finish the book?"

"I don't think I can stop," she assured him. "The words seem to be coming of their own accord."

"That's good! When may I read the rest?"

Judith looked at his eager face. That open countenance was so very dear to her. She longed to tell him that she'd come to Mount Street that very afternoon, but she hesitated, knowing that it would be unwise.

They were slipping back so easily into their old friendship. The thought was bittersweet. It would make it so much harder when she had to part from him for ever.

Why must she continue to torture herself? He'd been kind, but his love for her was dead. Now he could not even bear to touch her hand. She'd been deeply wounded when he'd dragged his own away so swiftly.

"Why don't you answer me?" he asked. "Is it Truscott? Did you not tell me that he is away?"

"He is," she admitted. "But I feel that I'm deceiving him."

"Why so? He had not forbidden you to visit your friends, so I understand."

"No, but it seems wrong of me to go about without a care when he may be in such trouble."

"Judith, he refused your help, possibly for the worthiest of reasons, but it will do no good to shut yourself away."

"I'd forgotten how persuasive you can be," she murmured.

"Have you? I can't agree with you. My efforts in that direction were not always successful…"

This reference to the past made her change the subject hastily. Six years ago they had each said all that there was to say. There was no point in recriminations.

"I'll try," she promised. "If it isn't possible I will send Bessie with the manuscript."

"Prudence will be disappointed. You have not seen her in these past few days." He paused and a shadow crossed his face.

"What is it, Dan? She is not sick, I hope?"

"She is not herself. Sebastian is worried, in spite of what the doctor says…"

"Oh, my dear! She will not lose the child?"

"There are no symptoms, but she is so restless, and the tears come easily. It is unlike her."

"She must be in some discomfort. I am told that these last few months can be a trial. Will Sebastian take her down to Hallwood? The change might do her good."

"I doubt if he would risk the journey now, but Pru is so bored and crochety that he fears it will affect her health."

"She is used to being active. For someone of her lively temperament the enforced rest must be a strain, but it will soon be over. Then she will have her babe, and all will be well again.''

Dan gave her a grateful look. ''Always a stalwart, Judith! I hope you may be right. This is an anxious time for all of us.''

Judith understood him perfectly. So many of the girls she knew had enjoyed but one brief year of marriage before succumbing to the dreaded childbed fever. It was a threat which loomed in many a woman's mind.

''Try not to worry,'' she murmured. ''Sebastian has obtained the services of the best physician in London.''

''I know it, but I can't be easy in my mind.''

Judith gave him an anxious look. She knew just how much Prudence meant to him. As a girl of seventeen she'd helped him to escape with her from a life of slavery in the cotton mills of the industrial north. She and Dan were bound by more than the common ties of friendship.

''I think you have forgotten the redoubtable Miss Grantham,'' she told him with a chuckle. ''Does she not interview your family physicians as to their views on cleanliness and a sensible diet?''

''She does! And she is forthright in expressing her opinions. The lady may be well into her eighties but she can still reduce the medical profession to a jelly.'' The idea cheered him, and he managed a smile. ''Elizabeth did us a great service when she and her aunt became members of the family.''

''I haven't seen Miss Grantham for some time,'' Judith told him. ''I always enjoy her company. She is an original…''

''True! But if you wish to see her soon you had best

make haste. This present Peace of Amiens has inspired her to consider yet another trip to Turkey.''

''At eighty-three?''

''Certainly! No one has yet been able to dissuade her, though Perry and Elizabeth have tried.''

''I feel like a feeble creature beside such enterprise.''

''Not you, my dear. I know your strength of character.'' Dan was unable to say more as they were now within sight of Rotten Row.

''You must leave us now,'' Judith murmured. ''We must not be seen together.''

''But when shall we meet again?''

''I don't know,'' she said uncertainly. ''Tomorrow I may visit Hatchard's to buy some books…''

''I'll be there,'' he promised.

He left her a prey to the most severe misgivings. Dan had complimented her upon her strength of character, whereas in reality she was weak-willed. Had she not vowed to forget him, and to prepare herself with fortitude for the life which lay ahead of her? Now she was behaving in a way which must be considered reprehensible.

The mention of a visit to Hatchard's in Piccadilly was not exactly the offer of a secret meeting. Or was it? Honesty compelled her to admit the truth. She could deceive herself no longer. When her choice lay between her obvious duty to the Reverend Charles, and the opportunity of a meeting with the man she loved, she knew that she would follow the dictates of her heart.

Poor Charles! He might at this very moment be sitting beside a sickbed. She was behaving in a wicked way, and it was only right that the happiness for which she longed should be denied her.

Chapter Seven

That gentleman was suffering in a different way.

On the day of his attack upon the child he'd left Judith in great haste to hurry back to the parish of St Giles. He'd no idea what he would find there, but he took the precaution of arming himself with a serviceable pistol in addition to the knife which he always carried.

A hackney took him as far as the entrance to "The Rookery", and there he dismissed the jarvey with an acid comment upon the reeking straw which covered the floor of the conveyance.

"Beg pardon, your honour!" the jehu sneered. "We ain't up to the standards of your own fine carriage." He backed away from the expression on his passenger's face.

This piece of impertinence did nothing to improve the preacher's temper. By the time he reached his destination he was in murderous mood. Someone should pay for the ruin of his plans.

When he reached his mother's door he didn't knock. Hopefully, he'd take her by surprise. Intent upon his purpose, he didn't hear the sound behind him until it was too late. Then a violent blow between his shoulder-blades sent him sprawling into the room. As a booted foot pinned him to the ground he heard an unfamiliar voice.

"Tie him up!" it ordered.

His wrists were seized and dragged together behind his back. Then they were bound together with a cord so thin and strong that it cut into his flesh.

"Up with him!"

He was lifted to his feet and thrust roughly into the single wicker chair. For the first time he was able to get a good look at his attackers.

The younger man he recognised at once. He'd been present at each of his previous visits to Nellie. His middle-aged companion was a stranger, though there was something about him which Truscott found it difficult to place. He searched his memory without success.

The only other occupant of the room was the child he'd used so cruelly. One of the boy's eyes was closed, but the other regarded him with such malevolence, combined with an unholy glee, that the preacher looked away.

"Where's Nellie?" he demanded.

"She's still alive! No thanks to you!" The younger of his two assailants bunched his fist, and delivered such a crushing blow to Truscott's jaw that both the chair and its occupant flew over backwards.

"Now, Sam, that ain't no way to treat our visitor! Remember, he's our ticket to a life of ease…"

"He's a murdering devil! You won't stop me from giving him a taste of his own medicine…"

"Later, Sam! However, I feel you have a point. Perhaps we should convince him that we are not to be trifled with. Fetch him through!''

"Best search him first," the child suggested.

"Certainly! An excellent plan! I promised you that pleasure, Jemmy, if your sharp eyes saw him first. Go ahead, my boy…!''

As the child approached him, Truscott was tempted to kick him away, but something in the older man's expression stopped him. Even so, Jemmy was careful to stand behind the chair, reaching forward to delve into pockets with all the skills of an experienced thief.

The preacher's watch and chain had caught his eye so he removed that first, laying it on the floor beside him. His next discovery was the pistol.

"Well, well! Were you expecting trouble, my dear sir? I think we shall be able to accommodate you.'' The smiles on the faces of both his captors were not encouraging.

Jemmy continued with his search, and the pile beside him grew as he added a leather bag of coin, two silk handkerchiefs and a bunch of keys. He stretched out a claw-like hand to open the purse, but this brought him a sharp reproof.

"Not yet, Jemmy! The share-out will come later.'' The man's eyes were on his captive's face. The preacher was too calm. He hadn't uttered a word of protest at the loss of his possessions. Perhaps there were still some to be found.

Then Truscott made a mistake. Stretching out his legs, apparently in an effort to ease his cramped position, he slid one booted foot behind the other.

His tormentor gave a grunt of triumph.

"Jemmy, the boots! You have forgot to search the

boots!'' He picked up the pistol and examined it. ''Loaded, I see! Now, sir, you will oblige me by not attempting to struggle. I have not the least objection to rendering you unconscious with a blow from the butt of this useful weapon.''

Truscott ground his teeth in fury as Jemmy pounced. When the child rose to his feet again he was holding the knife, which he then proceeded to brandish close to the preacher's eyes.

''No, no, my dear! The reverend gentleman will pay for your injuries in good measure, but you must not be too hasty. Now, Sam, bear a hand!''

Together the two men dragged Truscott to his feet and manhandled him out of the door, across the passage and into the room which faced them. There even Truscott, hardened though he was to villainy, could not repress a shudder. The place was a shambles. Ominous patches of some dark substance stained the floorboards, and the walls were bespattered to above head height with what he knew was blood. Some fearful struggle had taken place here.

''Sam, our visitor will wish to see his friends...''

Sam nodded. He walked over to a closet in the corner, and opened it in silence.

Truscott froze, his eyes starting from his head in horror as he looked at the two corpses. His two accomplices had been murdered with extreme brutality. The shirt of the nearest man was a mass of stab wounds whilst the other man was unrecognisable. His head had been beaten to a pulp.

The preacher swayed as the sweet and unmistakable stench of death assailed his nostrils.

"Dear me! Sam, our friend is not feeling well. We must persuade him to sit down…''

Sam closed the door to the closet and helped his companion to drag the preacher away.

This time his legs were bound. Trussed as he was, he felt completely helpless, and it took all his self-control to crush a rising sense of panic. He swallowed, wishing that his throat were not so dry. It was difficult to speak.

"What has all this to do with me?'' he croaked. "I've never seen those men before…''

"Strange! Before they died they were…er… persuaded to give us a full description of the man who had employed them…though naturally they weren't aware of his true identity.''

"Then why should you think that it was me? They did not know me as—'' Truscott stopped. He had almost given himself away.

"As the Reverend Charles Truscott? Of course not! But, sir, you shall not take me for a fool. I had been expecting something of this kind…''

The preacher stared at him. Who was this man? His speech was educated and his manner smooth. Perhaps an unfrocked parson, or a disgraced lawyer?

"I see that you don't remember me. I find that curious since we shared His Majesty's hospitality together. Well, well, my appearance has changed somewhat since then.'' The speaker patted his paunch. "The toll of the years, my friend! When we shared a cell in Newgate I was not as stout, and my hair was as dark as your own.''

"Newgate?'' As memory flooded back his captive paled. "Then you are…?''

"Margrave the forger.'' The man's face changed, and his eyes bored into Truscott's own. "I ain't forgotten you. You served me an ill turn when you stole from me to bribe the turnkey. That money was to buy my own way out…''

"You are mistaken. It wasn't me…"

"I'm not mistaken, though you weren't a reverend then. Some talk of murder, wasn't there? Can't say that I blame you in one way. You were no keener to get your neck stretched than I was myself, but it was a dirty trick…a dirty trick…"

"You must be mad," Truscott told him coldly.

"Oh, I ain't mad, though it turned my brain a bit at first. I searched for you for years, but you covered your tracks well. It was quite by chance that I fell in with Nellie. It was the name that brought you back to mind. Now you owe me, and you'll pay."

"I've said I'll pay. I told Nellie so…" Truscott gave up all pretence of ignorance.

He was desperate to escape. They wouldn't kill him, but they knew the errand upon which his accomplices had been sent. He might be in for a beating so severe that it would cripple him. He swallowed convulsively and his captor was quick to see it.

"Don't care for a taste of your own medicine, Reverend? You won't be harmed, much as I'd like to thrash you till you squeal. We have a little task for you."

"What's that?"

"There is the small matter of your friends next door. They must be disposed of. I believe a funeral is in order. Who better to conduct it than yourself?"

Truscott was silent.

"Nellie has it in hand. She is at this moment ordering two coffins… This evening will be best, I think. Less chance of your being recognised."

"Even if I were it would not be remarked," came the haughty reply. The preacher was recovering his confidence.

"Possibly not. You chose the right profession, but even here you aren't so anxious to be seen. Are you being followed?"

"Of course not!" Truscott snapped. "Why should I be followed? No one suspects—"

"Aye! You were always glib, but this time you over-reached yourself."

"I don't know what you mean…"

"Don't you? Remember the old saying, that if you want a job done well, you must do it yourself?"

Truscott stared at him.

"Didn't want to soil your hands? Even so, you might have thought of a better plan. Your friends from Seven Dials were known here. I spotted them at once. Why would men like that ply Nellie and her friends with drink, and then suggest a gin shop near the river? Too obvious, my dear sir."

Truscott ground his teeth. So that was how they had been caught. He felt no pity for them. His henchmen had behaved like fools, and richly deserved their fate.

Then he heard the clatter of feet upon the stairs. The door burst open to reveal his mother, with Sam's doxy by her side. Nellie paused for only a moment. Then, with a scream of fury, she rushed towards him, scratching at his face with nails grown as long as talons.

Margrave pulled her away.

"Nellie, my dear, you must control yourself! Would you destroy the good looks of our hopeful bridegroom even further? You won't wish to delay his wedding." Margrave pushed a bottle towards her. "Bring that along! We're all in need of refreshment after our exertions.'' He smiled pleasantly at his captive. ''I fear that we must leave you now, but we shall return this evening. May I suggest that you spend the time in composing a eulogy for the dead?''

Once alone, the preacher began to struggle with his bonds, but the strong cord would not give. It was cutting into his flesh, he was cold and thirsty, his mouth was swollen from the blow he had received, and the scratches on his face were bleeding freely.

He forced himself to ignore the discomfort. He must think. He was in no immediate danger. If his captors wished to gain their objective they must release him. The loss of his possessions had angered him, but he would recover them and more besides.

This scum would not defeat him. He'd go through with tonight's charade, and then let them take care.

That evening he walked through the streets ahead of the macabre procession, ignoring an occasional chuckle from Margrave. Once the coffins had been consigned to paupers' graves he turned.

''My keys!'' he demanded. ''I can't get into the vestry without them.''

Margrave handed them over. ''You won't forget us, my friend? Today's contribution won't go far. Perhaps another visit next week?''

Truscott nodded his assent. Let them believe that he was in their power. He walked away without a backward glance and made his way to the house in Seven Dials. Judith would not wonder at his absence for a day or two. It would take that time for his face to heal. It must be an appalling sight. His mistress confirmed his suspicions. She backed away from him in horror.

"What has happened?" she cried.

"What does it look like? I was set upon and robbed. Is there any money in the house?"

"Only a few coppers. You never leave much here."

"Brandy?"

"You finished it last time. There's gin…"

"Fetch it, and some food." He pushed past her, and pouring some water into a bowl he began to bathe his battered face. The deep scratches stung, but the consumption of more than a pint of gin served to deaden the pain. He no longer felt hungry. Ignoring the offer of a platter of bread and cheese, he threw himself upon the bed and slept till morning.

By the end of the following day he had consumed most of the food in the house and all the liquor. His demand for more brought a terrified response.

"Sir, they won't serve me without money…"

"Pledge your credit then."

"What with? Must I take this?" She picked up a handsome vase.

He took it from her with great care. Then he slapped her sharply across the face.

"Don't be a fool! You'd be set upon before you'd gone five yards. There are other ways of getting money."

She understood him perfectly, and she coloured.

"I…I don't know how to go about it. What must I do?"

"If you don't know, then I can't tell you. My God! Why must I be cursed with idiots?" He threw his boots at her. ''Take these! Tomorrow you'll be able to retrieve them.''

A plan was forming in his mind. Judith Aveton was the softest touch he knew. The girl must go to her and beg for charity. She would not be refused. He'd be in no danger. His mistress did not know him as Charles Truscott.

Next day he sent her off with strict instructions. She was not to approach the other ladies of the Aveton household. She must ask for Judith and no one else.

The girl came back empty-handed.

''They turned me away from the door,'' she explained. ''Don't hit me! I did my best.''

''Fool! You must try again tomorrow.'' Truscott realised that he had put himself in an impossible position. Without his boots he was trapped within the house. ''Approach the lady in the street. You can't mistake her. A tall creature, somewhat dowdy-looking, but a gentlewoman, for all that...''

''She didn't walk out today. I waited—''

''She must walk out some time. I'm losing patience with you, my girl. No more excuses, or you'll get a taste of my belt.''

He used her cruelly that night, and sent her out in an exhausted state. Waiting by the railings of the Aveton home she saw Judith almost at once, but hesitated to approach her. The lady was accompanied by her maid. Perhaps in the Park? But no! A gentleman had come to join her. The girl was in despair. She durst not return to Seven Dials to confess her failure yet again. It was only when Judith left the park that desperation forced her into action. She hurried along behind her quarry.

"Miss!" she cried. "Miss, of your charity, won't you help me?"

Judith didn't hear her. She'd been reliving the precious hour she'd spent with Dan. Then the girl caught at her sleeve.

"Be off with you!" Bessie attempted to shoulder her away, but Judith turned.

"What is it?" she asked quietly. "No, Bessie, please don't interfere! You may go indoors…"

Bessie ignored the mistress's request, choosing to remain on guard.

"Miss Judith, watch your reticule! I don't like the look of this one!"

A glance from Judith reduced her to silence. Her gentle employer did not often show displeasure, but when she did so Bessie felt it keenly. She subsided.

"Oh, please! I don't mean to rob you, but I must have money. We have no food, and Josh's boots are pledged… Miss, he can't go out until I get them back."

Bessie snorted in amusement, but Judith did not smile. There was fear in the girl's eyes, and she seemed to be close to collapse.

"I have very little money with me." Judith pressed all the coins she had into the girl's hand. "Come indoors, and I will give you more."

The girl backed away. "They won't let me in. When I asked for you they threatened to give me over to the magistrate."

"I see!" Judith tried to contain her rising anger. "Then we must meet again. Tomorrow I shall be in Piccadilly. Will you come there, to the bookshop?"

"Thank 'ee, miss. What time?"

"Shall we say at noon?" Judith gazed at the pale exhausted face, and suddenly she was puzzled. "You say you asked for me? How did you know my name?"

"Josh knows the Reverend Truscott, ma'am. He speaks well of you. Josh was sure that you would help us…"

"Until tomorrow, then?" Judith smiled at the girl. "Pray buy some food, my dear. I fear the boots must wait."

As the girl hurried away Judith went indoors. She was tempted to take the porter to task for his lack of charity towards their unfortunate caller. It was strange, she mused, how some servants, however lowly their position, showed little kindness to those who were less fortunate than themselves.

She held her tongue. This was Mrs Aveton's house, and here she had no rights.

She felt no such constraints when Bessie brought the subject up again.

"Boots, forsooth! A likely story! These beggars will tell you anything, Miss Judith, and bless me if you don't believe them!"

"You surprise me, Bessie!" Judith's look was stern. "I thought the girl was telling the truth, but even if not, you must have seen how weak and tired she looked."

Bessie flushed at the reproach. "You'd give your last penny, miss, and well you know it!"

"How foolish you must think me!" The words, spoken in Judith's usual quiet tones, were enough to persuade Bessie that she had gone too far. She raised her handkerchief to her eyes.

"No, don't weep! You may leave me now. I shan't need you again today."

This calm dismissal was too much for Bessie. "Oh, Miss Judith, don't send me away! I didn't mean—"

"Bessie, don't be such a goose!" Judith's smile returned. "You thought you were taking care of me. As for sending you away? I meant only that I shan't go out again today."

The explanation was enough to satisfy her maid, but when she left the room Judith took herself to task. Perhaps she'd been too harsh with this old friend who loved her so, but unkindness was the one thing which never failed to rouse her to anger.

And something else was troubling her. How odd it seemed that Charles had mentioned her name to one of his parishioners as a likely source of charity when he himself had access to the Fund for Paupers. Then she remembered. Charles was at a sickbed. The girl's case must be urgent, or he would have dealt with it on his return. Doubtless he had no idea when that might be.

Having satisfied herself on that point, she opened the drawer in her desk and examined her remaining funds. Her allowance for the quarter was largely untouched. She set aside a small sum for necessities, and put the rest into her reticule.

Hopefully, it would save the girl from immediate want for the next few weeks at least. The pale, stricken face could not be banished from her mind. How young she was, barely out of her teens, if Judith herself was any judge. And she'd looked so frail and weak, thin to the point of emaciation. Possibly it was due to hunger, but the pallid skin and the sunken eyes suggested something more. It seemed to her that the girl was ill.

Her anger rose. Who was this Josh…this man she'd mentioned? Not her husband, certainly. Judith had seen no wedding ring. But whether he was a relative or a casual protector, he might have taken better care of the poor soul.

When Charles returned she would speak to him about the case. There might be something he could do to help.

She was still preoccupied with the problem when she walked to Piccadilly on the following day. Dan was waiting for her by the door of Hatchard's, and he came towards her, his blue eyes sparkling with pleasure.

She was about to greet him when she saw the girl.

"Dan, will you excuse me for a moment?" she murmured. She thrust her purse into the girl's hand. "This will help," she said with her sweetest smile. "If you come to me next week, I may be able to do more for you."

To her surprise, the girl produced a folded paper and thrust it into her hand.

"Why, what is this?" she asked.

"It's a message, miss."

"From whom?"

The girl looked terrified. "I wasn't to answer any questions," she muttered. Then she disappeared into the crowd.

"A mystery?" Dan teased. "Who was that girl? Does she bring you a message from a secret admirer?"

"I doubt it!" Judith opened the note. It was brief, ill-spelt, and written in an illiterate hand on a torn scrap of paper. "I don't understand," she murmured as she handed it to Dan. "Can you make sense of it?"

"Parson sez as you ain't to worrit. Girl knows noth-

ing, so save your breath. Rev. comes back termorrer.''
Dan read the words aloud. "My dear, this is a mystery
indeed. The parson, I take it, is the Reverend Charles.
Why could he not write to you himself?"

"I don't know. Perhaps he feared to spread the infection…?"

"Did he not tell you that he was immune?"

"He did." Judith searched the crowd in vain for
some trace of the girl. "Oh, dear! I should have read it
before I let her go. She might have been able to tell me
what is happening…and given me some word of
Charles and his mother."

Dan's eyes rested on her face. "I fear she would tell
you nothing. You do not recognise the writing?" He
was beginning to have his own suspicions as to the author of the note, but wisely he did not voice them.

"No. It seems to be from a man…perhaps this Josh
that the girl has mentioned. Charles is acquainted with
him. That was how she knew my name and where to
find me."

"For what purpose?"

Judith coloured. "She was in need of help."

"So that was why you handed her your purse? My
dear Judith, Mr Truscott should have taken care of it
from the Parish Funds."

"But, Dan, he isn't there, and you could see from
her appearance that the case is urgent."

Dan wasn't satisfied, but he sensed that Judith felt
distressed. "Doubtless Mr Truscott will explain when
next you see him," he comforted her. He would not
betray his feelings to her, but his suspicions grew. It
was only with an effort that he forced a smile.

"Shall we go in?" He took her arm to lead her into the bookshop.

Judith shook her head. "You will think me a pea-goose, but shall you mind if we do not? I...I am not in the mood to choose a book today."

Dan guessed at once that she had parted with all the money in her possession.

"Not even one?" he urged. "I was hoping to make you a present of something that would please you."

"Oh, please...you must not!"

"Why not? It would be just a token of appreciation from an old friend."

"Appreciation? For what?" Judith was blushing. She looked so adorable in her confusion that he longed to take her in his arms and smother her face with kisses. If only he might do so...

"Why, for all the pleasure which your own book has given me," he said lightly. "I can't wait for the day when we see it displayed in Hatchard's window."

"You are dreaming!" Judith chuckled. "Take care, or you will give me a swollen head!"

"I hope not! I like your head exactly the way it is, and that bonnet is a triumph!"

"Dan! You never used to speak so foolishly," she reproached him, although she flushed with pleasure. She'd been doubtful about the full poke-front of the satin straw, but the puffs of ribbon trimming matched her new spencer so exactly that Bessie had coaxed her into buying it.

"Then I must have been a prosy bore...or blind," Dan joked. "Perhaps I saw the jewel, rather than the setting." He saw that this reference to the past had disturbed her. He had said too much, and he was quick to change the subject.

"I too have a message for you, Judith. Prudence would like to see you. She begged me to invite you to join us for a late nuncheon."

"I had supposed that visitors would tire her." The half-truth was excusable, but it was not Judith's main reason for ending her visits to Mount Street.

"She is alone today. Perry and Elizabeth are gone to visit Miss Grantham, and Sebastian has a meeting with his man of business."

"Oh, Dan, you should not have left her!"

"When I said that I might see you, she insisted. My dear, do come! As I told you yesterday, she is low in spirits at this time, and much in need of a change of conversation."

Judith thought for a moment. Nothing would give her greater pleasure than to accompany him to Mount Street.

"You have other commitments?" he asked anxiously. "Must you return to Mrs Aveton?"

Judith made a quick decision. "I shan't be missed," she said with a half smile. "When I come to Hatchard's I forget the time. Mrs Aveton will not look for me for hours."

Dan's face brightened, and he gave her a dazzling smile as he took her arm. "Then I shall steal you away," he said. "Shall we walk, or must I summon a hackney?"

"I prefer to walk in this fine spring weather." It was not the wisest of decisions in this crowded part of London, as Judith realised too late. They might be seen by some of their acquaintance. She comforted herself with the thought that at this hour most members of the ton were still abed. Polite society did not stir abroad much before five in the afternoon.

Even so, she turned to the left when they crossed Piccadilly.

"You don't wish to see the shops in Bond Street?" Dan teased.

"May we not take a quieter way? It will be quicker."

Dan made no objection. He fell into step beside her, and slipped her arm through his as they turned into Berkeley Street.

"Is speed essential, Judith?" He was glancing down at her with an expression which made her heart turn over. "I welcome the chance to have you to myself."

Judith looked away, and was surprised to see that one or two of the passers-by were smiling at them in fond amusement. She crimsoned. She and Dan must look like lovers. She pulled away from him.

"What is it?" he asked.

"We should have taken a hackney. Oh, Dan, this is all wrong. I shouldn't be here with you."

"Why not?" Dan continued to walk on beside her.

"Because...because I am betrothed, and you know it is not proper for us to walk alone."

"Bessie is but a yard or two behind us," he told her calmly. "Besides, we are almost there..."

"No!" she said. "I've changed my mind. I must go home."

He stopped then, looking at her gravely. "Judith, we have not spoken of the past. I believe it is time we did so." Without waiting for her reply he turned into Mount Street, but she did not follow him.

Dan retraced his steps and held out a hand to her. "My dear, you know that I am right. We cannot go on like this."

Chapter Eight

Judith found herself at a loss for words. Even then she might have fled, but she stood transfixed as she tried to resolve the chaos in her mind.

Dan stood in silence as he awaited her decision, and at last she gave him a look which was painful in its intensity.

"Perhaps you are right," she whispered. "Then we shall lay old ghosts to rest…"

It had been an agonising choice. She had no wish to discuss the past, or have old wounds reopened, or to relive the pain of parting all those years ago, but she couldn't pretend that it hadn't happened.

Above all, she didn't want to hear what Dan was so clearly about to tell her. He no longer loved her. She'd been deceiving herself to imagine that there was some-times more than friendly affection in his manner. Now she was making him uncomfortable, behaving in such a missish way, blushing like a schoolgirl at his compli-ments, and babbling on about the proprieties like some dowager.

She must pull herself together. There was such a

thing as civilised behaviour. Engagements were broken every day, but hearts did not break so easily. The world went on, and old lovers met again, but surely they could not suffer as she was suffering now.

And she had brought this suffering on herself. It would have been easier, so much easier, not to have agreed to meet him. She must have been mad. In two short weeks she would be married to another man. Now she was being fair to neither Dan nor her betrothed. Her behaviour was unworthy of any woman of character, and it must change.

Pale but resolute, she allowed Dan to lead her through the hall of the Wentworth mansion, and into the library.

He offered her a chair, and then he began to pace the room. She guessed that he was wondering how to begin.

"What did you wish to say to me?" she asked at last. The silence had become unbearable.

"So much that it would take a lifetime! Oh, my dear, I have no wish to distress you, but—"

"We haven't got a lifetime," she said dully. "In two weeks' time I shall be wed."

He came to her then and knelt beside her, taking her hands in his. "Look at me!" he begged. "I know that you aren't happy. I haven't seen you look like this since the day we parted all those years ago..."

Judith disengaged her hands and turned her head away.

"I'm tired, that is all. Brides have these attacks of nerves, or so I hear. It is the strain of all the preparations—" Dan silenced her with a finger on her lips.

"Dearest, this is Dan," he reminded her. "I know

your every look…your every gesture. Were we not once as close as a man and a woman could be?"

Judith took her courage in both hands. She must not allow him to suspect that the memory of their love had never faded. He must not know how much all remembrance of the past distressed her, or he would blame himself for her pain.

"We were very young," she whispered. "When I look back it seems to me that we were little more than children."

"You didn't think so then."

"I know, but it was all so long ago. In extreme youth one's emotions are at their most intense. It wasn't the time to make decisions for the future."

"You made yours," he said simply. "And it broke my heart. Oh, Judith, for years there was not a single day when I didn't feel your hand in mine, or sense your presence near me, even at the far ends of the earth."

"You knew my reasons…"

"I couldn't accept them then." Dan rose to his feet and resumed his pacing. "I tried to hate you for the way you sacrificed our love because of Mrs Aveton's slanders. I thought we might have faced them."

Judith was silent.

"Later I realised that I was wrong," he continued. "I must have been made to think that I could win you. What could I have offered you? A lad without breeding or fortune?"

"You would have made your way," she whispered.

"Through patronage, or as one of Sebastian's dependents? I would not have had it so, and neither would you."

Judith did not argue, though she longed to do so. She

cared nothing about his birth or lack of fortune, but at nineteen she could not see his life destroyed by the actions of an evil woman.

"Then perhaps it was for the best," she told him in a neutral tone. "Won't you take me to Prudence?"

"Not yet. Bear with me for another moment. For the sake of our old friendship, I'll ask you once again. Are you happy?"

Judith would not meet his eyes. "I am content," she murmured.

He slipped a finger beneath her chin and raised her face to his. "Tell me the truth! Do you love this man as we once loved? If you do, I shall not say another word."

Driven beyond endurance, Judith struck his hand away. "You have no right to ask!" she cried wildly.

"That's true, but you have given me my answer. Oh, my dear, won't you reconsider this betrothal before it is too late?"

"Stop!" She raised a hand to silence him. "You promised not to interfere. Why should I listen to you? What do you want of me?"

"Only your happiness, believe me. Give yourself time…"

"I can't." Judith rose to her feet. "I won't cry off now."

All hope had left her. She had given Dan his opportunity to tell her that he loved her still. He had not done so.

He'd changed more than she had at first suspected. The boy who once considered the world well lost for love had matured into a man who understood the values of the society in which he lived. Yet they were not his own. Dan would never seek the prize of a rich wife. He'd made it clear that he would make his way through his own efforts, or not at all.

She too had changed. At nineteen she would have scorned the notion of contentment as a basis for marriage. In those days love was all. She and Dan had shared something precious, something beyond a meeting of minds. In that halcyon time their passion had consumed them, giving their lives a radiance which she would never know again. In his every look and touch her world had been born anew.

"Oh, Dan!" It was a cry of despair. Unconsciously, she stretched out her hands to him.

If he'd taken her in his arms she would have offered him herself, her fortune and her love. Pride was a luxury which a woman in love could not afford.

He did not touch her. She did not know it, but he dared not or his resolve would have crumbled.

"Perhaps you are right," he told her stiffly. "I shall not speak of it again."

His situation was unchanged. All he could offer her was his love. He knew her tender heart. She might accept him out of pity, and that he could not bear. All he could do now was to protect her as best he could, putting her own happiness before his own.

"Prudence will be waiting," he said quietly.

Judith's hands fell to her sides. It had been a mistake to come here. Dan had asked only that she give herself time. Time for what? If she entered into another relationship, it would not bring her the happiness for which she longed. First love was an illusion, so she'd heard. It wasn't so in her case. Dan was all she wanted. She would love him, and him alone, for the rest of her days.

The look on her face destroyed his hard-won composure.

"Forgive me!" he murmured. "I have upset you. You were right. It was a mistake to speak of the past. We can't change it now…"

Judith was perilously close to tears. Perhaps they could not change the past, but they could change the future. She was about to tell him so, but his face was set, and she knew it would be useless to attempt to sway him.

Now she longed to be alone with her misery. To be so close to him was simply to prolong her torture, but there was Prudence to consider. She made a valiant effort to speak of something else.

"Have…have you heard from Admiral Nelson?" she asked.

"No!" he told her shortly. "I have long ceased to hope for miracles."

"Or even ceased to hope?" Judith lost her temper then as frustration and unhappiness overwhelmed her. "You disappoint me, Dan! Why won't you fight for what you want? Go to Merton! See the Admiral! What have you got to lose?" She rounded on him with eyes ablaze, only to find that he was smiling down at her.

"That's better!" he said gently. "I see that you haven't lost your spirit."

"Have you?"

"Judith, as I told you, I've tried for years to promote my own designs—"

"Well, try again! Oh, if I were a man I should not be so easily discouraged… Promise me that you will visit Lord Nelson!" In her eagerness to persuade him Judith had come alive again.

"Peace!" he begged as he backed away in mock terror. "I promise to obey you. Indeed, as I value my life I can do no other."

He was happy to see her smile, reluctant though it was. The years had dropped away, and now she was much more like the girl he'd known in his youth.

Unknown to Judith, he'd already made up his mind to go to Merton. The Great Man might refuse to see him, or worse, dismiss his ideas as totally impractical, but he had to try. The matter was urgent.

In suggesting that Judith give herself time to reconsider, he'd cherished the faint hope that if success should come his way at last, it might not be too late.

With the certain prospect of a career as a naval architect he would work until his reputation was second to none. Others had done it in different fields, with no better start than his. Sir Christopher Wren had rebuilt much of London, and so many of the churches were the work of Nicholas Hawksmoor. Inigo Jones had started his career apprenticed to a joiner, Dan thought in some amusement. It was a modest start for one whose genius as an architect was now well recognised.

If they could do it, so could he, but he needed time, and time was running out for him. He found himself praying that she would heed his words, and at least postpone her marriage.

Then, if all went well for him, he would woo her once again. Perhaps he was dreaming, but he could hope. There had been something in her manner when she'd flown out at him in fury which suggested that she still cared deeply what became of him.

Yet he must not raise her expectations, or his own.

It would be too cruel. He took Judith's hand and kissed it.

"Friends again?" he asked.

It was at this point that Sebastian entered the room. With his customary good manners he betrayed no surprise at finding Dan and Judith alone.

"Dan has persuaded you to visit us?" he said with a smile. "My dear, you are our saviour. Prudence will be delighted…"

He led the way across the hall, and up the massive staircase to his wife's room. Prudence was lying on a day-bed, turning the pages of her book in a way which suggested that it did not hold her interest.

Beautifully groomed, as always, her glorious hair was caught high in a bandeau which matched her embroidered negligée of sea-green gauze.

"My dear, you look quite lovely!" Judith exclaimed. "How do you feel today?"

"Much like a barrel!" Prudence said with feeling. "I wonder if I shall ever see my toes again."

"Nothing is more certain." Sebastian bent and kissed his wife. "My love, you ladies will have much to say to each other. Shall you mind if I steal Dan away for a few moments?"

"Secrets?" Prudence gave him a quizzical look. "Are we to hear about them later?"

"All in good time, I promise." He signalled to Dan, and walked swiftly from the room.

Prudence smiled at Judith. "I fear that I have a cruel husband. Tales of a mystery would have been a welcome diversion, but now I have your company, so I shan't complain."

"This is a trying time for you," Judith said with sympathy. "Can I do anything to make you more comfortable?"

"The pillow behind my back has slipped. If you could raise it a little…?" Prudence struggled to sit upright.

Judith slipped an arm around her and pushed the pillow into place. She noticed that Prudence was sweating.

"Would you like me to bathe your head?" she suggested. "It is so warm today."

"I should like that," Prudence murmured. "Oh dear, I am a dreadful bore at present! I wonder how Sebastian bears with me…"

"He understands." Judith poured water into a bowl and soaked a cloth. "You are the light of his life, as you know…"

"But sadly dimmed for the moment…" Prudence hadn't lost her sense of humour. "Oh, Judith, that feels so good!" She lay back and closed her eyes, enjoying the feel of the cool cloth against her brow. "Can you stay for a time?"

"Of course, if that is what you wish…" Judith continued with her task.

"I do. You are such a peaceful person. You don't fuss, or worry me with stupid questions. I cannot abide a fidget."

"Of course not!" Judith soothed her. "There is nothing worse than a busy person when one is feeling not quite up to the mark."

"I am not sick, you know." Prudence managed a weary smile. "But I have a million things to do. It is so galling to be forced to lie here thinking about them."

"Then don't." Judith had an inspiration. "You can help me if you will…just by listening as you lie there."

Prudence sighed. "My dear, I should not dream of offering you advice. Did we not promise not to speak of your betrothal?"

"It isn't that. Pru, how could you think that I should worry you about it? This is something else…"

"More secrets?"

"Well, yes, in a way." Judith looked a little conscious. "I'd like your opinion on…on my book."

"Your book?" Prudence opened her eyes and sat up suddenly. "You are actually writing a book? My dear, how wonderful! We said always that you should do so. Do you have it with you?"

Judith chuckled, though her colour rose. "It is not so wonderful that I must carry it about with me, but Dan has asked to see it, so I brought the manuscript today. Of course, I have not spoken of it to…to…"

"To anyone else? Never fear! Your secret is safe with me. I confess that I'm flattered to be asked for my opinion."

"I could be wasting my time," Judith told her gravely. "I am not the best judge of my own work. Dan liked the first few chapters, but it may be that he is simply offering me encouragement."

Prudence considered for a moment. "No, you are mistaken! I'm sure he would be honest, even if you did not enjoy his criticism. You are much too sensible to ask for an opinion if you did not wish to hear the truth."

"I'm glad you think as I do. Flattery is valueless. I prefer to have my weaknesses pointed out. It can be helpful to a novice."

"Hardly a novice, Judith! Have you not been writing since you could first put pen to paper?"

"That's true, but they were childish efforts—"

"And what of your essays which made us laugh so much? Is the book in the same amusing vein?"

"Perhaps you'd like to judge for yourself? That is, if it won't tire you to hear me read aloud?"

"My dear, it will be a godsend! I quite fancy myself a literary critic. How foolish I have been to trouble my mind with lesser matters! You have quite restored me. Read on, I beg of you."

"Now you are funning," Judith said severely. "I believe you to be the most complete hand...and quite as bad as Perry."

"Never doubt it! Sebastian despairs of me... I rely on the patience of my friends." Prudence leaned back against her pillows, but her expression was so comical that Judith began to laugh.

"No, Madame Author, pray be serious! This will not do, you know. We are to have a serious discussion..."

Judith gave up. She took the manuscript from her reticule, leafing over several pages until she reached the chapter which had pleased her most. Then, in her clear and beautiful tones, she launched into her story.

Prudence said nothing for a time. Then Judith heard a chuckle. Encouraged, she continued until the chuckle became an outright shout of laughter.

"Judith, I shall never ask you to another party, you sly creature! You sit there, looking as if butter wouldn't melt, whilst you look into our hearts as if we were made of glass."

"Not yours, Prudence, nor those of any of my friends. Have I been too cruel? I did not mean to pillory any one particular person. It is just that sometimes I feel that we...Polite Society, I mean...are like the froth upon a seething cauldron. Skimmed off, and thrown away, we should be no great loss.''

''Never say so, Judith!'' Prudence grew serious. ''Excellence may appear in the most unlikely circumstances. Take the Prince Regent, for example. He is extravagant, self-indulgent, almost certainly a bigamist, and an uncertain friend. Yet consider his achievements! The first member of the Royal Family for centuries with a true regard for culture.''

''Yes, but…''

''But his influence is felt throughout society. Look about you, not only in this house, but in others. Have you seen such craftsmanship in furniture, in decoration, in clothing, and…oh, I don't know…I suppose I must describe it as a way of life… You won't deny that it is civilised?''

''Of course not, but is it enough?''

''It isn't!'' Prudence gave her a straight look. ''Why do you think I am fretting so? Pregnancy? Not so! I am used to this condition, and happy to give Sebastian our children. Yet I can't forget the evils which surround us. I'd made a start in changing the conditions in the northern mills, especially for the children, but now I feel so helpless.''

''You will continue with the work. I wish that I might say the same.''

''Then that was why…? Forgive me, as I am being indiscreet, but we all wondered at your decision to marry a parson.''

''I hope I can be useful,'' Judith told her warmly. ''Oh, Pru, I know that you don't like Charles Truscott, but you don't know him. He means to devote his life to helping others.''

This sanguine belief was not echoed in the library below.

"You have news?" Dan had scarcely been able to contain himself until he was out of earshot of the servants.

"Yes! There have been developments. I thought it best to meet our Runner in a coffee house." Sebastian gave the younger man a hard look. "You will keep this to yourself, of course?"

"Of course! But tell me what has happened…"

"Truscott returned to the parish of St Giles. He spent the day in a certain house. When he emerged it was to conduct a funeral."

"Outside his own parish?"

"Unusual, perhaps, but nothing out of the way, except that one of the mourners was well known to our man. His name is Margrave."

Dan looked mystified. "You've heard of him?"

"So has half the world. Dick Margrave is a well-known forger. There were ugly rumours. He escaped the noose by a whisker. He was due for transportation when he disappeared."

"Our quarry keeps strange company," Dan observed.

"There is more. Truscott was well muffled, but at the graveside he was forced to reveal his face. He appeared to have been beaten…"

"A quarrel among thieves? I'm only sorry that they didn't kill him."

"You are jumping to conclusions, Dan."

"Am I? If he'd been attacked by strangers, why did he stay in 'the Rookery'? The obvious course would have been to lay a complaint before the magistrates. Instead, he conducts a *burial?*"

"One must wonder, of course. My man attempted to discover the identity of the two corpses, but he was unsuccessful. Paupers' graves are unmarked.''

"He might have questioned the other mourners.''

"Impossible! Margrave keeps his eye upon the three of them. He is suspicious of all strangers, and would probably have recognised our man.''

"Well, why do we wait? If this Margrave is a felon he must be given up to the law.''

"And lose our best chance of success? No, we must wait longer for certain proof of our belief that there is something wrong here.'' Sebastian paused. "When Truscott left them he went on to the house in Seven Dials.''

Dan's eyes scanned his face. "You do suspect him, don't you?'' he said earnestly. "Let me tell you what I learned today.''

He went on to describe the strange girl who had accosted Judith in Piccadilly, and given her the cryptic message.

"Now, Seb, you'll agree there's something smoky here? Why should Truscott mention Judith to these beggars in the first place? The relief of poverty should be his affair. And to send a message to her in this way...? Why could he not write to her himself? I may tell you I don't like it!''

Sebastian liked it even less, but he decided to keep the rest of his information to himself. The Bow Street Runner had kept track of him for some time, and a full description of Margrave's previous activities had been disquieting.

Sebastian had heard of him, but only as a forger. The

revelation of a long history of extortion, violence, and possibly murder made his blood run cold.

What was Truscott's connection with this man? And who was the girl who had spoken to Judith in the street, bearing a message to her from an intermediary?

"Nor do I!" he said slowly, as his gaze rested for a long moment on the younger man's face. Dan was already seriously alarmed, and he must do nothing to increase it.

"Of course there may be a simple explanation," he continued. "If Truscott has been injured, he may not wish to frighten Judith by appearing in his present state."

"Begging your pardon, Seb, but that won't wear with me! It's my belief that he's quarrelled with his cronies, and now he's gone to ground. I think he wrote the note himself!"

"You may be right," Sebastian told him mildly. "But if it's true, it's scarcely a hanging matter. Shall we join the ladies?"

"You mean you will do nothing?" Dan sprang to his feet. "I can't believe it! Judith may be in the greatest danger—"

"Not for the moment, I believe. If our suspicions are correct, Truscott will do nothing to delay his marriage. Judith will be in danger only if she decides to break her engagement. Do you understand me?"

Dan flushed. "You mean that I must not continue to persuade her?"

"I mean exactly that," Sebastian said in level tones. "I have no wish to alarm you further, but if we are right, Truscott won't allow his prize to slip away. You have seen how easy it is for anyone to approach her."

The colour left Dan's face, and he swallowed. "You can't think it possible that he would abduct her?"

"I don't know, but we must take no chances."

"Then I must warn her to be careful."

"You will say nothing!" Sebastian told him sharply. "She is still firm in her decision to wed him?"

Dan nodded, his face a picture of desolation.

"That's good! For the present it is her safeguard. Once let him doubt her willingness, and I won't answer for the consequences."

It was stern advice, but he felt obliged to give it. He knew Dan's heart. The years apart had not changed his passionate devotion for his first love.

He hadn't been so sure of Judith's constancy, though Prudence had assured him of it.

"You must be mistaken, my love," he'd argued gently. "Have you asked her?"

"Of course not!" His wife had taken his hand and held it against her cheek. "One needs only to see them together."

"You are a romantic!" He'd dropped a kiss upon her hair. "If it is true, then Dan must offer for her. Judith is not wed yet—"

"He won't do that!"

"Why not?" Sebastian was mystified.

"Need you ask? It is the fortune, my dearest. You know him. Would he ever take anything from you?"

Sebastian frowned. "No! That stubborn refusal of my help has been the cause of what few differences we have had, but this is another matter. The happiness of two people is at stake."

"I can't persuade him." Her eyes were sad.

It was this sadness more than anything which had

persuaded him to take such a close interest in Judith's affairs, though at first it had been much against his better judgment. Now he could only marvel at feminine intuition. Prudence and Elizabeth had been right to distrust the Reverend Charles Truscott. His determination to worst the creature hardened, but his expression was apparently untroubled as he reentered his wife's boudoir.

There he was delighted to find that his wife had been enjoying herself. She gave him a brilliant smile, and her eyes were sparkling with mischief.

"Feeling better?" he teased. "What have you been up to?"

"Not I, my love, but Judith! Now who would believe that beneath that air of calm reserve lies the wickedest sense of the ridiculous?"

"I would, for one, and so would Dan." Sebastian glanced at the scattered sheets of manuscript, and pretended to shudder. "Dan, I fear that we have been pinned to the board once more as interesting specimens."

Judith gathered up the pages. "How can you say so?" she reproached. "You know it is not true."

"Not even interesting?" Sebastian glanced at Dan and pulled a face. "I'm crushed, aren't you?"

"Now, my darling, I won't have Judith teased. You may not care to know it, but I've been working hard. I am now a literary critic…"

"But you always were…" Dan joined in the teasing "…the harshest one I've known, and always against the popular opinion. I had thought you must be sunk beneath reproach when you gave your view on Alexander Pope at Lady Denton's soirée."

"Turgid stuff! Besides, I was asked for my opinion. Would you have had me lie?"

"Perish the thought!" Sebastian sat beside her on the day-bed. "Shall you come down for nuncheon, dearest?"

"Great heavens! You must all be starving! Give me ten minutes and I'll join you. Dearest, will you ring the bell for Dutton?"

Sebastian did as he was bidden, and led their guest from the room. In the corridor he took her arm.

"Judith, how can I thank you? Pru is quite herself again today. Dan, don't you agree?"

Judith looked at her love, and caught her breath as she saw the warmth of his expression.

"How could it be otherwise?" he murmured slowly. "Judith has a certain quality which is not easy to explain…" He caught Sebastian's eye and looked away.

Their nuncheon was a gay affair, and Sebastian's chef, who had tried for weeks to tempt the flagging appetite of his mistress, was clearly on his mettle. Well aware that a lady in an interesting condition was likely to feel queasy at the sight of food, he had produced the lightest, freshest dishes imaginable.

Imaginative salads flanked the glazed ham and the platters of smoked duck. The épigrammes of chicken with a celery puree were tempting, and even lighter were the quenelles, tiny fish balls done *à la Flamande*. They were followed by a featherlight orange soufflé, and a selection of fruit jellies.

Sebastian smiled to himself. His more usual nuncheon, if he took one, consisted of a selection of cold meats and fruit. On this occasion, he announced that he was very hungry. Prudence beamed at him. Animated for the first time in days, she allowed herself to be helped to an excellent meal, almost without noticing.

Later he took Judith to one side. A plan was forming in his mind. It was a long shot, but it might succeed.

"What a difference you have made to Prudence!" he murmured. "Today, my dear, she is a different person. To see her so much more herself is a great joy to me."

Judith smiled. "I think you have no need to worry. She has enjoyed her nuncheon…"

"For the first time in weeks. I've tried not to let her see it, but I have been concerned about her."

Judith scanned his face with anxious eyes. "She tells me that she is not sick."

"No, Judith, she is bored to death. What she needs is stimulation. You have given it to her."

"You can't quarrel with her temperament. In the usual way she is so full of projects… These last few weeks are hard for her."

"My dear, I know it. How I wish that you might come to us, if only for a day or two! I have no right to ask. Your own marriage is so close, but is there the least chance that it might be possible?"

"I should like nothing more," she told him wistfully. "But Charles is to return tomorrow. I must be at home to greet him."

"Of course! It is selfish of me to put my own concerns before your own…"

Sebastian did not press her further. He knew that her affection for Prudence would lead her to stay at Mount Street if she could. That would be the answer for a time. Events were moving fast, and he trusted neither the preacher nor his friends.

Chapter Nine

The subject of his thoughts was still abed at the house in Seven Dials. Truscott was nursing an aching head.

He'd awakened in the worst of moods after a restless night. Sleep had proved elusive, and he'd tossed for hours, seeking in vain for some solution to his problems. This had required the consumption of the best part of a bottle of brandy, but it had served only to send him into a stupor.

Now he regretted his indulgence. He needed all his wits about him if he were to deal with Margrave. Damn the man! He'd seen the chance of easy pickings and he'd taken it. But he'd chosen the wrong victim.

He raised his throbbing head and glanced about the room to find that he was alone.

"Nan?" he yelled. Then he picked up one of his boots and threw it at the door.

"What is it, Josh?" The girl came hurrying to his side.

"Fetch me some ale, and be quick about it!" He caught sight of her face. "What happened to you? God, but you're a sight this morning!"

"You beat me, Josh." She touched her swollen face and winced.

"You must have deserved it!" He grunted and turned over. He had no recollection of striking her, but it was no matter. Women needed to be kept in line.

"I…I did everything you asked…and the lady gave me money…" At the look on his face she fled.

As Truscott sipped at his ale, the mists cleared from his mind. His decision to send the girl to seek out Judith had been a good one. He now had money enough for his immediate expenses, but better still the meeting had provided him with useful information which might prove vital at some future date.

How easy it had been for Nan, a stranger, to approach Judith in the street, and even to arrange a further meeting. Not for the first time he blessed the stupidity of her stepmother. How many young women were allowed to walk the London thoroughfares with only a maid for company, and unattended by either a footman or a groom for protection? It was Mrs Aveton's selfishness and spite which allowed Judith such infrequent use of the family carriage, and then only when she was to be conveyed to the homes of such members of the aristocracy as Mrs Aveton hoped to cultivate.

He'd wondered at it since the early days of their acquaintance, but he'd made no protest. His heiress must not be too closely guarded. If ever his original plan should go awry, he might turn that fact to his advantage.

He'd run no risk in sending Nan to Judith. The girl knew him only as Josh Ferris, and he'd warned her not to answer questions. All in all, it had been a successful operation. The note had been an extra flourish. He'd thought long and hard before putting pen to paper, and then it was not from a desire to reassure her as to his health.

He'd promised to call upon her on the following day. That should put a stop to any awkward enquiries from that long-nosed stepmother of hers.

"Fetch me a mirror!" he demanded. Close examination of his features showed that most of the scratches were healing, though one, across his cheek, was so deep that he would probably bear the scar for life. The purple bruising around his mouth and nose was fading. By the following day there should be little injury apparent.

If Judith mentioned it he would think of some explanation. Nothing, he vowed fiercely, would lose him his prize at his late stage. She'd hold to her bargain, as long as she continued to believe in him.

That was the danger now. His mother and Margrave had him firm within their grasp, with their threats of blackmail. He doubted if they would carry them out unless they wished to cast to the four winds all hope of sharing in his fortune.

The preacher's worries rested more upon his future. He'd never be allowed to enjoy the money in peace. And there was his reputation. His rise to fame had been meteoric, but he was not quite at the top of his profession. That would come when he was invited to preach at the Chapel Royal, in St James's Palace.

What a sermon he would give them! Let the fat old Royal Dukes comment upon it in stentorian tones, even as he spoke. He wouldn't care. It would be enough that they were there, and that he would be preaching before Royalty.

He could almost taste the feeling of power…the sensation of holding his audience in the palm of his hand.

He smiled to himself. More properly it should be called a congregation, but for him, standing at the pulpit, the entire setting was pure theatre.

Then a vision of Margrave sprang unbidden to his mind. The man would be constantly at his back, smiling, reminding him always that success must be bought at a price. The preacher's eyes narrowed. He'd no intention of spending the rest of his life in looking over his shoulder. Margrave must be removed, together with his cronies, but how? The man was as fast and dangerous as a striking snake.

He was still considering the problem when Nan came over to the bed and stood beside him, pulling nervously at her kerchief.

"What is it now?" he asked impatiently.

"I need some money, Josh."

"I gave you enough for food and drink. What else can there be?"

"It's the baby, Josh. I ain't been able to pay the woman for her keep—"

"That's none of my affair. I told you to get rid of it."

"I know you did, but it was too late when I found out. Old Mother Gisburn wouldn't touch me—"

"I'm not surprised! She must have thought that you'd have croaked on her."

"I wish I had!" The tears poured down Nan's face.

"Stop your caterwauling!" Truscott flung a coin at her. As he did so he eyed her with distaste. When her brothers had brought her from the country she'd been a plump and rosy wench, and a comfortable armful for any man.

They'd been aware of it, and hoped to earn good

money from her charms, but Truscott had seen her first. Now he considered that he'd had the worst of the bargain. Since the birth of her child Nan had grown scrawny and pale. Life seemed to have drained from her, leaving her dull and listless. Time for a change, he thought to himself. It wouldn't be difficult to replace her.

He was confirmed in this belief when she began to plead.

"Josh, let me have the baby here. I don't trust that woman down in Lambeth, and it would cost you nothing. She's but a few weeks old, and I want to care for her myself. I'll keep her quiet, I promise you!"

"Bring her here, and I'll keep her quiet for you…"

Nan could not mistake his meaning, and she backed away from him. "Your own flesh and blood? You can't be so heartless. I thought she would be company for me. It's lonely here without you. I ain't even seen my brothers for a day or two."

"They must be off on business of their own," he told her carelessly.

"I thought you asked them to do a job for you?"

"Didn't work out!" he said. "Get off, then, if you intend to go to Lambeth."

He waited until she'd left the house. Then he examined his outer clothing. She'd done her best to sponge away the traces of his enforced stay in that stinking attic, and, as always, he'd removed his collar and clerical bands before he entered the house in Seven Dials.

When he left here he would bathe and change before presenting himself to Judith, though he doubted if she'd notice anything amiss whatever his appearance. He could never guess what she was thinking. She seemed always to be out of reach, as if she lived in a world of her own. That would change, he vowed. He'd bring her down to earth.

He dismissed her from his mind. Judith was not his immediate problem. What mattered now was to find some way of foiling Margrave. He'd need all his guile. Truscott considered several possibilities.

He could lay evidence of the fellow's whereabouts before the magistrates. He guessed that the forger was still wanted by the authorities. It would not serve. If Margrave went down, he would take his former cell-mate with him in revenge.

As for paying him off? The idea was laughable. The forger and his friends would not be satisfied until their victim had no more to give. There was never an end to blackmail.

There was but one solution, and the preacher had known it from the first. His enemies must be silenced, and permanently. Next time he would not make the mistake of employing idiots. He would do the job himself, but how?

He was still considering the matter when Nan returned. Her eyes were red with weeping.

"Stop your blubbing!" he ordered. "I want some food."

For once she didn't hurry to obey him.

"Josh, please listen to me! The baby isn't well. I'm sure she isn't being fed...and I don't trust Mrs Daggett."

"She found you a wet-nurse, didn't she?"

"The woman is feeding several children. She hasn't enough milk for all, and two of those I saw last week have disappeared."

"Daggett don't keep them for ever...only till they are collected by whoever owns them."

"I...I can't be sure of that. Her neighbour says she is a baby farmer."

"What of it? If she sells them it's probably for the best. It saves a lot of trouble all round."

"*If* she sells them..." Nan burst into a storm of weeping. "Last week there were two bodies found in the river!"

"Brats die from natural causes," Truscott said impatiently. "Daggett can't afford to pay for burials." Her news didn't surprise him. If payment for a child's keep was not forthcoming, Mrs Daggett would solve the problem in the simplest way. It had been in his mind when he sent Nan to her with the child.

Now he gazed angrily at the weeping girl. "I said I wanted food," he growled. "Set about it, or you'll find yourself in the street..."

He was tempted to carry out his threat at once, but it would wait. He didn't want her running about the neighbourhood asking for her brothers. He doubted if they had discussed his orders with any of their friends, but it was best to take no chances.

Next day he left her with the unspoken resolve to throw her out as soon as it was practicable. After his marriage he would keep the house at Seven Dials, but he would have a change of mistress. Nan's connection with the murdered men would, in time, become a problem. He didn't fancy constant questioning. Besides, she was little more than skin and bone. His taste ran to a plumper armful.

With this decision made, he began to feel more cheerful. No solution as to the question of Margrave had, as yet, come to mind, but he would think of something. Meantime, he must not allow his enemies to suspect that he intended to outwit them. Robbed of his prey, Margrave would make every effort to destroy him, even to the extent of approaching Judith with his story.

He arrived at the Aveton household to find it in an uproar. The strident tones of Judith's stepmother were audible beyond the closed door of the salon.

When he was announced, Mrs Aveton looked up and paused for breath. Judith stood before her, flushed and silent.

Truscott raised an eyebrow in enquiry, but before he could speak he heard a gasp from Judith.

"Charles, your face! What has happened to your face?"

Involuntarily, he lifted a hand to touch the healing scratches. "A sad business, my dear! In her delirium my mother did not know me. She imagined that I was come to take her to the madhouse. It was difficult to restrain her."

"How dreadful for you! Is there no change in her condition?"

"Alas, she grows weaker by the day..." Truscott bent his head and covered his eyes.

"Oh, Charles, I am so sorry!" Judith came towards him. "There is still no hope of a recovery?"

"None! I fear I must return to her without delay." He was aware that Mrs Aveton had not uttered a word of sympathy and, looking up, he met her hard, suspicious eyes.

"Judith, you may leave us!" she snapped. "I wish to have a private word with Mr Truscott."

She waited until the door had closed before she rounded on him.

"Now, sir, what are you about?" she demanded. "Don't try to gammon me with your stories. Where have you been for these past few days?"

"Judith must have told you," he replied smoothly.

"Stuff! I don't believe a word of it. Smallpox, forsooth! Even if it were true, I don't credit you with sufficient Christian charity to spend your time beside a sickbed."

"Would you care to tell me what concern it is of yours?"

"It *is* my concern, and it should be yours. Sir, you are a fool! Here is Judith, constantly with her friends, the Wentworths, and in the company of that penniless creature who still dangles after her. Do you wish to lose her?"

"I won't lose her!" The preacher towered over Mrs Aveton, and there was something in his face which made her back away.

"You are the fool!" he told her softly. "Won't you ever learn? Must you always be at odds with her? What was it this time? The Wentworths?"

"Not exactly!" An angry flush stained his companion's cheeks. "That wicked, ungrateful girl had the impertinence to inform me that I...that we were spending beyond reason on her wedding."

"Really?" Truscott jeered. "She cannot be referring to her trousseau, since you tell me that her own purchases have been frugal. I take it that she's been alarmed by the accounts from your modiste?"

"There are three of us to dress," Mrs Aveton said defensively. "It is expensive."

"Especially when one provides for the whole of the coming season? No, don't bother to deny it. I fully understand."

She gave him an uncertain look.

"But there is something you must understand," he continued. "These bills will not be settled from Judith's estate. You will pay them from the share which I have promised you."

He almost laughed aloud when he saw her stunned expression. For a moment she was robbed of speech. Then she broke into a violent diatribe against him.

"And *I* shall not pay them," she said finally.

"Then they will remain unpaid…your credit will suffer with the London mantua-makers."

"You don't know Judith," she sneered. "She won't allow it. She has a positive abhorrence of debt—"

"Judith will have nothing to say in the matter," he said significantly. "Come, madam, I am well up to your tricks. You thought to milk the estate of as much as possible in advance. I won't have it!"

Mrs Aveton was silent, but the look she gave him spoke volumes. From now on she would be his enemy, but until her share of Judith's fortune was in her hands she must hide her feelings.

Truscott was undeceived, and again he wanted to laugh. She wouldn't receive a penny, and her bills would most certainly remain unpaid, but he'd thought it wise to frighten her a little. Their quarrel had drawn her attention from the questions she'd been about to ask. Sharp as a fox, he thought idly, but he was a match for her.

"Do you tell me that Judith spends much time with the Wentworths?" he enquired.

"Too much, in my opinion! You should forbid it, sir. Socialising as she does! Most unsuitable for a parson's wife… Of course, she is not yet your wife, is she?" It was a sly dig, and he was about to answer when Wentworth himself was announced.

Mrs Aveton's manner underwent a sea-change. No member of the Wentworth family had ever graced her home before.

Conscious of the fact that a carriage bearing a well-known coat-of-arms must at this moment be standing at her door, she was wreathed in smiles as she advanced towards her noble visitor.

"My lord, what a pleasure!" She sank into a curtsy.

Sebastian bowed both to her and then to Truscott, favouring them with one of his most charming smiles.

"I am so glad to find you both together," he said. "I am come on my wife's behalf to ask for your indulgence towards her."

Mrs Aveton begged him to be seated. Then she rang for refreshment.

"How is your good lady wife?" she asked in saccharine tones. "Believe me, my lord, if there is anything we can do to help…?"

"Well, ma'am, there is." Sebastian accepted a glass of wine. "Perhaps I should explain. My brother and his wife are gone to visit Mrs Peregrine's aunt, and the only other member of my household, my adopted son, is also called away from London at this time." He shot a covert look at the faces of his companions, guessing correctly that this final piece of information would aid his cause.

"The thing is that Prudence is sadly low in spirits,"

he continued. "She cannot go about in society at this time…"

"Of course not…so trying for dear Lady Wentworth." Mrs Aveton was flattered beyond measure to be taken into the confidence of this august personage whom she had previously considered somewhat distant.

"Ah, I knew you'd understand!" Sebastian leaned towards her. "You encourage me to ask if Judith might be spared for just a day or two. My wife is fond of her, and is much in need of someone to bear her company."

Mrs Aveton looked uncertain. "Lord Wentworth, if it had been at any other time…but Judith's marriage is now so close. I fear that it will be impossible…" She glanced at Truscott and subsided.

The preacher had been thinking fast. He'd sensed the purpose of Wentworth's errand from his lordship's opening words, and had given the matter his consideration.

Within these next few days he must settle with Margrave and his cronies once and for all. With Judith safe in the hands of the Wentworth family, Margrave and Nellie might threaten him to their heart's content. They would never find her.

Truscott smiled at Mrs Aveton. "Surely not impossible, ma'am?" he coaxed. "Consider! Is it not an excellent suggestion? Our little Judith has been looking tired. She too would be happy to spend time with her friends. We should thank Lord Wentworth for his kindness."

"The pleasure is mine. I must thank you for your understanding and forbearance, sir." Sebastian was puzzled. What was the fellow up to? He seemed positively thankful for the opportunity to remove Judith from the Aveton household.

"Shall we ask our little bride-to-be for her opinion of this invitation?" Truscott said archly. "I dare swear that she will be delighted to accept. Ma'am, will you send for her?"

Mrs Aveton raised no further objections, which also surprised Sebastian. He'd been expecting a much more difficult task. Perhaps it was the fact that Dan had gone away which had prevented a refusal.

Judith herself grew radiant when his proposal was explained to her.

"Of course I'll come—that is, if there is no objection...?" She looked at both Truscott and her stepmother, to find them nodding their agreement. "When will it be convenient?"

"I have my carriage waiting, and there is no time like the present," Sebastian chuckled. "I am rushing you, my dear, but perhaps your maid might be allowed to fetch your things this afternoon?"

"There now, his lordship has thought of everything. Off you go, my dearest one. You will give my duty to her ladyship?" Truscott was all smiles.

"Of course!" Judith thought that she had never liked him better. In the midst of all his troubles he was thinking only of her pleasure. "You will let me know how your mama goes on? Charles, I would come with you if you'd let me..."

"My love, it is out of the question, as I have explained. There is all the danger of carrying infection. Now you shall not keep his lordship waiting. I'm happy to know that you'll be with your friends whilst I am away." He took her hand and kissed it reverently, and was rewarded with a dazzling smile.

"Such a dear child!" he said when she had gone to put on her pelisse. "I am unworthy of her!"

Privately, Sebastian considered that a truer word was never spoken, but he contented himself with polite enquiries as to the health of Truscott's mother.

The man was glib, he thought to himself. He had all the symptoms of smallpox at his fingertips, but other than that Sebastian learned nothing of the whereabouts of the sick woman, or why she had not previously been introduced to Judith. He hadn't expected to, and no trace of his suspicions appeared in his expression.

Judith herself was smiling as he handed her into the carriage. The news that Dan was away had been bitter-sweet, but she prayed that he had gone to Merton to see Lord Nelson.

And if he had still been at Mount Street? Would she have agreed to visit Prudence? It was difficult to decide. She knew the danger. Her treacherous heart still longed for him. She should have been thankful that he had given her no encouragement, but the thought of her lost love still left her desolate. He was away, and she was safe from temptation. The knowledge should have comforted her, but it didn't.

Sebastian saw that she was looking pensive.

"Forgive me?" he asked.

"For what?"

"I stole you away without a by-your-leave. My dear, are you happy to come to us for a few days?"

"I am!" she told him simply. "Sebastian, you must now think better of Charles. You saw how much he wished for me to spend some time with Prudence. It was kind of him, when he might have raised objections—''

''Indeed! Judith, you must never think that we wish for anything other than your happiness. I suspect that Prudence and Elizabeth have no wish to lose you, even to your worthy preacher.'' He gave her a cheerful grin, hoping that she would believe this excuse for their objections.

His own suspicions had increased, and Truscott's ready agreement to Judith's visit to Mount Street had done nothing to allay them. The fellow was up to something, but what? To date the Bow Street Runner had brought no further news.

Sebastian glanced down at his companion. Once away from the Aveton household she was a different person. All her grave reserve had disappeared, and those large, expressive eyes were shining with pleasure as she questioned him about his boys.

''Inexhaustible!'' he said ruefully. ''They intend to make the most of this visit to London. Our next expedition is to be to Madame Tussaud's. The blood-thirsty little creatures have a taste for horrors.''

''It will be educational,'' she answered primly, but her face was alive with amusement. ''You must be delighted that they are anxious to improve their minds.''

They were still laughing when the carriage stopped and he helped her to alight. His plan had worked so far, and he was further rewarded by a cry of delight from Prudence.

''Oh, my dear, you've brought her! I had not dared to hope. Judith, am I very greedy to wish to have you here?''

It was the warmest of welcomes, and Judith flushed with pleasure as she shook her head. ''I was happy to come to you,'' she said.

Sebastian left them chattering gaily. He was content, at least for the moment, to have removed Judith from possible danger, but he was deeply concerned for her future safety.

He strolled down to the library and sifted through his morning post. It consisted mainly of invitations to one function or another. There was no message from the Runner.

For some time he was lost in thought. During his visit to Mrs Aveton he had watched Truscott closely. A shifty fellow, he decided, with something on his mind. Had he discovered that he was being watched? Sebastian thought not. This was something else, something which had caused a fleeting look of relief at his own suggestion that Judith came to Mount Street.

It was a riddle for which, at present, he had no answer.

Perhaps he imagined that the less he was in Judith's company the less likely it might be that she would change her mind and refuse to wed him.

Truscott appeared to be a consummate actor, but even he must find it a strain to keep up a front of benevolent respectability. There was always the chance that he would make a slip and say or do something to give her a distaste of him.

That was the danger now. Judith still thought kindly of her betrothed, or did she? Sebastian wondered if, at times, she were not a little too insistent as to his virtues.

He hoped that he was wrong. With Judith's fortune almost within his grasp, the preacher would not let his prize escape him. Should Judith break off her engagement, the man would stop at nothing.

Prudence, he knew, would say nothing further against the Reverend Truscott. She had too much regard for Judith's peace of mind. Elizabeth was more outspoken, but she and Perry were away.

And what of Dan, who loved her? He was the fiercest opponent of this marriage, yet he could put Judith into deadly danger if he betrayed his feelings for her.

Sebastian resolved that he would speak to Dan again, but it was not until late that evening that his adopted son returned.

Sebastian heard the bustle in the hall and strolled through from the salon in time to hear the butler announce that her ladyship had come downstairs and was at present with her husband and Miss Aveton.

"She's here?" Dan's face lit up. "I must go to them!"

"Dan, a word with you, if you please!" Sebastian threw open the door to the library.

"Isn't this great?" Dan threw aside his riding coat, and laid his crop beside it. "How did you manage to rescue Judith? At this hour she must be staying—"

"She is, but only for a day or two. Nothing has changed, Dan, and I must ask you once again to do nothing to persuade Judith to end her betrothal."

Dan's dismay was evident. "She is still to wed that creature? Then what is she doing here? The marriage is so close…"

"I am well aware of that." Sebastian paused, considering his words with care. "We must be patient for

just a little longer. I saw Truscott today. The man is
worried. I believe that something is afoot.''

"He knows that he is being watched?"

"I don't think so, but I've heard nothing from the
Bow Street man."

"Then what?"

"Who can say? He seemed relieved that Judith was
to come to us."

"That's strange! He is as fond of me as I am of him."

"He believes you to be away…" A faint smile
touched Sebastian's lips.

Dan frowned at him. "Why is Judith here? It can't
have been easy to persuade the old harpy to let her go."

"Prudence longed to see her."

"And that was enough to send you off to visit that
harridan?"

"As you know, my wife's wishes are of paramount
importance to me," Sebastian told him smoothly.

"I know that, but it ain't enough for me." Dan's eyes
were filled with suspicion. "There's something else…
something you aren't telling me."

"Dear me! How sceptical you are grown! You are
right, of course. Shall we say that I am hoping that
matters will resolve themselves within these next few
days. Judith will be safe with us."

"Then you think her still in danger?" Dan grew so
pale that the freckles stood out sharply against his skin.

"I was somewhat concerned to find that she is allowed to walk abroad without protection. It was much
too easy for someone to approach her in the street."

"Beggars and thieves, you mean?"

"No, I don't mean that!" Sebastian decided to lay
his cards upon the table. "I am come round to your

way of thinking. There is something very smoky going on. It is best to take no chances... For the moment, Judith's safety lies in the fact that she is still betrothed to Truscott. You must do nothing to put her in danger.''

"I'd like to wring his neck!" Dan said savagely.

"Agreed! In time I feel that someone may perform that desirable task for you, given the opportunity. Meantime, you will heed my wishes?''

"I will, but it won't be easy!" Dan rose to his feet. "May I see her now?"

"Of course!" Sebastian clapped him on the shoulder. "I know it won't be easy, but you would do more than that for her, I think."

"Anything!" Dan turned his face away, unwilling to say more.

"Well, then, let us join the ladies. They must be longing to hear your news."

"It isn't good!" Dan fell into step beside him as they strolled across the hall.

"Nevertheless, they will wish to hear it." Sebastian entered the salon and was greeted happily by his wife.

Judith said nothing. She looked up at Dan and her heart was in her eyes.

Chapter Ten

Prudence appeared to notice nothing. She patted her sofa invitingly.

''Come and sit down,'' she said. ''Sebastian has been keeping you from us. Was it to build up the suspense? How did you go on at Merton?''

Judith had recovered her composure, and now she smiled her encouragement for him to begin. She was both proud and pleased that he'd taken her advice, even to the point of telling Prudence and Sebastian of his plans.

Dan looked at the circle of eager faces, and then he grimaced. ''Foiled again!'' he joked. ''The Admiral was away from home.''

''Oh, my dear, what a disappointment! To go all that way for nothing!'' Prudence was dismayed.

''Not for nothing, Pru. Now that I've found my way to his door he'll find it difficult to be rid of me. I left my card, and I shall go again next week, when he is returned from Portsmouth.'' Dan grinned at her. He *had* been disappointed, but he wouldn't let her see it.

"That's the spirit! I'm glad to see that you don't plan to give up." Sebastian nodded his approval.

"Oh, I shan't give up!" Dan caught Sebastian's eye and then he looked away. His meaning had been clear, but he would heed the warning.

Prudence looked her relief. She'd been afraid that yet another blow to his hopes would depress his spirits, but the bright blue eyes were smiling fondly at her, with a tiny spark of mischief in their depths.

"And what have you been up to?" he demanded. "I mean, apart from abducting Judith with some cock-and-bull story about your failing health. You look positively blooming."

"Judith does me good," she confided. "It's such a pleasure to have an intelligent woman in the house when I'm usually surrounded by great clumping males." She peeped up at Sebastian from beneath her long lashes, laughing as she did so.

"Witch! Are you trying to put me in my place?" He picked up her hand and kissed it. "I won't have it! You wheedled permission to stay up until Dan returned, and now it is time you were abed." He lifted her in his arms, ignoring all her protests, and carried her from the room.

Silence reigned in the salon. Then both Dan and Judith began to speak at once. The confusion broke the ice and they began to laugh.

"You first, if you please!" Judith begged.

"I was about to say that it was a pleasant surprise to find you here. Prudence looks so much better…"

"She does, but she had such hopes for you, as did I. Oh, Dan, you must have been disappointed not to find the Admiral at home, in spite of what you told her."

"I was, but it is no matter. I won't be put off. Judith,

I think I must become a man of business. It is not the slightest use to spend my time designing if I can't sell my work.''

"Splendid!" Judith clapped her hands. "Have you a fat portfolio to take about with you? If Lord Nelson does not care for one idea, he may like another."

As she had expected, Dan was quickly launched upon his favourite topic. The technicalities were lost on her, but she was happy to watch his eager face, under the thatch of red-gold hair, alive with interest as he explained his latest invention.

How very dear he was. She loved everything about him, from the startling blue of his eyes to the dusting of freckles across his nose. And those fine hands were never still as he sought to make her understand.

Even he became aware of it.

"Tie my hands together, and I'm speechless," he joked.

"Never! That I shan't believe!"

"But you must be tired of listening to me. How do you go on?"

Her face changed at once. When she replied it was with an oddly closed expression.

"Much as usual," she said in neutral tones.

"But you are happy to be here?" he asked.

Her smile returned at once. "Of course. This is such a happy household. You had best prepare yourself. I fear you are to accompany Sebastian and the boys to Madame Tussaud's."

"That place in the Strand?"

"The very spot! I see you've heard of it."

"The boys mentioned some kind of a waxworks. It has just been opened, hasn't it? It sounds dull to me."

"Madame Tussaud had a great success in Paris with her exhibition at the Palais Royal. I believe it was started by her uncle, who taught her the skills of modelling. She is Swiss, you know."

"So now she has moved to London. Well, I suppose that travelling must be easier since the peace with France, but a waxworks? Shall you care to see it?"

Judith laughed. "I am not invited. This, I feel, is to be an expedition for gentlemen only."

She left him then. They had spent a pleasant hour together, and Dan had been friendly, but no more.

With burning cheeks, she went up to her room. What was she expecting? That by some miracle his old love for her had been revived? He'd given her no sign of it. Even if it were so, would he approach her now, when she was betrothed to another man? His own sense of honour would prevent it.

And he hadn't mentioned Charles Truscott. Knowing his feelings on the subject of her marriage to the preacher, she had half expected yet another attempt to persuade her to break off her engagement, but Dan had said nothing more.

At their last meeting she must have convinced him finally of her determination to wed Charles. The knowledge should have pleased her, but it didn't.

What a fool she was. She'd been clutching at straws, hoping that Dan would return from Merton basking in the approval of Admiral Nelson, and with the prospect of a promising career ahead of him. In her heart she'd wondered if it was her fortune which had changed his feelings. With his own future assured that barrier would have been removed, but he'd met with no success at Merton.

She must be wrong. He'd taken the reverse with the greatest of good spirits, and was fully prepared to wait until the Great Man should agree to see him.

It wasn't the bahaviour of a man whose only love was to wed another in ten short days. She must accept the fact that Dan no longer cared for her in the old way. It was a bitter pill to swallow. She tried to put him from her mind, but it was impossible. The face she loved so much would not be banished from her thoughts.

She climbed into bed and closed her eyes. Then she fell to dreaming. Things might have been so different, but she was drifting into a world of fantasy. Just for a second she allowed herself to wonder what she would do if Dan should offer for her now.

She knew the answer, and honesty compelled her to admit it. She held Charles in high regard, but Dan was the man she loved. She would fall into his arms in the wildest of raptures, forgetting her betrothal, the coming wedding, Charles Truscott's disappointment, and Mrs Aveton's undoubted fury. It was a small price to pay for a life of happiness.

Knowing that it could never be, it was long before she slept, but in the Wentworth household it was impossible to be miserable for long.

Judith wakened to find the sunlight streaming into her room as Bessie drew back her curtains. Then she was given the unexpected treat of breakfast in bed.

"Miss Judith, what will you wear today?" Bessie held up a gown in either hand. "I packed some others if these don't please you."

"Great heavens, Bessie, what were you thinking of?

I am to stay for only a day or two. You seem to have brought a large part of my trousseau…''

"I thought you'd like to look your best," Bessie said slyly. "There's no telling what you'll be needing…"

Judith gave her a sharp look, but Bessie's face was the picture of innocence.

"You know quite well that I am here to bear Lady Wentworth company. Her ladyship does not go abroad at present."

"No, miss, but you might do so…"

"Don't be foolish, Bessie." Judith glanced briefly at the garments. "I'll wear the blue today."

Bessie beamed at her.

"And you may take that expression off your face," Judith scolded. "Why you wish to turn me out as fine as fivepence I really can't imagine."

This wasn't strictly true. Bessie's intentions were transparent. Dan was to be so overcome by the charming appearance of her young mistress that he would offer for her without delay.

Her maid could have no idea of the true state of affairs, Judith thought sadly. Even so, when she was dressed she could only be pleased with her new gown.

It became her well. The soft blue was a perfect background for her delicate colouring, and the cut of the garment was excellent. It was of exquisite simplicity, the fine cambric caught with a matching ribbon from immediately below her splendid bosom, and falling in folds to a gathered flounce at the hem.

Judith glanced at her reflection in the pier-glass, pleased that she'd rejected the modiste's attempt to persuade her into buying extreme puffed sleeves. These were much more modest in design, swelling only slightly at the shoulder above the tight fabric which covered her arms as far as the wrist.

She smiled a little. For once she looked positively modish, though the morning-dress was quite suitable for a day at home. She left her room and made her way to the head of the staircase, but before she reached it a small hand slid into her own.

Judith gave a pretended jump of terror. "Why, Crispin, how you startled me! I thought I had been seized by some terrible monster…"

This brought a peal of laughter from Sebastian's youngest son.

"You didn't!" he accused. "You knew that it was me."

"How could I? I didn't see you. You crept up behind me like a redskin, and I didn't hear a thing."

"Truly?" His face grew serious. "I have been practicing, you know."

Judith nodded. "I can tell."

"I'd have come to see you earlier," the little boy continued. "But Mama said that you were not to be disturbed. We were very quiet this morning. You didn't hear us, did you?"

"Not a sound!" she assured him.

"Well, that's all right then." Crispin heaved an open sigh of relief. "I wanted to ask you…shall you come with us to the waxworks?"

"Not today, my dear one. Dan and your papa will go with you, and I shall stay with your mama…"

Crispin sat down on the top stair. "I hoped you'd come," he told her wistfully. "You always know the best stories."

"Well, suppose you try to remember all the things

you see. You might even write them down if you think you will forget. Then you may tell me all about them…''

He brightened at that, and hand in hand they walked down the staircase as Dan came out of the library.

The sight of Judith with the child struck him like a knife thrust into his breast. If they had married all those years ago she would now have sons and daughters of her own. Children adored her, and she was at her best with them, entering into their world without the slightest difficulty.

He was careful not to betray his feelings. He greeted her with a polite enquiry as to whether she was well rested.

''Very well rested, Dan, I thank you!'' Her radiant smile brought little response from him. ''Are you ready for your outing?''

''There has been a change of plan,'' he told her shortly. ''Prudence is not too well today. Sebastian has sent for the doctor. Naturally, he will wait for the man's opinion…''

''Then we are not to go to the waxworks?'' Crispin's lip began to tremble.

''Of course you are, my lad!'' Sebastian strode towards them, lifting up his son, and throwing the boy high into the air. ''I'm going to tease Judith into going with you. How shall you like that?''

Crispin squealed with delight. ''Better than anything!'' he yelled. Then he scurried off as fast as his fat little legs would carry him to impart the good news to his brothers.

''Spurned by my own flesh and blood!'' Sebastian mourned. ''Judith, you have much to answer for!''

As she began to smile he grew more serious. "Shall you mind accompanying them?" he asked. "I could send their tutor, or one of the servants to go with Dan, but it would not be the same…more of a lesson than a holiday, I believe."

"You think it will not be the same with me?" she teased. "My dear Sebastian, I intend to return one gentleman and three small boys to you with their minds quite over-burdened with useless information."

"What a dear you are!" Sebastian pressed her hand.

"Tell me about Prudence," she replied. "Sebastian, what is wrong?"

"Possibly just exhaustion. As you know, she insisted on waiting up for Dan. I sent for the doctor just as a precaution." He frowned. "She feels that this pregnancy is unlike any of the others… Believe me, it will be the last! I couldn't go through all this again, and nor could she." With that he walked away.

Judith was aware of Dan standing stiff and silent beside her. She could guess at his agony of mind. Prudence had been his first and only friend.

"Don't worry!" she said softly. "We must make allowances for Sebastian's natural concern. Prudence is strong, both in body and in mind. This may be nothing more than the weariness common in the last few weeks before a birth."

"You may be right." It was only with an effort that he forced a smile. "Forgive me, but I can't help feeling anxious about her."

"Of course you do!" She was searching her mind for further words of comfort when the boys came hurrying towards them, eager with anticipation.

"Are you ready, ma'am?" Thomas asked politely.

"Give me two minutes. I shan't keep you waiting.

She was as good as her word, and the little party was soon ensconced in the family carriage, and bowling over the cobblestones towards the Strand.

It was Madam Tussaud herself who greeted all visitors to her exhibition. Judith looked at her with interest.

It was difficult to believe that this dowdy-looking person in her old-fashioned high-crowned bonnet with a snowy pleated frill framing her face was in reality an astute business woman.

In prettily accented English she handed them a programme and left them to wander at will through the rows of models on display.

Judith was impressed. The wax figures were so life-like that it was easy to mistake them for living people, were it not for their splendid costumes of an earlier period. These were correct to the last detail, and Judith could only marvel at the amount of research which must have been involved. Madame must be something of a historian.

The kings and queens of both England and France were well represented, together with heroic figures from both countries, and the boys were soon attracted by the military men.

"See! Here is General Wolfe!" Thomas stood before his hero with shining eyes. "Papa told me all about him. He defeated the French in Canada, you know, at the Plains of Abraham—"

"But he was killed there," Henry murmured.

"It was still a famous victory," his brother insisted. "Don't be such a milksop! I bet you don't even want to see the Chamber of Horrors…"

This statement could not be allowed to go unchallenged and it was swiftly refuted. "Oh, yes I do! And Crispin will come too!"

"Well, I most certainly do not!" Judith told them firmly. "I was hoping that Crispin would stay with me. I've been saving one of my best stories for him."

She feared that scenes of executions would give the little boy nightmares and was tempted to suggest that Henry too should stay with her, but she was too wise to insist. She was well aware of the natural rivalry between Henry and his elder brother.

"We could hear it first and then go in," Thomas said hopefully.

"No, this one is especially for Crispin." She took the little boy's hand in hers and gave it a friendly squeeze. "It shall be our secret."

The promise quelled his likely objections to being left out by the others.

"It may be best," Thomas told her kindly. "Ladies don't care for things like death-masks and murderers being hanged."

"Ghoul!" Dan aimed a playful blow at him. "I wonder if you'll feel so brave when you get inside." Without more ado he led the boys towards the dreadful Chamber.

Judith moved away to seat Crispin beside the figure of King Canute.

"Now you shall tell me what you think," she said. "This king was very wise, but his courtiers thought he could do anything. He took them to the seashore to prove that they were wrong."

"How?"

"He made them bring his throne right down to the water. Then he sat down by the waves."

"What did he do then?"

"Can't you guess?" Judith sprang to her feet and stretched out an imperious arm. "He told the sea to go back…"

"But that was silly!" Crispin objected. "If the tide was coming in he'd get his feet wet."

"He did, but he knew that it would happen. It showed his courtiers that he had no power over it."

"Did…did he cut their heads off?"

"Oh, no! He was a kindly man, and he ruled England well. He became known as Canute the Great.

"I'll tell Papa about him. Do you know any more stories?"

"I know one which will make you laugh." Judith looked about her until she spied the figure which she sought. "Do you see this man sitting by a fire? What is he doing, do you suppose?"

"Cooking?"

"Not exactly. He was a king, you see, but at one time he was asked to watch some cakes upon the fire."

"Kings don't do that!"

"This one was in disguise. King Alfred was hiding from his enemies. He started to think how he might outwit them, and he forgot the cakes. When they burned the old lady in the hut was furious."

"What did she do?" Crispin was chuckling.

"I believe she beat him soundly."

"Well, he must have cut off her head, Judith."

"Good gracious, my love! I believe you to be every bit as bloodthirsty as your brothers. If you were king, would you wish to reign over a race of headless people?"

This nonsensical notion made him shout with glee, and he was still laughing when his brothers returned.

They were strangely silent, and Judith raised an enquiring eyebrow as she looked at Dan. He twinkled back at her.

"I think we've had our fill of horrors," he announced. "It's time for a treat. What do you boys say to ices at Gunter's?"

This suggestion met with cries of delight, and together he and Judith shepherded their charges towards the exit. As they gained the street again she saw an elderly couple smiling at the little group.

"What a charming couple!" the woman said audibly. "And so young to be the parents of those three stout boys."

Judith coloured, but Dan smiled at her.

"Don't take it so hard!" he whispered. "She did say that you were rather young to be a staid mama."

"Yes, I know. It is just that…well, I must suppose that it was easy to make the mistake. I am not in my first youth—"

"Nor in your dotage, Judith. Prudence isn't much older than you are yourself. Would you describe her as being at her last prayers?"

"Of course not!" she told him roundly, thankful that he had imagined that her evident confusion arose from the fact that the woman had supposed her to be older than she was. It had not. She'd been startled because she and Dan had been taken for husband and wife.

She peeped up at him, but there was nothing in his expression to indicate that he felt the same. Smiling blandly, he was handing the boys up into the carriage.

At Gunter's, the ices disappeared with lightning

speed, but as Dan was about to order more, Judith nudged him.

"No more!" she pleaded in a whisper. "The boys have had enough excitement for one day. We shall be in trouble if we take them home with upset stomachs."

He laughed at that. "In my experience small boys don't suffer in that way."

"Don't be too sure! You won't be too pleased if Crispin casts up his accounts over your fine breeches."

Dan shuddered. "You are right, as always. Let us return our monsters to their loving parents without delay."

It was a tired but happy party which turned the corner into Mount Street. Then Dan frowned as he saw the carriage standing at the door.

"Brandon?" he murmured in surprise. "What in the world brings him to Mount Street at this time of day?" He was out of the carriage in a flash.

Judith realised that his anxiety was for Prudence. Was she worse? If the family had been summoned there must be something wrong. It was with a sinking heart that she allowed him to lead her into the salon.

A glance at Sebastian's face told her that her fears were unfounded. His visitor was not the Earl of Brandon, but Amelia, his brother's wife.

With his customary good manners, Sebastian was engaging her in polite conversation, but as she and Dan entered the room, followed by the boys, she saw the look of relief in his eyes.

"Amelia, I think you know Miss Judith Aveton? And Dan, of course? Boys?"

At a nod from their father, his sons advanced towards their aunt and bowed.

"Growing fast, I see. What great creatures they are! Sebastian, you will soon have a full quiver."

Sebastian chose to ignore her last remark.

"Amelia is come to enquire about Prudence. I was happy to be able to tell her that the doctor is quite satisfied with her progress."

"I shall go up to her." The Countess gathered up her shawl and her reticule. "Such a mistake for a woman in her condition to be giving way to fads and fancies and to be keeping to her bed. I hope to advise her to think better of it."

"No, ma'am!" Sebastian's tone held a hint of steel. "Prudence is forbidden all visitors for the moment. I will give her your regards."

"Good of you!" The Countess glared at him. "Then I must wonder what this lady is doing here. I understand from her stepmama that Miss Aveton was invited for the purpose of keeping Lady Wentworth company."

"That is correct." Sebastian was unfazed by her angry look. "Judith did so yesterday, and will do so again tomorrow. On this occasion she has been kind enough to accompany the boys upon their outing. Such a relief to me!"

"You might have sent their tutor, or a servant with them, if this...er...gentleman was unable to control them on his own."

"I might have done so, but I did not. Is your memory failing, Amelia? This is Dan, my adopted son. You cannot have forgotten him?"

An ugly flush stained Amelia's face. It went much against the grain, but she was forced to acknowledge

Dan with a brief nod of her head. His own bow was perfection.

Judith felt dismayed. She was in no doubt as to the reason for Amelia's visit. Since it was clearly impossible for Mrs Aveton to invite herself to Mount Street, she must have begged her friend to pay this visit with the promise of a tasty piece of gossip.

Prudence and Amelia were not favourites with each other. To Judith's knowledge the Countess had not called before with enquiries as to the health of her sister-in-law. Amelia was here to spy, and to carry her tales back to Judith's stepmother.

How gratified she must have been when Judith arrived with Dan. It had been the most innocent of outings, but Judith felt consumed with guilt. The look of triumph in Amelia's eyes did nothing to reassure her.

She murmured some fictitious excuse, and was about to hurry away when the door to the salon opened.

"Miss Grantham!" the footman announced.

That lady swept towards Sebastian with all the dignity of her advancing years. Her authoritarian manner put the Countess of Brandon in the shade.

"Well, my boy, how do you go on?" She gave him her hand to kiss.

"I am well, ma'am, as you see." Sebastian's smile was dazzling as he led her to a chair. "As for you, I have no need to ask, I think. Your energy puts us all to shame."

"It ain't what it was, but I'll do for a year or two yet…" Miss Grantham settled herself more comfortably and looked about her.

"At your age you should take more care, ma'am," Amelia murmured spitefully. "I believe I have been misinformed. I heard some talk of your venturing abroad, to Turkey, of all places. Pray assure me that it isn't true. It would be so unwise—''

''Thank'ee for your advice, Amelia. When I want your opinion, I'll ask for it! You ain't been misinformed. I leave within the week.''

''Oh, Miss Grantham, you are making game of us,'' Amelia tittered. ''To joke is all very well, but you must not tease your friends.''

''I never joke, and I wasn't aware that you were any friend of mine.'' The old lady eyed the Countess coldly. ''Wouldn't do for you, of course. You'd never stand the journey. You're getting fat, Amelia. Keep on eating as you do, and you'll never get out of your chair.''

Judith heard a choking sound behind her, and cast a reproachful look at Dan. She felt that it was time to intervene in what promised to become an ugly scene.

''Won't you tell Miss Grantham and your aunt about the waxworks?'' she said to Thomas in desperation. She'd noticed that the boys had retreated behind their father's chair. It was their usual manoeuvre when in the presence of their formidable aunt.

Miss Grantham would have none of it. She beckoned to Thomas.

''Come here, boy,'' she ordered. ''Waxworks, indeed! What have you learned today?'' Her tone was sharp, but Thomas was encouraged by the twinkle in her eyes.

''The figures looked like real people, ma'am. We saw the kings and queens of England, and of France.''

''Recite them!''

Thomas made a creditable effort and was rewarded with a nod of approval.

"And what did you like best?"

Thomas looked at Judith and was urged on by her smile.

"We went into the Chamber of Horrors, ma'am. We saw Charlotte Corday murdering Marat in his bath." His look of relish brought a sharp reproof from the Countess.

"Disgusting!" she snapped. "Sebastian, I wonder that you allow your children to be exposed to such dreadful sights. It is enough to turn their brains."

"Crispin didn't see them," Judith said swiftly.

"Miss Aveton, you too have surprised me, though your stepmama assures me that you puzzle her. What could you have been thinking of to behave in such an irresponsible way? I say nothing of your companion's bahaviour. Some gentlemen have not the slightest notion of what is proper."

Judith saw Sebastian's face grow dark. Under his own roof he would not insult a visitor, but she was in no doubt that he was very angry. He opened his mouth to speak, but before he could do so Miss Grantham intervened.

"Stuff!" she said rudely. "Amelia, you put me out of patience with your nonsense. The child has had a history lesson. Would you have him learn anything other than the truth? The past was not all sweetness and light, however much you care to stick your own head in the sand..."

This was too much for her adversary. Amelia rose to her feet and, bidding the company farewell in icy tones, she took her leave of them. Sebastian accompanied her to her carriage.

"I have never been so insulted in my life," she said

in awful tones. "Brandon shall hear of this. Why you tolerate that rude old woman I can't imagine! Her age leads her to believe that she may go beyond the bounds of what is permissible."

Sebastian smiled down at her. "You shouldn't have offered your advice," he said gently.

Amelia tossed her head. "It was merely out of some small regard for Miss Grantham's safety," she replied. "Believe me, I shall not make the same mistake again. The woman should be in Bedlam."

With that, she stepped into her carriage and was borne away.

When he returned to his elderly guest, Sebastian found her unrepentant.

"Seen her off?" she cried cheerfully. "Thank the Lord for that! Her face is enough to turn milk sour." Miss Grantham glanced slyly at her host. "I hope you ain't expecting me to apologise?"

"Ma'am, I know you better! The thought never crossed my mind." With all the ease of an old acquaintance Sebastian took a seat beside her and tapped her wrist. "I should scold you, you wicked creature. You don't change in the least. I believe you take a positive delight in making mischief."

Miss Grantham beamed at him. "I do indeed! It is one of the pleasures of old age." Her impish grin was that of a five-year-old.

"One day you will meet your match," he warned.

"My dear boy, whoever it is had best be quick about it. I ain't immortal."

"Does that mean that you are going to die quite soon?"

Judith was amused to see that all three boys had gravitated towards their visitor, recognising a fellow rebel, however unlikely in appearance. It was Henry who had asked the question, and his elder brother nudged him.

"You shouldn't ask that," he whispered. "It isn't polite."

"Nonsense! It's a perfectly sensible question." The old face, which resembled nothing so much as an ancient walnut, cracked into a smile. "I meant only that I can't hope to live forever. A great pity! Life is so interesting. Don't you think so?"

"Yes, I do." Henry thought for a moment. "The waxworks were interesting, but I didn't like the blood in Marat's bath."

"It wasn't blood…it was dye," his brother told him in disgust. I know…I tasted it!''

This brought a ripple of amusement from his listeners, and Miss Grantham was moved to congratulate Sebastian.

"You have bred a scientist, I see. Well done, Thomas! Never accept the obvious without question. Always test if you wish to know the truth."

A lively discussion seemed likely to ensue until Sebastian intervened. "I think I must send my scientists off to find their supper, ma'am." Smiling, he dismissed the boys, and with a murmured promise to return, Judith followed them from the room.

Dan too begged to be excused, and Sebastian was left alone with his visitor. He looked at her and raised an eyebrow in amused enquiry.

"Aye, you may well wonder, sir! I've come to get to the bottom of this mystery, which you are all keeping to yourselves."

Chapter Eleven

Sebastian stared at her. "You know?"

"I know nothing, but I suspect that something is afoot. To me, your brother's face is like an open book. Dissimulation was never a strong point with Perry, as you well know."

Sebastian smiled as he was forced to acknowledge the truth of this pithy statement.

"As for Elizabeth…she, too, has looked preoccupied. My dear boy, what is wrong? Is it Prudence? Are you keeping something from us?"

"Prudence is well, ma'am, though she has been trying to do too much. At present she must rest, but the doctor is satisfied with her progress."

"A sensible fellow! I'm glad you took my advice when you engaged him. At least he doesn't believe in this fashionable notion of starving pregnant women and robbing them of their strength." She was about to assure him that her protegée also washed his hands before examining a patient, and engaged also in the eccentric habit of boiling his instruments before use, but she thought better of it. This was no time to remind Sebastian of those hideous implements.

"Yes, ma'am. I believe him to be the best in London, and I thank you for bringing him to our attention." Sebastian began to chuckle. "What does he say to your plan to travel to Turkey?"

"He don't know of it," Miss Grantham replied in triumph. "I ain't consulted a member of the medical profession in years, and I don't plan to do so now."

Sebastian shook his head in mock reproof. Then he began to laugh. "In spite of what you told my boys, I believe you are an immortal."

"Don't change the subject, sir. You haven't answered my question."

"There is something…" he admitted. "Both Prudence and Elizabeth are worried about Judith."

"The girl is to wed quite soon, I'm told, to some fashionable preacher?"

"Yes, ma'am." Sebastian was reluctant to go further.

"Well, marriage ain't a hanging matter, though some would disagree with me. I shouldn't choose a preacher for myself, of course. They are a sanctimonious lot, always happy to get their feet beneath someone else's table… Is that the trouble? Don't they like the fellow? I ain't seen him myself, or heard his rantings."

Sebastian hid a smile. Miss Grantham's humanist views were well known to him. It was highly unlikely that she would ever listen to a preacher, however fashionable.

"Something like that," he agreed.

The old eyes rested on his face. "You ain't the man to be swayed by female fancies. There's more to this than you will tell."

"Yes, ma'am. I wish I could be more open with you, but it would not be wise. I have so little information…"

"Is there anything I can do?"

Sebastian shook his head. "All we can do is to wait."

"I don't like it," she said decisively. "But I shall not trouble you further by poking my nose into matters which you prefer to keep to yourself."

He looked up then and saw the anxiety in her face. On an impulse he took her hands in his.

"Don't worry!" he said gently. "All will be well. You need have no fears about Elizabeth, or any of us."

He could see that her lips were trembling. Then she straightened her back.

"I should hope not!" she announced with some asperity. "Now, sir, I must go. Perry and Elizabeth brought me to you, and now they shall take me home. You will give my love to Prudence?"

"Won't you go up to her?" he suggested. "She is so fond of you, and will be sorry not to see you."

"Flatterer!" Miss Grantham hesitated. "It will not tire her if I stay for just a moment?"

"Of course not!" He led her through the hall and up the staircase, a hand outstretched to help her if she found the climb too much.

She had no need of it. Miss Grantham ate sparingly and was a firm believer in the value of walking as an exercise. There was surprising strength in the thin, wiry figure and she marched along beside him without a pause to catch her breath.

She was greeted by a cry of pleasure from Prudence, and was persuaded to sit down for a brief five minutes.

Then Miss Grantham reappeared and joined Sebastian in the hall.

"Nothing to worry about there!" she said with satisfaction. "Only your precious mystery need concern you now." She began to draw on her gloves. "Sebastian, you will take care?"

"Certainly, ma'am."

"And you might look to Dan. He's changed in these past years."

Sebastian could only marvel at her shrewdness. Dan had been in her company for so short a time, and they had barely exchanged a word.

"You ain't thinking of playing Cupid, are you?"

Sebastian laughed. "I'm not the build to be a cherub, ma'am. Look about you! Do you see a bow and arrow?" He bent and kissed the withered cheek.

She pushed him away, but he could see that she was pleased. Then Perry and Elizabeth came towards them.

"There you are, my dears! Come, we must make haste! I have still to pack my books and papers…"

Perry began to tease her. "And don't forget a sharp knife, Aunt. In a month or two you will be dining on camel and yaks' tails."

"Yaks? In Turkey? Bless me, the man is totally uneducated. Yaks, my dear Perry, are found only in Tibet." With this quelling statement Miss Grantham allowed herself to be led away.

Sebastian returned upstairs to find his wife convulsed with laughter.

"Oh, my dear!" she gasped. "I have been missing all the fun. Judith tells me that Amelia was well and truly routed."

"Wicked creature!" he said fondly. "Where is your spirit of Christian charity?"

"I haven't one where Amelia is concerned. Dear Miss Grantham! Is she not a treasure?"

"She is a wise old woman. What's more, my love, she found you looking well. You must not spoil it. Will you dine up here this evening?"

"Only if you will join me." Prudence looked up at him, her eyes aglow with love.

"Would you have me ignore my duties as a host?"

"Judith will not mind. She and Dan have always so much to say to one another. They are fast friends, just as we are ourselves."

Sebastian dropped a kiss upon her hair. Then he looked at Judith. "Shall you mind, my dear?"

"Not at all!" It wasn't strictly true. Judith had sensed a growing estrangement between herself and Dan. Was it her imagination, or did he seem to be growing ever more distant? She racked her mind to find an answer.

Their outing with the boys had been enjoyable. She could think of nothing that she might have done or said which might account for his strange reserve.

It didn't matter now, she thought sadly. The Countess would lose no time in carrying her tale to Mrs Aveton, and then she would be summoned home.

Whilst she dressed for dinner, she tried to fight off a growing feeling of depression.

In an effort to raise her spirits Bessie had laid out a gown in the softest shade of rose-pink muslin, with appliqué at the hem.

"Bessie, I am not attending a ball," she protested.

"I should think not, miss. Otherwise, you might have worn the yellow brocade."

"Great heavens, you did not pack that too?"

"No, I didn't!" her maid said firmly. "I packed only

those which were suitable for wear at home. Now, miss, do give over with your arguments, or you'll be late for dinner."

Judith submitted to the ministrations of her maid without further protest, though she refused the offer of an attempt to train her fine soft hair into a high knot, with ringlets arranged to frame her face.

"Bessie, you know it is a waste of time," she laughed. "My hair will be down about my ears before I reach the dining-room."

"Very well, miss. At least the bandeau matches your gown, and you do look a picture, if I do say so myself."

"You'll turn my head with your nonsense," Judith predicted darkly. "I shan't be late abed tonight, but you need not wait up for me."

"As if I wouldn't, Miss Judith." Bessie hid a secret smile. Nothing would have persuaded her to retire before her young mistress. Besides, she had great hopes of the coming dinner *à deux*. A look at Judith's face would tell her how it had gone.

Judith found Dan waiting for her in the salon. The door was slightly ajar, and her ribbon-tied silk sandals made no sound upon the carpet.

"Dan?"

He turned, caught off guard, and his eyes glowed as he looked at her. That look was quickly banished, but it was enough to make her heart beat faster. Had she imagined it?

He gave her a smile which held no more than a friendly welcome.

"Judith, you are in famous looks tonight. I had thought that our outing might have tired you."

"No, no!" she protested. "It was the greatest fun. How much the boys enjoyed it!"

"Perhaps we should do it again. Have you any ideas? There are military reviews in the Park, balloon ascents, firework displays and Astley's Royal Amphitheatre, all guaranteed to delight the heart of any boy..."

"And mine, too, I make no doubt."

"I was sure of it," he grinned. "At Astley's you may see a spectacular piece called *The Flight of the Saracens,* unless you prefer *Make Way for Liberty.* Confess it, they sound irresistible..."

Judith returned his smile. "The boys are keen to go there. I have had a full description of the sawdust ring in which John Astley and his wife show off their equestrian skills."

"It could be a mistake," he teased. "I foresee broken bones when Thomas and Henry return to Cheshire. Thank heavens they have no ponies here, or we should be treated to similar attempts at acrobatics."

At the sound of the gong he took her arm and led her into the dining-room. Two of the leaves had been removed from the table to provide a more intimate setting, and the light from a single candelabra shone softly upon fine silver and antique glass.

Judith gave a sigh of pleasure as she looked about her. Tonight this lovely room, with its panelled walls, seemed like a haven of peace. Just for once she would be self-indulgent, revelling in the prospect of a precious evening alone with the man she loved.

Sebastian's chef was a master of his craft, but Judith was in a dreamlike state, unaware of what she was eating. She nibbled at a tiny lobster vol-au-vent and allowed herself to be helped to a serving of broiled fowl, but she waved aside the preserved goose, the dish of ham in maderia sauce, a fine serpent of mutton, and the chef's speciality, neats' tongues dressed to a jealously guarded recipe.

"My dear Judith, you will cause the wizard in the kitchen to pack his bags if you spurn his efforts," Dan protested. "You haven't eaten enough to keep a bird alive."

"I'm sorry, I wasn't thinking." Judith collected her wandering thoughts. "The syllabub looks delicious, and so do the fruit jellies." She took a little of both dishes, hoping to restore herself to favour with the god below stairs.

Dan signalled to the butler to replenish her glass.

"No, thank you!" She laid her hand across the rim.

"Nonsense, it will do you good! Red wine, you know, is said to be the answer to all ills." He removed her hand, and watched as the ruby liquid flowed.

Judith laughed. "Not if it results in a dreadful headache," she protested.

"Two glasses cannot hurt you."

"But, Dan, I shall be chattering like a monkey."

"It will be a change. You have been quiet tonight."

"Have I? I beg your pardon. I didn't mean to be a dull companion."

"You are never that, my best of friends, but you have not spoken for the past ten minutes."

"Forgive me! It is just that...well...I was enjoying the peace in this lovely restful room."

"Is peace so rare with you, my dear?"

"It has been," she admitted. "Life at home is not always pleasant."

He sat back then, his eyes intent upon her face.

"I would describe that as the understatement of the year, Judith. I can't think how you have survived your life with Mrs Aveton. I had thought you must have married long ago. Were you never tempted?"

"No!" she said briefly. "You will wish to enjoy your port and a cigar. I told Bessie that I should not be late tonight. Will you excuse me if I leave you now?"

"No, I will not! Must you run away? I don't want port and I don't want a cigar. What I do want is to talk to you. Shall we go into the salon?"

Judith glanced at the butler, and at the impassive faces of the footmen. To refuse might lead to an undignified argument before the servants. In silence she preceded him from the room.

"Cross with me?" he asked lightly.

"Of course not!" Judith felt uneasy. She had been foolish to bring up the subject of Mrs Aveton. Her face clouded. By tomorrow that lady would be in full possession of the news that Judith had accompanied Dan to Madame Tussaud's with no other members of the family present except for Sebastian's boys.

Then, unwittingly, Dan added to her worries.

"I'm still waiting for your decision," he said.

"About what?"

"About your next expedition. Is it to be to Astley's, to the fireworks, or to the balloon ascent?"

A lump came to Judith's throat. "I doubt if I shall be here," she whispered in choked tones.

"Why ever not? I thought that the dragon had given you permission to stay for several days."

"That was before she knew that you were likely to return. Oh, Dan, don't you see? The Countess will tell her. Then I shall be summoned home."

"I think you haven't reckoned with Sebastian."

"It won't make any difference. If she insists he can do nothing. Besides, I feel so guilty as it is…" A slow tear trickled down her cheek.

"Ah, don't!"

Neither of them seemed to move, but suddenly she was in his arms, her cheek pressed to his coat. Through the fine fabric she could feel the pounding of his heart, and it seemed as if, at last, her dearest wish was to be granted. Now he would tell her that his affections were unchanged, and he still loved her.

She lifted her face to his, longing for the kiss that would wipe away all memory of those years of loss and desolation. Her heart was in her eyes as she looked at him, but he made no move to seek her mouth.

Gently he placed his hands upon her shoulders, and held her away.

"I can't bear to see you so distressed," he murmured. "Trust Sebastian, Judith! He won't allow you to be taken away so soon."

She couldn't have been more stunned if he had struck her. She'd have preferred it. A blow would have sent her spinning into oblivion, unaware of the agony of mind which now possessed her.

She had thrown herself at him and been rejected. Her passionate embrace had been so warm that he must have known that she was offering her heart. He had refused it. Judith felt that she wanted to die. She grew so pale that he helped her to a chair. She did not notice that he too was trembling.

His anguish matched her own. Nothing in his previous life had caused him so much pain as that bleak refusal to tell her of his love, but he dared not. Her safety must be his sole concern.

In silence he poured out a glass of brandy. ''You are upset!'' he murmured. ''You had best drink this.''

She waved it away and stumbled to her feet. Dan reached out a hand to steady her, but she drew back sharply.

''Please...don't touch me!'' The despairing cry cut him to the heart, but Judith fled before he could reply.

She wanted to run and to hide herself away, but her limbs were leaden. To climb the staircase felt like wading through a morass which tugged her back with every step, but she reached her room at last.

As the door opened, Bessie sprang to her feet expectantly. Then she saw Judith's face.

''Why, miss, whatever is it? Here, you had best sit down. You look as if you've seen a ghost.''

Judith did not speak. She *had* seen a ghost, but it was a ghost of the past which had vanished, never to return. She sat on the edge of her bed, staring into space. Now she could no longer hope, and only the black void of her future lay before her.

It was all too much for Bessie. She gathered her mistress in her arms, rocking back and forth, and crooning gently to Judith as if she'd been a child.

''There, don't take on!'' she murmured. ''Things always look bad at night. You'll feel better in the morning.''

The love and sympathy in her voice was Judith's undoing. The tears came then, and she wept as if her heart would break.

''I can't bear it!'' she cried in anguish. ''Oh, Bessie, if you only knew...''

Wisely, Bessie did not question her. There was no need. Something had gone wrong between her young mistress and the man she loved, but there was nothing she could do to put matters right. All she could offer now was comfort.

"Let's get you into bed," she murmured. "Then you shall have a drink of milk and honey to send you off to sleep." She drew Judith to her feet, and began to undress her. Then she settled the unresisting figure into a chair, and began to brush her hair.

The long, slow strokes were soothing, and Judith closed her eyes. Then Bessie laid aside the brush and placed a hand on either side of Judith's temples, moving her fingers in circles at each end of her brow. It was Bessie's favourite remedy for a pounding headache.

"Better?" she asked.

Judith nodded.

"Well, then, drink your hot milk, and don't you dare get up for breakfast in the morning. You are living on your nerves, Miss Judith, and it won't do. Next thing we'll have you falling sick, and where will you be then?"

"In bed, I expect." Judith managed a feeble smile.

"It's no joke!" Bessie insisted. "You won't wish to worry Lady Wentworth. I thought you'd come to cheer her up. You won't do that if you go about like that there Sarah Siddons…!"

Judith caught her hand and looked at her with fond affection.

"Don't scold!" she begged. "I won't behave like a tragedy queen."

Bessie's expression softened. "I know that, miss. You keep up a brave front. It's only me as knows…

well, I won't say more.'' She blew out the candles, and crept softly from the room, leaving her mistress to stare into the dark until nature won the day and emotional exhaustion sent her off to sleep.

Below, in the salon, Dan was sitting by the dying embers of the fire. He'd refused the footman's offer to build it up, or to replace the candles which were now guttering in their sockets.

The shadows matched his mood. Judith's unhappiness had shaken him to the very core of his being, and his endurance had reached its limit. Nothing in the world was worth this misery. Beside it, his own stiff-necked pride was meaningless. He cursed himself for a selfish prig. Judith did not care about her fortune, and he knew now that she loved him. Was it right to allow his own principles to stand in the way of their happiness? Suddenly it seemed like nothing more than vanity.

He reached a decision at last. Tomorrow he would ask Sebastian to release him from his promise. If he and Judith were to marry quickly, she would no longer be in danger.

He stubbed out the butt of his cigar. He'd picked up the habit of smoking the rolled tobacco leaves whilst in the West Indies, and he preferred it to the more fashionable custom of taking snuff.

Suddenly, his feelings of depression vanished. He'd been a fool not to think of the obvious solution before. With Judith's fortune out of reach, the avaricious parson would be forced to look elsewhere.

As for himself? Let the world accuse him of marrying for money. It wouldn't even be a nine-day wonder. The *ton* would see him as no better or no worse than any other bachelor on the look-out for a rich wife. Was not matchmaking the main objective during the coming Season?

It was his own pride which had caused him to reject the notion. Now it was high time that he considered Judith rather than himself. Neither of them cared for the opinion of Polite Society, and in time his own talent would be recognised.

Lost in thought, he strolled across the hall. Tomorrow he would ask Sebastian how to procure a special licence. There was still a little worm of doubt in his mind. Could he persuade Judith to accept him? And even if she did, would she agree to this hasty marriage? She might reject all notion of such a hole-and-corner affair, but he dared not wait. Sebastian had warned him what might happen if Judith tried to break off her engagement to Charles Truscott.

Then he noticed a streak of light beneath the library door. Sebastian must be reading late. He tapped a brief tattoo and entered the room.

Then he paused. Sebastian wasn't alone. Seated opposite him was the brawny figure of the Bow Street Runner.

The man gave Dan a brief nod of recognition and then fell silent.

"It's all right, Babb! You may continue to speak freely. I have no secrets from my adopted son." Sebastian signalled to Dan to take a seat.

"Well, my lord, as I was saying…our quarry is on the move again. Today he went back to the rookery in St Giles, and spent the afternoon drinking with Margrave in a gin shop."

"So they are friends?" Sebastian frowned.

"It would appear so. I didn't see the other three to-day."

"Were you able to get close to him...to hear?"

"No, my lord. Margrave knows me, and he's as wary as a cat. I thought you wouldn't wish him to suspect that there was anything in the wind, so I kept out of sight."

"But you must have got some impression? Were they quarrelling?"

"Thick as thieves, they were! Laughing and joking for three hours... Then Truscott left. I followed him to Seven Dials. He's there for the night, as usual, I believe, so I came to you."

"Quite right! You must follow him again tomorrow. Do you need more men?"

"Not for the moment, sir. I'll let you know. Now I'll be off, if I'm to make an early start tomorrow."

Dan waited until the door had closed behind him.

"What's happening, Sebastian?"

"I don't know, but I don't like it..."

"Nor do I. We are getting nowhere. It's all much too slow. Judith will wed that creature before we know it."

"My dear boy, I did counsel patience. Let us wait for another day or two..."

"I can't!" Dan told him flatly. "I've made up my mind. I wonder that I didn't think of it before. If I wed Judith now...tomorrow...she will be safe."

Sebastian shook his head. "It isn't the answer, Dan. I warned you of the danger. Suppose that something should go wrong?"

"How could it? We could leave this house in secret, and be wed within the hour. How can I get a special licence?"

"That may prove to be the least of your problems," Sebastian said deliberately. "Have you spoken to Judith of this plan?"

Dan coloured. "No, I haven't, but, well, I don't think she's indifferent to me. I thought so at first, especially as she had agreed to marry Truscott, but now I am certain that her affections have not changed."

"You may be right, but how will you explain to her the need for this sudden haste?"

"I'll tell her the truth about Truscott."

"And will she believe you? You have no proof of your suspicions."

"Does it matter?" Dan cried impatiently. "If she loves me she'll agree to wed me, whenever and however."

"I wish you'd reconsider." Sebastian rose from his chair and began to pace the room. "Are you quite sure that this is what you want? There is still the matter of Judith's fortune…"

Dan coloured. "You guessed that it was the stumbling block? We haven't discussed it, you and I."

"There was no need. I know you well, my boy. Can you stomach the notion of being dependent on your wife?" His words were cruel, but Sebastian was desperate to prevent what he considered to be an act of folly.

Dan's colour deepened. "That's hitting below the belt," he said with dignity. "If you must know, I'm ashamed of my own pride. I've let it stand in the way for much too long. Now Judith's safety must come first."

"This is not the way to ensure it. Truscott must be taken beforehand."

"I've almost given up hope of that. Sebastian, I hate to go against your wishes, but I've quite made up my mind."

"Very well. Bishop Henderson will provide you with a special licence. I'll give you his address." He scribbled a few lines on a card. "Now, if you'll excuse me, I must go up to Prudence."

"You'll say nothing to her?" Dan's face was anxious.

"Certainly not, and nor will you! The only advice I'll give you now is to keep this plan to yourself." Sebastian looked grave as he walked away.

Chapter Twelve

Dan was up betimes next day, but obtaining the licence was not as easy as he had at first supposed.

The bishop was not receiving visitors before morning service, and later he had a number of appointments. The day was well advanced before Dan was admitted to his presence.

Another hour passed as he was well catechised as to the reasons for his unusual request. The bishop was adamant that he would issue no licence in aid of an elopement.

"No, my lord bishop. It is nothing like that, I assure you. It is just that...well, the matter is urgent."

Bishop Henderson looked at Dan's troubled face, and sighed. He had long since ceased to marvel at the tangles into which young people fell so readily. At last he reached into a drawer and drew out a form.

"I may tell you, sir, that were it not for the fact that you are connected to Lord Wentworth I should have no hesitation in refusing you. Does his lordship know of this?"

"He does, Your Grace. I spoke to him last night. It was he who suggested that I came to you."

This succeeded in disposing of any further argument, and when Dan hurried back to Mount Street he had the precious piece of paper safely in his pocket.

To his chagrin he found that for the rest of the day it was impossible to get Judith to himself.

Perry and Elizabeth were to dine at home that evening, and Prudence, much rested, had elected to join the family party for their meal.

Dan glanced at Sebastian in despair, but the bland face told him nothing. Sebastian made no enquiries as to the success of his adopted son's mission, whilst Judith herself seemed determined to avoid all his efforts to speak to her alone.

When the ladies retired to the salon, Dan was impatient to follow them. The licence was burning a hole in his pocket, and he paid only scant attention to his two companions. He had eaten nothing.

Perry passed the port, but Dan waved it away.

"Sickening for something, Dan? Great heavens, man, when *you* lose your appetite it must be serious. You were always a famous trencherman…" Perry grinned at him.

Even Sebastian smiled. "It's too early in the season for raspberry tart. When I first met Dan I suspected that he had hollow legs. He demolished two full tarts on our first day together. Even after that there was no way of filling him."

Dan responded to the teasing with a reluctant smile, but he couldn't hide his impatience to be done with the custom of the gentlemen lingering in the dining-room after their evening meal.

"You'll have to watch him, Seb, old chap," Perry murmured slyly. "Our Dan is becoming quite a ladies' man."

Goaded beyond endurance, Dan was tempted to make a sharp retort, but a look from Sebastian stopped him.

"Dan is right," his lordship murmured. "We had best join the ladies. It grows late, and Prudence must not overtax her strength."

Dan shot him a look of gratitude, but his optimism was short-lived. When Prudence decided to retire, Judith went with her. He was forced to spend another sleepless night wondering how he might manage to approach her and tell her of his plans.

On the following day it seemed that everything conspired against him. It was Henry's birthday, and he had promised the lad a gift of a Pedestrian Curricle. This interesting machine consisted of two wheels with a saddle slung between them. The rider propelled it forward with his feet until he attained sufficient speed. Then he lifted them and coasted for as long as possible.

Prudence had at first protested that Henry was too young to manage this alarming vehicle, but she had been overridden by a chorus of male voices. Now Dan and Perry were to take the boys in search of Henry's birthday gift.

The celebration continued with a visit to the New Mint which boasted gas lighting and a fascinating collection of steam engines. They were even allowed to watch the stamping of the coins, but by the time they returned to Mount Street the day was gone.

Overwhelmed with expressions of youthful thanks, Dan went up to change for dinner.

He would wait no longer. Tonight, he vowed, he would speak to Judith, if it meant asking her for a private interview within hearing of the rest of the family.

He couldn't hope that she would be allowed to remain with Prudence for much longer, although her fears that she would have been summoned home on the previous day had proved unfounded. He wondered at that. The Countess must, by now, have informed Mrs Aveton that he had returned and was squiring Judith about the town. It seemed strange that his old enemy should prove to be so unexpectedly compliant.

This was far from true. Mrs Aveton had been furious, but mindful of Truscott's wishes she had not set for Judith.

Again Dan struggled through what seemed to him to be an interminable meal. He made a valiant effort to take part in the usual lively conversation, aware that Judith too was doing her best to play her part. Pale but composed, she confined most of her attention to the ladies, refusing to meet his eyes.

Then Sebastian took pity on him. When the ladies had left them he cut short Perry's enjoyment of the port with the laughing excuse that Prudence had taken him to task on the previous evening.

As he left the dining-room he drew Dan aside.

"Are you still of the same mind?" he murmured.

Dan nodded.

"Then best get it over with. You will let me know how you go on?" With that he led his companions into the salon.

Scarcely able to contain his eagerness, Dan made his way to Judith's side.

"I must speak to you alone," he murmured.

At first she seemed not to have heard him, but Sebastian had drawn the others to the far side of the room, and he was able to repeat his words.

Judith flushed painfully and shook her head. Then, with a muttered excuse, she moved away.

"Judith, my dear, I wonder if you'd mind? Prudence has left her vinaigrette upstairs. I'm sure you will know where to find it." Ignoring his wife's astonished look, Sebastian smiled at their guest.

As Judith hurried away, he gave Dan an imperceptible signal, and turned back to the others.

Dan needed no second urging. He followed Judith from the room, and caught her at the foot of the stairs.

"Please, I beg of you! Won't you listen to me for a moment?" He took her arm and attempted to lead her back into the dining-room.

Judith tried to pull away. "No!" she cried in desperation. "Please leave me alone!"

"Not until you've heard me out."

"Very well, then." Judith was aware of the footman standing in the hall. The man's face was wooden, but the story of an undignified struggle would, she knew, be a source of gossip in the servants' hall.

She felt very angry, and when he closed the door behind him, she rounded on Dan with blazing eyes.

"Must you put me in this position?" she asked coldly. "I thought I had made my wishes clear. I won't listen to you, Dan. I'm tired of being worried and hounded and driven to distraction. Everyone knows what is best for me, with the apparent exception of myself."

Dan tried to take her hand, but she drew away.

"Please don't presume upon our friendship. Say what you have to say, and let me go."

"Won't you sit down?" Dan drew a chair towards her, but she turned her back on him, standing very stiff and straight.

"You aren't making this easy," he murmured. "I'm asking you to marry me."

She spun round then, and he thought he had never seen her look so angry.

"How dare you?" she cried. "Must you offer for me out of pity?"

It was Dan's turn to lose his temper. "Do you think so little of me? I'm asking you because I love you."

"You have a curious way of showing it. I don't believe you—"

"But you must." He drew the licence from his pocket. "Judith, we could be wed tomorrow, if only you will have me."

Her eyes fell upon the paper. "A special licence? You surprise me! Why this sudden haste? Since you returned I've seen no sign that your affections are unchanged."

Dan stood as if turned to stone. Sebastian's prediction had come true. It would be impossible to explain his actions with any hope of success.

"There were reasons," he said lamely. "I mean... there was your fortune to consider."

"I still have it."

"And, Judith, I couldn't be sure that you still cared for me. You were betrothed to Truscott."

"You didn't ask." Her voice was almost inaudible.

"I'm asking now. Oh, my dear, tell me that you won't marry him!"

"So that's it! You'll have your way, no matter what. This is unworthy of you, Dan. Who are you to judge Charles Truscott? He, at least, does not pretend to a passion which he does not feel."

"Then you won't change your mind?" Dan was shaken by her fury. Her face was set, and to go on would only make matters worse. He made a last despairing effort. "You are mistaken, Judith. I love you more than life itself. Will you condemn yourself to a life of misery with that creature?"

"Stop! I'll hear no more of this! How dare you presume to criticise the man I am to marry? Charles is good, and kind, and I want to marry him. I do! I do!" Bursting into tears, she fled from the room.

Dan sat down suddenly, feeling that the void had opened beneath his feet. He'd played his part too well. Judith didn't believe that he loved her, and now he'd never be able to convince her. She thought him merely mean and spiteful.

If only he'd been able to offer her some proof of Truscott's villainy. He had none, and that was the truth of it.

In an agony of mind he cursed Truscott, himself, the Bow Street Runner, and the cruel fate which had kept him away from England for so long.

Now he had lost his only love for ever. He buried his face in his hands.

He hadn't moved when Sebastian came to find him some time later. Dan felt a sympathetic hand upon his shoulder.

"Well?" Sebastian asked.

"She won't have me. I can't believe it! I was so sure that she still loved me."

"Don't give up hope, old chap. This may be for the best."

"Oh, I know you warned me. I've only made matters worse. She said that I'd offered for her out of pity and…and an unreasonable dislike of Truscott. She won't hear a word against him. What could I say to her? Now she's more determined than ever to marry him."

"Judith isn't married yet. Will you come back to the ladies, Dan? Prudence has been wondering where you are."

Dan shook his head. "Will you make my excuses? I can't face Judith just at present."

"Judith has retired. She claimed to have the headache." Sebastian rose and led his companion back into the salon.

Judith had not lied. At that moment she was lying on her bed with her hands pressed to her temples in a vain attempt to dull the pain.

The memory of Dan's astonishing behaviour only made it worse. Two days ago he had rejected her, thrusting her away when he must have known how much she loved him. He hadn't even tried to kiss her.

Now it seemed that she was to fall into his arms in simple gratitude for being rescued from a marriage of which he disapproved.

The sight of the special licence had disgusted her. There could be no reason for such unseemly haste unless he had determined to get his hands upon her fortune. His plan to interest Admiral Nelson in his drawings had met with no success. Perhaps he had given up all hope of a promising career.

In her heart she knew that it wasn't true. Dan cared nothing for her money, and he still believed in his own talent.

If only he'd told her of his love when she'd thrown herself into his arms. She would have believed him then, but the pain of rejection was still with her.

He didn't return her affection, though tonight he'd tried to convince her. She closed her eyes in pain. It had been the coldest of proposals. Dan had made no attempt to crush her to his breast and silence all her objections with his lips against her own.

Instead he'd been at pains to convince her of her own folly, her lack of judgment in accepting Charles Truscott. She'd have no more of it. Reaching out, she rang her bell for Bessie.

''I'd like you to pack my things without delay,'' she said.

''Tonight, Miss Judith?'' Bessie looked her surprise.

''Tonight, or first thing in the morning. I must leave tomorrow.''

''But, miss, I thought you was to stay? Won't Lady Wentworth think it strange of you to rush away?''

''Don't argue with me, Bessie! Her ladyship won't find it strange at all since the date of my marriage is so close. There must be a thousand things to do.''

Bessie sniffed. ''I'll pack tomorrow, then.'' As she undressed her mistress she made her disapproval clear, but Judith ignored her mutterings.

She'd made her decision to leave and she would stand by it. Prudence would be disappointed, but she would understand. After all, this visit was intended to be short.

Judith prayed only that she might be allowed to leave the house without the need to bid farewell to Dan. If that could be managed she would be wed before they met again, and safe from further persuasion. She felt that she could take no more.

Her wish was granted. Sebastian had foreseen that she would wish to go, and had sent Dan off on some errand of his own. He had also warned Prudence that she must take Judith's probable departure with good grace.

Prudence obeyed him, though it went much against the grain. She held out her arms to Judith and clasped her friend in a warm embrace.

"My dear, I'm sorry that I shan't be with you on your wedding day," she murmured. "I wonder…shall you like Sebastian to give you away? Mrs Aveton hinted at it when he came to fetch you."

Judith felt a twinge of panic. The suggestion brought the date of her marriage so much closer. Then Sebastian smiled, and she felt reassured.

"That would be kind," she said. "It is good of you. I have no male relatives, you see."

"It will be a pleasure." Sebastian bowed, though he felt that the lie must choke him. He still hoped that Truscott would be unmasked. If not, Judith must be assured of his support. He couldn't shake off a sense of deep foreboding, but his worries were not apparent as he settled Judith into the family carriage.

Judith swallowed a lump in her throat as she was borne away. Parting with her friends had not been easy. When she saw them again she would be Charles Truscott's wife.

* * *

This fact was recalled to her attention by Mrs Aveton. Summoned to that lady's presence, she was left in no doubt of her stepmother's opinion of her conduct.

"Of all the sly, deceitful creatures, you must be the worst!" the older woman shouted. "Did you imagine that I should not hear of your disgraceful behaviour?"

"Disgraceful, ma'am? I am not aware of it."

"How else would you describe yourself? Don't play the innocent with me! Will you deny that you spent the day alone with that...that pauper?"

"We weren't alone, ma'am. We had three children with us... Besides, I am not yet wed."

"Nor likely to be, if Mr Truscott hears of this. What will he say, I wonder, to the idea of you and your old paramour whispering and making sheep's eyes at each other in dark corners?"

"I must hope, ma'am, that his mind is rather more elevated than your own."

"Why, you impudent baggage! How dare you speak to me like that?" A dark flush stained Mrs Aveton's face, mottling her nose and cheeks with dull red. "When I think of what you owe to me, bringing you up as one of my own!"

Judith's patience snapped. Tall and straight, she eyed her stepmother with contempt.

"I owe you nothing, ma'am, except for some plain speaking. Since my father died, you've done your best to make my life a misery. I haven't forgotten all I've suffered at your hands. I thank heavens that it is almost at an end. Carry your tales to Mr Truscott if you wish. It will make no difference. Wed to him or not, I fully intend to leave this house."

Mrs Aveton knew that she had gone too far.

"You…you can't do that," she said uncertainly.

"Why not? I now have the money to set up an establishment of my own."

A snort of disbelief greeted this remark.

"Nonsense! Young women do not live alone. It would cause a scandal!"

Judith smiled, but there was no amusement in her eyes. "Do you suppose that gossip would worry me? I have no fears of your mischief-making in that direction. Scandal harms only those who care for the opinion of Polite Society. I do not."

Her words struck a chill in Mrs Aveton's heart. Her hopes of a share in Judith's fortune were disappearing fast, and Truscott would be furious. If the truth were known, she was a little afraid of him.

"You misunderstand me," she said more calmly. "I was thinking only of your future happiness."

"Since when?" Judith turned on her heel and left the room.

Her mood had changed completely and she now felt much more cheerful. When confronted, Mrs Aveton had collapsed like a pricked balloon. Perhaps that was true of all such bullies. For the first time, Judith felt in full command of herself. She should have spoken out years ago.

With a fine disregard of all depredations to her trousseau, she decided to wear her most expensive gown that evening, and she made no objection when Bessie offered to dress her hair in the latest and most fashionable style.

It was a subdued Mrs Aveton who was moved to compliment her upon her appearance. Judith nodded an acknowledgment, but she wanted to laugh. No such praise had ever come her way before.

The Aveton girls gazed at their mother in astonishment, but she bid them sharply to get on with their meal. Then she turned to Judith.

"Did you hear from the Reverend Truscott whilst you were at Mount Street?" she enquired.

"No, ma'am. He sent no messages here?"

Mrs Aveton shook her head. Then she forced a smile. "I think we need have no fears about him, Judith. With sickness it is never possible to predict the course of a disease with any certainty. It is much to his credit that he refuses to leave his mother's bedside. For the present, his thoughts will be for her alone."

"As they must be, ma'am. I offered to go with him, but he wouldn't hear of it."

Mrs Aveton was unsurprised by this news. Of a naturally suspicious mind, she'd never trusted her accomplice. What fool would believe his story? Truscott was not the man to waste his sympathy on the sick.

This cock-and-bull tale about his mother's illness was pure fiction. Only a guileless creature like her stepdaughter would be taken in by it. Truscott was up to something, and she would have given much to know the truth of it. Whatever his activities, she was convinced that they would not bear inspection. What a comfort it would be to have some hold over him…some threat which she might use to force him into keeping his part of their bargain.

There was little likelihood of that. The preacher had always evaded her attempts to learn anything of his past life. Now she found herself wondering as to his present dealings.

She wasn't overly concerned. The avarice of the Reverend Charles fully matched her own. He'd surprised her with his willingness to leave his bride-to-be in these few days before their marriage, and with his obvious wish for Judith to remove herself to Mount Street, but he must have good reasons. Charles Truscott took no decisions without giving them careful thought.

She was right. Three days earlier the preacher had returned to the house in Seven Dials to consider all the options open to him. After much deliberation he had hit upon the solution to his problems.

Margrave was the main danger. The forger was the brains behind the plot against him. He must be dealt with first. Cut off the head of a venomous snake and the writhing body of the reptile could do no further harm. Deprived of Margrave's leadership, Nellie and her friends would present no problem. He could deal with them at his own leisure.

And he would handle all these matters himself. His last attempt to dispose of his enemies had convinced him that he could trust no one to follow out his orders.

First, he must get close to Margrave. It wouldn't be easy. The man was as wily as a fox, and as wary.

Truscott lay upon his bed for hours, until the answer came to him. Then a grim smile played about his lips as he remembered the old adage: "divide and rule" was excellent advice. He would follow it without delay.

He threw back the coverlet and called to Nan to fetch his clothing.

Her reddened eyes told him that she had been weeping. He'd used her cruelly the previous night, but she had given him no pleasure. She might have been a block of wood for all the response she offered.

God, but he was tiring of her constant whining, and the endless questions about her brothers. She'd have to go. He'd see to it before the week was out, but now he had other matters to attend.

Wrapping his cloak about him, and with a slouch hat pulled well down to hide his face, he set off for the parish of St Giles.

His mother's house was empty, but he knew where to find her. Turning into the nearest gin shop, he saw her sitting in the corner with her friends. As he had expected, Margrave was one of the party.

"This is an unexpected pleasure, Charlie." The forger gave him a sly smile.

"I promised, didn't I?" Truscott pulled out a leather purse and laid it on the table.

Nellie's claw-like hands reached out, and then she gave a little yelp of pain as Margrave rapped her across the knuckles with his cane.

"Don't be greedy, Nellie!" he reproved. "I'll take charge of that."

"There's plenty for all, and more where that came from," Truscott told him carelessly.

"Thought it over, have you?" the forger jeered. "Very wise! I never thought you a fool."

"I'm not! I don't waste my time bemoaning anything I can't change."

"Splendid! Nellie, I must congratulate you upon your son's good sense." Margrave tipped out the contents of the purse. Then his lips pursed and he shook his head. "A modest offering, I fear. You must do better than this."

"I'm not such a fool as to carry gold about me in this place. If you want more you'll have to come with me to fetch it."

Margrave laughed in his face. "To Seven Dials? Charlie, do you take me for a plucked 'un? I'd as soon walk through the gates of hell as go to your house alone."

"I shouldn't ask it of you. I leave no money there. It's safest at the church. There's always a tidy sum from the collections."

Margrave leaned back in his chair, and eyed Truscott with great deliberation. Then he shook his head.

"I don't think so. I don't trust you, Charlie. You've been at pains to keep us all away from your precious parish. What is so different now?"

"I don't mean all of you," the preacher cried impatiently. "I can't have Nellie about the place, but you would pass for one of the congregation."

"Thank 'ee! I'm flattered, but not convinced. You'd best come here every day, and bring as much as you can."

"I can't do that. I'm to be wed next week. My absence is already giving rise to comment with the lady's stepmother. Would you have me lose my bride?"

Margrave looked shocked. "My dear sir, I hope that you will not do so. The lady is to be the source of all our fortunes, is she not?"

"Then heed my words. I cannot come to you again before my marriage. After that, I cannot say. You claim that this present sum is modest. I agree. For the present the only money at my disposal is locked within the vestry. It will provide for you for several weeks. After that, there will be papers to be signed and perhaps a lengthy wait before I am in possession of my wife's inheritance.''

"So you are offering us your savings? My dear chap, how very generous of you, though sadly out of character, I fear. We must prepare ourselves to wait, I believe.''

"As you please!'' Truscott rose to his feet, and prepared to take his leave of them. Then Nellie intervened.

"We can't live on this!'' she snarled. With a quick movement of her hand she scattered the coins across the table in disgust. "Don't trust him, Dick! Once he's wed he won't come back.''

"Oh, I think he will, but you are right. We can't live on air. Very well, sir, I will go with you, but I warn you. I am armed.''

Truscott ignored the implied threat. His plan was going well, and he was in no hurry. He allowed his companion to comment upon the fine spring weather as they strolled along together, and permitted himself a smile at Margrave's pleasantries.

"This is better,'' the forger observed as he gave his hat a jaunty tilt. "Charlie, you ain't short of brains. We ought to be good friends.''

"I agree. It's a pity you have the others hanging on to you. A fortune shared between you won't go far.''

"You express my own thoughts to perfection, but for the moment I have no alternative. There is safety in numbers, as you know.''

"Careful, as always?'' Truscott chuckled. "I was thinking only that we might come to some arrangement, just the two of us. You might be useful to me. As I say, you would pass for a member of my congregation…''

"A partnership? It's certainly worth of consideration. Shall we step into this hostelry?"

They were now well away from the pauper colony, and he turned through the doors of a nearby inn. Avoiding the noisy taproom, he led the way through to a small parlour with smoke-blackened walls and windows so heavily leaded as to admit only the faintest trace of light.

The two men seated themselves in the far corner of the room, almost concealed by the shadows. Truscott looked about him.

"You know this place?" he asked.

"I've used it on occasion. No questions asked, you understand, and plenty of warning if strangers are about. Can't always tell who's in the taproom, naturally, but it will be quiet enough in here."

Truscott nodded. He was well satisfied with this quiet spot in which to pursue his objective.

"This plan of yours?" the forger continued. "What's in it for me?"

Truscott considered his next words carefully. At no time must he alert his quarry to the fate in store for him.

"You have certain skills," he said at last. "It may be that at some time in the future there will be a need to alter various documents in my…in our favour."

"Very true! That should present no problems."

"Aside from that, you have a smooth address. Why not make use of it? The fools of women who attend my services are begging to be parted from their dibs." Deliberately, he used thieves' cant as he grinned at his companion. "We might even make a preacher of you!"

"No, no! I'll leave all that to you. You could always talk, and you might have made your fortune on the boards. As for me, my face is too well known in certain quarters. I believe in keeping low.''

''Just as you wish, but my offer holds. Work with me, and I'll make you a rich man. Now, what do you say?''

''I'll think about it.'' It was as far as Margrave would go. ''There's only one thing worries me. You were always a selfish devil, Charlie, looking out for number one. Why the sudden change?''

''Oh, I haven't changed, but I don't close my eyes to facts. Let's say I'd rather have you with me than against me. You know the old saying 'If you can't beat 'em, join 'em'?''

''You're a marvel, sir...a positive marvel!'' The older man gave his companion a look of admiration. ''It's a pleasure to do business with you.'' He downed his drink in one. ''Now about this money? Shall we go?''

''Dick, you must give me an hour or two. I shan't be wasting my time. You'll agree that I must keep the lady sweet? I've been neglecting her in recent days. I'd best go to see her.''

Margrave's look was speculative. ''You wouldn't be trying to do me down? I warn you—''

''No, no, it's nothing like that! We are in full agreement, aren't we?'' Truscott favoured his companion with an encouraging smile. ''Why not come to my church tonight? If you attend the evening service you'll see what I mean. When you cast your eye over those plump pigeons ready for the plucking, you'll hesitate no longer.''

''Why must it be tonight?'' Margrave was immediately suspicious.

''The church will be full. Your presence will go unnoticed, and I'll give you the money after the service. You won't object to adding tonight's collection to your purse, will you?''

Greed fought with suspicion in the forger's mind. Then, as Truscott had expected, he agreed to the plan, albeit with some misgivings.

''No tricks, mind!'' He tapped his pocket significantly, comforted by the weight of the pistol which reposed there.

Truscott shook his head in apparent sorrow. ''You must learn to trust me. Would I be likely to attack you in full view of my congregation? Didn't you say something about there being safety in numbers? I thought you'd welcome the idea.''

With that he strode away. He was well pleased with the result of this interview with Margrave, and not all of his story had been false. He *had* been neglecting Judith. By now she must be wondering what had become of him. It was time to pull the strings and draw his puppet back to him.

Now he had no fear that any of his enemies would approach her. Margrave would see to that. She must return home without delay. Mrs Aveton would be happy to send a note to that effect to Lady Wentworth.

He was surprised to learn that Judith had already parted from her friends. Was she anxious for her wedding? He doubted it, but his lips curved in pleasurable anticipation. He banished that smile as he was shown into the salon, but he sensed at once that Mrs Aveton was not her usual bombastic self.

"Thank heavens you are come!" she said with feeling. "Sir, it was folly to leave us for so long."

"Is something wrong?"

A bitter laugh greeted his words. "You may judge for yourself. Judith is much changed…"

"How so?" Truscott was alarmed, but his face was bland as he looked at her.

"Why, she is very much upon her mettle, and is lost to all sense of propriety. Whether it is the influence of her friends, or the thought of her inheritance I cannot say, but she answered me in such a way! I must say, I was shocked by her pert behaviour."

"Have you been quarrelling with her?" There was something in his eyes which made her back away.

"I had cause to speak to her upon a certain matter," she said defensively.

"Ma'am, you are a fool! Did I not warn you to keep the peace? When will you learn that you must leave her to me?" Truscott's face was working as he took a step towards her.

"Let me send for her," she said hurriedly. She retreated to the far end of the room and tugged at the bell-pull.

"I won't tell you again," he warned. "You will keep a still tongue in your head. God knows what damage you have done!"

His fears were stilled when Judith entered the room. She came towards him quickly.

"Charles, you have news? How is your mama?"

"Sad news, my love! She is gone, alas, and is at this moment in the presence of her Maker." He sat down suddenly, and covered his eyes with a shaking hand.

"Oh, my dear, I am so sorry. At least you were with

her. That must have been a comfort in her dying moments..." She rested a gentle hand upon his bowed shoulders.

He seized it and pressed his lips against her fingers.

"Too good, my angel! Now I have only you. You are all that is left to me." Truscott lifted his face to hers, ignoring a sardonic look from Mrs Aveton. "I must be strong," he murmured. "There will be much to do in the days ahead...the funeral, you know."

"Shall...shall you wish to postpone our wedding? At a time of mourning, it would be unseemly for the ceremony to take place."

"Ah, my dearest, how like you to consider me, but I made a death-bed promise. It was my mother's dearest wish that our marriage should go ahead, just as we had planned. We cannot bring her back to us, but before she died she urged that nothing must stand in the way of our future happiness."

"Then the delirium passed?"

"At the last her mind was clear, and I thank God for it. She knew me, Judith, and gave us both her blessing." Truscott managed to squeeze out a solitary tear. "You will not allow conventions to stand in the way of the wishes of a dying woman?"

"No!" she said quietly. "It shall be as you promised." She felt ashamed that even in the midst of her pity for him she'd felt a sudden lightening of her heart at the thought of a possible postponement of her marriage. In the usual way there would be at least a year of mourning for a close relative, but it was not to be.

She crushed the tiny flicker of hope which had flared, however briefly, in her heart. She was being selfish. Now, when Charles was most in need of her, she was thinking only of herself. In a gesture rare with her she took his hands and pressed them warmly.

Chapter Thirteen

Truscott almost fainted with relief. In his play-acting, he had overlooked the possible consequences of his news.

The stupid girl might have upset all his plans with her foolish notions of propriety. Left to her own devices she would probably have gone into black for at least a year. Any postponement of his marriage would be sure to finish him, for Margrave would not wait.

His throat felt dry, and when he looked down at his hands he saw that they were trembling. It was no matter. Judith would attribute his pallor and his inability to speak to a natural distress. He glanced at Mrs Aveton for support.

"Our dear Charles is right," she said at once. "His filial sentiments do him the utmost credit."

She wanted to laugh aloud. Truscott thought himself so clever, but this time he had overplayed his hand. She'd been alarmed herself, but he had made a swift recovery, twisting the situation to his own advantage. She could only admire the speed with which he had extricated himself. It hadn't made her like him any better.

Now he stumbled to his feet and took his leave of them. There was much to do to prepare himself for Margrave's visit, but he'd had a shock and his nerves were still on edge. He forced himself to walk more slowly, drawing in deep breaths. He must be calm. If his plans for the forger were to go well he needed a cool head.

Judith returned to her own room and sat down at her desk. Since her return, and after the confrontation with Mrs Aveton, she had felt curiously detached from the world about her.

The only reality was her book. In writing it she could forget the sad thoughts which beset her. In her unhappiness she'd been convinced that she would never write another line, but it wasn't so. She'd learnt to leave a sentence unfinished when she put aside her work. To complete it led her into the next, and soon her pen was flowing swiftly over the pages.

Bessie eyed her doubtfully. She was deeply troubled. Lost in a world of her own making, her young mistress was at peace, but in company there was a certain brittle brightness in her manner which was out of character.

Bessie stole quietly from the room. Then she stationed herself beside a window which overlooked the street. Taking out her handkerchief she waved to a figure opposite. The man turned quickly and walked away.

She returned to her vantage point at the same time on the following day. This time the family carriage was waiting at the door. As Bessie watched, Mrs Aveton left the house accompanied by her daughters, intent upon an outing to the Park at the fashionable hour of five o'clock.

Bessie opened the window slightly as the carriage rolled away. Then she beckoned to the watcher in the street. Silently she stole downstairs and let him in by a side-door.

Then, with a finger to her lips enjoining silence, she motioned to him to follow her up the back stairs.

Bessie had chosen her time well. Freed from the demands of their importunate mistress for an hour or so, none of the other servants were about. She guessed that they would be resting, or playing cards in the servants' hall, glad of the respite before the bustle attendant upon the evening meal.

She paused before Judith's door and tapped, but there was no reply. Throwing caution to the winds she opened it and departed, leaving Dan to enter the room alone.

Judith didn't raise her head. It was not until he stood behind her and laid his hands upon her shoulders that she turned.

''You!'' she cried in disbelief. ''You must be mad! What are you doing here, and how did you get in? The porter has orders never to admit you.''

''Judith, I had to see you. Why did you run away?'' Dan was very pale, but the blue eyes held her own.

''Need you ask?'' she said coldly. ''You had best go at once, before my stepmama returns.''

''Not before I've had my say. Oh, my dear, I tried to tell you of my love. Why won't you believe me?''

''I judge by actions, not by words, and I will have no arguments. Will you go, or must I call the servants?''

Dan stood his ground. ''Only if you wish me to break

their heads. Judith, you must listen to me, if only for the sake of our past friendship—''

''You presume too much upon it, sir. What am I to hear? Another tirade about the man I am to marry?''

''I didn't intend to speak of him...only of you.''

''And what of me? You have a curious notion of friendship, Dan. Do you care nothing for my peace of mind? I won't be worried in this way. Heaven knows I have enough to bear without your constant pestering! How can I make you understand?''

''You'll never do so. Judith, you don't love this man. Will you lie, and tell me that you do?''

''Love, so I'm told, is not a prerequisite for marriage. Is it not said to come much later?''

''You don't believe that, and nor do I!''

''I wonder that my feelings should concern you. You have no right...no right at all to question me!''

''Once, long ago, you gave me that right.''

''All that is past, but you won't accept it, will you? Dan, I have grown up. I'm not the girl you knew. You mentioned friendship? If you still wish to be my friend you will respect my wishes.''

''I'd be happy to do so if I believed that this marriage is what you wish with all your heart.'' He moved towards her, intending to take her in his arms, but she put out a hand to fend him off.

''No!'' she cried sharply. ''Please don't touch me!'' Judith could not trust herself. Once in his arms, with his mouth on hers, she would be lost. And lost to what? To a man who had offered for her only out of pity? She could not bear it.

Dan's face grew ashen. She had recoiled from him so fiercely that his arms fell to his sides.

"Forgive me!" he said simply. "I won't trouble you again. May I offer you my wishes for your future happiness?"

Dan's spirits were at their lowest ebb. What happiness could Judith hope for with a man whom he knew to be a villain? Without proof, there was no way to convince her. Her determination to wed Truscott seemed unshakeable.

Judith rang the bell for Bessie. She did not look at her maid.

"Show this gentleman out!" she ordered coldly. "When you have done so you may return. I have much to say to you."

Dan lost his temper then. Wild with frustration, he spun round.

"Don't take your anger out on Bessie, please. The fault is mine, if fault there is. Believe me, I have no wish to repeat it." With that he strode towards the door. "Bessie, you need not trouble yourself. I'll find my own way out—"

"Not that way!" Judith flew after him as he started down the main staircase. "Someone is sure to see you."

Her warning came too late, though she had a restraining hand upon his arm. At that moment the front door opened and Mrs Aveton entered the house, accompanied by her daughters and Charles Truscott.

The sight which met her eyes robbed her, for the moment, of all power of speech. Judith, scarlet with embarrassment, was in much the same condition.

Then Mrs Aveton found her voice. "Why, you little trollop!" she hissed viciously. "You should be whipped at the cart's tail!"

Ignoring Truscott's warning look, she turned to Dan.

"Out!" she ordered. "Or must I have you thrown into the street?"

Truscott thought in time to intervene. "My dear ma'am, are you not a little overwrought? Judith, I'm sure we are agreed, is welcome to receive her friends at any time."

"In her bedroom?" It was a scream of fury. "Oh, the disgrace!"

Truscott became aware of the sniggering girls beside him. He bent a stern look upon them. "Your daughters must be tired after their drive, Mrs Aveton. Doubtless they will wish to retire…"

It was clear that the girls had no such wish. Judith had been caught in the most compromising circumstances and the scene which must surely follow was far too good to miss. They longed to defy him, but there was something in his dark gaze which sent them scurrying away.

He turned to Judith's stepmother, jerking his head in the direction of the goggling porter. "This is hardly the place for a discussion, ma'am. May we not go into the salon?"

"Not him!" Mrs Aveton glared at Dan.

"But certainly this gentleman shall accompany us. My dear sir, I well remember you. You are Lord Wentworth's adopted son, I believe?"

Dan murmured something unintelligible in reply. His thoughts were in turmoil. Due to his own folly he had placed Judith in an impossible position.

He dared not look at her, but he knew how she must be feeling, and the thought of her present agony of mind almost broke his heart.

What a fool he'd been to come here. He'd forced

himself upon her, though she'd made her feelings clear that night in Mount Street. Why could he not accept that she cared for him no longer? In his arrogance he'd succeeded only in compromising her reputation.

"Perhaps a little refreshment, ma'am?" Truscott suggested smoothly.

For Mrs Aveton this was the last straw.

"How can you sit there speaking of refreshment, sir? Have you no notions of propriety? This girl deserves her fate. Mr Truscott, pray have no regard for my own feelings. Since all must be at an end between you, I shall excuse you if you wish to leave my home."

"I had no such thought." The preacher smiled at her, but there was no amusement in his eyes. "In less than a week, Judith will become my wife. Her conduct is now my concern, not yours, I think. Nothing she might do or say will give me a poor opinion of her. I trust her implicitly."

Judith lifted her head and looked at him in amazement. Another man might have placed the worst construction upon the situation.

"I...I'd like to speak to you alone," she whispered.

Dan sprang to his feet. "Then if you will excuse me?" He bowed to the assembled company and left the room. Judith was lost to him for ever. He knew it now.

Once in the street he looked about him blindly. Then he began to walk though he was unaware of his surroundings. For all they meant to him he might have been wandering on another planet.

His thoughts were all of Judith. He couldn't have made matters worse if he had tried. Now Mrs Aveton would humiliate her with all manner of vile accusations, and there was nothing he could do to protect her.

His fears were unnecessary. Truscott had seen at once that his bride-to-be was at the limits of her endurance. Her nerves were as taut as bowstrings. One false move, and he would lose her. If Mrs Aveton persisted with her disgusting insinuations, Judith herself might break off her engagement, feeling that she was unfit to marry him.

He moved towards her and took her hands. "Your stepmama will excuse us, dearest one." Over her head he cast a warning look at Mrs Aveton. It was a clear dismissal and she obeyed him, though she was loath to do so.

"My love, this has been most unpleasant for you," he murmured soothingly. "Won't you sit down, Judith?" He attempted a little joke. "Now, you shall not look at me as if you are a guilty schoolgirl!"

"I do feel guilty," she admitted quietly. "What must you think of me?"

"I think as I always did…that you are true and good. I could never doubt you."

His kind words tested her self-control, but she forced herself to speak.

"I owe you an explanation," she whispered. "I did not know, you see, that Dan would come here—"

Truscott placed a finger against her lips. "No explanations, dearest. None are needed. Now let us forget the matter. We shall not speak of it again."

"You are very good." Close to tears, she fled. Now she was confirmed in her belief that he was a man of generous spirit. If she didn't love him, at least she could admire him.

Truscott helped himself to a glass of wine. He was well satisfied with the way he'd handled her. In his apparent charity he had done his cause no harm at all. He had her now. There would be no further difficulty in the wooing of this witless creature.

He permitted himself a smile. He knew her well enough by now. There would have been no romping on the bed with his rival. Had they quarrelled? Either way, it did not matter. But how had the man gained access to her room? He thought he knew the answer. Bessie must be dismissed, but not until he was safely wed.

His spirits began to lift. It was high time he had some luck. That day he had awakened in the worst of moods. Margrave had let him down the night before, though he had waited for the forger until long past midnight.

Had his quarry grown suspicious? He went over their conversation, but he could think of nothing which might have alerted him.

Still, time was growing short. Cursing the necessity, he took himself back to the parish of St Giles.

There was no sign of Margrave in the gin shops. Then he bethought himself of the inn. To his relief Margrave was sitting in the corner, but he was not alone.

Truscott bowed to the bold-eyed wench beside him.

"Getting worried, were you, Charlie?" Margrave's look was sly.

"Not in the least!" Truscott seated himself and signalled to the waiter. "Ma'am, may I offer you something, and you too, my dear sir?"

"Quite the gentleman, ain't he, Jenny? I said that you would like him."

"Oh, I do!" The girl leaned forward, giving Truscott a full glimpse of her magnificent bosom. "He's just the sort of gentleman as appeals to me."

"My dear!" Truscott raised his glass in tribute to

their fair companion. The girl had possibilities, unless, of course, she was Margrave's doxy.

"My niece!" the forger said mendaciously. He might have admitted that she was his insurance against treachery. With Jenny keeping an eye upon the preacher, he felt he might be safe.

"The dear child turned up last night," he lied. "I couldn't desert her. She knows no one here in London town."

"And no work, nor a place to stay," the girl confided. Her plump thigh was pressed close to Truscott, and he felt a stirring in his blood.

He pretended to consider for a moment. "That need present no problem," he said at last. "I own a house at Seven Dials. As it happens, I'm in need of a housekeeper for the place. Have you any experience?"

"Plenty!" she leered. "I wouldn't disappoint you, sir."

"I'm sure of it." His hand strayed beneath the table and lifted her skirt. Her face remained unchanged as his fingers wandered.

"Well, then, perhaps you'd care to meet me there tomorrow?" Truscott gave her the address. "Shall we say at noon?"

"Right then, Jenny, be off with you!" Margrave waved her away. "We have matters to discuss!" He turned to his companion. "Tonight?" he asked.

"Leave it until Sunday. That is when I preach again."

"We're getting short of dibs," the forger told him.

"Then you should have come to me last night. I waited long enough…"

"Couldn't be done!" Margrave felt it unnecessary to

explain that he had, in fact, been among the congregation on the previous evening. He knew that Truscott was a ruthless man, and he had feared a trap.

Now he was satisfied. In that milling throng of worshippers no harm could come to him. Jenny had been an afterthought, an insurance for the future. Truscott, he knew, had a weakness for the ladies.

It was a weakness he despised. In giving way to his lusts a man might expose himself to danger. Women were unpredictable creatures.

His face betrayed nothing of his thoughts.

"Then Sunday, for certain?" he suggested.

"For certain!" Truscott hurried away. Today he must get rid of Nan. The girl had been a thorn in his flesh for long enough.

Yet he was surprised by her tenacity. Even his beatings seemed not to have deterred her.

"I won't go!" she'd cried. "You can't turn me away. How am I to live? How am I to pay for the child?"

"You should have thought of that before." His tone was brutal. "I told you to get rid of it."

"But I didn't! She is your flesh and blood! How can you abandon us?"

He'd been deaf to all her pleas. Taking her keys he'd thrust her from the door. Spineless, that's what she was! In her place he'd have stuck a knife in his tormentor.

He'd locked the door against her, summoned a hackney carriage, and returned to the West End.

When Mrs Aveton came to join him in her salon he didn't rise to greet her.

"Well?" She was still in a towering rage.

"Very well, no thanks to you! You fool! You couldn't hold your tongue if it should hang you!"

"Don't use that tone with me, sir! What of you! Perhaps you've no objection to taking damaged goods?"

"Save your lies for those who will believe them."

"Such nobility!" She gave an angry titter. "Judith does not know you—"

"And nor do you, apparently. Do you suppose that it was her virginal purity that persuaded me to offer for her?"

"I know it wasn't." Mrs Aveton glared at him.

"Then for God's sake, woman, use your head! We are too close to lose her now. You might have ruined all our plans..."

"What was I to do? You think yourself so clever, sir, but suppose I had said nothing? Judith is no fool. Her suspicions would have been aroused at once. Would you have her guess that we had come to an arrangement?" Her look grew crafty. She thought she had him there.

"You had no thought of that when you spoke out. Let me remind you that I'm not one of your feeble-witted friends..." Truscott paused. "Even so, you've done me a service. Judith now believes that I'm a model of all the gentler virtues."

Mrs Aveton began to speak again, anxious to justify herself still further, but he waved her to silence.

"Your ill temper is a serious threat to us. I'll have no more of it. Judith must expect to be punished. You will confine her to her room until the wedding. Send up her meals and do not speak to her again."

Mrs Aveton bridled. "You shall not give me orders in this house!"

"I shall, believe me!" There was so much menace in his tone that she backed away from him.

"I'll do as you say," she promised hurriedly.

"You would be well advised to do so. What's more, you must keep a sharp eye on the maid."

"On Bessie? What has she to say to anything?"

Truscott looked at her in pity. "How do you suppose that Ashburn entered this house?"

Mrs Aveton's colour rose once more. She sprang to her feet and tugged at the bell so hard that she almost broke the rope.

"I'll turn her off at once," she cried.

"You will do no such thing. Have you learned nothing, you stupid creature? I'll deal with Bessie in my own good time." Without further ceremony he left the house.

Unaware of the fate in store for her, Bessie was at that moment enduring a most unpleasant interview with Judith.

"How could you be so underhand?" her mistress demanded sternly. "You have surprised me, Bessie."

The maid stood her ground. "I ain't sorry, miss. You may turn me off without a character if you like, but you won't make me sorry for helping Mr Dan."

"You haven't helped either of us. In fact, you have made matters very much worse, to say nothing of distressing me…"

Bessie's face crumpled. "I didn't want that, but, Miss Judith—"

"No! I'll hear no more excuses. You may leave me now. I'd like to be alone."

Still and composed, Judith turned away. She felt

drained of all emotion. Her sufferings that day had been severe, but now she felt nothing. Perhaps there came a point where the mind would accept no more.

She wished to speak to no one, but Mrs Aveton would certainly wish to see her. It didn't matter. The expected tirade of abuse would wash over her like a stream across a rock.

She stayed in her room until the light began to fade. Then she heard a tapping at the door. It was Bessie with a tray, and her reddened eyes told Judith that she had been weeping.

"Don't distress yourself," she murmured. "I was too hard on you. I know you thought you were acting for the best."

"Oh, miss, it isn't that. I was to tell you that you ain't to leave your room before your wedding. Madam don't wish to see you."

Judith managed a faint smile. "You think it a punishment, Bessie? I could wish for nothing better."

Bessie set down the tray. "Then you'll eat your supper, miss?"

"At present I feel that food would choke me. Take it away!"

This brought a further flood of tears from Bessie. To cheer her Judith took a few mouthfuls of the food, but it gave her a feeling of nausea.

"I believe I'll go to bed," she said at last.

She stood in silence as the girl undressed her, though she was distressed to see that Bessie's tears still flowed.

"Don't worry!" she said gently. "In four days' time we shall be gone from here."

Bessie was too overcome to speak. With a hand pressed to her mouth she fled.

Judith lay on her bed in a trance-like state. Only four days to her marriage? It didn't seem possible that she would then become Charles Truscott's wife. She had a curious floating feeling, as if she were detached from everything about her. It was comforting, and she prayed that this sense of unreality would last. Whilst it remained, nothing more could hurt her.

Wisely, Truscott did not attempt to see her for the next two days, though he sent her flowers and messages.

Jenny was now installed at the house in Seven Dials and, as she'd promised, she hadn't disappointed him. The wench had all the experience which he craved to satisfy his lusts. He left her on the Sunday morning with reluctance, promising to return as soon as possible.

"But you're to be wed," she pouted. "You'll tire yourself with your new bride..."

"You think so?" His eyes glowed as he looked at her. "I'm more likely to tire you!"

"Never, Charlie! I'm a match for you!"

He was still laughing as he strode away. He'd rest that afternoon, recruiting his energies for the evening service.

He always preached at night, well aware of the theatrical nature of his setting. With the side aisles in darkness, and the body of the church lit only by four massive candelabra, he could sense the power he wielded over his congregation.

A single lantern hung above his pulpit, placed carefully to shed its light upon his face, throwing into high relief each plane and contour, and emphasising the hollows in his cheeks. It gave him a fanatical appearance, and he was pleased with the effect.

He might have been some latter-day Savonarola, he thought with satisfaction. The Italian monk had achieved the pinnacle of success with his preaching. A pity that he'd overreached himself at the last, and had been executed. Truscott ran a finger around his collar. Strangling wasn't a pretty death. He thrust the thought aside.

That night he was at the peak of his own powers. He'd never preached better and he knew it. Taking as his text ''What doth it profit a man if he gain the whole world, and suffer the loss of his own soul?'', he launched into his sermon. When he paused for effect there was total silence in the church.

He spared his listeners nothing, and was rewarded by the sound of an occasional moan. When he drew the sermon to a close his garments were clinging to him. He had given his all that night. The only thing lacking was the sound of wild applause.

As was his custom, he moved into the church porch when the service ended, greeting his parishioners with a grave face, and accepting their congratulations upon his forthcoming marriage with great dignity.

At no time did he acknowledge by the flicker of an eyelid that he had seen Dick Margrave standing by a pillar, but he felt a fierce spasm of pleasure. His quarry was within his grasp.

He waited until the last of the crowd had left by the lych gate. Then he turned to the forger.

''Satisfied?'' he asked cynically.

''More than satisfied, Charlie. You've got some prime ones there. I've said it before and I'll say it again. You're a blooming marvel.'' Margrave began to laugh.

"That text! I thought it must have finished me! I had to go outside."

"I thought you'd appreciate the irony. Now what do you say to a drink? My throat is parched…"

"No, I don't think so. This ain't a social call. Give me the money, and I'll be gone."

"It's in the vestry," Truscott told him smoothly. "If you'll follow me…?"

Margrave laughed again. "I ain't such a fool. I don't know what little surprise you might have rigged up for me. I don't stir a step from this doorway. You can fetch the money to me."

"Still suspicious?" Truscott shook his head in apparent sorrow. "We must learn to trust each other, Dick, but if you insist… Wait there! I shan't be above a moment."

When he returned he was carrying several leather bags, and, unknown to Margrave, a heavy cudgel beneath his flowing robes.

"Will you count it?" he said carelessly.

"No need! You won't trick me if you know what's good for you." Margrave held out his hands for the money.

Somehow, in passing over the bags, Truscott contrived to drop one. He'd tied it loosely, and the gleaming coins began to roll in all directions.

"Gold?" Margrave was transfixed by the sight. He bent, picked up a coin, and weighed it in his hand.

"What else? These people wouldn't insult me by offering pence." Truscott fell to his knees and started to collect the gold. "Give me a hand!" he cried impatiently. "Unless you're satisfied with what you've got!"

"Nay! I'll not leave this!" The forger's eyes were

glittering with avarice. The sight of the money had driven all thought of danger from his head. He began to crawl about the flagstones.

"Let me get the bag!" Truscott rose to his feet, withdrew the cudgel and brought it down with sickening force. One blow was enough to fell his enemy.

The preacher stepped out of his gown, folded it, and wound the cloth about Margrave's head. He'd no desire to leave a trail of blood. Then he seized a leg in either hand and dragged the inert figure into the churchyard to where a mound of fresh-turned earth rose above the surrounding grass.

He'd hidden a spade behind a nearby tombstone. Now he worked fast to toss the earth aside until he'd made a shallow excavation, thankful that the moon appeared only briefly from between the scudding clouds.

It was the work of a moment to roll the body into the hole and pile the soil above it. When he'd finished he surveyed his handiwork with satisfaction. Next week the family of the original occupant of the grave would erect a handsome tombstone, sealing Margrave in the cold earth for ever.

He was unaware that his every move was being watched. The Bow Street Runner was hardened to all kinds of villainy, but even he could not repress a shudder. He remained in hiding as Truscott returned to the church, gathered up his gold and locked the doors. Within minutes he was gone.

The Runner decided not to follow him. His quarry wouldn't go far, believing himself to be safe. It was more important to mark the exact position of the grave. Now Lord Wentworth should have his proof. Truscott had not removed his cassock from about the head of the dead man. That alone was enough to link him to the crime.

The Runner moved closer to the grave, and then he froze. The earth was moving. With his bare hands he tore wildly at the mound of soil. If the man was still alive he'd have a witness. Then a dreadful figure rose towards him and iron fingers closed about his throat. He knew nothing more.

Chapter Fourteen

On the day before her wedding Judith had a visitor. She hadn't left her room for days, but when Sebastian arrived she was summoned to the salon.

He took her hand and gazed into her eyes, troubled by the dark, bruise-like smudges beneath them. Yet Judith was perfectly calm, standing before him with a grave, contained stillness.

He longed to shake her, to bring some life into that gentle face. If only he might have saved her from what could only be a miserable future. Now, he feared, it was too late.

"I am come to make arrangements for tomorrow," he murmured. "At what time is the ceremony?"

She looked at him without expression. "At noon, I believe."

"Then I shall take you in my carriage. Shall we say at a quarter to the hour?"

Judith nodded, not daring to ask the question which was uppermost in her mind. She was praying with all her heart that Dan would not be in the congregation as she made the vows which should have been made to him.

Sebastian understood. "Prudence sends her love," he told her. "And Perry and Elizabeth will be there." There was no point in distressing her with the news that Elizabeth had at first refused to go until Perry had insisted.

A silence fell as the unasked question hung in the air between them.

"Dan sends his regrets," Sebastian continued. "But I have some news which I know will please you. Nelson has sent for him. Dan left for Merton earlier today."

He had all her attention then. Judith raised her head, and for the first time her face grew animated.

"The Admiral is pleased with his work?"

"We can't tell yet, but it seems likely. We must wait until Dan returns before we can be sure."

"I'm sure! Oh, I am so very glad for him. You will tell him so?"

"He will know it, Judith. Until tomorrow, then?"

"How kind you are!" Judith gave him her hand, and even managed to force a smile.

She must be glad for Dan. She must...but if only this news had reached him earlier. It might have made all the difference. Then she remembered. Dan no longer loved her. Her heart was breaking, but no one must guess. She went back to her room.

As Sebastian returned to Mount Street he found himself regretting the impulse which had led him to offer to give Judith away. It had all the overtones of leading a lamb to the slaughter. Judith appeared to be in a state of shock, but it was nothing to the shocks which were likely to await her.

Damn the Runner! Where on earth was the man! It was now a matter of hours before the wedding. Was there still time to stop it? At this late stage it was folly even to hope.

Later, Judith could remember little about the morning of her wedding day.

She had a vague memory of Bessie pressing her to eat something, however little, but she pushed the tray aside. When she tried to speak she seemed to have lost her voice.

"Drink your chocolate!" Bessie ordered. "If you go on like this, Miss Judith, we'll have you fainting at the altar." Even as she spoke she wondered why she was insisting. Privately she considered that to faint was now Judith's only hope of escaping the clutches of the Reverend Truscott. Yet her mistress, she knew, would not collapse. Judith's face was set. She would go through with the ceremony.

Bessie choked back a sob. This should be the happiest day of any woman's life. No bride should look so pale and listless. She drew the curtains about the old-fashioned bed and summoned the waiting footmen to remove the boxes and portmanteaux which contained her mistress's possessions. They would be sent on ahead to her new home.

Within the curtained bed, Judith lay inert. She had the oddest sense of looking down at her own body from some point far above. The fantasy would pass, together with this feeling of unreality. Soon she would begin to be aware of what was happening to her.

It was strange. She'd expected to feel a pang of regret at leaving this shabby room which had been her sanctuary for so long.

In this room she had wept for her dead father, found consolation in her books and her writing, and on occasion had managed to escape the cruel strictures of her stepmother. The months after Dan had left were far too painful to remember, but it was all so long ago.

When Bessie drew the curtains back she looked about her, willing herself to feel something. Anything, even the pain of loss would be preferable to this dreadful feeling of inertia. Now the room looked impersonal. Her pictures, her books and her few trinkets had gone. It might have belonged to a stranger.

She bathed in silence, hoping that the water would refresh her. Then, statue-like, she stood obediently as Bessie dressed her in the unbecoming gown of dull lavender which had been Mrs Aveton's choice.

Even the matching bonnet with its tiny clusters of flowers beneath the brim did nothing to improve her appearance. In Bessie's eyes, her mistress looked like a ghost.

"Miss, don't wear this!" she begged. Then she remembered. The rest of Judith's gowns were packed and gone.

"It will do!" Judith closed her eyes. "I think I'll sit down for a moment." She walked over to the window-seat and rested her cheek against the cool glass. It was difficult to decide if she felt hot or cold.

She knew that she must pull herself together. She was being unfair to Charles. He deserved better than to wed the marionette which she felt herself to be that morning.

It took a supreme effort of will to force herself to

think about him. She tried to bring his face to mind, but she could see only a pair of bright blue eyes beneath a crop of red-gold hair. Memories followed each other in quick succession. Dan teasing her, laughing, entering into all her hopes and plans with the eagerness peculiarly his own.

Then the picture changed to a vision of his stricken face, pleading, angry, and finally despairing. She wouldn't think of him. It was just that she couldn't seem to recall the face of her betrothed at all.

It was madness. Charles had been so good to her. Always pleasant and courteous, his kindness was unfailing. She'd always be able to rely on him, and she would not soon forget his staunch support in a situation in which most men would have thought the worst of her.

And yet she could not love him, she thought despairingly. What did she want of a man? The answer to that lay only with Dan. Never again would she feel that leap of the heart whenever he walked into a room, and the joy which filled her soul. She closed her eyes, remembering his smile, the thrill of his touch, and even the very scent of him.

What had he called her? ''My best of friends''? There was more to it than that. Beneath the friendship there had once been the bonds of a love so passionate that it promised to last for an eternity. That love had vanished, and with it all her hopes and dreams.

A tapping at the door recalled her from her reverie.

Bessie answered it, returning with the news that Lord Wentworth had arrived.

''Oh, is it time?'' Judith asked quietly.

Bessie wiped away a tear. Her young mistress might

have used just those words if she'd been summoned to the tumbrils in France, and on her way to a dreadful death by the guillotine.

Judith pressed her hand. "Don't look like that!" she pleaded. "Charles is a good man, and he will care for me."

With that she took Bessie in her arms. They clung together for just a moment. Then Judith disengaged herself. With her head held high she left the room.

There were four people in the salon, but it seemed to Judith to be excessively crowded, due to the fact that Mrs Aveton and her daughters were *en grande toilette.*

Judith looked at them in wonder, amazed by the profusion of lace, satin, feathers, ribands and jewellery which graced the persons of the three ladies. The purple satin turban of her stepmother was crowned by an immense aigrette, and the spray of gems sparkled and shook each time she tossed her head.

Now Mrs Aveton hurried towards her, conscious of Sebastian's penetrating eyes.

"Dear child!" she gushed. "How beautiful you look today!" She'd intended to embrace the bride-to-be, in an effort to convince Sebastian of her fondness for the girl, but Judith turned away. Such pretence disgusted her.

Sebastian took her hand and kissed it. Then he turned to Mrs Aveton with a significant glance at the clock.

"If you leave now, ma'am, we shall follow you," he said. "You will wish to arrive before the bride."

"Why, yes, of course! How like you to consider me! I hope that our dear Judith appreciates your condescension in giving her away, my lord. So good of you, and far more than she might expect!"

"Judith is a dear friend." There was something in his tone which silenced her. Her colour heightened as she hurried her daughters to the waiting carriage.

Sebastian looked at his companion, noting her grave, contained manner.

"Judith?"

"I'm ready," she said quickly. "Shall we go?"

In silence he offered her his arm. There was nothing left to say. He longed to beg her to change her mind. It was not too late. His carriage would take her to Mount Street and to Prudence, but the tension in her slight figure warned him against such a suggestion. All he could do now was to lend her his support throughout the coming ceremony.

She would need it. He thought he'd never seen another human being quite so close to breaking down completely.

In an effort to divert her thoughts he began to speak of Prudence.

"Your visit helped her, Judith. The doctor now believes that her time is closer than we thought. The child could arrive within these next few days."

"Oh, Sebastian, should you have left her?" Judith turned to him at once in her anxiety for her friend.

He patted her hand and smiled. "These things don't happen in minutes, my dear. I offered to send Perry in my place, but Prudence would have none of it. She insisted that I kept my word to you."

"But—?"

"No buts, Judith! Elizabeth has stayed behind to be with her. She will send word if anything should start to happen. I have no fears on that score. Our beautiful hothead can be a tower of strength upon occasion, as I'm sure you know. Elizabeth won't lose her wits.''

Judith smiled for the first time. ''I know it! She has so many of the qualities of her aunt. Miss Grantham has left for Turkey?''

Sebastian nodded. ''Two days ago. Perry swears that she'll return with a Mameluke or two in tow.''

''He's teasing you. Will you give my love to Prudence? You will all be so relieved when this is over and the babe arrives.''

''I should be used to it by now, but I suffer through these times almost as much as Prudence. At least I'm not as bad as Perry. He was like a man demented on both occasions when Elizabeth gave birth.''

Judith squeezed his hand. ''All will be well, I'm sure of it.'' She looked up as the carriage stopped, and paled a little.

''Are we there?''

''Yes, my dear.'' Sebastian gave her his hand and helped her from the carriage.

She hesitated only once, as she saw the open doorway of the church. Then she straightened her shoulders, lifted her head, and together they walked slowly down the aisle.

Heads turned towards her as she passed, but Judith was oblivious of the sea of faces. Her eyes were fixed upon the altar and the man who stood before it, awaiting her.

As she reached his side he gave her a tender smile, but she did not respond. She was still possessed by a sense of unreality. This could not be happening to her. The girl who stood beside Charles Truscott wasn't herself. It was some stranger taking part in a ceremony which meant nothing.

Truscott then gave his full attention to the bishop, and Judith became aware of the opening words of the marriage service.

"Brethren, we are gathered together in the sight of God and this congregation to join this man and this woman in holy matrimony…"

The bishop paused. Then, as church law required, he asked if any knew of the existence of an impediment to the marriage.

It was a formality, but a silence fell for what seemed to Judith to be an eternity. Then, as the bishop was about to continue, a faint voice reached him.

"This man is the father of my child!"

A gasp like the sound of the rushing wind across a sea of corn seemed to ripple around the church, and beside her Judith felt Charles Truscott stiffen.

When he spun round to face his accuser she heard him curse beneath his breath. Then he regained his self-control and walked towards the figure standing in the aisle.

Judith recognised the girl at once. This was the frail creature who had accosted her in the street, and later had given her the mysterious message from Charles.

Now he disclaimed all knowledge of her. "The woman is demented," he announced. "Tell me, my dear! What is the name of the father of your child?"

"It's you…Josh Ferris! Will you deny your own flesh and blood?" She drew aside her shawl to reveal a puny child which lay within the crook of her arm. The little creature seemed too weak to cry.

Truscott looked about him with a sad expression,

anxious to dispel the astonishment in the faces of his guests.

"Pitiful!" he murmured. "The girl has lost her senses! I am not Josh Ferris, my dear. My name is Truscott…the Reverend Charles Truscott. Now let me get some help for you…" He looked towards the ushers who had hastened down the aisle.

The girl pulled away from the restraining hands.

"You shan't deny me!" she cried wildly. "I don't care what you call yourself. The child is yours!"

Truscott turned to Judith. "I am so sorry, dearest, to have you exposed to this. I do not know this woman."

Judith answered him then, and in the silence her clear voice carried to all corners of the church.

"That isn't true!" she said quietly. "This girl brought me a message from you."

There was another gasp from the assembled guests.

Then Judith moved towards the young mother. "This is no place for you," she said. "Let us go into the vestry."

Suddenly, Mrs Aveton was tugging at her sleeve.

"What are you about?" she hissed. "The ceremony must go on. Let them take this creature away. She should be in Bedlam."

Judith looked down at her. The contempt in her grave grey eyes might have caused a lesser woman to shrivel, but Mrs Aveton was undeterred.

"Suppose this child is Charles's by-blow?" she murmured in an undertone. "What has that to say to anything? A sensible woman would ignore it."

"Then perhaps I am not sensible." Judith removed the clutching fingers from her arm, and turned to the bishop. "My lord, I must have the truth of this."

"Of course!" he agreed. "We shall break off at once in order to investigate these allegations."

"No!" Truscott's face was dark with rage. "Judith, this is no impediment. You must believe me!"

"Even so, the lady is entitled to make enquiries." Sebastian found it almost impossible to hide his relief. Now he took Judith's arm. "The vestry?" he said quietly. "You won't wish for a public scandal."

"Leave her!" Truscott shouted. "How dare you interfere? You and your family have done your best to give her a dislike of me. Now, I suppose, you will persuade her to believe these lies?"

"Judith wishes only to discover the truth, sir." Sebastian's voice was cold. "If you are innocent you need have no fear—"

"Guilty? Innocent? Who are you to judge? You with your money and your arrogance? My wife shall end her connection with you from this moment!"

"My dear sir, you are making a spectacle of yourself. Have you no consideration for Miss Aveton?"

"Miss Aveton is it, now?" Truscott attempted to seize Judith's arm. "Don't listen to him. They are all against me…"

At this point the bishop was moved to intervene. "Lord Wentworth is right. This is a most unedifying scene. It should not be taking place in public." Frowning, he strode away.

"No, my lord, don't go!" Truscott hurried after him. "Am I not entitled to defend myself…to refute these allegations?"

"You may do so, and I will hear you out, but not before the altar. Later, if you can explain yourself to the lady's satisfaction, the ceremony may continue."

Truscott returned to Judith's side, attempting to thrust himself between her and Lord Wentworth. With the dashing of his hopes all his composure deserted him. Now he was babbling wildly.

Judith ignored him and moved towards the girl.

"What is your name?" she asked.

"It's Nan, miss. Please, you must believe me. I wasn't lying. Josh turned me out. I had no money for the child. I think she's dying…"

Judith looked at the tiny figure lying in her arms.

"Don't give up hope!" she said. "You shall have all the help you need. This man you know as Josh? He is one and the same as the man I was about to marry?"

"Yes, miss. Does he claim to be a preacher?" Her eyes grew bitter. "He ain't no Christian gentleman. He would have left us both to starve."

"I think you are very tired," Judith said gently. "Let us go to a more private place. There you may sit down." She looked up at Sebastian and he nodded. Then he raised a finger to summon one of his servants, despatching the man for food.

In a last desperate effort, Truscott tried to intervene.

"No!" he shouted. "I'll help! I'll give her money, but, Judith, you must listen to me!"

"I'm quite prepared to do so." She slipped her arm about the girl, leading her through the door into the vestry. She was followed by Sebastian, and the frantic figure of Truscott.

Standing before his bishop, the preacher changed his tactics, adopting a bullying demeanour towards the girl.

"Wench, you will burn in hell!" he shouted. "That is the fate of those who lie before God!"

"Spare us your threats!" Sebastian turned on him.

"You will keep a still tongue in your head. My lord bishop, will you question the girl?"

Nan looked terrified, but encouraged by Judith's gentle manner she began to tell her story.

"Seven Dials?" Truscott cried at one point in her tale. "I don't know the place."

"Strange, considering that you have a house there!" Sebastian studied his fingernails with interest. "You have been seen entering and leaving, and so has Nan. It is Nan, isn't it?" He smiled encouragement at her.

The preacher's face took on a ghastly hue, but he tried to recover his position.

"I might have guessed it," he said savagely. "You have set men on to spy on me. Much good may it do you! As a man of God my work takes me to all parts of London upon errands of mercy. I don't always know the names of the places which I visit."

"Nor, apparently, are you able to recall the faces of those you tend." The bishop's face was stern. "Why did you claim not to know this girl?"

"Why, my lord, I can't be expected to remember all those who come to me for help. There are so many…" Truscott cast a pleading look at Judith.

She didn't glance at him. Memory had come flooding back. Here, in this very church, she had caught him beating a small child. Nausea overwhelmed her as she realised the truth. She had been mistaken in him all along.

Sebastian hesitated, but not for long. Judith must now hear the truth, however unpalatable it might be.

"Do your duties require you to stay overnight upon these errands?" he asked quietly.

A purple flush stained Truscott's face. "I may have stayed on one occasion...but it was by a sickbed."

"Ah, yes, these sickbeds! There are so many, are there not, and all at the house in Seven Dials? I'm told that your presence was required there for several days at a time."

"Judith knows about it," Truscott said defensively. "My mother has been suffering from the smallpox—"

"You are lying, sir. Your mother lives in the parish of St Giles, in that salubrious part of London known as 'The Rookery'. To my knowledge she is suffering from nothing more than neglect on the part of her disgraceful son."

Judith rose to her feet. She did not look at Truscott. "I have heard enough," she said with dignity. "My lord bishop, this marriage will not now take place. What you choose to do about this man I will leave to your own judgment. Sebastian, will you take me home? Nan and her child shall go with us."

"Judith, you can't!" Truscott ran after her into the main body of the church, empty now, except for Mrs Aveton and her daughters. "It's lies, I tell you, naught but a pack of lies. They'll stop at nothing to take you from me."

"Nay, Charlie, it ain't lies! Who knows that better than you, you murdering devil!"

The voice came from the shadowy porch. It was low, but so chilling that it stopped Truscott in his tracks.

He fell back, all colour draining from his face.

"Who is there?" he cried fearfully.

"A dead man, who else?" Margrave stepped into the light, and as he did so, Mrs Aveton screamed.

The forger was a terrifying sight. His face had the

pallor of the grave, except for the patches of scarlet blood which seeped steadily from the cloth about his head and trickled down one cheek.

"Thought you'd killed me, Charlie? I ain't so easy to get rid of. Now it's your turn. Did you think I'd let you live to enjoy this lady's fortune?" He raised his pistol and levelled it at Truscott's heart.

"Wait, Dick! Hear me! It was a mistake! I fell against you. Then I thought that you had cracked your head. What was I to do? I couldn't have you found here…"

"So you decided to give me a Christian burial?" The forger's laugh struck terror into those who heard it. "Lucky for me that there wasn't a tombstone handy. I'd never have left that grave."

Judith found that she was trembling, but it was Sebastian who spoke.

"Sir, will you be a witness? If this is true, you may leave this man to the authorities—"

"Nay, I'll not do that. Lord Wentworth, ain't it? My lord, the authorities are no friends of mine. I'll handle this myself. I'm sorry, ma'am, that you are to be soon a widow."

"I am not married," Judith whispered.

"Really? Ah, I see!" He looked at the girl beside her. "Our little Nan got there before me!"

Judith moved to stand in front of the shrinking girl.

"You are making a mistake!" she said steadily. "Will you commit murder in this church? Please do as Lord Wentworth has suggested. You cannot take the law into your own hands."

"Count your blessings, ma'am, and stand aside! I know what I'm about. They won't catch Dick Margrave!'' As he raised his pistol once again, Truscott grabbed Judith to his breast.

Holding her as a shield, he thrust her ahead of him towards the porch. She felt the pricking of his knife against her ribs.

"Don't struggle!" he advised. "I have nothing to lose."

"Let her go!" Sebastian's voice was calm. He was almost within touching distance. "This is naught to do with Judith. Your quarrel is between you and this man…" Imperceptibly, he moved closer.

"Back!" the preacher shouted. "Unless you wish to have her blood upon your hands!"

Judith was terrified, but she kept her head. Truscott should not find it easy to drag her from the church. Apparently on the verge of collapse, she leaned heavily against him. Then she felt what seemed to be a sharp blow as he pulled her upright.

"No tricks!" he ordered roughly. "Move!"

Now he had an enemy on either side. Margrave was ahead of him, blocking his exit from the church, and Sebastian was behind.

"You first!" he told Sebastian. "Walk ahead of me!"

He cast just one brief glance at the horrified faces of Mrs Aveton and her girls, the bishop, and finally at Nan.

"You'll pay for this!" he promised. "I'll be back!" His face was a mask of evil as he looked at her, and none of his listeners dared to move.

Then, thrusting Judith ahead of him, and using Sebastian's tall figure as a further shield, he began to edge his way towards the porch and freedom.

Margrave had moved to one side. As his enemy

passed it would give him a better shot, but Truscott sensed his purpose.

"Out!" he ordered.

For a long moment Margrave hesitated and Judith closed her eyes. She meant nothing to the man, and there was murder in his face. In his desire for vengeance he was more than likely to fire through her.

Sebastian's murmur was audible to no one but the forger.

"No!" he said. "Not yet! You'll get your chance.

It seemed at first that Margrave would disobey him, and for Judith it was the longest moment of her life. Then the man walked out of the church.

Judith felt the sunlight warm upon her face. Again she felt a sense of unreality. Could this frightful scene be taking place here, in the quiet surroundings of the churchyard?

Sebastian's carriage was already at the lych gate, ready to bear him home.

"Summon your man, my lord! If you wish this lady to live you will obey me. He is to open the carriage door, let down the steps, and stand away. Then your coachman must drive off at speed when we are safe inside."

Sebastian stopped suddenly. "You can't be meaning to take Judith with you?" he exclaimed in horror.

Truscott ignored the question. "Do as I say!" he shouted.

"No, listen to me! She will slow you down."

Judith felt the prick of the knife, and she gave a tiny gasp of pain. "Do as he says," she pleaded.

Sebastian's lifted hand brought a groom running to his side. The man's eyes widened as he realised what was happening. He was a burly fellow, and with his arms spread wide in a wrestler's stance, he started to move forward.

"No!" Sebastian was quick to stop him. "Do as I bid you! This lady is being held at knife-point."

"Very wise, my lord," the preacher mocked. "Now stand aside."

Judith's view was partly blocked by Sebastian's massive figure. Then she heard the sound of running feet.

"Seb, am I too late?" Dan came tearing around the corner of the church. "The Runner has news. I've brought him with me. Pray heaven we are in time!"

"Indeed you are!" The preacher's voice was a paean of triumph. "In time to bid your lady-love farewell. Now, sir, his lordship has been most amenable. I trust that you will follow his example and do nothing foolish?"

As Sebastian stepped aside, Dan took in the situation at a glance. Beside him, the hand of the Bow Street Runner strayed towards his pistol. Then Dan saw the terror in Judith's eyes.

"We shall do nothing foolish," he agreed. "You are free to leave, but you shall not take Judith with you."

"And how are you to stop me?" Truscott jeered.

"I fear that we cannot." Dan paused. Then he looked at Judith. "Why, my dear, you have forgotten the pearl necklace…"

"Pearls?" Even Truscott was startled. What was the fellow thinking of to speak of a necklace at this time?

Judith raised her head, and for a long moment grey eyes locked with blue.

"Yes," she murmured. "I had quite forgot." She bent her head again. Then, with a sudden movement, she thrust it back with all her strength, catching Truscott full in the face.

He gave a cry of agony and staggered back as Dan ran towards him, twisting Judith from his grip.

Two shots rang out in unison, but Truscott had already dodged behind a tombstone. Then he began to run, zig-zagging between the graves.

The Runner raised his smoking pistol and took careful aim, but Margrave thrust him aside.

"He's mine!" he said with great deliberation. He fired one more at the running man, and this time he did not miss.

Frozen with horror, Judith watched as the preacher's head exploded in a red haze. Then Dan hid her face against his coat.

"Get her out of this!" Sebastian muttered. "I'll see to matters here…"

Dan needed no urging. With the aid of the groom he half led and half carried Judith to the waiting coach.

"Back to Mount Street!" he ordered briefly. Then he gathered his love into his arms.

"Why, Dan, you are trembling!" Judith murmured in wonder. "I am unhurt…"

"Then what is that?" With a shaking hand he pointed to her skirt.

Judith looked down to see a long rust-coloured stain creeping from the bodice of her gown down towards the hem. "It's only a graze. He…he pricked me with the knife."

"He might have killed you. Oh, my darling, I thought you lost to me for ever." He covered his eyes and turned away to hide the agony in his heart.

"Dan, look at me!" Judith pleaded. "I must know! Can you ever forgive me?"

"Forgive you? For what?" he groaned. "I should be asking your forgiveness for exposing you to danger."

For answer she took his beloved face in both her hands.

"You tried to warn me," she said tenderly. "Don't blame yourself! I wouldn't listen. How could I have been so blind?"

"You weren't alone, my love. Truscott deceived everyone—"

"Not you! Nor any member of your family."

"Prudence and Elizabeth had seen another side of him."

"Oh, my dear, if they had only told me the whole…"

"Would you have believed them? Besides, Sebastian insisted that they must not meddle. He was unconvinced until quite recently."

"But you?"

"I hated him on sight," Dan told her simply. "But I was mad with jealousy."

"You hid it well."

"I had to, Judith. In the end we came to believe that you were safe only as long as you remained betrothed."

Her eyes widened. "I was in danger? Why did you not warn me?"

"We had no proof until today. The Runner arrived as I returned from Merton. He'd seen Truscott's attempt to murder Margrave."

"Margrave was the man who shot him dead?" Judith closed her eyes as if to shut out the memory of that dreadful scene. "He is dead, isn't he?"

"He is, my darling, but he was a man who lived by violence and in the end it killed him."

Judith began to shudder. "I'll never forget it. It was a frightful ending…"

"Try not to think about it, dearest." Dan turned her face to his. "It's over. Now we shall think only of our future."

He kissed her then, and as his mouth came down on hers the long years of their separation sank into oblivion. They were still locked in a passionate embrace when the carriage came to a halt.

Judith felt light-headed, and when Dan tried to help her down her limbs refused to obey her. She looked down at her skirt and saw that the ominous stain was spreading rapidly.

"Don't tell Prudence!" she said in a queer, high voice. "I'm sorry, but I think I'm going to faint."

She fell towards him, and into darkness.

Chapter Fifteen

Judith awakened as the first grey fingers of dawn began to creep across the sky. She looked about her in bewilderment. This was not her room.

She tried to move and winced with pain. Cautiously she touched the firm binding around her ribs with her right hand. Her left was held so tightly that it was impossible to disengage her fingers.

In the corner of the darkened room a single candle was guttering low, and by its faint light she could distinguish a figure sitting by her bedside.

Dan seemed to be asleep, but he stirred as the door was opened.

"You must get some rest," Elizabeth whispered. "You've been here all night. Go now! I will stay with Judith."

"I won't leave her!" came the obstinate reply. "I want to see the surgeon."

"So you shall, my dear, but he won't return at dawn. I promise to call you the moment he appears."

Dan shook his head. "He thought there might be a fever. I must stay in case she needs me."

Judith felt a cool hand upon her brow. "She isn't feverish, Dan. Do go! At present you look worse than Judith. You mustn't frighten her. When she wakes she will wish to speak to you."

"I do!" Judith opened her eyes. "How long have I been here?"

"Since yesterday, my love. You fainted in the carriage..."

Dan's haggard face alarmed her, but she managed a weak smile. "That was foolish of me. It must have been the shock."

Elizabeth bent over her. "Judith, you were stabbed. Do you not recall?"

Judith shook her head. "I was pricked by the knife at first. Then I felt a sort of blow...more like a punch to my ribs."

"You received a deep cut, Judith, but it isn't serious. By some miracle it missed the vital organs."

"But you aren't out of danger, my beloved." Dan was beside himself with anxiety. "There is the risk of fever."

"I shan't get a fever," Judith promised as she laid a loving hand against his cheek. "But I do feel sleepy. Won't you rest, my darling? Come back to me later..."

It was only with the greatest reluctance that Dan left the room, with so many instructions to Judith not to excite herself, nor to worry, and most especially to get some sleep, that in the end Elizabeth seized his arm and thrust him through the door.

"He's been like a man possessed," she said ruefully. "You gave us such a fright! That villainous creature! We should have warned you. Then we might have spared you this experience—"

"How could you, when I wouldn't hear a word against him? Oh, I have been such a fool!"

"No more than the rest of London, Judith. He was a cunning devil, and old in the ways of evil."

"But he paid in the most horrible way..." Judith covered her face with her hands, as if to shut out the hideous memory.

"It was quicker than a hanging," Elizabeth said briskly. "Don't waste your pity on him, love. He got what he deserved...and to stab you as he did? We may be thankful that the surgeon was already here when you arrived."

Judith looked up quickly. "Prudence?"

"Prudence gave Sebastian two fine daughters not an hour ago. Her pains had started before Sebastian left but she didn't mention it to him. That was why I stayed behind. You didn't wonder why I was not at the church?"

"I was in a daze, I think. I didn't notice anyone. But twins? Oh, my dear, what a night you must have had!"

"It wasn't dull!" Elizabeth began to smile. "Perry went for the surgeon as soon as Sebastian was safely out of the way. Wait until you see them, Judith. They are adorable..."

"And Prudence?"

"She's tired, but very happy. As for Sebastian?" she threw her eyes to heaven. "Between them, he and Dan were most in need of the doctor's services."

Judith caught at her hand. "Sebastian should not have left her."

"My dear, she wanted him to be with you. She felt that you would be glad of his support."

"How like her! She was right! I was so glad to have

him with me. I still can't believe what happened. It seems like some frightful nightmare. But didn't Sebastian wonder why you stayed behind with Prudence?''

Elizabeth blushed. ''Not really.'' She looked a little conscious. ''I had been behaving badly, you see.''

''In what way?''

''I made a dreadful fuss about your marriage, Judith. I didn't wish to see you wed to that monstrous creature. Sebastian thought I'd seized on the excuse when the doctor said that Prudence was very near her time.''

''I wish I'd listened to you.''

''You are not to think about it. Now you must try to rest. Is there anything I can get for you?''

Judith shook her head. ''I just want to sleep.'' She closed her eyes.

Later, the doctor's visit was a trial, but not a sound escaped her lips as he changed the dressing on her wound.

''May I not dress and go downstairs?'' she pleaded. ''I promise to sit quietly, but I'm making extra work for everyone whilst I am up here.''

''What's all this?'' Dan was standing in the doorway.

''Why, sir, this young lady has her own ideas about her convalescence. I'm trying to persuade her to follow mine.'' He turned to Judith. ''Miss Aveton, you have been fortunate. Your wound will heal quickly if you take my advice. Otherwise you may go down with the fever.''

''Miss Aveton will obey your orders to the letter,'' Dan said sternly. ''I will see to that.'' He bowed the doctor out.

Then he strolled over to the bed, sat down and took both of Judith's hands in his.

"Goose!" he said fondly. "Haven't you given me enough cause to worry about you? I've aged ten years in these past few weeks."

Judith peeped up at him from beneath her lashes.

"I can see no sign of it," she said demurely. "Your hair has not turned grey."

"It was white, my love. I was forced to dye it."

"More play-acting, Dan? You have certainly deceived me—"

"With my red hair? Oh, dear, and I thought it looked so natural."

"Of course not! Don't joke," she pleaded. "I thought you didn't love me. That was why I wouldn't listen to you."

Dan took her gently in his arms and kissed her tenderly. "Do you still believe that I have changed?"

Rosy with pleasure, she rested her head against his shoulder. "I should never have doubted you. Oh, my darling, there has never been anyone else for me. I, too, have never changed in all these years. I used to think of what we had, and our parting almost broke my heart. I felt that my life was over. Nothing seemed to matter. That was why…"

He silenced her with another kiss. "All that is past. We shall not speak of it again."

"But we must, my dearest. So much is left unanswered. I cannot rest until I know."

Dan looked at her with loving eyes. "It may be best," he agreed. "But then you must lay the ghosts to rest. Will you promise me that?"

She nodded, tucking her hand within his own as he began to speak.

He skirted as lightly as he could over the beginning of his tale, mentioning Truscott's mother only briefly. He said nothing about the murder of Nan's brothers. There was no point in distressing her with that, though Margrave's cronies had betrayed him and given a full account of the affair.

Judith tensed when he told her about the house at Seven Dials.

"So Nan was telling the truth?" she whispered.

"She was, my love. The child is Truscott's."

"Oh, the poor creature! Where is she now? I promised to help her."

"She's here, my darling. Sebastian brought her with him. The servants are making a great fuss of the little one, and the doctor holds out hope for her."

"Thank God!"

Dan patted her hand. "I knew you'd be relieved. Shall I go on, or have you heard enough? The rest of the tale is unfit for your ears, I fear."

"Oh, Dan, I have the right to know."

"Very well. We had our information from a Bow Street Runner. Sebastian set him to follow Truscott several weeks ago. His discoveries were disturbing, but there was no proof of actual wrongdoing."

"He could explain his visits to these places?"

"Sebastian did not challenge him. He thought it best to wait until… Oh, Judith, I should never have agreed. When I think that we might have been too late!"

Judith pressed his hand. "Don't blame yourself, my dear one. This man—Margrave, do you call him—he was intent on murder. I knew it when I looked into his eyes. I should have been a widow before I was a wife.''

''You could never have been Truscott's wife. He was wed some years ago.''

''To Nan?''

''No, I believe the woman lives in Essex. Frederick sent word this morning.''

''The Earl of Brandon? He, too, was involved in this? I can't believe it!''

''Elizabeth pressed him into service. She was so sure of Truscott's villainy, and Frederick had sources which are closed to lesser mortals.''

''How shall I ever thank you all?'' Judith murmured.

''Well, my love, you might begin by kissing me again.'' Dan slipped a finger beneath her chin and his mouth came down on hers. In that passionate embrace all the bitterness of the past was washed away, and Judith's heart was filled with an overwhelming joy.

Then he held her away from him. ''I was warned that you must rest,'' he teased her. ''This can't be good for you.''

''Nothing could be better,'' Judith whispered. She was blushing furiously.

Dan was tempted to kiss her again, but with admirable self-control he managed to restrain himself.

''Temptress!'' he accused. ''You are driving me to distraction. Just listen to the pounding of my heart!'' He took her hand and held it against the fine cambric of his shirt. ''Would you have me faint with happiness?''

''No, my love.'' Judith's eyes grew misty.

''Well, then, allow me to continue with my tale. Sebastian was right. Truscott decided that before his marriage he must rid himself of his worst enemy. He tricked Margrave into meeting him, and then he tried to kill the man, burying him in a recent grave.''

Judith grew stiff with horror, and he slipped an arm about her, drawing her to his breast. "He didn't succeed, my darling. The Runner saw it all, but when he tried to help, the forger attacked him, thinking, perhaps, that Truscott had returned to lay a tombstone over him." Dan glanced down at his love in some concern. "Judith, I should not have told you."

"I'm glad you did. Now it is all clear to me. It all seemed so unbelievable, but now I see why Margrave killed him. Did he get away?"

"No! He was taken in the street. He was a wanted man, my dear. Forgery is still a hanging matter. Now murder must be added to his crimes."

"I'd call it judicial execution!" Elizabeth had come to join them. "The man deserves a medal, not a hanging."

"Bloodthirsty wench!" Perry tugged gently at his wife's dark curls. Then he walked over to the bed.

"How are you feeling, Judith?"

"Oh, Perry, I'm so much better. There's really nothing wrong with me—"

"Apart from the odd stab wound?" he observed with some amusement. "You ladies are a hardy lot. You put us all to shame!"

"Now, Perry, you shan't tease!" his wife reproved. "Judith, do you mean it? Will you take a little broth? It will help you to regain your strength…"

Judith nodded, smiling, and Elizabeth whisked away.

"What a pair you are!" Perry sank into the nearest chair and stretched out his long legs. "Never a dull moment! What's this I hear about some necklace? Sebastian couldn't believe his ears when Dan mentioned it at the church…''

''It must have seemed strange,'' Dan admitted. ''But it was all I could think of at the time.''

''Well, I've heard of defeating one's enemies with swords and pistols, but never with a string of pearls. What on earth were you about?''

Judith began to blush. ''Dan reminded me. It was just a story which I wrote some years ago.''

Dan's eyes began to twinkle. ''It was your first.'' He turned to Perry. ''Judith was an admirer of Mrs Radcliffe, and her tales of Gothic horror. *The Mysteries of Udolpho* persuaded her to try one of her own.''

''I'm no wiser,'' Perry said blankly.

''Well, in 'The Pearl Necklace', the heroine escaped her fate by doing exactly what Judith did yesterday.''

''Ah, now I understand! That was quick thinking, Dan. I doubt if I'd have remembered it myself.''

''I haven't forgotten anything.'' Dan took Judith's hand and squeezed it fondly. ''Dearest, I can't tell you what it means to have you safe at last, and here with all your friends. You shall never leave me.''

''Mrs Aveton?'' Judith murmured. ''Has she been asking for me?''

Perry gave her a grin of unashamed delight. ''When she'd finished drumming her heels and tearing out her hair she closed the house and scuttled off to Cheltenham with her charming daughters. Sebastian persuaded her that it would be for the best…the scandal, you know.''

''Is someone taking my name in vain?'' Sebastian put his head around the door. ''Judith, should you be holding court, my dear? You must be very tired…''

"No, I'm not! Oh, do come in! I so wanted to congratulate you. Prudence and the babes are well?" Judith held out both her hands to him.

"They are fine!" Sebastian's face was radiant with delight. "And you?"

"I feel wonderful! Oh, my dear, I am so happy for you. Now you have got your heart's desire."

"I think I am not alone in that." Sebastian looked at Dan and Judith. Then he bent and kissed her. "Welcome to the family," he said softly.

"Great heavens!" Elizabeth walked into the room accompanied by Bessie. "Judith, are you holding a reception? It won't do, you know." She frowned at the circle of gentlemen seated around the bed.

"Off you go!" she ordered. "Our patient is supposed to rest." Her smile robbed her words of all offence.

As Perry and Sebastian left, Dan rose as if to follow them, but Judith clutched his hand.

"Don't go!" she whispered. "I don't want you to leave me."

"But, dearest, you must eat," Elizabeth protested.

"Dan won't stop me. Oh, please, don't send him away."

"No chance of that if you want me here, my love." Dan took the tray from Bessie. "I am quite capable of handling this."

Elizabeth threw up her hands. "Come, Bessie! Let us leave these love-birds. We are not needed here."

"She was right, my darling," Dan murmured when they were alone. "Our need is for each other. Tell me again that you still love me."

"I never stopped." Judith gave him a misty smile and suddenly she was beautiful. "Just hold me, Dan."

The soup was forgotten as he stretched out on the bed beside her and cradled her in his arms. His tender kisses rained down upon her brow, her eyelids and her cheeks, until she sighed with rapture.

"Can it be true that we shall never part again?" she whispered.

"Never, my dear love. Shall you mind if we don't live in London after we are married?"

"No, I will go anywhere with you, but why do you ask?" She sensed that he was chuckling. "Are you keeping secrets from me?"

"Just one, but you may hear it now. The Admiral will order frigates built to my design, but it will mean that we must move to Portsmouth."

"Oh, Dan, as if that mattered! I am *so* happy for you."

He cradled her head against his shoulder. "Judith, that is the least part of my joy. I have you…"

He bent his head and found her mouth in a kiss that sealed their love.

* * * * *

*Don't miss the conclusion of Meg Alexander's Regency duet in **Volume 4** of The Regency Lords & Ladies Collection, available in October 2005.*

MILLS & BOON®

The *Regency*

LORDS & LADIES
COLLECTION

*Two glittering Regency
love affairs in every book*

1st July 2005	The Larkswood Legacy *by Nicola Cornick* & The Neglectful Guardian *by Anne Ashley*
5th August 2005	My Lady's Prisoner *by Ann Elizabeth Cree* & Miss Harcourt's Dilemma *by Anne Ashley*
2nd September 2005	Lady Clairval's Marriage *by Paula Marshall* & The Passionate Friends *by Meg Alexander*
7th October 2005	A Scandalous Lady *by Francesca Shaw* & The Gentleman's Demand *by Meg Alexander*
4th November 2005	A Poor Relation *by Joanna Maitland* & The Silver Squire *by Mary Brendan*
2nd December 2005	Mistress or Marriage? *by Elizabeth Rolls* & A Roguish Gentleman *by Mary Brendan*

*Available at most branches of WH Smith, Tesco, ASDA, Martins, Borders,
Eason, Sainsbury's and all good paperback bookshops.*

REG/L&L/LIST

MILLS & BOON®

The *Regency*

LORDS & LADIES
COLLECTION

Two Glittering Regency Love Affairs

BOOK FOUR:
A Scandalous Lady *by Francesca Shaw*
&
The Gentleman's Demand *by Meg Alexander*

Available from 7th October 2005

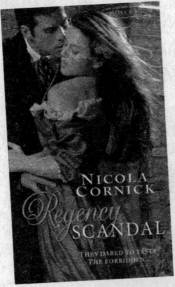

Featuring

Lady Allerton's Wager

&

The Notorious Marriage

Two feuding families…

Two passionate tales…

Against the enchanting backdrop of an island in the Bristol Channel, international bestselling author Nicola Cornick brings you two captivating stories of the feuding Mostyn and Tevithick families – and the star-crossed lovers who may bring their wilful battles to a sensual end!

On sale 7th October 2005

Available at most branches of WHSmith, Tesco, ASDA, Borders, Eason, Sainsbury's and most bookshops

THE ENGAGEMENT
by Kate Bridges

Being jilted was a humiliation no woman should have to
bear – but Dr Virginia Waters had survived it. Now she
anxiously awaited her wedding to Zack Bullock – the
brother of her former fiancé! Zack had vowed to do the
honourable thing in marrying Virginia. But neither had
predicted the danger looming – a danger that
threatened to keep them apart…

THE LIGHTKEEPER'S WOMAN
by Mary Burton

Caleb Pitt, solitary lighthouse keeper, once
believed love was eternal, for Alanna Patterson
promised him for ever. But then she left him to
drown in disgrace. Now she's reappeared in his life,
as beautiful and seductive as ever… Faced with
marrying another, she has returned to discover if
Caleb still holds any feelings for her…

SOMEONE LIKE YOU

By *USA TODAY* bestselling author

SUSAN MALLERY

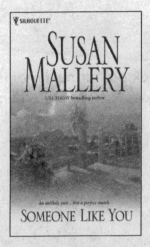

They were an unlikely pair...

When a messy divorce sends Jill Strathern back to her small hometown, she's surprised to find that burned-out cop Mac Kendrick – the guy who rejected her in high school – has also returned for reasons of his own. And even more surprised to find she's still attracted to him!

...but a perfect match.

On sale Friday 16th September 2005

To be or not to be…his mistress!

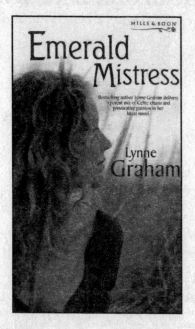

When Harriet's world crashes down, the
unexpected legacy of a cottage in Ireland seems
like the perfect escape — until she discovers that
the man who cost Harriet her job is entitled to
half her inheritance! Rafael's solution is to make
her his mistress — while Harriet's is to resist this
sexy neighbour…if she can.

On sale Friday 7th October 2005

*Available at most branches of WHSmith, Tesco, ASDA,
Borders, Eason, Sainsbury's and most bookshops*

Be whisked
away to an age
of chivalry,
where passionate
knights and
innocent ladies
face danger
and desire…

The Knight, the Knave and the Lady
by Juliet Landon

Marietta Wardle *never* wanted to be someone's
wife, but Lord Alain of Thorsgeld had
no scruples about compromising her into
marriage…

My Enemy, My Love by Julia Byrne

Kept hostage during a royal feud, Isabel de Tracy
held fast to the memory of tough, yet tender
knight, Guy fitzAlan…

On sale 2nd September 2005

*Available at most branches of WHSmith, Tesco, ASDA,
Borders, Eason, Sainsbury's and most bookshops*